WARRIOR PRINCESS ASSASSIN

ALSO BY BRIGID KEMMERER

YOUNG ADULT NOVELS
Forging Silver into Stars series
Forging Silver into Stars
Carving Shadows into Gold

Defy the Night series
Defy the Night
Defend the Dawn
Destroy the Day

Cursebreaker series
A Curse So Dark and Lonely
A Heart So Fierce and Broken
A Vow So Bold and Deadly

Elemental series
Storm
Spark
Spirit
Secret
Sacrifice

Standalones
Thicker Than Water
Letters to the Lost
Call It What You Want
More Than We Can Tell

WARRIOR PRINCESS ASSASSIN

A NOVEL

BRIGID KEMMERER

AVON
An Imprint of HarperCollinsPublishers

This is a work of fiction. Names, characters, places, and incidents are products of the author's imagination or are used fictitiously and are not to be construed as real. Any resemblance to actual events, locales, organizations, or persons, living or dead, is entirely coincidental.

WARRIOR PRINCESS ASSASSIN. Copyright © 2025 by Brigid Kemmerer. All rights reserved. Printed in Italy. No part of this book may be used or reproduced in any manner whatsoever without written permission except in the case of brief quotations embodied in critical articles and reviews. For information, address HarperCollins Publishers, 195 Broadway, New York, NY 10007.

HarperCollins books may be purchased for educational, business, or sales promotional use. For information, please email the Special Markets Department at SPsales@harpercollins.com.

Avon, Avon & logo, and Avon Books & logo are registered trademarks of HarperCollins Publishers in the United States of America and other countries.

FIRST EDITION

Designed by Diahann Sturge-Campbell
Interior map designed by Nick Springer, Springer Cartographics, LLC

Library of Congress Cataloging-in-Publication Data has been applied for.

ISBN 978-0-06-345087-5
ISBN 978-0-06-339166-6 (hardcover deluxe limited edition)

25 26 27 28 29 RTLO 10 9 8 7 6 5 4 3 2 1

*For anyone who's ever felt lost and alone
and found sanctuary in the pages of a book . . .*

This story is for you.

A NOTE FROM THE AUTHOR

Warrior Princess Assassin is a romantic fantasy written for adult readers. Within the story, readers will find mature language, violent imagery, and explicit romance. Additionally, situations involving past trauma and abuse (including sexual abuse) are mentioned—alongside themes of faith, trust, survival, and hope. Please read with care.

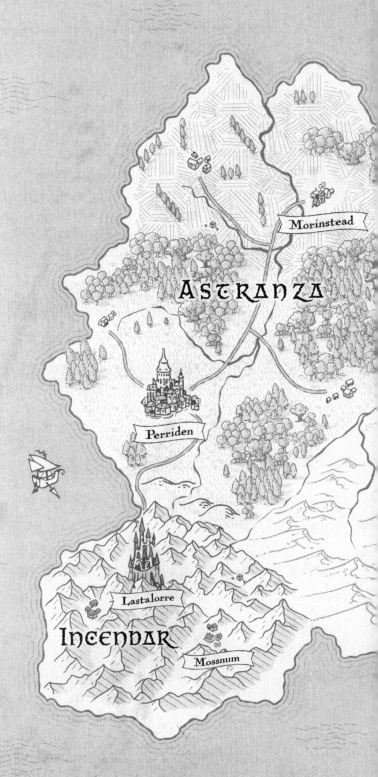

Copyright © MMXXV Springer Cartographics

Chapter One
THE PRINCESS

The bells stopped tolling hours ago, so it must be near midnight. It's certainly dark enough. Cold, too, especially in my chambers. My breath makes a thin cloud every time I exhale, and I inwardly curse my father's decree that any flame in the kingdom needed to be doused at sunset. It's impossible to escape the bone-deep chill that's settled over the palace.

This is surely the worst time for a dress fitting—especially for a wedding gown I have no intention of wearing.

A pin jabs into my shoulder, and I make a tiny sound, but I try to keep still.

The seamstress notices anyway. "Forgive me, Your Highness," she says, blowing on her hands in an attempt to warm them. She's middle-aged, with a round figure and graying dark hair that's wrapped in a braid. "I can barely feel my fingers."

She's one of my dressmaker's assistants, but I don't know her name. Normally her mistress would be here to supervise, but this is my fifth fitting of this wedding gown, and I'm certain the prim and delicate Mistress Revelle considered the cold and the dark and wanted nothing to do with it.

It makes no difference to me. They could ask one of the stable hands to pin the dress together for all I care.

I glance at the window, where each pane is clouded with frost, gleaming in the moonlight. My heart thumps, and I hope for a flicker of motion outside, some sign that Asher has returned, that he's hiding in the shadows, waiting for me to be alone.

If he were here, this wouldn't all be so terrifying.

If he were *here*, I could beg him to help me escape.

Another pin pricks my shoulder, and I stifle a yelp. "Surely we can light the hearth for a short while," I say. "The contingent from Incendar isn't due to arrive until dawn."

The seamstress looks hopefully over my shoulder toward Charlotte, my first lady-in-waiting. "My lady, if the princess insists—"

"No," Charlotte says to her firmly. "All flames were to be doused before dark. The precinct officers have been out for hours, enforcing it all over Astranza. The king of Incendar must be within our borders by now, and there shall be no fire to draw his power, most definitely not in this room. Your father issued the order, and Prince Dane was *very* clear in delivering it."

Well, my father isn't half-naked and being treated like a pincushion, or I rather think his orders would be different.

Then again, it's Father's magic that's making it so cold.

Another pin pokes me, and I bite my tongue and try not to jump.

Charlotte draws close, coming into view. She's a bit older than I am, with mouse-brown hair that she always twists back into a knot, and very sharp features that make her seem closer to forty than thirty. She's been with me for years, but she's never quite been a friend. Dane has too many lackeys and spies in the palace for me to fully trust anyone on the staff, so my only true friend has been Asher.

That said, Charlotte is one of the few people who seems more loyal to me than to my brother. If she refuses to allow a fire, then he must have been very clear indeed.

She confirms it when she adds, "Your brother is not willing to take any chances with Maddox Kyronan and his temper. Not until the king has made his marriage proposal and you have given your . . ." She hesitates. "Your response."

She means when I say *no*.

If profanity from the princess wouldn't cause a scandal, it would be *fuck no*.

I glance at the moonlit window again. *Asher, please.*

But I haven't seen him in months.

Worry flares in my gut, and I try to tamp it down. Of anyone I know, Asher can certainly take care of himself, and I have bigger problems.

Like this marriage proposal that's supposed to seal our alliance with

Incendar. Dane may have spent months negotiating for this union, but as far as I'm concerned, he can spend a few more. I refuse to be sent away to a barren, sun-scorched kingdom as some kind of payment for their king's brutal magic on the battlefield.

The instant I have the thought, a new twinge of worry pierces my belly.

Because I know why Dane is so desperate for this alliance. The war heralds bring news to court every evening, so I heard the gasps when they announced that Maddox Kyronan won a narrow victory against Draegonis by setting an entire regiment of soldiers ablaze. Thousands of Draegs burned to death on the field. Any survivors were finished off with arrows and steel.

Dane would give anything for Astranza to be so victorious. We can barely keep Draegonis from breaching our borders. And as Father grows older, there have been rumblings from the people asking how we will manage to keep Astranza secure.

But we've all heard darker stories about Maddox Kyronan. A day maid whispered that he once sketched sigils in the air and turned a man to ash right in the middle of his throne room, leaving his advisers aghast. Another one said that the touch of his skin can cause blistering burns, searing right through muscle and bone if he refuses to let go. I shuddered when I heard that, but it's not even the worst of it. There are rumors that Maddox Kyronan keeps his people obedient by scorching their limited fields and leaving them hungry, too. When they complain, charred, blistered bodies are strung from pikes along the road, ghastly reminders of his power.

And Dane just plans to hand me over.

Something inside me curls up, tight and afraid. I need to stop thinking about this. No one can be *that* powerful. My own father's magic always seems vast, allowing him to harness the weather and keep Astranza's fields bountiful and prosperous—a king providing for his people. Rumors about his magnanimous abilities swirl through Astranza, too.

But they're not all true. Even Father has limits.

The seamstress pokes me again, and I have to suck back a yip. It's so cold that I'd honestly let them light this dress on fire while I'm wearing it. I hope the pins are drawing blood, because there will be sparks of crimson on the bodice in the morning, and that might be reason to delay the wedding.

Maybe that's worse. Maybe this vicious king would *like* specks of blood on my dress.

I glance at the window again, but there's nothing. Just the silent moon, taunting me.

My chest tightens. Asher's duties have taken him far from the capital city in the past, but it's rare, and he's never been gone for so long. But if something happened to him, no one would even think to tell me. An assassin from the Hunter's Guild would never be associated with the prim and proper Princess Marjoriana.

But Asher is my dearest friend. My *only* friend.

I glance at the frosted windowpane again. He could be hurt. He could be *dead*.

The very thought makes my throat go tight, and I have to swallow.

Charlotte reaches out and squeezes my hand, and I blink away tears.

"Maybe he won't be *so* horrible," she murmurs.

She's still talking about Maddox Kyronan, and she probably thinks I'm overwhelmed with emotion about the proposal. I huff a laugh, because it's better than letting a tear roll down my cheek. "Every hearth is dark," I say. "Clearly everyone else expects him to be horrible."

She frowns and says nothing—which is answer enough.

Charlotte said the king and his retinue are inside our borders, so they must be riding toward the palace right now. I've never been to the southern border, so I don't know how long the journey would be in this weather. Will they be riding through the night? I wonder if Father is allowing the snow to fall to hide the vastness of our fields, or if this is just an example of his power, meant to impress visiting royalty. Maybe both. Incendar might have mountain ranges full of valuable iron ore, but it's no secret that they've been struggling with barren fields for years now—regardless of whether their king is causing it. All the iron in the world won't feed starving people.

No one here in Astranza ever goes hungry, not with our miles of farmland. Father's magic brings the perfect balance of sunshine and rain to let our crops and livestock flourish. I've heard army generals warn my brother that Maddox Kyronan could one day turn his sights on Astranza—and I wonder if this is part of the reason Dane and my father have sought an alliance *now*.

A rap sounds at the door, and before Charlotte can cross the room, it swings wide. My brother strides in without hesitation—without even asking if I'm willing to receive him.

"Marjoriana," he says crisply. He's ten years older than I am, with gray threading the hair at his temples, though at thirty-five, his beard is still full and black.

"Dane," I say, my tone just as cold. "By all means, come in with no regard for whether I'm dressed."

"I will," he says, because he refuses to acknowledge sarcasm. He walks past the women, who both hastily curtsy, though he ignores them. He studies the heavy train of delicately beaded fabric that's carefully draped over a chair behind me, and then his eyes shift to the two dozen pins surrounding my décolletage.

"I expected to find you sleeping," he says, "but your guards indicated that the dressmaker was *still* at work."

He sounds upset, and the seamstress flinches. Though honestly, Dane always sounds upset about everything. He's been that way for as long as I can remember. When I was young, I used to hear whispers that my birth was a blessing, because my mother had had numerous miscarriages, but Dane never saw it that way. He's always been the crown prince, off learning to hold a sword and ride a horse and rule a country, while I've always been the baby princess, sheltered and coddled and kept away from any danger.

He never hated me as a child; he simply didn't care—especially since there were more important things to worry about. Rumors of attacks from Draegonis had just begun to spread, and Father's weather magic suddenly had to protect our borders instead of simply providing our people with food. Back then, no one was panicked, especially since Dane was still young. There was still the potential for the crown prince to develop skills with magic, just like Father.

But then he didn't.

In peacetime, it might not have mattered. But Draegonis sought our fertile farmland—and Incendar's steel. Attempts to negotiate for peace went unanswered. When the Draegs attacked, they came on strong. They're the largest country on the continent, and they'd clearly been planning to overwhelm our borders for some time. We were lucky to have Father's weather magic, because he could call pummeling storms to the border anytime we received word of an invasion.

The Draegs attacked Incendar, too, but they weren't able to make much progress. Maddox Kyronan's kingdom might be the smallest, but the mountains of Incendar provide a natural barrier, and weapons forged from Incendrian steel are nearly unbreakable. The king's army is fierce and violent—to say nothing of his fire magic.

Astranza, by comparison, struggled. We'd never been a warring country, and our people began to worry about what would happen if Draegonis managed to breach our borders—if our king were to fall. My father was kept off the battlefield, his magic protected. When it became clear that Dane didn't inherit his talents, everyone's desperate sights turned to me.

I was given tutors and guides, and I spent years trying every sigil, every potion, every rune, waiting for any sign of a gift. It's known that magic—while rare—runs in families, and when the magic skipped Dane, everyone was *certain* it would manifest in me.

I used to sit beside Father, practicing the sigils, always so hopeful when I could generate a flicker of power in the air—then crestfallen when nothing further would manifest. If he wasn't present, I couldn't summon so much as a spark.

Mother always sat beside me, her smile gentle and encouraging. "Don't fret," she'd say when I got frustrated. "The magic will find you when it's ready, Jory."

It's never been ready.

I shouldn't feel regret and remorse for that, but I do. Mother died a year later, when I was fifteen, killed when thieves ambushed a carriage she was riding in. Maybe if I'd had magic, I would've been able to stop it.

As it was, Asher and I could do nothing but watch. We were riding in the carriage behind, and Asher dove to cover me when the bandits started shooting. My mother took two arrows through the chest before we even knew what was happening. Asher's mother, Lady Clara, was the queen's first lady-in-waiting—and Mother's closest friend. I still remember the sound of her screaming. *Not like this*, she kept shouting. *Not like this.*

Asher's mother died, too. But not during that attack. Because of it. Those desperate words were repeated at her trial. My brother said they confirmed her guilt, that she was somehow involved in the crime. I always felt they were a declaration of her sorrow.

I shouldn't be thinking about this. Memories of Mother are too painful, and my heart already aches from everything happening *now*. When Lady Clara was bound for execution and Asher was exiled, I begged Dane to intercede. He refused. Our mother was dead, and he stood there coldly while my closest friend was dragged out of the palace in chains. I sobbed at my brother's feet, pleading for him to make it stop.

That was ten years ago, and I've never forgiven him.

He's still glaring at the seamstress, who's stopped sliding pins through the fabric and now looks ready to cower.

"It's dark," I snap at Dane. "And freezing. Maybe your staff can handle their work in these conditions, but intricate stitching requires fingers that *aren't* frozen. But by all means, we can stop immediately."

"You are to meet your future husband in the morning. It's nearly midnight."

"Oh?" I say breezily. "I thought I was to meet the king of Incendar. Is he bringing my future husband with him?"

He clenches his jaw. "*Marjoriana*—"

"And I simply do not know why you care about the state of my sleep or my gown or anything to do with me at all," I add. "You're clearly determined to send me away."

"You are not being *sent away*," he seethes.

"You're right. I'm not. I've told you a thousand times that I will not be accepting this proposal. Just as I won't be pawed at by some land baron who wants to advance his political ambitions, I refuse to wed some king who wants a trophy for slaughtering men on the battlefield. You could have saved everyone a lot of trouble if you'd listened to me a month ago." I look down at the seamstress. "Please continue," I say gently. "You must be tired."

Dane glares at me, his jaw set. The woman gives him a narrow glance and moves to adjust another pin. This time when she pokes me, I don't move a muscle.

Charlotte looks from me to my brother and clears her throat. "Perhaps I could call for some tea—"

"Yes," says Dane. "Leave us. Both of you."

The seamstress bobs another quick curtsy, and then she practically runs from the room.

Charlotte doesn't. Her eyes are on me, and she's waiting for *my* answer.

"Tea would be lovely," I say, meaning it. I'm absolutely freezing. "Thank you."

Though as soon as she's through the door, I realize the tea will be just as cold as everything else right now. I frown.

"Marjoriana," my brother says, stepping close to me. "I have endured your silly rebellion long enough. I will not have you making declarations of your *refusal*—"

"My rebellion isn't silly. The fact that you chose to engineer an alliance without my participation was silly."

"I am the crown prince! Acting regent in Father's stead! I do not need to *defer* to you."

As if he ever would. "I am your sister," I say. "You could spare a thought to my well-being."

"Your well-being!" He looks like he wants to knock me off the stool.

"Yes. You're marrying me off to a man who burns people to ash when they displease him, so it's only a matter of time."

"You're being ridiculous. Your well-being has been thoroughly negotiated. The terms of our alliance are very clear."

"Oh, really!" I exclaim. "I would love to read the details, then. Am I to bed him on certain nights? Is there a monthly quota I must fulfill?"

He clenches his jaw again, and thunderclouds roll through his eyes. But he says nothing.

My eyes flare wide. "Dane!" I say. "Surely that is not in your contract."

"As I said: thoroughly negotiated."

I step down off the dressmaker's platform and stride forward, my hand swinging before I'm even fully aware of what I'm doing.

I should know better. Dane trains with the best soldiers in the army, and I . . . don't. My brother catches my hand in midair, gripping my wrist tight as I struggle. His fingers dig in tight before he lets me twist free. The action leaves me panting and glaring up at him, a few of those pins poking into my breast now. I won't give him the satisfaction of seeing me rub my wrist.

His hands are in fists, however, and his eyes are dark with anger. For an eternal second, my breath catches. He's never hit me, but the air carries the promise of what he *wants* to do.

When he speaks, his voice is deathly quiet. "I cannot believe this," he says. "I've spent *months* trying to protect Astranza, and you're going to spend five minutes undoing it. You act like I'm tying you to his bed for the rest of your life. You *know* a magical heir would only benefit Astranza."

I do know that—but I hate that I'm being forced to produce this magical heir with a man who could set me ablaze in the process. "Have you promised that he can do it as soon as he gets here? Should I be ready on the bed?"

"You're being a child."

"I'm being a princess. I should be involved in these negotiations. I care for Astranza just as much as you do."

"If you care for Astranza, you should be thinking of your *people*. He's coming here in good faith, to pledge his armies to defend us."

"Good faith!" I point at the cold hearth. "If he's coming in good faith, then why is every hearth dark?" I point at the frost-edged window, where snow swirls in the moonlight. "Why is the entire *kingdom* dark?"

"He can't call fire from nothing. You know that."

"You think his soldiers won't carry flint?" I say. "What's to stop him from lighting his own fire?"

That muscle in his jaw twitches again, which genuinely makes me think Dane hasn't considered this.

Idiot. This is why I should be a part of the negotiations. I wonder what else he hasn't considered.

"If you're so worried about his magic," I say, "why don't you just have the archers shoot him when he gets here? It's not as if he's bringing an army."

"Would you stop being so ridiculous?" he demands. "We're forming an alliance to have a chance at *ending* this war! I'm not starting another one!"

"But you're worried," I press. "You're worried he's *not* coming in good faith and he's going to turn us all to cinders in our beds. And you're still willing to send me away with some wicked, spiteful, terrible man I've never seen—"

"I'm not worried about him," he snaps. "I'm worried about *you.*"

"Well, you certainly don't seem very worried."

He takes a rage-filled step toward me. "I'm worried about *you* and your headstrong ways ruining everything Father and I have worked so hard to arrange. That's why every hearth is dark. That's why we're preparing every luxury to welcome the king." His expression darkens, shadows falling across his features as his voice rises. "*That* is why I am here, to make sure you stop with your dramatics."

I raise my chin defiantly. "Incendar has a princess," I say. "The king's younger sister. Why don't *you* marry *her?*"

Something about that gives him a jolt. Dane draws back. "I offered that first. He refused."

Oh. That makes my heart pound a little harder. I'm only second in line for the throne here in Astranza. Maddox Kyronan is already king. As much as I hate it, my marriage to him would be weighted in our favor.

For him to refuse feels significant. I wonder what it means.

Dane's voice drops. "If we had another way to signify unity between our nations, we would do it. But every hearth is *dark* because I'm worried you're going to tell this man exactly what you think of him. I'm worried that by nightfall tomorrow, we won't have *one* enemy, but *two.* You want to declare that you're a princess? Why don't you consider your *kingdom.*"

"I *am* considering our kingdom! His armies are known to kill wantonly. He has turned his magic on his *people*. Why would we ally with someone like that? *Why*, Dane? Father is powerful, but he has never been outright cruel to—"

"Father is dying."

He says this so simply, so *quietly*. The words drop into the shadows between us, and suddenly I'm frozen in place.

"Very few people know," he adds, and his voice grows no louder. "And it is essential that it stay that way. I am only telling you now so that you understand the absolute need for this alliance. Once Father is gone, the entire kingdom is at risk."

Because neither of us shares his magic.

I stare at Dane in shock. "Does Incendar know?"

"Absolutely not."

"How long have *you* known?"

"Nearly a year. It wasn't as bad in the beginning, but the palace physician sees to him daily now. His heart won't last must longer."

"And the healers—"

"They have all tried."

The breath eases out of my chest. I cannot believe they've kept this a secret as long as they have—and I'm hurt that they've kept it from *me*. For the last few months, Father has been slowly allowing Dane to act as regent. It's commonplace—expected, even, for an aging king—though it's widely assumed that Father has been overseeing Dane's decisions. But Father is barely seventy. He isn't so *very* old, and he hasn't said one word about illness or conceding the crown. No one has suspected anything like . . . *this*.

They've worked very hard to keep this private, because I haven't heard one single whisper.

No wonder they didn't consult me. No wonder they're willing to let this brutish, violent king drag me across a border to do whatever he wants with me.

Without Father's magic, Astranza will have limited defenses against Draegonis. We'd have limited defenses against Incendar, for that matter. If the alliance isn't in place before Father dies, Maddox Kyronan could simply take what Dane is currently offering. Astranza needs that power as an ally, not an opponent.

No wonder marriage is such an essential part of the deal.

I swallow tightly. As the king, my father is always busy, always distant, always tethered to Dane. I often go days without seeing him. Sometimes weeks. We haven't been close in years. Not since Mother died. When he sentenced Lady Clara to death and exiled Asher from the palace, it broke something between us that he's never tried to mend.

But he's still my father.

"Can I see him?" I say softly.

"No. If you go rushing to Father's bedside, it will be apparent that something is wrong." Dane pauses. "But do you understand now?"

Yes. I do. I hate it, but I do.

He must read it on my face, because he gives me a sharp nod. "The king of Incendar will arrive at dawn, and Father and I will greet him to review any final details of our alliance. You will meet him at midmorning, and he will issue his proposal. And then the choice is yours."

But there's no choice at all. If I refuse, I'm condemning my kingdom.

Charlotte raps at the door, then calls, "The tea has arrived, Your Highness."

Dane takes a step back. "I will leave you to your attendants." He strides for the door and exits so brusquely that he nearly collides with Charlotte and her tray. The seamstress cowers behind her when he passes.

I smooth the panels of the dress and give them both a nod, trying not to let any of what I learned show on my face. "Continue," I say to them both. "It's growing late, and tomorrow will be a busy day."

But my head is spinning. My earlier fear has wrapped up with dismay and anguish, and I don't see any way out.

Charlotte sets the tray on my side table and pours me a cup. "Yes, Your Highness."

I can't help taking another glance at the moonlit window.

Asher. I need you.

No shadows move at all.

Maybe it doesn't matter. Maybe it's better that he's gone.

Because there's no escape for me. Not anymore.

Chapter Two
THE PRINCESS

My ladies added two extra quilts and a fur to my bed when I finally retired, but I still can't stop shivering. I toss and turn, tucking the bedding around me more securely, then shift to face the door. I'm sure Dane expects me to be prim and demure tomorrow, but at this rate, I'll be awake all night. When the king arrives, I'll end up yawning through a curtsy, and Maddox Kyronan will set the tapestries ablaze because he's so offended by my rudeness.

I'd laugh if it weren't all so tragically possible.

Instead, I want to scream into my pillow.

If Asher were here, he'd lift my spirits. He'd call Dane an uptight ass and threaten to poison his tea. Maybe he'd hang one of my stockings from a nail high in the rafters, so I'd have to stifle a giggle in the morning while my ladies tried to figure out how it got up there. We'd sit in the shadows and I'd beg him for gossip from the distant corners of Astranza that I never get to see. He never stays too long, but sometimes the night will grow dark and quiet and he'll linger. We'll share memories from our childhood, from before our mothers died and the world became too dark and lonely to think about.

Once I'm in Incendar, I'll be completely alone.

My throat tightens, and I sniff back tears before they dare to form.

I wonder if I could figure out a way to send word to the Hunter's Guild in the morning, to inquire about Asher and his whereabouts. Dane could surely do it, but he's the last person I would ask. Officially, the Hunters never work for the Crown, because no one in the palace would ever admit to hiring them, but I know it's been done. When some nobleman or high-ranking soldier needs to be dealt with discreetly instead of publicly.

I asked Asher about it late last summer.

"Does Dane use your services?" I said primly.

"My *services*?" he echoed. We were in the midst of a game of cards in the moonlight, and I saw his lip quirk up under the hood of his jacket. Ever in the shadows, even in the dead heat of summer. "Jory, I'm not polishing the silver. I'm hired to kill people."

My heart always stutters a little at the casual way Asher talks about his occupation, but I pressed on. "Then does he *hire* you?"

The smile fell off his face. "Not me. I won't take your family's money."

It was one of the last times I saw him. He often disappears for weeks, though I rarely know where he's been. An assassin wouldn't be very successful if he broadcast his whereabouts. But this is the longest he's ever been gone, and it's not as if Astranza is *so* very large. When he was first exiled from the palace at sixteen, he was sold into indentured labor to pay his "debts to the Crown," but even then he'd manage to slip away, finding his way back to me time and time again.

I toss myself sideways and face the window, willing Asher to appear.

He doesn't. Not that he'd simply *appear*, anyway. He'd never be that obvious. I might see a flicker of shadow, or the draperies might flutter.

Tonight there's nothing.

I heave an exasperated sigh and punch the pillow, then bury my face in it.

"Stars in darkness, Jory. What did that pillow ever do to you?"

I gasp and sit bolt upright. "Asher."

"Careful." He draws out the word slowly, and his low, quiet voice is like a caress. "I don't think your ladies are asleep."

He sounds close enough to touch, but I don't see him anywhere. That doesn't necessarily mean anything. He's quicker than lightning, and he can move through darkness like a ghost.

My heart is leaping in my chest, but I drop my voice to a whisper. "Where are you?"

"Up here."

I look up, and there he is, perched on one of the dozen rafters that artfully stretch across the room. The decorative beam seems too narrow to be comfortable for lounging, but somehow Asher manages. He's dressed all in black, from the soles of his boots to the strap of his pack. Black leather, black canvas, black wool, black buckles. Even his weapons are specially forged so they don't reflect the light: there's not a speck of gleaming steel anywhere. The only brightness is Asher himself. He's pushed back his hood far enough for me to see the shock of white-blond hair that hangs into his eyes, and the fair skin that rarely sees the sun. His eyes are in shadow, but I know they're a bright, vivid blue. When we were children, the ladies at court would always comment that he'd grow out of that hair color, that his eyes would darken once he got out of childhood. They were wrong on both counts.

I wonder if any of the older ladies ever think of Asher, or if they cast him out of their minds as soon as he was exiled. They never offered him an ounce of pity or mercy when he desperately needed it, so I doubt it.

My jaw is set now, my joy at his presence replaced with protective anger over the boy he once was.

Asher pulls a cookie from somewhere and bites off a piece. "What's with the look?"

I force my features to soften. "I've been so worried," I say. "How did you get up there?"

"Jumped."

"That can't be comfortable."

"It's not." He takes another bite of the cookie and shifts his weight, and then he simply falls off the beam.

My breath catches—but I should know better. Of course he doesn't *fall*. His knees hook the wood, letting him hang upside down right over my bed. It would be comical if half his weapons spilled free, but he'd never be so careless. The hood of his jacket hangs loose behind his head, but all of his gear stays tight and intact to his body. Those blue eyes are always a bit gray in the dimness of my room, moonlight etching the curves of his face.

He's so close that my eyes fall on the dark lines ink-branded on his left cheek. I have no idea what they mean, but I don't think it's anything good. When he showed up with the first one, the edges were still raw and red, but he refused to tell me what happened. I'd never seen anything like it, so I asked one of my ladies if they knew what an inked line on a man's cheek could mean. Her eyes flicked around warily, and she whispered, "Judgment marks, Your Highness. From the slavers."

"The slavers!" I exclaimed. We have no slaves in Astranza.

She winced. "That's what the indentures call them."

When Asher showed up with two, I asked what he'd done to deserve judgment.

He snorted. "I got caught."

"By the slavers?" I said, and his eyes went dark, closed off.

"It doesn't matter," he said. Then he disappeared for weeks.

By the time he had four, I learned to stop asking.

Now he has seven.

I quickly jerk my eyes back to his own, because he hates when I stare at them. "It's been months," I say. "Where were you?"

"North." I don't expect more of an answer than that, but he adds, "I had duties in Morinstead." He takes another bite of the cookie. "There were complications."

His voice is so bland that he could be talking about delivering a sack of grain, but I know better. I keep my voice equally bland, because nothing chases him away faster than digging for details. "Killing duties?"

"Yes."

When he first told me he'd been accepted into the Hunter's Guild, I knew what it meant. I'm not *that* sheltered. But Asher read the horrified judgment on my face before I could say a word. It was two years ago, just after he earned his freedom from indenture, and I will never forget the flare of betrayal in his eyes.

"So your brother and his soldiers can be killers on the battlefield," he said, "but you save your contempt for me, just because I'm not in uniform?"

"That's *different*."

"It's not. I'm still taking orders, still being trained for violence. Would you rather I go back to the slavers?"

"Of course not. But surely it wasn't as bad as *killing* people—"

"It was *worse*."

I'd never heard his voice like that—so tight, so angry. It drew me up short.

"How?" I whispered.

He stared back at me, and for an instant, anguish flickered in his gaze. But then he blinked, and the emotion was gone. "It doesn't matter." He gestured at the lines on his face. "No one will hire a marked man for honest work. So, what now? I should *starve* so I don't insult your delicate sensibilities, Princess Marjoriana?"

"No one in Astranza *starves*, Asher—"

"Oh, you don't think so? You have no idea what it's like outside the palace. *None.*" He drew back, putting distance between us. Then he knocked a vase off my dressing table, making the porcelain shatter on the stone floor. He leapt for the rafters, disappearing into the night air, knowing I couldn't call after him when the guards and my ladies came rushing in to see what caused such a racket.

Now I flick my gaze along his upside-down form while he takes another bite of cookie. He looks as lean and muscled as ever, and he's hanging from his hooked ankles like he could do this all night.

"What kind of complications?" I say. "Were you injured?"

"Not really."

That probably means *yes*, but I bat my lashes at him, teasing. "Did another woman catch your eye?"

He takes another bite, lifting one shoulder in an upside-down shrug. "Eh."

I lose the smile. "*Eh!* What does that mean?"

His eyebrows go up, and he grins. "Jealous?"

Yes. It's like a hot flare through my chest, and I have no right to feel it.

I glare at him anyway. "You're going to choke."

"I think that's quite literally impossible."

"You're dodging my question."

"You're being ridiculous. No one caught my eye." His voice is so deep and gentle, his eyes simultaneously tempting and taunting, a complete contrast to the deadly weapons that are nearly invisible against his body. He breaks the remaining cookie in half and holds out a piece between two gloved fingers. "Want some?"

My heart skips. He's been gone for so long, but every time he reappears, it feels like it's barely been five minutes.

I crawl forward on my knees. I'm tempted to bite the cookie right from his fingers, because there's something in Asher that always makes me want to drag him into my bed and forget everything else exists.

But he wouldn't like it. Sometimes I'll forget myself and hug him, and he'll stiffen like a statue. "You're a princess," he'll say. "I'm nothing. I'm no one."

He wasn't always like that. When we were younger, we'd sneak out of the palace all the time. I still have vivid memories of the night I slipped away from my fifteenth birthday celebration and met Asher in the stables. The party had gone on for hours, and no one cared very much about *my* involvement anymore. We climbed the ladder to the shadowed hayloft, sharing gossip about the lords and ladies we'd seen at the party, both of us a little tipsy from the blackberry wine. The night started out very innocent, very chaste. But as darkness closed in, our words turned soft and serious. We spread a blanket over the hay so we wouldn't dirty our clothes, then lay beside each other, our fingers carefully wound together—until they weren't. His fingertips boldly traced my cheek, my jaw, my neck. It wasn't the first time we'd touched each other, but it was the first time in the dark, in private, with so much heady emotion between us. I shivered and found the courage to explore the soft hollow of his throat, twisting the hair that drifted across his forehead, and finally dragging my thumb across his lower lip.

I'll never forget the way his breath caught, how his hands closed on my waist to pull me closer. I'd heard Mother's ladies giggling over the men at court, the way they gossiped about someone's trousers growing tight, or a man's hardness pressing against their thigh. I'd never understood what they meant until that night, because when Asher pressed against me, I felt the hard ridge of him through our clothing, and something inside me seemed to bloom. He tugged at the hem of my skirts, his fingers slipping over my ankle, then my calf. With each brush of his hands, he caused a tightening in my belly, a clenching between my legs. His eyes were fixed on my lips, his breathing a little quick. His mother was the queen's lady, and I was the princess, and if we were caught, it would've been a scandal beyond measure. I remember being terrified that he'd close the distance between us.

I desperately wanted him to do it anyway.

"Jory," he whispered, my name like a promise. When his mouth found mine, I drowned in the taste of him. His tongue brushed my lips, that daring hand finding its way along my knee, his fingers grazing my thigh.

Then a night watchman strolled into the barn down below, whistling while he went about his duties. Asher and I snapped apart, our hearts pounding. The moment was broken, our roles remembered. We snuck back to the party, perfectly behaved. It was my first kiss. My only kiss.

A week later, my mother was killed, his mother was executed for treason, and Asher was dragged out of the palace in chains.

And now I've been promised to another man.

I take the piece of cookie with my fingers. "Thank you."

His eyes trace my face. "You're welcome." He pauses, and his voice turns solemn. "I'm sorry it's been so long."

I inhale to answer—but my breath catches. It's been months . . . and I suddenly realize it could be forever. I don't even know if Asher could cross the border into Incendar. Or if I'd be able to visit home.

I take a bite of cookie to try to cover it up.

Asher isn't fooled. A tiny line appears between his eyebrows. "Ah, Jory." He swings his body upward, twisting in the air as he releases the beam. He lands neatly on the bed in front of me, every movement as agile as a cat. He drops to sit cross-legged, knee to knee with me like we're young again, staying awake to whisper long after the maids have doused the lanterns.

"Do you know what's happening?" I say, and my breath clouds faintly with the words.

"Which part?" he says quietly. "That you've been sold away to Incendar? Or that your father is dying, and without this alliance, Astranza could be razed by Draegonis?"

I gasp and look up at the crisscrossed rafters climbing high above me. They go all the way to the ceiling, where he would have been invisible in the shadows, especially with every fire doused. "How long have you been here?"

He shrugs a little. "Long enough."

"*Long enough?*" I whisper furiously. "I've been thinking I would never see you again!" I punch him in the shoulder.

Or I *try*. He catches my hand effortlessly within his gloved one. Contrary to the way my brother grabbed me, his hand is gentle, and I don't fight him at all.

"I know," he says, his voice full of contrition. "I was thinking that might be better."

"It wouldn't be *better*, Asher."

"We've always known our lives would one day be divided. Even before . . . *before*."

Before our mothers died. Before our lives were inextricably altered. But he hasn't let go of my hand, and I don't pull back either. Though he's speaking of distance, all I can focus on is the urge to lace his fingers through mine and pull him closer. He so rarely lets me touch him anymore. I hold very still, trying to gauge what he is thinking, afraid to break the spell.

His thumb brushes over my knuckles.

My breath catches, but when I examine his face, it's only regret I see etching his features, not desire.

"What if I never come back?" I say softly.

For a moment, he says nothing, and his thumb goes still. But then he shrugs. "I'm sure you will, with half a dozen Incendrian babies in tow."

"Half a dozen!"

He continues as if I haven't said a word. "They'll all be quiet and docile and perfectly behaved, until the moment they come to visit their uncle Dane. They'll put spiders in his bed and honey in his shoes, only he won't be able to do anything about it, because their father would set him on fire."

It should make me laugh, but it doesn't—because the father of these imaginary children is a man who can cause blisters with a brush of his fingers. "I know what everyone expects, but there will be no babies." A shudder rolls through me. "I'll marry Maddox Kyronan to protect the kingdom, but I'm not letting him touch me."

Asher takes another bite of his cookie. "Do you think everyone has to call him that?"

"Asher."

"I just feel like it would be remarkably tedious."

He's trying to lighten the mood, but my mouth stays locked in a line. So the smile fades from his. "I'm sorry about your father."

I doubt that's true.

My expression must shift, giving it away, because Asher offers half a shrug. "I'm sorry for *you*."

I sigh, twisting my fingers together. "You don't need to be. He's . . . he's a stranger, Asher. I barely see him anymore." I pause. "And now he's forcing me to leave."

Now *his* mouth forms a line.

"What if Father dies, and the king feels he's been tricked?" I say. "Then I'm trapped in Incendar." I take a breath. "As his prisoner."

Asher goes still as if considering that, his expression darkening dangerously. But maybe the mood has grown too heavy, because he blinks, then lets go of my hand and sits taller. He taps his jaw, just below the seven lines of ink across his cheek. "Here, punch me again. Show me how you'd really hit him."

"Asher."

He grins, and it lights up his face.

But then the door latch clicks, and he all but *vanishes*. He's so quick that I'm not even sure which direction he went.

A wisp of a voice comes from the shadows, just before the door opens. "Cookie, Jory."

I look down at my hand to see the rest of the cookie I haven't eaten. I shove it under my covers just as Charlotte comes back into my chambers with another quilt.

"You *are* awake," she says softly. "None of us can sleep. I thought you might need another blanket."

"Oh," I say, surprised by this unexpected kindness. I remember the way Charlotte waited for *my* order and ignored my brother. Maybe I should give her more credit. "I—yes. Thank you."

She gives me a small smile, then fluffs the quilt over me. I wonder if they're all awake because they're cold, or if it's really that they're afraid of the king of Incendar. I doubt Charlotte is afraid, though. She might be very simple, but she never seems to flinch from anything. Not even my brother.

A new thought suddenly occurs to me: maybe they're all awake from fear of what *I'll* do.

"I'm going to say yes," I say, even as the words twist in my gut. "Please tell my ladies that no one needs to be afraid of . . . of repercussions."

Her eyes meet mine, and her hands go still. After a brief hesitation, she smooths the last bit of the quilt and nods. "I'll tell the others," she whispers.

With a quick curtsy, she's gone. My heart is pounding again.

I hold my breath, my eyes searching the darkness for Asher. When he drops off a beam and lands right in front of me, I nearly have a heart attack. His hood is fully up now, cloaking his face in darkness.

I want to punch him again. "Stop *doing* that!" I hiss.

"She hardly gave me any warning." He pulls at my quilts until he finds the cookie. He blows some lint off the edge, then holds it up in front of my face. "Are you going to eat this?"

"I cannot believe you're worried about food at a time like this."

"So . . . that's a no?" His eyes are gleaming at me from under the hood. I would give anything to see him in the sunshine again.

This time I lean forward and take a bite, right from his hand.

Something in his gaze tightens, a spark of heat flickering in his eyes. The sugar dissolves on my tongue, and my gaze flicks to his mouth. I have to lick the crumbs off my lips.

He inhales, and a note of desire in his breath makes my belly clench. I think of the way he was just pawing at the blankets, how I'm wearing nothing more than a thin sleeping shift under these quilts. I'm suddenly warm, the cold hearth forgotten.

But he doesn't move. His throat jerks as he swallows.

We've found this point before. If I push, he'll pull away. I know from experience.

"I wish *you* were stealing me away," I whisper.

He scoffs. "Please. If I kidnapped the princess, I'd never keep my head."

"I was going to beg you to help me escape."

"*Escape.*" He frowns. "Where would you go, Jory? You don't even know what life is like outside the palace."

"That doesn't matter. I'd be with you."

He goes very still.

"It could be like when we were younger," I say. "I'd find a maid's uniform and slip out of the palace to meet you by the stables."

His eyes are intent on mine. "Would you?"

He says this so earnestly it's like the prelude to an offer. As if I could say *yes* and he'd tell me to lace up my boots right now.

The very thought makes my heart race again, because I desperately want to. I could be dressed and ready in minutes. He's right—I have no idea what my life would be like outside the palace. But I'd be away from the political machinations of my *brother*. I wouldn't be forced into marriage.

And I'd be with Asher. Just like when I was young; that alone is tempting.

But I'm not fifteen anymore. If what Dane said is true, the entire country *is* at risk. If I disappear, Father's magic will eventually be gone, and everyone within our borders could be slaughtered by soldiers from Draegonis.

And it would all be my fault.

I stare into Asher's eyes, and it takes everything I have to shake my head. "I can't."

"I know." He draws a rough breath and looks down. "I shouldn't have come. It would have been easier. For both of us."

He looks toward the window, and my heart breaks. Desperate, I roll up on my knees and grab his hands.

He goes tense immediately, his mouth a line. "Truly, Jory. I should leave."

"Asher. Please."

He looks down at my fingers wrapped around his gloved ones. Since the day he was taken away, this might be the longest he's ever let me touch him.

My heart beats so hard. I can't bear the thought of this being our final moment together. "If I'm never going to see you again, I wish . . . I wish you'd stay. Please. *Please.*"

His shoulders are fixed and rigid, his eyes locked on our hands. He's going to refuse. I can feel it. Asher never stays long, and he hasn't stopped talking about how it would've been better if he hadn't come at all.

But then he sighs, and the sound of his breath is like a balm. "I'll stay. Lie down."

I'm so startled that I bounce on the bed like a little girl who's just been promised a bowl of sugared berries. "What? Really?"

He tsks under his breath. "Be a good princess, or you won't get what you want."

I pout at him, then slither down beneath the covers, tucking the quilts up to my chin.

"Roll over," he says. "Face the window."

The gentle command in his tone makes me shiver in an entirely new way. I don't realize I'm still staring at him until he raises an eyebrow and adds, "*Now*, Jor."

A curl of heat forms in my belly as I obey, turning to face the window. My skin feels charged, making me very aware of every thread in my sleeping shift. When Asher lies down behind me, it's so unexpected that my amusement simply vanishes. His arm comes around my waist, over the blankets—because of course he wouldn't risk trapping himself under the covers. But he tucks me against him, and his breath is sudden and warm against the back of my neck. My body goes very still, frozen in place, as if my heart refuses to believe this moment is real.

But Asher must notice my tension, because he draws back a bit. "Is this all right?"

I nod fiercely, and he laughs, low and soft against my skin. I relax into him, feeling the hard muscle of his body, the edges of his weapons, even through my layers of blankets.

We might have kissed when we were teenagers, but he's never held me before. Not like *this*. Not as a man holds a woman.

I reach for the hand that's fallen against my waist, and I tug gently at his glove. This time he does pull away, his fingers curling, resisting.

I let go at once. "I'm sorry," I murmur.

He says nothing, but his breathing slows against my hair. After a moment, he begins to draw back fully, shifting away from my body.

I feel the absence of him instantly. "No! Asher, please—forgive me—"

"Shh." That gloved hand goes over my mouth, but gently.

I turn in the bed so I can look up at him. He's propped on one arm, his hand still over my mouth. Those blue eyes stare down into mine.

"Why won't you ever let me touch you?" I whisper against his fingers.

For an instant, his eyes shutter, going dark, revealing nothing. But then his still-gloved thumb brushes over my lips. He's staring at my mouth like a starving man desperate for a meal. Half his body is against mine, and I suddenly realize it's not just weapons I'm feeling. Heat blooms in my abdomen, and I shift my weight, sliding my legs against each other. He inhales deeply.

"Asher," I whisper, drawing out his name like a plea. He's gone still, so I take hold of his wrist, tugging at the glove again. This time, he lets me. Suddenly, his hand is bare: long, tapered fingers, short nails, velvet soft skin. I press his palm to my cheek, and when his thumb brushes over my lip, I shudder. My breathing has quickened, and I want to drag his hand lower. I want his touch everywhere. I'm desperate for the taste of him.

I have the satisfaction of hearing his breath tremble, just a bit. His lips part, and so do mine, ready and willing.

But then he says, "No."

I hold my breath, because I couldn't possibly have heard him correctly. My body is frozen, staring up at him. "You don't want me?"

He closes his eyes and inhales. He's so close that I can hear the desire in his breath. "It's not a matter of *want*."

"Then why?"

"Because I'm not the boy you remember." His eyes open, dark and intent and fixed on mine. "And you're about to marry another man."

Tears spring to my eyes, hot and sudden.

Asher strokes a thumb across my cheek. "Hush, lovely. No tears. We knew this day would come." He nods at the pillow. "Roll over again. Let me hold you."

Lovely. He's never called me that before. Warmth swells in my chest again, but it's a request I can't refuse, because I'm worried he really *will* leave. When I roll over, those tears slip down my cheek to land on my pillow. But I'm rewarded by his arm coming around my waist again. This time I clutch my hand over his, and it's my bare skin against his own.

His arm is tense, but he settles behind me, his warm breath easing along my neck again. It's so sweet and so comforting—and a reminder of everything I'll never have. My heart wants to mourn and rejoice at the same time. I've always wanted to be with *him*—but Asher is right. Our paths have always been destined to divide. Maybe I've simply been fooling myself all this time.

"Dane says he negotiated for how many times the king is allowed to bed me," I say.

Asher snorts. "I overheard that part, too."

I consider how his life outside the palace always makes him seem so much more worldly, and I wonder again whether other women have caught his eye. "Can I ask you something?"

"Anything."

"Do you know if it'll hurt?" I say, and my voice is very low, very quiet.

He goes absolutely silent, as if he's startled by the question.

I twist to look at him. "I'm sorry to be so bold."

For a moment, I think he'll tease again, but his eyes stay serious. "You're not being too bold," he says softly.

I swallow. "Do you know?"

"It shouldn't hurt." He pauses. "Not if it's done right."

That makes me go warm again. But I'm imagining *him* now, not the man who's going to drag me away to Incendar.

Asher is so still behind me. "*Never*, Jor?"

I turn away and shake my head against the bedclothes. My cheeks are growing hot. Of course *never*. I'm never alone, never unguarded, never unchaperoned.

Except for now.

I twist to peer back at him. "Have *you* been with many women?" He hesitates, so I flush immediately, turning away. "Don't answer that."

He's quiet for a long moment, and then his voice is low against my hair. "I don't want to be indelicate."

I flush deeper. I'm such a fool. That probably means he's been with dozens of women.

Well, of course he has. I have eyes.

But he won't let me *touch him.*

Is that just because I've always been destined to wed someone else? I don't know. I don't know if I want the answer.

Especially since he's touching me now. He breathes against me, and I relax into his warmth.

After an eternity, a new thought occurs to me.

"What if he hurts me?" I whisper. This time there's no keeping the fear out of my voice.

At my back, Asher goes still, and I feel the tension in every muscle of his body as he reacts to the question. "You'll meet him tomorrow. Be brave, be strong, and be smart." He pauses, and a dark note enters his voice. "And if you need me, send word."

"How?" I whisper, and my voice shakes. "I'll be alone."

"You'll find a way." He strokes that bare finger over my lips, and that simple touch causes my flush to spread everywhere. "Even in Incendar," he says. "I'd find my way to you. King or not, magic or not, I'll do whatever needs doing."

My eyes meet his and hold them. He's so protective. The swirling fears in my gut stop churning quite as forcefully. The tension in my body eases away again. *Asher is here.*

For now.

My lips part as I gaze up at him, and his gaze flicks to my mouth again. I want him to kiss me so badly—so when he closes the distance between us, it feels like a dream. But his mouth is warm and real against my own, and my heart hums. I taste his breath, sweet like the cookie, then feel the slight brush of his tongue against my lip. As soon as I feel it, I want *more:* my body seems to crave him. His hand twists in my hair, and I reach for his face, pulling him closer, desperate, wanting. Molten honey seems to flow through my veins, and I press myself fully against him, my legs shifting against his. His strength is apparent in every touch, and I long for him to press me into the bed, to feel the weight of his body on mine.

But he draws back, his mouth releasing mine.

The kiss is over. Gentle. Chaste.

And nowhere near enough.

My breathing has quickened, and I stare up at him. He says nothing, but then I realize that his kiss wasn't a beginning—it was an ending. A *goodbye*.

Tears suddenly prick at my eyes, and we settle into a silence that seems to stretch into an eternity. His body is so warm against my own, and I can almost believe that time has stopped, that morning will never come, that we can stay like this forever.

"Sleep," he says softly, his voice so lovely and deep. "Just sleep, Jory."

I nod, then turn to stare out at the moon, but this time it's not mocking me. Not with Asher here, safe and warm, where I can lose myself to the weight of his arms. The chill has slipped away for the first time all night.

I don't want to sleep, because if this is all we'll have together, I want to savor every last moment of it. I'll remember that kiss until the moment I take my last breath. Even now, I'm replaying it, wishing he would do it again, wishing *that* could be our eternity. But like everything else in my life, my body doesn't care what I want. I seem to blink, and when my eyes open, my room is lit with the first threads of sunlight, my breath fogging in the frigid air.

Asher is gone.

My throat threatens to close up with emotion. But when I shift my blankets back, there's a folded up maid's uniform, a tiny slip of paper tucked under the apron.

Just in case. —A

A sob breaks free of my throat. As much as I desperately want to escape all of this, I can't. I *can't*. I won't condemn my country for my own selfish desires.

But I stroke a hand across the fabric, and I remember all the mischief we used to get up to when we were younger. We'd sneak through the palace in disguises just like this one, practically invisible because no one ever looks at a servant. It's no different from the way Dane wouldn't look at Charlotte and the seamstress. He never looks at anyone he perceives as beneath his station.

As soon as I have the thought, I go still.

Dane, who's going to be meeting with a warrior king this very morning—a meeting I wasn't invited to.

You'll meet him tomorrow. Be brave, be strong, and be smart.

My chest is still tight, but I take a deep breath. There will be plenty of time for tears later. I swing my legs out of bed and shake out the uniform Asher left.

The kingdom is at stake. No matter how badly I want to, I can't run away.

But I can choose how to face my destiny.

Chapter Three
THE WARRIOR

It's nearly dawn, and we're already late—clearly the perfect time for one of the carriages to get stuck in the snow.

I raise a hand, calling a halt to my short cadre of soldiers. The driver snaps his whip and chirps to the horses, but the carriage doesn't move. Wood cracks.

Fuck.

We've been riding for hours in the frigid moonlight, without a single lantern, torch, or bonfire to be seen for miles. The darkness has been absolute, creating wide swaths of gloom in every direction, making travel reckless and challenging. On any other night, I'd draw a ball of flame to sit on my palm, something strong enough to warm my men and light our way. But I gave my word that I wouldn't use magic on Astranza's soil, and I'll keep it.

Then again, I made that promise when I thought this kingdom would have at least *one* torch lit somewhere. The mountains of Incendar have never felt as bleak as these windy, snow-covered fields. I wonder if this is normal for this time of year or if it's a vicious display of King Theodore's power—possibly an attempt to bait me into using *mine*. Whichever it is, I can't imagine his citizens are grateful. We're supposed to be allied nations in a matter of days, but this feels like the prelude to an attack. The entire country seems to be trapped in a snare of apprehension.

Or maybe that's just me. Even in the dark, we're too exposed. A coil of tension wrapped around my spine hours ago, and it refuses to let go. I've been searching the swirling snow for any sign of movement, just waiting for an arrow to snap out of the shadows and pierce *something*.

I'm exhausted. And freezing, which is a good bit of irony.

Sevin Zale, the captain of my First Regiment, sits astride his own horse beside me. He's been quiet for at least an hour, and that's unlike him. I wonder if the weather and worry are getting to him, too. When the horses can't clear whatever stopped the carriage, Sev heaves a sigh and dismounts. He looks at the four soldiers behind us, then jerks his head toward the carriage. "Callum. Garrett. Let's push it free."

My men obey, but they're as silent as he was. No one is having fun on this journey.

Callum and Garrett throw their strength into the task, their boots slipping in the snow as they attempt to shove the carriage free. Wood cracks again, and one of them swears.

"It must be stuck in a rut," Roman calls from behind me. "You'll have to lift it a little."

Garrett snaps his head up to glare at him a little breathlessly. "Why don't *you* get down here and lift it a little?"

If they start bickering, we won't move at all—and we're an easy target out here in the snow. I swing down from my own horse. "We need to keep moving. If you two lift, I'll help push."

But just as my feet hit the snow, shadows shift, and a figure takes shape in the darkness.

Without a thought, I have a weapon drawn. Every muscle goes tense, ready for battle. Garrett and Callum have shifted to block me, and moonlight glints on their own blades. Nikko and Roman are still on horseback, but their bows are raised, arrows nocked.

A male voice cries out in alarm. "Stop!" he shouts, and his voice sounds old, thin and cracking. His Astranzan accent turns every consonant flat. "Please! I came to see if you needed help!"

Moonlight beams down as clouds shift overhead, and I can see him more clearly. The man *is* old, with thick gray hair in a swirl around his head—and he's alone. He also appears to be unarmed, with nothing more than heavy boots and a thick cloak. His gnarled hands are empty.

My heart settles—but only a little. It could still be a trap. I don't put away my weapons. Neither does anyone else.

"Where did you come from?" I say.

The man points behind him, and I realize there's a small house a short ways off, almost invisible among the shadows and snowdrifts. "Just there."

While I'm staring, the man draws closer, his hands raised. He's short and stocky, with a heavy gut and a lumbering gait. He peers at Garrett. "Your armor—Is that—" He breaks off, his eyes going wide when they fix on the circular crest stamped into the leather. Even in the moonlight, the silver markings clearly reveal a sword and a hammer crossed over the outline of a mountain.

"Incendar," he whispers. His eyes skip over us all, then flick to the gilded carriage that's sitting a little crookedly, trapped in the snow. "You're escorting your king to the palace in Perriden."

Sev cuts me a glance, but all he says is, "Yes. We are."

The man wrings his hands. "He'll stay inside there, won't he?"

My jaw goes tight. "Who?" I say flatly—because I *know* who.

The man draws back another step. "Your mage king," he says quickly. "I don't want any trouble. We've followed the orders."

I sheathe my sword and sigh. This man is too anxious to be setting a trap for a wild hare, much less a contingent of armed soldiers. I move forward to brace my shoulder against the carriage beside Sev. "Have no fear," I say, resigned. "Our 'king' will stay in the carriage."

"Good, good," says the man. But he wrings his hands again.

At my side, Sev murmurs, "You really *should* be in one of the carriages, Ky."

He's right. I probably should. Negotiations for this alliance took months. I'd get reports from couriers and advisers about the demands from Astranza, and I often thought we might never come to terms. It's clear these people don't want me here. Not really. But appearances matter, and a king shouldn't show up to make a wedding proposal in battle-worn armor. I should be in full court finery, reclining on a velvet bench, watching the snowflakes drift down through a tiny window.

But I'm not stupid.

"If anyone attacks, they'll go for the carriages first," I mutter under my breath.

Sev flicks his eyes skyward. "On my count," he calls to the others.

Garrett and Callum take hold of the rear wheels, and Sev counts to three. We push, they lift, and a moment later, we're all breathless—but the carriage is free.

Still on horseback, Nikko and Roman have lowered their bows—but arrows are still nocked. Their attention is split between the man and the horizon.

We've all seen far too much violence to fully trust any stranger on the road.

The man has backed away another step. He's shivering now. "That's it, then?" he says hopefully. "You'll be on your way?"

I swing aboard my horse. "We'll be on our way." But then I realize what he said, and I frown. "Wait—you said you followed orders. What orders?"

"To douse all the flames at sunset." The man's eyes flick to the unstuck carriage again, then at the other two ahead of it. "So as not to tempt your king's power."

I set my jaw again. No wonder it's so dark and cold.

"Well done," I say, and my voice is still flat. I pull a coin from the pouch at my waist and toss it to him as we begin to ride away.

He catches it eagerly. "Thank you, soldier!" he calls after us.

I grunt in response.

Then we're on our way again. My four soldiers fall into formation behind me and their captain. Sev is as quiet as he was the instant we stopped.

I glance over to find his eyes scanning the darkness to our east. "No stories tonight?" I say.

"I'll have a good story tomorrow about why my balls are frozen solid."

It makes me smile—until he falls back into silence. Then my face shifts into a frown. I usually count on Sev to talk my ear off when the world is tense and uncertain. In fact, it's how we met.

Ten years ago, we were twenty, alone and cornered by two groups from Draegonis who'd killed the rest of our battalion. We'd taken refuge in a narrow culvert near the border, sweat-soaked and bleeding. We were nothing more than strangers in matching armor, united by fear and a will to survive. I didn't know it at the time, but enemy soldiers had already torn my father apart, limb from limb. As the crown prince, I was their next target. My magic was still new and wildly unpredictable, and in my exhaustion, I could barely summon a spark. I was certain the Draeg soldiers would find us, and we'd both be killed—or worse, taken prisoner.

I didn't even know his name, but Sev must have seen my panic. Or maybe he was trying to hide his own. The Draegs were closing in on us from both sides, shouting from outside the culvert that they'd found our tracks. I kept desperately sketching sigils in the air, trying to draw fire so we could drive them back, and Sev . . . he just started *rambling*. He started with a story about the girl he tried to charm by leaving tokens of affection at her door—only for her to confide that she was actually madly in love with his sister. Then he told me about bedding a girl who ended up being the captain's daughter, resulting in him eating slop for a week.

By the time he got to his fourth failed conquest, Draeg soldiers were pouring through the opening—but his distraction had worked. I was ready to punch him to get him to shut up, but I wasn't panicking. My sigils flared, pulling fire from the enemy torches, swirling into an inferno that I turned back on the attackers. Some escaped the flames, and it was then that I quickly learned why Sev had survived to make it into the culvert with me, after the rest of our regiment had been destroyed. He was shockingly good with a sword. Together, we fought back the remaining soldiers, until we were the only two left standing. We were soaked in blood and both a bit singed from the flames, and it took us two days to make it home to our commanders.

Sev never left my side.

The battle was recorded as my first victory as king. Sev has fought beside me ever since. Now that he's an army captain himself, he has no shortage of women to woo and charm. I feel like I hear about a different one every week.

I'm surprised I'm not hearing about one *now*.

"*You* could ride in one of the carriages," I say to him. "I'm sure 'the king' would like some company."

He gives me a look. "At least we know why there's a complete and total lack of firelight in this kingdom. They don't trust you."

I snort, then bite the fingertips of the glove on my right hand to tug it free. I gave my word, but now I'm curious, so I sketch a sigil in the air. Normally, it would pull any fire within a mile right to my hand.

Tonight, the sigil barely emits a faint glow before going dark.

Sev shakes his head. "Do these Astranzans think we don't have flint?" he scoffs. "We can start our own fire if we need to."

"No." I pull my glove back on and glance out across the dark horizon again. "It would make a beacon out of the whole procession. If they hate me this much, I'd have an arrow in my back in under two minutes."

"Eh. Five minutes. Like you said, they'd go for the carriages first."

That almost makes me smile.

"Do you really expect an attack?" he says. "I thought that man was going to faint when he saw the crest on Garrett's armor."

I frown. The man seemed so relieved when we rode away. It makes me wonder what stories they tell about me here.

Then again, the stories they tell in Incendar are becoming just as bad.

Sev glances my way again, because I haven't answered his question. Maybe that's answer enough.

His eyes return to the landscape, and he blows out a breath through his teeth. "For all this drama, I sure hope the girl is beautiful."

He's baiting me, but I shrug. It doesn't matter. I don't care what she looks like.

But Sev presses. "You aren't the least bit curious?"

"No."

"You must have *some* idea."

"No."

"You're going to ask her to marry you! Not even a *portrait*—"

"Bleeding skies, Sev! I negotiated from the battlefield! You were right there half the time. I haven't seen her."

That shocks him into silence. But it shouldn't. This is a political alliance, nothing more. The proposal is a formality. A marriage to unite our kingdoms and reassure the people of Incendar before another spring drought leaves more crops barren and more people hungry. I can protect Astranza's soldiers in the war if King Theodore's magic can make sure my own don't starve. I've already heard reports of cellars and food stores running empty, and while we don't have these heavy snows, we have another month of winter left at least.

My advisers have also begun to report that rumors have turned darker in nature, too. People have begun to speculate that my fire magic is somehow *causing* the droughts.

It's not, but I won't deny it. The truth is worse.

My friend is still watching me. "So you don't care at *all*?"

I keep my eyes on the frozen landscape and shake my head. Any girl who clings to the comforts of her palace in the midst of a war is probably spoiled and lazy—and likely downright conceited, if her eldest brother's attitude is anything to go by. Princess Marjoriana didn't appear for any of our negotiation meetings, and that says a lot about her opinion of Incendar. At least Prince Dane is familiar with a battlefield—though it didn't take me long to figure out that he's the type to sit safely in a tent and give orders from a distance.

My own father was always right in the thick of battle, so it's never occurred to me to lead any differently. On the day I first met the crown prince of Astranza, I answered his summons fresh from a skirmish on the border, with blood on my knuckles and dirt clinging to my armor. Astranza's forces had been involved as well, but Dane looked like he hadn't seen a drop of bloodshed in his life. When I found him in his tent, he was sitting bored in a chair, without so much as a scuff on his polished boots. Before I could say a word, he looked down his nose at me, contempt plain on his face. "You there. Tell your king I am ready to receive him now."

It's a miracle we ever came to terms.

Honestly, it's a miracle I didn't shove him up against a tent post and remind him why they sought Incendar for an alliance at *all*.

But this is why I don't care what the princess looks like. I remember the arrogance and disdain on her brother's face, and I end up imagining how it will manifest in her own.

Fine. She can hate me if she likes. I've long known that marriage would be a matter of political convenience—if not outright strategy—so I learned to guard my heart. As long as she stays away from my sister, she can do whatever she wants. I'll give the princess a corner of the palace where she can complain to the stars.

But every time I have that thought, I hate the tiny part of *me* that flickers with hope, that maybe she won't be horrible and scornful. That maybe this union could lead to something more than political scheming.

That maybe there's a part of her that wants this alliance to work as badly as I do.

When that flicker appears, I stamp it out, like smothering a fire before it can wreak havoc. I'll offer hope to my people, but it's dangerous to allow it to take root in myself.

I grit my teeth. "It doesn't matter. I'm rarely in the palace. As long as she leaves Victoria alone, I don't care what she's like."

Sev smiles. He can always see right through me. "You care a *little*."

I don't smile back. I can't afford to care. We both know what's at stake.

Maybe it's better if she's spoiled and selfish and wants nothing to do with me. It's not as if I'd be any kind of husband. My life is on the battlefield. Not the bedchamber.

When I don't answer, the smile slips off his face, and Sev falls silent again. The only sounds are the creaking of saddle leather and the swish of hooves through slush and snow. My soldiers aren't bickering now, but I'm not sure their silence is better. They're likely as cold and irritated as I am, and it's never wise to have unhappy men at your back.

In the distance, farmhouses and other structures are barely visible in the moonlight, but the first threads of sunlight appear on the horizon. I look out across the snow, wondering about that man, the way he said the people had been ordered to douse every flame. Not a single candle twinkles in a window.

Was that a spot of movement, though? I automatically pull a glove free.

But there's no fire here. Magic won't help us. I shorten my reins a few inches in case we need to bolt.

Sev follows my gaze. "I told you we should have brought the entire First Regiment."

There's a part of me that wants to go back and get the whole army. "I don't want to show up looking ready to wage war. It's supposed to be a wedding proposal."

He glances my way and gives me a once-over. "Oh, so that's why you're back here with a dozen weapons strapped to your armor. You're prepared to be *romantic*."

"Forget what I said. I liked it better when you were quiet."

He laughs.

But then a shadow flickers across the snow somewhere in the distance, and his laughter cuts short. He has a bow tethered behind his saddle, but he unstraps it now. Mine is already in hand.

Whatever moved has disappeared—or gone still—and we see nothing further. I don't put away my bow, though.

Sev doesn't either.

I wonder again about traps. Was something planted in the snow? Could that man have been sent out to delay us?

I shake off the questions. We're not at war. This is a journey toward peace.

It still doesn't feel like it. "How much farther, do you think?" I say, keeping my voice low.

"To Perriden? Less than five miles, I'd say. But at this pace it'll take another hour." He glances at the hint of sunlight along the horizon. "How serious do you think they were about you showing up at dawn?"

Very serious, and knowing Prince Dane, he'll take any delay as the highest of insults. We'll spend an hour trading barbs about it, and then he'll threaten to unravel the entire alliance unless I yield something *else*.

But another hour feels interminable, especially with threats hiding in the darkness and men at my back who are already freezing and frustrated.

No one has complained, but they're my best soldiers. They won't.

I sigh and consider the horses, the snow, the way we're sitting ducks out here in the darkness—and how very deliberate that is.

Then I consider the way Prince Dane didn't even realize who I was on the day we met, how they're surely expecting the king to arrive in style, with a full retinue of servants and courtiers and guards, despite everything he knows about me.

Maybe it's better if they *think* we're late—without me being late at all.

I draw my horse out of the line and ride parallel to the others. "Nikko," I say to the soldier behind Sev. "Hold the line." I nod at the carriages. "Keep protecting the 'king.' Sev and I will ride ahead."

Nikko gives me a nod, but Sev looks at me like I'm insane.

"They'll think we're heralds," he says. "Or outriders. You're *the king*, Ky."

I roll my eyes and tether my bow. "I know who I am. But they won't. This will give us a few minutes to determine whether Prince Dane is genuine—or if this is a trap."

He still balks. "A *trap*? Then you stay. I'll take Roman and—"

"Are you coming or not?" I say. Sunlight begins to crawl over the horizon, so I don't wait for an answer; I just touch my heels to my horse's sides.

If this is a trap, I don't need Astranza's fire to protect my people. I can start my own.

Chapter Four
THE PRINCESS

When we snuck through the palace as children, Asher and I never really worried about getting caught. No one would punish a princess, and Asher's mother was the queen's first lady-in-waiting. It's very possible that we weren't fooling anyone, and the actual staff simply endured our antics because of who we were. But it felt powerful, like by changing our clothes we could also change our skins, becoming someone else entirely. When we were teenagers, we learned to be stealthier, but it wouldn't have been a huge scandal if we were caught.

If I'm caught dressed as a maid on the morning Maddox Kyronan is due to arrive, it would absolutely be a scandal.

When I slip out of my bedchambers in the stolen uniform, the halls are quiet and dark—and cold. Soft voices echo from somewhere nearby, so I scurry away from my door, keeping my head down.

It's early enough that few people are out and about, and it helps that the lack of torches and lanterns keeps the halls *very* dark. When I pass a footman in crisp livery, I keep my eyes on the floor, but he doesn't glance in my direction. I chance a look up, but I can barely make out his features in the shadows.

Maybe this will be easier than I thought.

By the time I make it to the central atrium of the palace, the soft hum of activity is echoing off the vaulted ceilings. I'm at the top of the main staircase, allowing a wide view of the sprawling room below. Servants and footmen and guards are everywhere, standing along the wall, arranging flowers, dusting fixtures, placing chairs, fluffing the tapestries. There's a bit more light here, from the stained glass along the front wall that paints vibrant shades of blue and orange along the walls, to the massive windows beside the main doors that allow the first glow of dawn into the room. I search faces, but there's no sign of my family. My gaze stops on Drewson, the head butler, who seems to be engaged in a tense discussion with two men in black armor.

Black armor! Are these soldiers from Incendar? I creep closer to the steps.

"You there!" a woman hisses from behind me. "What are you doing?"

I whirl, choking on my breath. A hall maid stands behind me, and she's older and pencil-thin, with hair drawn back in a tight bun. When she meets my eyes, I expect her to gasp and curtsy and say, "Oh, Your Highness," in appalled shock.

But she doesn't. She repeats her demand with more emphasis. "*What* are you *doing?*"

I stare at her, my mouth working, but no sound coming out.

She snaps her fingers and points past me. "The servant stairs are that way," she continues in a furious whisper. "You new girls can't seem to manage to follow the simplest rules. You're not serving mead in an alehouse anymore. What is your name?"

I can't help but stare. I don't know if I want to snap at her for being so irascible or if I want to hug her for not recognizing me.

When I don't answer, she gives an aggravated sigh. "Well, I obviously won't need to know it for long. Get out of the main stairwell!" She points behind me again, like I'm a disobedient hound. "Get! Go on, *get!*"

I *get*.

But as I cross over to the servant stairwell, I realize one of the soldiers is looking up at me. His hair is brown—no, dark blond. There's a night's worth of beard growth along his jaw, too. The crest of Incendar is stamped into the black leather of his armor, though he's too far to make out much detail beyond the sword and hammer. It's his eyes that catch me, because he's staring up at me so boldly. My heart kicks again, giving an odd little flutter, and I have to remind myself that I'm dressed as a maid. No common soldier would *dare* stare at the princess.

A flare of challenge sparks in my gut, and it takes me by surprise. No one ever challenges me, not really. I'm protected. Sheltered. Dismissed. Ignored. Never *challenged*, not even by Asher. I want to stop for a moment, just to stare back and see who yields first. But that maid is still behind me, clearly waiting to make sure I obey, and these brutes from Incendar might stare at everyone. I avert my eyes and hurry along.

As I cross to the other side, I can't help glancing back at the soldiers. The man isn't looking at me anymore, and it sounds like Drewson is arguing with them now.

"You will stand to the side," the butler is saying, his tone exasperated. It sounds like he's given this directive more than once. "We will alert His Highness as to your arrival once your *king* is in attendance."

The darker haired soldier draws himself up sharply. "You are speaking to the—"

"As you say." The blond one gives Drewson a nod, then looks to his companion. "You heard the man, Captain. We will wait."

Then I can't hear any more, because I've reached the narrow entrance to the servant stairwell. Once I've gone down a few steps and around a tight bend, it's suddenly pitch-dark from the lack of torches and lanterns. I can hear my own breathing, and I freeze on the steps.

I'm not afraid of the dark, not really, but the hair on the back of my arms stands up. For a terrifying moment, this feels beyond reckless. There are strangers in the palace, and I'm hiding in a dark stairwell. I think of Asher, the way he slips through the shadows. Someone could kill me right now, and no one would have a clue who did it.

But if I turn back, that old maid is going to pitch a fit, and I'm going to have to tell her who I am. She'd be humiliated, and likely punished if my brother heard about any of this.

And those soldiers are at the base of the stairs. Would they hear what was going on? Would they report back to Maddox Kyronan?

Or . . . would I be at risk? They have no idea who I am, and everyone seems to be afraid of these men and their king. Perhaps this is the most reckless part of my plan at all.

But I'm so desperately curious—especially since Dane kept me away from the negotiations. Everything I know about Incendar has always been a matter of rumor and hearsay.

But these are real soldiers, and they're *right here.*

The steps end at a door, and it's so dark that I nearly walk right into it. I push gently, unsure of what's on the other side, hoping I don't find another maid waiting to yell at me.

Instead, I find myself on the main floor of the atrium, in a bit of an alcove between two tables full of striking flower displays.

I'm also right behind the two soldiers.

I catch my breath and hold it. From behind, there's something very tense about the set of their shoulders, the way they've taken a spot to the side of the room. They stand at ease, like soldiers awaiting an order, but they're speaking in low tones to each other.

This close, I can hear every word.

The dark blond one from earlier is saying, "Now it's a power play, Sev. We'll be forced to wait for the others."

His voice is low, but he has an accent that I didn't expect, softening every word. Does everyone from Incendar speak like this? My lungs are screaming, so I let out my breath slowly to keep from making a sound. I wonder who's making the power play, whether they're talking about my father or my brother—or maybe they just mean Drewson.

The other soldier is an inch taller, but not quite as broad through the shoulders. His hair is pitch-black, and long enough to be pinned in an unruly knot at the back of his head. "Well, we didn't *have* to wait for the others."

The first man snorts, then turns to look at him. He breaks off sharply as he spots me instead.

I bite my lip and quickly busy myself with arranging flowers that don't need any arranging.

"We have an eavesdropper," he says. His accent softens his *r*'s and lengthens his vowels in a way that's almost . . . tender. For soldiers who are known to burn armies to the ground and cut up what's left, I can't believe one of them can sound like that.

To prove him wrong, I completely ignore him, fluffing leaves, tilting stems this way and that.

I expect them to fall silent and stand at attention now that they're aware I'm here, the way soldiers from Astranza would, but this one turns fully to face me.

"Or perhaps a spy," he adds.

I don't dare look up. I can't tell if there's a hint of warning or intrigue in his voice, but either way, my cheeks are growing warm. "Surely you can see that everyone is working. I just happen to be working near you."

"Ah. Coincidentally, I'm sure."

That gets my attention, and my hands go still. I look up at him. "Are you accusing me of lying?"

I'm being too bold for a servant, and his eyebrows go up. He's taller than I thought, and he seems to be more heavily armed than necessary. Something about him is making my heart pound, and I can't decide if it's his closeness, his weapons, or the fact that I'm definitely not supposed to be here, and he's very likely not supposed to be talking to his king's future bride.

"No." His voice drops, his accent curling around every word. "I'm accusing you of spying."

I fix my eyes on the flowers and set my jaw. "I'm not going to be questioned about my integrity by an Incendrian soldier."

He takes a step closer to me. "You think Incendrian soldiers lack integrity?" he says, and there's a note in his voice that's simultaneously dangerous and amused.

"I know of your reputation," I say, though my heart is pounding now.

"Truly," he says in surprise. "Tell me about my *reputation*."

That flicker of challenge flares in the air between us, tugging at my heart, drawing at me in a way that's new and untested. I should turn away and find another task, the way a *real* servant would, but I can't walk away from this now. "I know you're ruthless and cruel," I say, and my cheeks grow warmer. "I've heard about your brutality on the battlefield."

He regards me evenly. "Is our brutality not the exact reason your king seeks an alliance?"

My heart gives a little skip. The words are chilling—because it *is* why.

"Perhaps," I say. "But apparently your cruelty is not confined to the battlefield." My hands fidget with the blossoms, and a few petals fall. I lock my eyes on the arrangement in front of me, tugging at stems haphazardly. "Your king torments his own people, does he not?"

His fingers catch my wrist, making me break off in a gasp. It forces me to look up at him.

I'm somewhat shocked at the audacity, even for a soldier with a maid. But despite the sudden motion, his grip is gentle and his fingers are warm. This is nothing like the way Dane grabbed me last night, and it steals my ability to speak for a moment. So do his eyes, which are brown with flecks of gold. *Kind* eyes, I realize as I stare up at him, because his gaze isn't flickering with anger, but instead something like regret.

He nods at the flower arrangement. "Thorns," he says.

I follow his gaze, spotting the roses in the midst of the arrangement. *Oh.*

But then he leans closer. His hand is so warm against my skin. "Go on," he says softly. "Tell me more about Incendar's wicked king."

I flush, flustered, and I realize he's been holding on to my wrist for a good long while—and he has no right to touch me this way. I square my shoulders and twist free of his grip, then smack his hand away, *hard.*

His eyes flare wide. The dark-haired soldier beside him lets out a breath.

And then I discover everyone in the atrium is staring at us—including my brother, who's just come down the stairs.

The soldier's back is to him, but clearly a skirmish between an Incendrian soldier and a member of the palace staff is enough to earn my brother's focus. Dane's eyes light on my face, and all of a sudden, he looks like he's swallowed his tongue. If it were any other moment, I might enjoy this.

Dane strides between maids and footmen who scurry to yield a path, and then he shoves past the soldiers without paying them a glance. His face is like thunder, and he takes hold of my upper arm like he's going to give me a good shake. He's so rough and so harsh, and it's so completely contrary to the way the soldier just did it. His fingers dig into my bicep, and I make a small sound before I can help it.

Dane's eyes blaze into mine. "You will return to your quarters at *once*," he hisses under his breath. "You're lucky you were only seen by—"

"Let her go."

It's the soldier with the dark blond hair and the velvet accent, but there's nothing quiet about his tone now. He probably has no idea who my brother *is*, or he wouldn't be ordering the crown prince to do anything at all.

Dane ignores him anyway. His fingers squeeze into my arm again, and I give another little squeak of pain.

"*Now*," he growls at me. "And do not show your face until I—"

"Dane," says the soldier. "Let her *go*."

When the man uses my brother's given name instead of his title, some of the servants gasp. *I* nearly gasp, because I don't know anyone who'd dare.

Dane's entire expression ices over, and he inhales sharply, likely preparing to excoriate the soldier for his insolence—or possibly to call for guards to have him dragged out of here.

But when he turns his head, my brother simply . . . freezes. His mouth works for a moment, no sound coming out.

"*Now*," says the soldier. His expression has turned cold and hard, his voice full of promised violence if Dane doesn't obey.

To my absolute shock, my brother does. His hand slips away from my arm, and his mouth clamps shut. It leaves them glaring at each other, until I wonder if there's any chance for an alliance, because these two men are going to start a war right here. The silence in the room is thick enough to wade through, and it ticks on for a full minute.

The soldier with black hair tied back in a knot clears his throat. His expression is a fascinating combination of resignation and amusement.

"Your Highness," he says to my brother, his tone dry. He has a similar accent, but his voice is a little lower, a little rougher. "As you may recall, I am Captain Sevin Zale, of the First Regiment of the Incendrian Army. Our herald has been detained, so I have the honor of presenting His Majesty, King Maddox Kyronan."

I nearly yelp. I'm glad I had all the practice with the seamstress and her pins, because I'm able to keep perfectly still. I taste copper, and I realize I've bitten my tongue. I need to slow down my breathing or I'm not going to be able to hear anything else.

But I have no idea how to proceed. *This* is the king? I'm not supposed to meet him until later, and definitely not like . . . like *this*. Will he remember me, or will this interaction be forgotten?

I lock my eyes on the floor, so all I see are their boots. First my brother's, polished and shining without a buckle out of place. Then the soldiers'—well, the king's and the captain's—which are full of scuffs and scrapes and mismatched stitching where they've been repaired. Much like the rest of their armor, really.

I never would have taken either of these men for royalty.

"Your Majesty," my brother is saying. He must have recovered from his shock, because any harshness has been erased from his tone. "Forgive me. We did not realize you would be traveling ahead of your party. Welcome to—"

"Enough." The king says this like he's had his fill of my brother's nonsense—and it's shocking. *No one* talks to Dane like that. I want to look up, to see what expression is on this man's face, but I don't dare. I'm desperately hoping he wasn't looking at me too closely before. Because as cruel as my brother has been right now, he'll be worse later in the privacy of my chambers.

The king's fingers catch my wrist again, just as gentle as before. "Did he hurt you?"

I snap my gaze up. Those golden eyes hold mine.

He's definitely going to remember.

"Of course I didn't hurt her," Dane says immediately.

But the king doesn't look away from me. "I'm asking her."

There's a note in his voice that nearly makes my breath catch, and I can feel the strength hiding behind the softness of his grip. *This* is the man who sets armies on fire and cuts them into pieces? The man who starves his people? The man who's rumored to burn men to ash with nothing more than a touch?

And then I realize that his hand is touching my bare skin, and just like before, his fingers are warm despite the chill in the air.

A shiver rolls through me, and I draw back.

I watch the movement register in his eyes, and he frowns. "Forgive me." His hand drops. "I didn't mean to frighten you."

"You took me by surprise." My heart keeps skipping along, but I square my shoulders again, the way I did before I knew who he was. "I'm not afraid of you."

I sound bolder than I feel, and the king's eyebrows go up. "You didn't answer my question," he says. He glances at my brother. "Are you afraid of your employer?"

Dane is staring daggers at me, and I know he wants me to excuse myself and flee, in some vain hope that the king will meet me later and have no recollection of this moment. For Dane, maybe that would be possible. My brother barely pays attention to anyone below his station. It's the only reason he didn't recognize Maddox Kyronan before grabbing hold of my arm to shoo me back to my chambers.

But as I look into his golden eyes, I know the *king* won't forget. There's no sense in trying to hide my identity any longer. Besides, I rather like that he slipped in here without anyone recognizing him.

The same way I did, really.

It's the biggest surprise of all, especially when I didn't expect to like anything about him. I almost offer him a smile, as if we're co-conspirators, trapped by this arrangement.

But I think of those warm fingers that touched my arm, surely a sign of the power he wields. I think of all the rumors that preceded his arrival. I think of the magic that Dane desperately wants. The talent to call fire that can kill thousands on the battlefield.

Is our brutality not the exact reason your king seeks an alliance?

My smile stops before it can form. I won't allow myself to be fooled by a gentle voice and kind eyes. I felt the strength in his grip. I see the power in his frame.

But I can go into this alliance on equal footing.

I take hold of the maid skirts and drop into a curtsy. "Your Majesty, it is an honor to finally meet you. I am Princess Marjoriana."

The king goes absolutely still. Shock washes through his eyes before his expression locks down, closing off. He's frozen in place, and he says nothing.

Wind whispers along the main doors, and someone nearby gives a little cough, but the king doesn't move. The silence stretches on for so long that I begin to feel a bit foolish.

And then I realize that we're not co-conspirators at all—not really. Maddox Kyronan showed up to secure an alliance between nations, while I snuck into the atrium dressed as a maid—as a *spy*, just as he said. He might not have announced himself to me, but it's not like he showed up in rags and hid his identity.

And then I practically accused him of lacking integrity and tormenting his people.

Heat floods my cheeks. I'm suddenly terrified he's going to say something that will humiliate me as effectively as my brother.

But he doesn't. His rich golden eyes simply blaze into mine, and I can't read anything in them.

Captain Zale is the one to finally speak. The man claps his king on the shoulder in a casual gesture I've never seen anyone use with my brother—*or* my father.

"There you go," he says. "I told you I'd have a good story later." He looks past us all and finds a footman along the wall. "Rumor says you have good whiskey here. Which one of you can bring us some?"

That breaks the king's silence. He snaps his head around to look at his captain, and his expression is aggrieved. "It's barely dawn, Sev."

"Well, I've been up all night, and there's apparently no heat in this country." Captain Zale nods at the footman who's stepped forward. "That means we're going to need twice as much."

Chapter Five
THE ASSASSIN

The gathering room of the Hunter's Guild is never busy at dawn. We do nighttime work for a reason, and most everyone sleeps the day away. By dusk, the room will be as packed as any tavern, with just as much wine and ale poured, because anyone is welcome to spend money here. Hunters are well trained and discreet, and we're not *always* killers. Technically, we're only hired to find people. Everything we do afterward is just a matter of how much someone is willing to pay.

This morning, the gathering room is nearly deserted, the scuffed wood floors smudged with dirt and sticky with spilled ale, along with a few darker spots of blood from where discussions grew a little too heated. Sunlight shines through the windows near the ceiling, but it does nothing to warm the space. Every torch is unlit, the hearth just as cold as the ones in the palace.

Only two people are present. One is Hammish, the old man who cleans during the day, though it doesn't look like much of that has happened yet. A mop bucket sits near the wall, a thin crust of ice on the water, but Hammish is pouring himself a glass of whiskey behind the bar. The other person is Rachel, the daytime keeper of the books. She's well into her fifties, and she's been doing this a long time. Possibly as long as I've been alive.

She whistles low when she sees me. "Asher. I heard you were back."

I push back my hood and approach the cage where she sits. Steel bars stretch from the ceiling to the floor, forming walls that are ten feet wide, trapping her inside with a desk, two chairs, and a series of chests along the stone wall at her back. It would give the impression of a cell, but the locks are all on the inside, blocked by panels of steel that are too wide to reach around and too thick to break. I've seen men try.

Rachel doesn't just keep track of our assignments. She holds the money, too.

"I'm back," I say. "I checked in last night."

"I saw." She taps the book. "Only ten percent pay because of the delay. That's unlike you."

The *job* wasn't delayed, just my return, but excuses don't matter here. I was lucky to get any pay at all. I shrug. "I ran into difficulties up north."

"Tanja said you lost your room over the mill, too."

Tanja is the night keeper. I didn't tell her that I lost my lodging, but I'm sure the miller came looking for his coins when I stopped paying rent. I shrug again. "That happens when you disappear for three months. I'll find another place."

And I will—eventually. Though losing most of the pay on that job hurt dearly. So does losing most of my belongings. But I've started with nothing before. I can do it again.

I've just never done it in the middle of winter. When the order to douse every flame came ringing through the streets last night, I genuinely thought I might freeze to death somewhere.

But then Jory offered her bed.

I keep thinking of the way she fell asleep pressed against me, the way she clutched my hand to her chest. How small her voice sounded when she said, *What if he hurts me?* Or the way she trusted me to take care of it if he did.

I'm probably the last person anyone should trust. But she's so innocent. So sheltered. I've heard the wonder in her voice when she asks for stories about the far corners of Astranza. She was ready to beg me for escape—without having *any clue* how difficult her life would be outside the palace. Without having any clue how difficult *my* life is.

Though some of that is my fault. She's only ever known the Asher who was her companion as a child—and the Asher who dares to visit her at night.

I've never had any desire to share anything in between. Not then, and not now.

I have no desire to think of it myself, honestly.

There was something so comforting about the feel of her heartbeat against my chest, the softness of her body yielding against mine. I'd forgotten that touch could *be* like that, simple and gentle and without expectation. I've spent so many years at the mercy of others that I never let anyone touch me anymore—and I certainly don't fall asleep. But her chambers are always full of memories, and I long to return to what my life was once like. To be seen as someone other than . . . than what I am. Her warmth pulled the tension out of my body until I drifted off for a few hours, the sound of her breathing in my ears. When I woke in the dark, it took everything I had to let her go.

But I had to. That kiss was almost my undoing. I left her the uniform, then hid in the shadows, waiting for daybreak. I spent hours clinging to the darkness, torn between wanting her with me and knowing it was a mistake.

When she emerged from her room in the maid's uniform, my heart leapt, and I expected her to head for the stables.

Instead, I clung to the rafters and followed her to the throne room. I watched her meet the king and his captain.

I watched her choose her fate, and in doing so, she sealed mine.

I need to stop thinking of Jory. It's over.

But my heart gives a wrench. I truly have nothing.

Rachel is still studying me. "What happened in Morinstead, Ash?"

Hammish is still behind the bar, fidgeting with something I can't see, but his head is canted in this direction. He's listening to hear what I say, hoping for gossip.

They don't mean any harm, but as with Jory, I won't tell either of them the truth. "It's not important."

"You have somewhere to sleep?" she says.

My eyes flick up. Any of the other Hunters would smirk and say, "Is that an offer?" They always cajole and flirt in an attempt to charm the keepers into higher percentages, but I don't like to play those games—which is probably why her question sounds like there's genuine concern behind it.

"I'll be all right," I say.

She lifts two folds of leather from the desk. "I have two new assignments. They were delivered at dawn, directly from Pavok."

Pavok is the Guildmaster. My eyes go from her to the leather. Each fold is stitched closed, all the way around. *Sealed*. That means the Guildmaster is the only one who knows the targets—and who paid.

Often that means someone of importance. Possibly someone in the palace.

My heart thumps. Jobs like these are rare. My share from two sealed assignments would have me in new living quarters before the end of the week.

But jobs like this are only ever offered to the most skilled Hunters. The most loyal. I'm very good, but I haven't been part of the Guild long enough to earn assignments like that.

I look back at Rachel and frown. "It's not like you to break the rules."

She lifts one shoulder in half a shrug. "I'm not breaking the rules. There's a time limit, and you're the first Hunter I've seen."

I'm certainly not going to argue. I take a step forward and put out my hand. "I'll take both."

"You'll take one. And only because I don't want a Hunter sleeping in the street when the kingdom's been ordered to freeze."

"They're both stitched closed. What if the targets are together? You want the death of one to tip off the other?"

Her eyes narrow.

Hammish laughs under his breath. "He's got you there, Rach."

"You won't see Logan or Gunnar until nightfall," I add. "If then." They're the two best Hunters in the Guild, the men who'd usually get first crack at opportunities like this.

They're also the best sleepers, because they earn enough silver to keep them well-housed and well-fed.

Rachel taps the bound leather against her hand. "Both jobs are to be done by sundown," she says. "If they're not, I'll have to send another Hunter, and they'll only pay half."

It's not a lot of time for two jobs, but I give her a sharp nod. "Even more reason to give them to me now."

She doesn't move. "If they only pay half because you got cocky, you're covering the rest." Her eyes flick to the lines on my cheek, the punishment marks left there by the slavers. "And you know where the Master will get it."

I stare at her, weighing the implications of that.

It's almost enough to make me drop my hand.

She stares back. "Still want both, or do you want to think about whatever *delayed* you in Morinstead?"

She's implying that I got caught up in a romance, or gambling debts, or any of the other vices that distract Hunters when they're new.

"What happened in Morinstead wasn't anything like that," I say evenly. "I got the job done."

Behind the bar, Hammish catches a glimpse of my expression, and he laughs. "You were gone a long time," he calls. "The others were starting to lay bets on why. Bekka was disappointed that you came back so soon. She bet we wouldn't see you inside of a year. Sorrel thought maybe you were in prison again."

I scowl. That's a little too close to the truth.

But now that the opportunity has been offered, I don't want to see it yanked away. I keep my hand extended, then swallow hard. "Please, Rachel."

She heaves a sigh and stands, carrying the leather folds to the bars, but she hesitates before coming close enough to pass them through. "It's my neck on the line, too, Asher. I'll give you till midday. If they're not done, I'm telling Pavok to send someone after you."

My eyebrows go up. It's barely dawn. Shortening my deadline doesn't give me a lot of time.

But I nod. "They'll be done."

She slips the folds of leather through the bars. "I'm looking out for you." Her eyes flick to the ink-brands on my cheek again.

I scowl and pull up my hood so she can't look at them anymore. When I reach for the assignments, the leather is so rich and smooth—I've rarely felt anything like it since I lived in the palace.

"You're looking out for the Guild," I say.

But maybe she's looking out for me, too. She didn't have to offer these to me.

She doesn't deny it, though. "*Midday*, Asher."

I nod. "Understood." If she has to send another Hunter after me, I wouldn't hear the end of it. I could kiss any decent assignment goodbye.

It would almost be worse than disappearing for months and having everyone think I was whoring my money away.

Then again, Pavok would probably sell me back to the slavers anyway. I'd rather he send someone to kill me—though I suppose that wouldn't put any coins in his pocket.

There's a space under the gathering room where Hunters can go to privately read their orders—and then burn them. But it's underground and windowless—and likely freezing right now. Without the hearth or a lantern, I wouldn't be able to read anything at all.

Anyone else would have private quarters where they could go, but I have nothing. If I open these orders here, Rachel and Hammish are surely going to watch, but it doesn't matter. I'll dunk them in the mop bucket when I'm done.

I carry the bound leather to one of the distant tables near a window, then draw my dagger to cut the lacings. When I slice through the first, a smooth piece of parchment slips free. A sheen of gold is stamped at the top, and it gives me pause.

The royal seal. This order was sanctioned by the Crown. That means it's someone of political importance—likely someone in the palace.

My heart gives a kick, but I keep my face perfectly still.

I read quickly, looking for the name of the target and the location where they can be found. Sometimes a requested method is even included, and for this amount of money and preparation, I expect it.

When I get halfway down the page, my eyes freeze on the name.

MADDOX KYRONAN, KING OF INCENDAR

Of *course* it's him. I should have figured. Half the country is afraid of the man—including Dane, considering the way he spoke to Jory. I probably should have guessed before I even sliced the leather open. No one is paying this kind of money to put a blade in some simple nobleman.

But . . . sanctioned by the Crown? Does that mean King Theodore? Or Prince Dane? Neither makes sense. The death of Maddox Kyronan would put an end to their precious alliance.

Unless that's the intent. I just don't know *why*.

But it doesn't matter. He's powerless without his magic, and Jory's terrified of him. With the king dead, she'd have no reason to leave Astranza. An hour ago, I thought I would never see her again, but now my blood is rushing at the possibility of coming through her window once more.

More confident, I slice through the lacings of the second order. If the first is for the king, then this will likely be someone in his retinue, someone too close to the king to be left alive.

But it's not.

MARJORIANA, PRINCESS OF ASTRANZA

At first, I think I must have misread. But as my eyes rove over the letter, catching on her name again and again, reality grabs hold of my heart.

Jory. This can't be possible. I want to shove these orders back at Rachel and refuse.

But of course I *can't*. I've already read them, so I'm committed now. I've seen Hunters executed for less. We all take an oath, and we all know the penalties.

Besides, even if I did, the Guild would just assign these killings to someone else. No one here cares who the target is. We're paid *not* to care. If I refuse, they'll pass this on to someone like Gunnar, who'll read them impassively, sharpen his blades, and have throats slit before breakfast. He'll be sitting here laughing with the barkeep before the bodies are cold.

Rachel and Hammish are still watching me, so I will my heartbeat to slow. I keep my eyes fixed on the order, as if there are numerous details I need to commit to memory.

I force myself to breathe. To read. To *think*.

There's no royal seal on this one, so it's not sanctioned by the Crown. Maybe these really did come in separately. Though I can't imagine Master Pavok would accept an order to kill the princess—unless the price was high enough. With a sealed order, this would be the only proof that the Guild was even involved.

I skip to the bottom, looking for details. I see how much was paid, confirmed with the Guildmaster's receipt mark and signature.

But then my eyes stop. It takes a moment for me to figure out why, and then I realize what's unusual. I see *how* it was paid.

Incendrian silver.

My blood goes cold. Not with fear. With fury.

I might have been trapped in Morinstead for months, but I still have my weapons, and I still have my skills. I keep my expression neutral, but I roll up the orders, folding them down into the palm of my hand. Then I stride across the room to dunk my fist in the bucket of icy water, giving it a little splash for good measure.

"Midday, Ash," Rachel calls.

As if I need the reminder. I lift a hand in acknowledgment, then slip into the shadows.

Once I'm alone, I check for the familiar weight of my blades, and rage grips my spine.

What if he hurts me?

Her voice was so small. So innocent.

Ah, Jory.

I made her a promise, and I meant it.

I know what I have to do.

Chapter Six
THE WARRIOR

The sun is fully up now, and my men are finally sleeping.

I, however, am not.

My instincts have been screaming at me since the moment we arrived in the palace. Honestly, since we crossed the border. We've only been here for an hour, but every shadow seems to hide a spy, every sound seems to indicate an impending attack.

Then again, it's possible I'm just exhausted.

We've been given a *very* fine set of rooms, with platters of food and pitchers of wine, along with a full decanter of whiskey after Sev expressed an interest. All of it is ice-cold, but the servants have clearly been ordered to spare no expense to ensure my soldiers and I are comfortable.

Sev could have his own quarters, but he's sprawled on the chaise longue in mine, two blankets drawn up to his chin. He drank two shots of whiskey, so I'm not surprised *he* can sleep. He's still wearing every weapon, though, still buckled into every inch of his armor, right down to his boots.

So am I.

I think the others are, too—the only sign that I'm not alone in my worries. They've heard about how my potential bride dressed as a maid to spy on the Incendrian "soldiers," so maybe they're all just biding their time, waiting to see how bad this gets.

Your king torments his own people, does he not?

Her words cut like a blade.

A shadow flickers across the stone wall, and my eyes snap to the windows, scanning each one for movement. My hand has already gone to the hilt of my sword.

But there's nothing. Just the piercing blue sky of early morning. Not even a shifting cloud.

I run a hand over my face. I need to relax. A part of me wants to wake Sev, because we could find the bottom of that bottle together.

But I won't steal sleep from my men when they can find it. Instead, I walk a patrol, as if we're in drafty tents on a battlefield instead of elegant rooms lined with polished mahogany and gleaming marble. I slip through my doorway and glance into the next room, where Roman is sound asleep under a pile of furs, though the edge of his armor is visible. To my surprise, Nikko is wide awake and alert in the chair by the window. A gray fur is thrown over his lap, and a book sits on top of it.

I raise my eyebrows and glance at Roman, then back at Nikko.

He uses two fingers to tap under his right eye twice, then makes a circular motion to indicate the room. It's a common soldier signal, and I know it.

Keeping watch.

So maybe I'm not the only one who's anxious.

Mindful of the man asleep on the bed, I lift a hand and signal for him to follow me, peeking into the other rooms as I go. The next one is empty, and when I glance into the third, I see why: Callum and Garrett have shared the bed, doubling their ration of blankets. A dagger hilt sticks out from under Callum's pillow, his hand right beside it. I can't see Garrett's pillow, but I'd bet he's done the same.

When I turn, Nikko is by my side, waiting. I don't want to wake my sleeping soldiers, so I lead him back to the quarters that Sev left untouched. Once we're inside, I half close the door and gesture to the plush chairs arranged near the cold bricks of the hearth.

He must be tired, because Nikko doesn't need any more encouragement than that. He eases into one, so I do the same.

Nikko will go hours without speaking unless someone drags a conversation out of him, so I say, "Did Sev make you sit sentry?"

"No," he says, his voice low and unnaturally rough. "We drew for it."

"You should sleep, Nikko. I'm not going to."

"I'll wake Roman in a bit."

There's a familiar resolve in the way he says that. A refusal that's not a refusal. Even if I ordered him to sleep, he'd lie in bed and stare at the ceiling until whatever predetermined time they agreed on. At thirty-six, Nikko is the oldest of our group, and he's been a soldier long enough that he served under my father before me. He has black hair that he wears short, and skin the color of driftwood that turns to a rich brown in the summer. Dark, deep-set eyes, too. When we visit the taverns, he's never lacking for admirers—though I've never seen him leave with anyone. I rarely even see him *talk* to anyone.

He's not shy. Just . . . aloof. Especially with strangers. Few people know that under his armor, the left side of his body is marked with burn scars from shoulder to ankle. Three years ago he was part of a small contingent that was captured by soldiers from Draegonis. Half of his group was killed, including his captain. The other half were tortured, set on fire over and over again in an attempt to gain information—and later, to lay a trap for me. The Draeg soldiers wanted to get my attention.

They got it, just not in the way they wanted.

After we rescued those who were still alive, I discharged the most badly injured, allowing them to return home with pay. Nikko was among them. I didn't expect any of them to return to service. Their injuries were too severe, the harm too great. But Nikko reported right to me on the first day he could manage to strap on his armor.

At first, Sev told me to be careful and privately advised me to turn him away. We'd both seen the effects of torture, the way dormant fear can make someone falter in the worst moments. How a drive for vengeance can make someone reckless and wild.

But I liked that Nikko was quiet and reserved when he came to me, unlike the ones who are full of blustering swagger. I'm always reluctant to turn away an experienced soldier who wants to fight, too. So I gave him a chance, and I told Sev to keep him close so we could be sure.

I've never regretted it for a second.

Nikko glances at the cold hearth, and I watch him bite back a shiver, but he says nothing. He's probably wishing he brought that fur in here, but he won't complain about it.

I rise from the chair, grab the two quilts off the unused bed, and toss them both at Nikko. Then I drop back into my chair.

He smiles and untangles the blankets, then tosses one onto me. "We don't *both* have to freeze."

"I actually think that's their intent," I say.

He laughs softly, but then he sobers when he sees I'm not kidding.

When the palace footmen first showed us to these rooms, Sev said, "They can't order *us* to keep the hearths cold, can they? Garrett, where's your flint?"

Garrett pulled it from his belt almost instantly—but I told him to put it away. No matter how desperate I am, everything in this palace is too tense. The last thing I'm going to do is start a *fire*.

Nikko's expression is serious, and he studies me. "Roman sketched a map of what we've seen of the palace," he says. "He's got most of their guard placements down. It might be a challenge while the sun is up, but we know where the horses are kept, and our footmen aren't far. We could disappear before nightfall if you want to move."

Roman is my best tactician. I'm not surprised he's already mapped out an escape route, and he accounted for everyone in our party.

I hate that we're talking about this.

A flicker of motion from above nearly makes me jump. Nikko's eyes lock on the window, too, but there's nothing. I frown.

I rub a hand across the back of my neck and sigh. My thoughts are too twisted up for this. I keep thinking about the way the princess appeared, hiding her identity, creeping behind me and Sev to listen to our conversation. Was that a clumsy attempt at subterfuge? Prince Dane seemed furious to see her there, so it clearly wasn't planned by him. Was it King Theodore? I've met the man on two occasions, and I simply can't see him dressing up his daughter to spy on me. Why risk her at all?

Which means it had to be *her* decision.

But if it was . . . then what was Princess Marjoriana planning? I was prepared for her to hate me, but this . . . this feels altogether different.

I know you're ruthless and cruel.

She's right. I am.

Did she think I wouldn't remember her? Did she really think we could have any sort of accord if our first meeting was spun from a lie?

Nikko is still looking at me, waiting for a response about whether I want to leave.

I glance at the sunlit window and think of my sister, sitting back at home. I hope Victoria is enjoying a peaceful morning. Painting, perhaps, or walking in the gardens.

I hope she isn't causing any more trouble.

I scrub a hand across my jaw. "I don't want to move yet."

"Have *you* slept?"

"I will." Maybe.

He nods at the bed. "I'll keep watch."

I hesitate, because it's tempting, and I trust Nikko at my back. I trust everyone I brought with me. I just . . . don't trust anyone else in the palace.

But my sleep is never peaceful. Horrors from the battlefield like to haunt my dreams, especially when I'm anxious. I doubt being *here* would make that any better. My hand absently sketches a sigil in the air, a force of habit from when I'm stressed, but there's no flame to draw. The sigil barely glows before vanishing, and I frown.

Nikko is looking at me with something akin to pity, and I curl my hand into a fist.

"I wish I knew what her goal was," I say. "I wish . . . I wish her brother hadn't interrupted us quite so quickly."

"Why?"

It's a good question. I don't fully have an answer.

I frown. "Because . . ."

My voice trails off. Because she might have been spying, but she didn't *seem* like a spy.

A scratch against stone sounds from above. It's barely a whisper of sound, but I jerk my head up.

Again, nothing. This is ridiculous. It's probably just birds roosting in the snow.

Maybe my instincts are screaming about nothing at all.

The thought is striking. Perhaps I really have spent too many days along the front lines of battle. I've been looking at everything like a plotted attack, as if Astranza's royalty sought to lay a trap—as if armed men might storm in from above at any moment.

I realign my thoughts and attempt to reevaluate the way the princess entered the room, the way the other woman scolded her on the steps, the way she was rearranging the flowers behind us. She couldn't have known who I was. No one knew who *she* was.

When Prince Dane appeared, he was scolding her. He gripped her wrist so tightly. I heard the sound she made.

Of course I'm not hurting her.

That's what Dane said. But the *princess* never answered.

For hours, I've been wondering if Princess Marjoriana devised this as a plan to get access to me or my soldiers, as if her scheme was part of some master plot to work against Incendar. As if she hoped to hear secrets that she would later report back to her brother or father.

But for the first time, I consider another reason a princess would feel the need to sneak and hide—and it has nothing to do with subterfuge.

"Wake Sev," I say to Nikko. "There's still work to be done."

Chapter Seven
THE PRINCESS

Dane has been yelling at me for an hour.

It's been going on for so long that my ladies eventually held up a sheet so they could help me change out of the maid uniform and into something more appropriate for a princess. Now I'm at my dressing table while two of them braid my hair, Charlotte supervises, and Dane continues ranting behind me.

I have no idea what he's saying. I stopped listening forty-five minutes ago.

Instead, I'm thinking of Maddox Kyronan. His oddly compelling accent. His golden-brown eyes. The way he ordered Dane to let go of me—after I basically accused him of torturing his people.

Did he hurt you?

My heart skips a little, and I tell my heart to knock it off. He's a rough-edged soldier with a reputation for violence. I don't know him. He doesn't know me. But no one other than Asher has ever given a passing thought to the way my brother addresses me.

I simply can't imagine that a man known for eviscerating his enemies would *care*.

"*Marjoriana*," my brother intones. "Are you even listening to me?"

I pick at my fingernails. "I think the entire kingdom is listening to you, Dane."

One of my ladies stifles a laugh, and Charlotte clears her throat, trying to cover for her.

Dane storms forward, and my ladies jump. One braid goes spiraling loose.

No one is smiling now.

A sharp knock sounds at the door.

My brother draws back and folds his arms. "*What?*" he calls flatly, but no one answers.

I scowl at him. "It's *my* room." I glance at Charlotte in the mirror. "Please see what requires my attention."

She bobs a curtsy and moves to the door. A moment later, she gasps, then closes it.

"Your Highness," she says to me. "His Majesty has asked to speak with you alone."

I look at her sharply. "Father?" I whisper.

Even Dane takes a step back. I was ready for my brother's wrath, but I didn't consider how our *father* would react to my transgressions this morning. I still haven't seen him since Dane spoke of his illness. Dane warned me not to go rushing to his side, but now I wonder if my reaction to his presence will give it away.

But Charlotte shakes her head. "The king of Incendar."

That's worse. I go rigid, unsure how to react.

Before I can figure it out, Dane declares, "Absolutely not. Have his herald send back a refusal immediately."

Charlotte inhales sharply. "But—it's not—"

"*No.*" Dane cuts her off, making a decisive motion with his hand. "He may have tricked the porters at the gate to slip into the palace unnoticed, but we agreed upon a set chain of events. Father and I will meet with him at—"

"I tricked no one," Maddox Kyronan says clearly from outside the door. "And you are correct that we agreed upon a set chain of events, which Astranza has already abandoned. So before we proceed, I would like to speak with the princess alone, as our conversation was interrupted this morning. Otherwise, Prince Dane, I will take my people, and I will be on my way."

Dear lord, he's *here*? The king came to my door *himself*?

Charlotte's eyes are as wide as saucers in the mirror. Mine match.

Dane appears at my side in an instant. His eyes are like fire, and he grabs hold of my wrist to jerk me around to face him. My hair yanks hard as one of my ladies gets knocked out of the way, but I refuse to make a sound.

"You will undo whatever mess you have made," Dane hisses at me. "You will do whatever he asks, and you will—"

"You have three seconds to accept," says the king, and there's nothing soft about his accent right now. He immediately begins counting. "One. Two. Thr—"

"*Open the door,*" I call to Charlotte. "For goodness' sake, let him in."

She draws open the door.

The king is in the shadowed hallway, and it looks as though several of his men have come with him. My own guards are against the wall behind him, looking alert and prepared—and unsure how to proceed.

But Dane still has hold of my wrist, and he's practically looming over me. This becomes sharply apparent when Maddox Kyronan's gaze locks on us both.

"Let her go," he says.

Dane snatches his hand back as if he's been scalded. But he stands his ground. "You will not come here and make demands of me or my sister," he says evenly.

"I agreed to your terms," the king says. "I traveled to your kingdom. I yielded *my* magic for *your* comfort. I demanded nothing. I asked for a moment of privacy."

They glare at each other, the tension thickening to a point where I'm almost glad I wasn't part of their negotiations. I wonder if every meeting was like this.

I turn back to the mirror. "Come in, Your Majesty," I say. "If you'll forgive me, I was in the middle of preparing for the day. My ladies hadn't finished." I shoo them away and pick up a hairpin myself.

The king steps across the threshold, but his men remain in the hallway.

Dane looks between us. "You should have guards, at the very least, Marjoriana—"

"I'm fine," I say breezily, jabbing the pin in place and reaching for another. Inside my chest, my heart is hammering. My ladies have scooted through the doorway, but Charlotte is still hovering, waiting to see what transpires.

Dane glances through the door, and then at Maddox Kyronan. "I am not leaving you alone and surrounded by Incendrian soldiers before our alliance is finalized."

I expect the king to argue about that, but he turns his head to look back at his men. "Roman, remain in the hallway. Sev, take the others and withdraw to our quarters." Then he looks at my brother and raises his eyebrows.

Dane's jaw is clenched. His eyes find mine in the mirror, but I say nothing to him. My stomach is churning, but I simply pick up the dropped braid and reach for another pin, carefully tucking it into place.

"Go ahead, Charlotte," I say. "We shouldn't make the king wait any longer. Given why he's here, I'm sure we can have a few moments to speak."

She dips a curtsy to me, and then, to my surprise, she offers a trembling one to the king before dashing through the doorway.

My brother is the only one left. His jaw twitches, and he moves to stalk past the king, too.

But Maddox Kyronan puts out a hand to stop him, and he leans in to say something low and private before Dane can pass. A chill rolls down my spine as I suddenly remember my brother saying just how specifically they arranged for *every* detail. Could this be about that?

Dane doesn't respond, but I watch their interaction in the mirror. I can tell from the set of his shoulders that my brother is not happy about whatever is said.

But then he's gone and the door falls closed, leaving me alone with the Incendrian king.

The man is still trussed up like he's ready to fight a war, while I don't have a single weapon on me. Not that it would matter—he's pretty big, and his hands look like they could snap my bones as an afterthought. I study him in the mirror as I slide a hairpin into place, securing a lock of dark hair. When I reach for the next one, I take two, tucking one into my palm.

When my eyes shift back to his, he says, "I'm not here to harm you."

I wonder if he saw me hide the pin, or if he's just offering reassurance. "We'll see," I say. "I'm not used to men forcing their way into my chambers while I'm still dressing."

"You're not? Your brother was welcome, then?"

That strikes with a bit more precision than I'm ready for, and I have to glance away. I fuss with one of my braids, smoothing a strand into place. "I understand the terms of the alliance were well negotiated. Are you here to inspect the goods? Or do you have an inquiry about the prescribed services?" That hidden hairpin feels hot against my palm. "You'll have to forgive me. I haven't reviewed the contracts. If you'd like for me to perform a demonstration, I'm not sure if I belong on the bed or the floor first."

His eyes narrow. "Is that truly why you think I'm here?"

My heart is pounding so hard. "I have no idea why you're here."

"I wanted to talk to you without the added weight of your brother's presence." He folds his arms. "But if you've prepared a demonstration, feel free to begin wherever you like."

I whip around, because I genuinely can't tell if he's mocking me or if he's calling my bluff.

The king looks back at me implacably, and honestly, it feels like he's issued a challenge.

I've met some of Astranza's most decorated warriors, and they're usually slobbering brutes who talk with their mouths full and sweat too much. All the rumors about Maddox Kyronan and his victories on the battlefield led me to believe he'd be the same. I wasn't ready for this honey-voiced soldier who somehow has the talent to make even my brother scurry. I thought his magic gave him an edge in this war against Draegonis, but now that I've had the chance to meet him, I sense there's something more.

I'd *never* say these words out loud in the palace, but I can tell that this man does not fuck around.

I like it.

It *scares* me how much I like it.

He nods at my hands, which have fallen into my lap. "Why don't you start with whatever you meant to do with the hairpin."

That's unexpected again, and I'm off-balance. The small length of metal is still tucked under my knuckles, and this feels like another challenge.

"What hairpin?" I say lightly.

He smiles, but it's cunning. "Shall I show you what hairpin?"

My heart skips, and a little thrill races through me.

But no. That's terrifying. I have no idea what's happening here. My mouth goes a bit dry, and I twist the pin between my fingers until it's visible, glinting in the light. "I was going to stab you in the eyes if you got too close."

"Right for the eyes? That's vicious, Princess." He doesn't sound too upset about it, though.

"You're the one who forced your way in here."

"You keep speaking of force. I made a request."

"You made a *demand*."

He scoffs and shoots a dark look at the door. "My request only became urgent when your brother turned it into a pissing match."

A little heat flares on my cheeks. I don't think I've ever heard a man at court say the words *pissing match* right to my face. I rarely hear profanity at all, except from Asher. I'm not offended, but it feels scandalous.

It scares me that I like this, too.

I keep the pin between my fingers, because setting it down would feel too much like yielding something. "What did you say that made Dane so angry?"

"Which time?"

That's frank and startling and almost makes me smile, especially since he's not kidding. "Just now. When he was leaving."

"I said that if this alliance is to proceed through marriage, he will not lay a hand on you again. If he does, I will consider it an act of war."

"You think I can't defend myself?"

"You're prepared to stab me in the eyes. I absolutely think you can." The king's gaze holds mine. "I wanted to make it clear to Prince Dane that I will not just protect Astranza. As you are their princess, I will defend you as well."

I stare at him. I'm not sure what to say. No one ever is ever willing to defend me against Dane. No one but Asher.

But this man is a stranger. I'm no one to him. Maybe his vow should make me happy, but instead, my throat is tightening, and I can't quite define why.

I think of Asher curling up in my bed last night, the warm weight of him at my back. Every moment between us has always been . . . easy. So sweet and simple—the exact opposite of all this.

I'm not the boy you remember. And you're about to marry another man.

Maybe he was right. Maybe it would've been easier if he'd stayed gone.

A line appears across the king's brow. "Does that upset you?"

"No," I say, and my voice is a bit rough. I glance at the doorway. I'm sure everyone is hovering, wondering what he's doing to me. "What did you want to talk about?"

The king unfolds his arms, but then he hesitates. "May I come closer? Or are my eyes still in danger?"

The hairpin stops spinning between my fingers, and I give a humorless laugh, then drop it on the table. "You're wearing a thousand weapons. I doubt it would be a fair fight."

"I've seen men taken down by less than a hairpin." He reaches for a buckle on his forearm. "But I'll disarm for you, Princess."

I inhale to tell him that he doesn't have to, but his fingers slip the leather through the buckle in a way that's so quick and deft that I can't help but stare. Before I realize it, his left bracer is gone, revealing six hidden knives on his forearm. He unsheathes each one to set it on the dresser along the wall. Then he bends to pull a longer knife from his boot, adding that to my dresser as well. His movements are smooth and deliberate in a way that reminds me of Asher. But Asher is lean and quick, like a panther. I can't see this man slinking through the shadows and flipping down from the rafters like a jungle cat. No, the king prowled right into my quarters like a lion.

By the time he reaches for the buckle of his dagger belt, I'm transfixed, watching the movement of his fingers, the slow slide of leather across steel. That goes on the pile as well, and he finally reaches for the buckle of his sword belt, which is wider, and hangs a bit lower.

When I realize that I'm just staring, my cheeks flush again. But I don't want to look away.

He doesn't either, because his eyes hold mine the whole time.

When the sword is on the dresser as well, he stops. "Armor, too?"

he says, and his accent curls around the words in a way that should be criminal.

"Ah, no." I have to clear my throat again. "Thank you, Your Majesty. That will . . . suffice."

He must take that as some kind of invitation, because he closes the distance between us, and without warning, he sits right down beside me. Out of all the plush furniture in my chambers, the king of Incendar is sitting on one of the tiny velvet stools of my dressing table.

"I do have other chairs," I say.

He glances at the hairpin. "I thought you might want your weapon within reach."

I can't tell if he's being funny or serious. A little of both, I think. It's cold enough that I can't catch much of his scent, just a hint of leather oil from his armor, and maybe something a little deeper, a little masculine. The slight beard growth on his chin is gold in the morning sunlight, and his eyes are shadowed.

I think of how early he appeared in the atrium with his captain. They must have ridden all night. My brother would have slept in a carriage, but I doubt this man did.

"Before we begin," he says, and his voice is a bit quieter, "I should ask for your forgiveness. I did not intend to give the impression of force. If you do not wish to speak with me, I will leave."

That's unexpected—and generous. But I think of what he said when he was speaking through the door, to say nothing of Dane's threats that I need to *fix this*. "You'll leave Astranza?"

He winces. "No. But I will leave you in peace until we are to meet officially—if that is what you prefer. "

He sounds so sincere. I'm a little breathless now that he's right in front of me. "I'll talk to you." I set my shoulders. "I would have talked to you without the threat of unraveling the alliance."

"Good. Because I would like to begin anew. With truth between us, Princess. I have made no secret of how badly Incendar needs King Theodore's weather magic. Your people are well-fed, and mine are . . . struggling. I long to help them. Draegonis is making advances against

Astranza's armies, and I believe I can lead my forces to stop them. This alliance will help us both."

I nod, but my heart catches, thinking of what I know of my father and his illness.

I would like to begin anew. With truth between us.

Is he only talking about what happened this morning? Or does he suspect the truth about my father? Did his men hear something? Have the servants been gossiping?

Maddox Kyronan picks up the hairpin I was hiding between my fingers. "I'd like to ask you a question," he says, and his voice is grave. "If your answer is a lie, it's possible you'll fool me—for a time. But it will set a course of distrust that can't be undone." He pauses. "I don't want to begin that way."

He says this so earnestly, and I can see in his eyes that he means every word.

"I don't want to begin that way, either," I say quietly, and the words hurt to say. Because I'm bracing myself. If he knows about Father, I'll have to lie. I have no choice.

"Very well. Why did you dress as a maid this morning?"

I jerk back a little, because it's not at all what I expected—it's *worse*. It's humiliating. I'm a grown woman. A princess who's supposed to be his future queen. In the moment, sneaking into the atrium felt brave and maybe a little reckless, but just now, it feels silly and childish.

I have to look away. I want to snatch the hairpin out of his fingers and stab *myself* with it.

When I say nothing for a full minute, the king says, "So this *is* how we're to begin?"

"I'm not *lying*," I say, my eyes on the edge of my dressing table. "I don't like the answer."

He considers this. "When you did not participate in any of our negotiations, I thought perhaps it was an indication of disdain for Incendar. Of unwillingness to proceed."

"What?" I snap my head up. "*No.*"

He smiles, but again, there's no real humor to it. He spins the pin across his knuckles. "It's clear you don't trust me."

"That's *not* why I didn't attend the negotiations," I say hotly.

"Then why?"

"I wasn't *allowed*."

He frowns, then sets down the pin. "You see, this did not occur to me. Your brother was so contemptuous that I assumed you were alike in thought. Your father was so distant that I assumed you shared his pride. Your future is to be bound to mine. Had I known you were deliberately excluded, I would have insisted on your presence."

I think about Dane saying that he'd offered to marry Maddox Kyronan's younger sister, but the offer was rejected. "If the situation were reversed, would you allow *your* sister to participate in the negotiations?"

Now it's his turn to jerk back, which is surprising. "Victoria? I wouldn't refuse. But she is . . . she is not interested in political matters."

Interesting.

"Not at all? She doesn't care who she marries?"

"My sister prefers her solitude." At his side, his fingers twitch, and there's the tiniest glow in the shadows, gone so quickly that I might have imagined it.

"That's a summoning sigil!" I say. "Are you calling *magic*?"

He gives a little jump, like I've truly surprised him. But then he draws back, regarding me a little more warily. "You know the sigils?"

"Yes. Both Dane and I were tutored when we were young."

He pauses, and intrigue lights in his eyes. "Do you share your father's power?"

For an instant, I want to lie. I want to say *yes*. Because it would give us a cover in case Father's illness is discovered.

But as quickly as I have the thought, I shove it away. My lack of power would be obvious the instant anyone needed a demonstration.

"No," I admit. "Though . . . there was hope."

"Ah." He pauses, studying me. His eyes are so intent, and I can tell that this is a man who sees *everything*. "You'll have to forgive me, Princess." He holds up his hand, flexing his fingers like they've betrayed him. "An unfortunate force of habit. But the magic is powerless. There's no flame to draw."

An unfortunate force of habit. I wonder if that means he's nervous. About me? About the alliance? About his sister?

I wet my lips. "Do it again." When he hesitates, I look from his face to his hand. "As you said, there's no flame to draw."

He considers this for a good long while, and I wonder if he thinks this is a trap. But he must decide to trust *me*, because he sketches a sigil in the air, and the faint glow appears again before disappearing.

"If there were fire anywhere near," he says, "I could call it to my hand."

"How far?" I say.

"Quite a distance. Does your father's magic not work similarly?"

I shake my head. "It's not the same. He draws weather across the sky." Last night, I was terrified of Maddox Kyronan and his magic, but now that he's in front of me, I'm intrigued. "Would you show me?" I say. "With real fire?"

A light sparks in his eye, and he leans in. For a breathless span of time, I think he's going to say *yes*. It's like that moment in the atrium when he felt like a co-conspirator, when we were both hiding but we had the same goal.

But the king seems to catch himself, because he goes still, then sits back. "I'm reluctant to risk the alliance when we've come so close." His voice finds that gentle purr again. "Once we are in accord, Princess, I will show you anything you desire."

I have to take a deep breath and remind myself of all the reasons I was prepared to hate him. All the reasons I was ready to beg Asher to help me escape.

All the reasons I kept that hairpin tucked in my palm.

But it's hard to reconcile the stories about his brutality when he sits in front of me and talks about trust and truth and feeding his people. When he defends me against my brother and apologizes for using force.

"You have quite the talent for dodging my questions," he says. "You still haven't told me why you dressed as a servant."

That flush on my cheeks returns. But maybe his admission about a nervous habit has loosened something inside me, because I admit,

"I was curious." A line appears between his eyebrows, and I add, "I wanted to see you on my terms."

For as fierce as he seems, something in his gaze gentles. Softens. "So you took it upon yourself to dress in disguise."

"Yes." The word lands between us with weight, because it really was that simple. I consider his lines about truth and integrity and everything he assumed when I wasn't present at the alliance negotiations. I've been sitting here wondering if I'd survive the humiliation, but I suddenly realize that he's been worried about something entirely different: that my appearance this morning was part of something nefarious, instead of desperate and innocent.

His eyes are too intense. I have to look away.

"What did you discover?" he says.

"I didn't know you were . . . *you.*" I reach out and tap the worn, scarred leather over his forearm. "You certainly aren't dressed as a king."

He catches my hand, lightning quick, and I remember the way he did the same thing in the atrium. Like before, I can feel his strength, but his grip isn't painful. It's warm. Soothing.

"I fight alongside my soldiers in battle," he says. "If I look like a king, I become the primary target."

I look at his hand on mine, and my heart thrums. Some of it is fear—but some of it isn't. "The rumors here say that your touch burns," I say.

He looks right back at me. "It can."

That's sobering. I almost pull away.

But he turns my wrist, using his other hand to push back my sleeve a few inches. There, on the pale skin of my forearm, a few dusty blue marks reveal where Dane grabbed me last night.

Maddox Kyronan's eyes flick back up to mine. "A man doesn't need magic to cause harm, Princess."

I swallow.

"Thank you for taking the time to speak with me," he says.

"We've set a course," I say.

That makes him smile—and there's nothing cunning about this one. His eyes have lit with surprise, and for an instant, the flicker of hope his expression is almost boyish. It makes me blush in a way that I feel to my core.

"Forgive me for interrupting your morning," he says. "I'll leave you in peace." He lets go to stand.

But this is the most peace I've felt since I woke up, and I want to beg him to stay.

As he straps his weapons into place, he says, "I'll have Sev—Captain Zale—bring you the contracts so you can review them before our meeting. If you wish to have any terms struck, send word by midday."

I stare at him, because this is said with such cool practicality that I almost can't comprehend it. "You will?"

"Yes. Strike the entire section about your . . . ah, *prescribed services*, if you wish." He threads the sword belt through the buckle. "*I* didn't add those passages. I'm not going to bind anyone to my bed with a *contract*." His gaze darkens. "Your brother said it was all you were willing to offer. I thought it might be an affront to reject it."

Of course Dane allowed him to think I was involved with the negotiations from afar.

I stand up to face him. "What if I want to strike the whole thing?"

The king's hand goes still on a strap of leather, and he looks at me. "Then we'll strike the whole thing, and we'll begin anew." He finishes with that buckle and steps close again. "My people are in need. I want to help them."

He means that. He truly means it.

"We're in need, too," I say.

He nods. "I know. We can help each other."

The air shifts between us, and for the first time in my life, I feel like *I* have a shred of power, instead of everyone in my life keeping it out of reach. I feel capable instead of forgotten. I thought this alliance would mean yielding to this man, but instead, it seems to mean taking control of something. Something *good*, something *meaningful*.

But I can't get ahead of myself. My father is dying. The alliance might well be a farce. Maddox Kyronan wants the best for his people—but I'm not sure Astranza can offer it for very long.

So I take hold of my skirts and offer him a curtsy. "Thank you, Your Majesty."

He reaches out to take my hand, and despite the rough edges and common armor, he proves he's still a king. He offers me a perfect courtly bow, and when he straightens, he doesn't let go of my hand.

"Ky," he says.

My eyebrows go up. "Ky?"

His eyes flick skyward, and if anything, his expression turns a bit sheepish. "Maddox Kyronan is far too long."

It startles a giggle out of me, and he grins—possibly the first real smile I've seen on his face. It robs him of some of the severity—and it scares me how much I like this, too.

"Jory, then," I say to him. "Because Marjoriana is *far* too pretentious."

"Jory," he says, and it's startling to hear it in his accent. Warmth crawls up my neck.

He offers me a nod, then lets go of my hand. "Until later, Princess."

Then he's through the door, and I let out a breath, pressing my hands over my heart. Absolutely *none* of that went the way I thought it would.

Ky really meant everything he said. The desire rang in every syllable he spoke. It's the only reason he's putting up with Dane's antics at all.

But so many people are afraid of him. So many people have horrific stories about him. That must mean *something*.

A shadow passes across my window, and I think nothing of it. A bird, perhaps.

But then it happens again, followed by a scrape of metal along my windowsill.

My heart leaps to my throat. If it were the middle of the night, I'd know it was Asher.

But it's midmorning—and Asher is gone.

A bitter draft swirls through the room. The window is open, a man in black coming over the sill. Terror grips my chest, and I think about the four thousand weapons the king was wearing, and I almost wish he were still here. I scrabble for another handful of hairpins, inhaling sharply to scream for the guards.

The intruder is quicker than thought, because he has a hand over my mouth before I can make a sound, and his other hand clamps around my waist. He wrenches me away from the table before I can grab anything, and I swing an elbow into his midsection, then clamp down hard with my teeth on his gloved hand. My attacker grunts, and I earn an inch of freedom, so I reach out, swiping a hand along the surface of the dressing table. My fingers finally close on one of those hairpins.

I don't think. I stab back.

The man grunts again, tightening his grip. "Jory, *stop*!" he growls against my hair. "It's me!"

Asher.

I freeze. As soon as I go still, he lets me go.

I whirl around and smack him on the arm. Twice for good measure. My heart is still pounding. "What are you doing?" I begin to shout, but he slaps a hand over my mouth again.

"*Guards*, Jory." His face is in shadow under the hood of his jacket, but he's breathing like he's run a race.

My own heart won't stop pounding. I shove his hand away from my mouth, but I keep my voice down. "What is *wrong* with you!" I whisper furiously. "Why did you *grab* me?"

"I've been waiting for him to go. You need to leave." He shoves back his hood. "You need to leave *now*."

I suddenly can't process what he's saying. I haven't seen Asher in the sunlight in ten years.

His hair is still so blond, but it glistens in the sunlight. I always thought he was pale, but his skin is like warm desert sand at midday, and the ink-brands on his cheek are stark. I never knew they were vaguely different colors, but in the bright light of day, I discover some lines are blue, some are black, one is purple. I wonder if it means anything.

"Jory," he's saying urgently. "Are you listening to me? You must *leave*."

It jolts me out of my reverie. "What? *Why?*"

"Because I've been given orders to kill you. If I don't do it, they're going to send another Hunter. We need to make it look like you ran, that you fled the marriage. That you're rejecting the alliance to Incendar. I'll hide his body, then lay tracks to make it look like he went after you."

There are too many shocks in that statement. "Asher—"

"Now, Jory. You don't understand the kind of men who will come after me if I fail. Who will come after you. We'll arrange a place to meet. You must go quickly—"

"What are you *talking about?*" My voice is rising, and I don't care. "What body? What—"

"Damn it, would you listen to me? There are two people I've been ordered to kill. *You* can escape, but I don't want Incendar to pin the blame on you. You need to be gone before I do it."

I stare at him. "Asher. What are you saying to me?"

"The Hunter's Guild has been hired to kill you *both*." His blue eyes are so fierce. "So now *you* are going to run."

"And what are you going to do?" I say, but my voice is small.

Because I already know. My brain has caught up.

"I'm going to kill Maddox Kyronan, the king of Incendar."

Chapter Eight
THE ASSASSIN

Jory is staring at me desperately, wetting her lips like this is a new puzzle she has to solve. "Asher," she says firmly. "You cannot kill the king—"

I slap a gloved hand over her mouth again, then cast a glance at her chamber doors. "Maybe you could say that a little more quietly."

She hesitates, then nods, so I let her go.

I reach into my jacket and withdraw the tightly folded orders that I hid from Hammish and Rachel when I dunked my hand in the bucket. "You need to see this," I say as I unroll them. "I've been ordered to kill you both. If I fail, another Hunter will be sent. Soon."

She inhales like she's going to keep arguing, but her eyes must lock onto something on the parchment, because she finally snatches both pieces out of my hands to read. Her eyes scan the paper and stop on Maddox Kyronan's name, then flick back up to the royal seal at the top.

"This has to be fake," she says. "It has to be. You heard Dane yourself. He'll do anything to ensure this alliance. He's not going to have the king killed *now*—"

"Or he laid a trap where the king has no access to fire just so he *could* have him killed. Read the next one."

She huffs a breath as if we're children again and I'm being stubborn, but she flips to the next piece of parchment and reads.

A line appears between her eyebrows when she reaches her own name.

"Look at the bottom," I say. "It was paid with Incendrian silver. And the order was received this morning."

"This doesn't make any sense."

The only thing that doesn't make sense is the fact that she's not wrapping herself up in a cloak and sneaking through the servant passageways.

"These are fake," she says. "Someone is tricking you." Jory thrusts the crumpled parchment at me with finality. "Ky wants this alliance, too."

I was in the middle of wondering if I should just drag her over the windowsill, but my thoughts trip and stall when she calls him *Ky*.

I don't care. I don't.

I *can't*.

My expression must shift anyway, because spots of pink appear on her cheeks. She squares her shoulders and stares up at me boldly. "I talked to him, Asher. He wants to protect his people. He didn't do this."

I take a tight breath through my teeth and cast a glance at her door. We surely only have moments before one of her maids returns. "Two hours ago, you were terrified of him."

"That was before he came to speak with me privately."

I have no idea how she can be so bold and so naive at the same time.

Actually, I do know, because I was the exact same way when I was first exiled from the palace. I earned the first stripe on my face because of it.

I stare down at her. "He spoke to you for ten minutes, and you suddenly believe he wants peace and light and happiness? The man is responsible for cutting through entire regiments on the battlefield. He sets enemy soldiers on fire and watches them burn. So would you please consider that *Ky* could have engineered a situation where an assassin could dispatch you without conflict?"

She blanches a bit when I mention the king's atrocities, but then her eyes narrow. "Why would he need an assassin at all?" she demands. "We were alone! He could have killed me with his own two hands!"

The door clicks, and I snatch the parchment out of her fingers and leap for the rafters. I don't have the favor of nighttime now, and even though the hearth and sconces are dark, the room is full of sunlight. I dig my fingernails into the wooden beams and climb as high as I can before going still in the shadows alongside a wooden beam braced against the wall.

I'm mostly hidden, but I'm not invisible. Those pieces of parchment are half-crumpled in my hand because I had no time to tuck them away. I'm frozen in place, pressing that hand into the beam to keep it still. Nothing draws the eye like a hint of movement. My heart might be pounding, but I barely allow myself to breathe.

Especially since Dane has stepped into the room.

He stops directly below me. I could drop right on top of him if I wanted to.

I wish *his* name was on one of those parchments.

When he speaks, his voice is cold. "What did Maddox Kyronan say?" he demands. But then he stops short, and I realize Jory is staring back at him, wide-eyed. "What?" he says. "What did he do?"

I doubt he's concerned about her well-being, but it's clear Jory is still rattled by my presence. I hold my breath, worried she's going to glance in my direction and give me away. I'll have a dozen men trying to fill my back with arrows a second later.

But Jory squares her shoulders. "It's nothing, Dane," she says, her tone level and strong. "Your precious alliance is not in danger."

I let out a slow breath. *Good girl.*

"Then what did he want?" Dane says.

Jory moves away, returning to her dressing table. She sits on a velvet stool and picks up a hairpin, tucking an errant curl into place. "He wanted to make sure I was privy to everything Astranza was agreeing to. He said he would have his captain bring me a copy of your contracts."

"For what purpose?"

She tucks another curl. "So I could strike any terms I find unsatisfactory." She reaches for a tiny pot of pink cream and dabs some on her left cheek. "Up to and including the whole agreement."

Dane storms forward, his arm outstretched like he's going to grab her, and rage fills my chest, just like any time I'm this close to him. I was never fond of Prince Dane, not even when I lived here. He's always been arrogant and disdainful, and as the child of a servant—even a high-ranking servant—I rarely earned his attention.

True hatred for Dane didn't set in until the moment I was dragged out of the palace in chains. I shift my weight, ready to leap down to stop him.

But Jory doesn't flinch. She's glaring at him in the mirror. "The king *also* told me that if you lay a hand on me again, he'll consider it an act of war."

Thunder has rolled across Dane's expression, but he stops short.

Jory simply dabs more cream onto her other cheek. The tension is so thick it's practically holding me in place. An entire minute ticks by.

Which brings us an entire minute closer to another Hunter coming to kill her.

Jory finally breaks the silence. "Dane, if you're done standing there, I would rather like to finish getting ready." She reaches for another pot of cream, rose-red this time. "I believe you have to make some preparations yourself?"

"Fine," he grates out. "I'll send in your ladies."

Jory dabs the darker cream on her lips. "No. Please tell Charlotte that I would prefer some time to myself. I'll need some privacy to review the contracts once they arrive."

Dane doesn't even answer. He's already slamming through the door.

Once he's gone, she looks up, scanning the beams until she finds me tucked against the wall, fifteen feet above.

"Come back down," she calls softly.

I shake my head and glance at the door. "Not yet."

She makes a frustrated sound and rises from the little stool. Her cheeks are more pink now from the cream, her lips more vibrant. I remember what she looked like as a girl, and she was always pretty in an understated way—the way children born to privilege often are.

In adulthood, however, her beauty has depth.

I think of the way my heart leapt when I watched her emerge from her chambers in the maid's uniform. The way she went to meet *him*.

"Did you hear what he said?" she whispers. "Why would Dane care about the alliance if he wanted to kill the king?"

"Maybe he's making sure everything proceeds as normal until a killer has time to work." I hold up the parchment, which is crumpled from my rough treatment along the beam. "The Guildmaster *knows* the king and the crown prince—he would have verified these orders himself. This one can't be a fake." I pause and shift between them. "I sincerely doubt the other one is either."

"Why would they both issue these orders at the same time?"

"I don't know that they did. I just received them this morning—and it was after Maddox Kyronan arrived." I tap the parchment and read off a line below his name. "*Payment of three hundred coins received in Incendrian silver.* So he absolutely could have sent one of his people to the Guild to arrange it. He and his men didn't arrive together. One of them could have done it before arriving in the palace."

She considers that—but I'm right, and she knows it.

I glance at the door again, but I haven't heard a sound. I'm still not ready to risk dropping to the ground. "Jory," I say. "*Please.* Pack a few things and go. I can help you—"

"Asher! I am not throwing away this alliance because you showed up with these orders! Simply go back and tell them *no.*"

It's my turn to make a frustrated sound. I finally uncurl from where I'm hidden and spring from beam to beam until I land in front of her. "You think I can tell them *no*? I could be executed just for keeping these orders! Just for *telling* you! And even if I refused, what exactly do you think would happen? They'll give back the payment and say the Hunter didn't *feel like it*?"

Her cheeks are flushed now, her breathing rapid. "Why did you even accept it at all?"

"I didn't know you were the target until I opened it! You don't know how lucky you are that it was given to *me.*" As soon as I say that, I realize how true it is. If I hadn't strolled through the gathering room this morning, Jory might be facing another Hunter—or not facing him at all, as the case may be.

"You must run," I say firmly. "If you and the king aren't dead by midday, they will send another Hunter to finish the job—and then there will be nothing I can do to save you. We are oath bound to track our prey until the job is done. Your brother wants the king of Incendar dead—so he will be. The king wants *you* dead—so you will be."

"Then I'll tell the guards, Asher! I'll tell Dane—"

I step forward, spin her around, and trap her arms before she can even inhale. I use enough force that I have her body pinned against my chest, unable to struggle. A blade is already in my hand, and I touch the metal of the dagger hilt against her chin. She squeals and her chin lifts an inch.

I can feel her heart pounding through her corset, through the buckles of my jacket, through the leather of my glove where it sits against her throat. Her breathing hitches once, a sound full of fear, and I almost let her go. This is a side of myself that I've *never* wanted her to see.

But she needs to be afraid. She needs to understand.

She wrenches at my grip, but I hold fast. My mouth is close to her ear now, the floral scent of her hair filling my nose.

"Another assassin wouldn't wait," I say, keeping my voice low. "Your throat would already be cut, your blood on the floor."

Her breathing shakes again, and her fear swells in the air between us. Her entire frame is rigid, tight against me.

Good. I hate it, but *good.*

I let her go, and she falls away from me, gripping the edge of her dressing table, her breath heaving.

"Do you understand now?" I demand.

She doesn't nod. Instead, she whirls and punches me square in the face.

The strike snaps my head to the side, because I really didn't see it coming. I might even taste blood. I have to fall back a step so I don't fall down.

"Don't you *ever* do that again," she says, her voice ragged.

"You weren't listening!" Stars in darkness, that was a good strike. I had no idea she could hit like that. When I touch a hand to my lip, it stings like fire, and my fingertips come away with blood. I don't know if I should be impressed or angry, but this definitely feels like a time for both. "*Fuck.*"

"You put a knife to my throat!" She rubs at her neck, then checks her fingers as if expecting to find her own blood.

"It was just the hilt," I growl. "I wanted to *show* you, not hurt you."

She stares at me, her chest still heaving a bit. Her eyes are dark and full of censure, but I don't care. I dab a drop of blood away from my lip.

After a moment, Jory sighs and pulls a small handkerchief from the bodice of her dress, then reaches for my face.

I jerk back without meaning to. It's an automatic motion, but she freezes. Her hand hangs there, outstretched, but then her eyebrows flicker into a frown.

She's looked at me like that before, and I hate it. I draw up the hood of my coat and look away. "We're wasting too much time," I say. "Lead a horse into the woods, then mount and head north. There's an inn about five miles from here, called Three Fishes. It's off the main road. I'll take care of the king and follow in a few—"

"Asher." She tucks the handkerchief away and faces me with her shoulders squared—exactly the way she faces down her brother. "I'm not running, and you can't kill him."

She's so brave—but this is infuriating. And heartbreaking.

I give a ragged sigh and fold up the slips of parchment, then set them on her dressing table. "I'll leave you with the proof. Hide them where they'll be found so Incendar has some evidence that you aren't responsible." I scowl. "But *you* didn't believe me, so who knows what they will think." I leap for the rafters again.

"Where are you going?"

"I can't stay. I've been given a deadline. If you change your mind, I'll meet you at the inn." I swing high, gripping tight to each beam.

"Asher." Her voice catches me just before I reach the highest window. "I believe you. I'll go."

My heart leaps.

Then she says, "But you can't kill the king."

"I can. Without his fire magic, he's just another soldier." I snap the latch beside the ledge. Cold air swirls into the space, tugging at my hood. "And it doesn't matter. If I don't kill him, someone else will."

"I know," she says. "But you said that if I needed help, I could send word. You said you'd *do whatever needed doing*."

I look down at her. She has no idea what I'm risking here. "That's exactly what I *am* doing, Jor."

"No. That's why you're *not* going to kill him. Astranza needs the king and his magic—and Incendar might be to blame, but I don't believe *he* is." Her voice isn't small anymore. It's strong and brave and clear, reminding me that she might be naive about the world outside these walls—but she's still a princess, and she's got a solid grip on my heart.

"If we need to run," she says, "we're going to take him with us."

Chapter Nine
THE WARRIOR

By the time I return to our quarters, my men are awake, with the exception of Nikko, who's finally asleep in the back room. *I haven't slept yet, but my mood is lighter than it's been in months, and it doesn't go unremarked.* When I come back through the doors, Sev takes one look at me and grins. "*Don't care what she's like,* my ass."

That makes me blush before I can help myself, and Callum and Garrett both whoop and clap me on the shoulder until I tell them to knock it off. But it's good to see them so lighthearted after so many hours of riding in the dismal cold—and after months and months of battling near the front, while food stores ran empty and Draegonis seemed to gain ground with every assault.

"I believe we understand each other," I tell them when they ask about the princess. "And I believe our goals are in accord."

"*And* she's beautiful," Callum coughs, and Garrett smacks him in the arm before I have to.

But warmth clings to my cheeks, and their gentle ribbing starts up again. I truly meant what I told Sev earlier—it doesn't matter what she looks like. I'm certainly no ideal husband, and I would've married a stone pillar if it meant helping my people.

Princess Marjoriana *is* beautiful, though.

Jory, I think. I don't tell my men about that part, because it feels too personal, like a secret between us. Prince Dane never used a nickname when describing his sister. I still can't quite believe that she resorted to disguising herself when she wanted to see me. It's simultaneously so brave and so . . . *innocent.* Like the way she was ready to put my eyes out with a hairpin, but then she blushed like a schoolgirl when I unbuckled my weapons. I remember the spark in her gaze when she asked me to show her my magic, how badly I wanted to pull my flint right there.

I haven't said a word, but Callum grins and whistles low through his teeth, and this time I do punch him in the shoulder. He laughs.

Roman smiles too, but his reaction is more reserved. "It's good that you found some common ground with the princess." There's a gravity to his voice that sobers the others, and I realize that it's not just the endless fighting or the cold ride that's been weighing on them. It's the prospect of this alliance—and the risk of failure. Roman himself sketched out a means to escape this palace before he even went to sleep. They all know how tenuous my relationship is with Prince Dane—and how dire the circumstances have become in Incendar.

They also know my reputation, and what's at stake.

My people are in need, I said to her. *I want to help them.*

She said her people were in need, too. That she wanted to help them all.

My chest clenches. Hope is so dangerous, but I let it settle in my heart for the first time.

"She wants this alliance to succeed as badly as I do," I say, and I know that same hope rings in my voice. I envision healthy spring crops that provide enough food to store for the winter, farmers with fat livestock bragging about the size of their spring calves, soldiers returning home and having more to eat than bone broth, fish stew, and stale bread. I imagine returning to my capital city of Lastalorre, finding my people waiting to greet me with bright eyes and welcoming faces.

The images are so powerful that I'm surprised to feel emotion tightening my throat. "We're so close to bringing home a new kind of victory."

That emotion must capture them, too, because no one is smiling now.

After a moment, Sev stands and puts out a hand. "By fury and flame."

The first line of our battle rally. It's rarely spoken so solemnly, especially by him. But more than anyone else in this room, Sev knows how very desperate I am to make this work.

I stand and clasp his hand to say the next line. "For valor and truth."

The others slap a hand over their heart. *"For Incendar."*

I've heard it a thousand times. Maybe more. But it strikes a different chord this time. "For Incendar," I say back.

Sev pulls me forward into half an embrace, clasping my shoulder before letting me go. His dark eyes hold mine, and I can see the flicker of relief there. He's been a captain long enough that he never reveals anything less than cool confidence to his soldiers, but we've been *friends* long enough that he'll let me see it.

He blinks the emotion away, then steps aside so the others can do the same thing.

When Garrett lets me go, he winces and glances over his shoulder at the small hallway that leads to the other rooms. "Nik is going to hate that he's missing this."

I think of the soldier who rode all night, then stayed awake to sit sentry so the others could get some sleep. "Don't wake him," I say. "Nikko needs to rest."

A knock sounds at the door, and the others snap to attention. Any warmth in my chest ices over. This is probably Prince Dane, ready to resume our pissing match. I'm sure he's full of vitriol over the way I chased him out of his sister's room.

I'll chase him out of this one just as quickly.

"Enter," I call, and Sev automatically steps to the side, ready to block if necessary.

But the door swings open, and instead of an angry prince, I find the princess—and she's alone.

My eyebrows go up. "Princess," I say in surprise.

"Ky." Her eyes flick to my men, and she seems to falter, just for an instant. A bit of pink flares on her cheeks. "Ah... *Your Majesty.* Forgive me for interrupting."

I find it fascinating that she can be so demure in one moment, and so courageous the next. It's like the way she smacked my hand when she was still dressed as a maid.

"There's no interruption. You are welcome here."

"Thank you." But she doesn't move forward through the doorway.

There's something apprehensive about her gaze, and I consider that she first hid that hairpin out of genuine fear. I wonder if the others are frightening her, or if it's still me.

Then I think of the bruises shadowing her wrist and the way Dane loomed over her.

Maybe she's afraid of her own brother.

A bit of fury coils in my gut as I remember that he first proposed a marriage between himself and my sister. If he ever has occasion to loom over Victoria like that, I'll turn him into a pile of ash piece by piece, starting with his favorite appendage.

But as I regard Princess Marjoriana—*Jory*—I think maybe it *is* my men. Her eyes flick from them to me. To their credit, they've fallen back to stand at attention, abandoning any hint of lighthearted banter now that she's here. But they're my most lethal soldiers, and they definitely don't look harmless. I can feel the weight of their focus, so I'm sure she can, too.

"You didn't have to come here alone," I say. "Would you prefer to summon your attendants?" I pause. "Or would you like to speak somewhere less private?"

"No," she says quickly. But then she lifts her chin. "You said you would allow me to review the alliance contracts."

"You didn't have to fetch them." I glance at Sev. "I was just asking Captain Zale to deliver them to your quarters."

She lifts a hand. "It won't be necessary for me to review every detail. The discussions have taken months. I don't want to prolong them further." She pauses. "But I did have a few questions for you."

"Of course."

She glances at my men again, then crosses the threshold, her skirts whispering against the floor. She might be afraid, but she's brave, her green eyes piercing as they hold mine. In her chambers, I said I would defend her against her brother, and the promise seemed like an affront. I can already tell that this is a woman who's always had to defend *herself*, with no one at her back, no one to fight at her side. The air between us is charged, and for a searing moment, I want to step close and offer reassurances.

We are to be allies. You don't have to be afraid.

But I've only just met her, and she has no reason to trust me. Perhaps that would feel like an empty promise.

So I keep my distance. "Ask anything you like, Princess."

"Could we be alone again?" she says softly. "If you please, Ky?"

Every pair of eyes snaps to me. Behind her, I swear Callum is smirking now. Sev might be, too.

If they make me blush again, I'm going to kill them.

"Leave us," I say, and my tone is sharper than I intend. But they obey, moving into the hallway, letting the door fall closed.

Once they're gone, she finally moves closer, and some of the tension slips out of her frame. Maybe the others *were* frightening her. "Did you bring a hairpin?" I tease. "Or are my eyes safe this time?"

She smiles and lifts her hands, revealing her palms. "Completely harmless."

That makes me smile. "I rather doubt *that*."

"*You're* not, though." She reaches out to trace a finger along the buckle of my bracer. Even through layers of leather and steel, I'd swear I can feel her touch, and it sends a pulse of warmth right through my body. I suddenly feel the need to adjust the lacing of my trousers.

This is terrible. I need to get it together.

"Shall I disarm every time we meet?" I say.

Her eyes flick back to mine, and I expect her to smile, to tease back—but instead, she sobers. I wish I could figure out her expression, but I don't think it's fear. Something has changed in the short time since we spoke before. Is it her brother? What has happened? My eyes narrow.

"Yes," she says after a moment, and there's a note of finality in her voice. "Disarm. Then we can face each other as equals."

"As you say." But when my hand lands on a strap of leather, I hesitate.

In her room, this didn't feel reckless.

I'm not sure why, but this time, it does.

She lifts her chin, and she finally smiles, though it's small. "Are you afraid of *me* now?"

No, not really. I certainly can't see her overpowering me, even without weapons—but my instincts are pricking at every nerve ending I have.

My eyes flick past her, toward the doorway. No one else is here, and my men are surely just on the other side of the door.

"I'm not afraid," I say. "I'm curious." I slip the first strap free, and as before, she watches the movement. I feel the weight of her eyes on my fingers. She's closer than she was before, when we sat in her chambers, and I can hear each whisper of her breath. The sunlight has warmed the space better than before, too, and I can even catch her scent, something warm and inviting, like cinnamon or vanilla.

The bracer comes free from my forearm, and I toss it onto the chair, but she hasn't said anything.

My eyes flick up. "Princess?" I pause, remembering the pulse in my heart when she called me *Ky* in front of the others. "*Jory?*"

That earns a full smile, and the pink on her cheeks deepens. "You spoke passionately about your people," she says. "And I believe you want to help them."

I start on the second bracer. "I do."

"And you seem earnest in your desire to begin our . . . our *marriage* from a place of honesty and truth."

"I am." These buckles slip free, and I toss this one onto the chair as well. A shadow flickers over the room, and I cast a glance up at the window, but there's nothing there.

Those birds again. My instincts aren't quite screaming at me, but my fingers hesitate as I reach for my sword belt.

The princess reaches out to rest her fingers over mine, and it drags my gaze back down to meet hers. Her hand is faintly trembling, and I frown. I think of that man in the snow who seemed so terrified of my soldiers—and me.

"What has happened?" I say. I yank at the buckle that holds my sword in place, then toss it onto the chair with my bracers. The dagger quickly follows. "My commitment to this alliance is genuine, I assure you."

Her breathing has quickened. "I want to believe you," she says. "I just . . ." Her voice trails off, and she presses her hands to her mouth, inhaling deeply.

Then I notice the broken skin across the knuckles of her right hand, the slight swelling of her knuckles.

She definitely didn't have that before.

Maybe this is why my instincts are screaming. Maybe she's trying to tell me she's in *danger*.

I swiftly step forward and take hold of her hand. "You hit someone. Who hurt you? Was it your brother?"

She inhales sharply, her eyes searching mine. There's a pleading there. A *need*.

"Tell me," I demand, and this time I make no effort to hide the fury in my voice. "Believe *this*, Princess. If Dane is threatening you in regards to our alliance, I truly will consider it an act of—"

Metal scrapes over stone from somewhere above.

I snap my head up, but all I see is a dark blur. A heavy weight slams straight down into my shoulders with enough force to bring me to my knees. I barely stop myself from crashing face-first into the floor. My hands reach for weapons that aren't there, and I inhale to shout for my men.

Before I make a sound, a thin rope snaps tight against my throat.

Well, *fuck*.

I automatically go for the rope, but it's drawn so tight that I'm already seeing stars. There's weight on my back, and what feels like a knee pressing into my rib cage. I try to fling myself back to dislodge my assailant, but there's no wall behind me, and whoever it is grips tight. I try to roll, to use my weight to my advantage, but the rope goes tighter. I surge against the ground, reaching back, striking at anything I can reach.

I hit something vital, because my attacker grunts, telling me it's a man. That rope goes slack, but it snaps tight before I can get more than a second of air. It's enough time for me to strike again.

He's ready for it. He catches my wrist and wrenches it back so fiercely that my shoulder might dislocate. The sudden sharp pain brings me to the ground, the rope still tight around my throat. Now there's a knee in my lower back, digging into my kidney, and another just over my spine. The stone floor grits against my face, and my eyes are beginning to water from the lack of air.

The princess isn't screaming. Has someone attacked her, too?

I have one hand free, and I press against the ground, but whoever's on my back has too much leverage. My lungs are beginning to scream.

Jory's skirts are visible in my blurring vision. She's still on her feet. I fight to speak, but the rope is too tight. *Run*, I think. *Scream.*

The man speaks from behind me, his voice low, the tone tight with strain. "Jory. His dagger belt. Quick."

Oh.

I'm an idiot.

Desperate, I sketch a sigil against the stone floor, praying someone has lit a fire *somewhere*.

Nothing.

"Jory!" the man says again. "*Now.*"

"Asher," she says breathlessly. "Asher, you're hurting him."

"You knew he wasn't going to walk out the door!" the man growls. "I need you to tie his hands."

Asher. I search my memories for the name and come up with nothing. It's possible the lack of oxygen isn't helping. I let my muscles go slack, hoping that will earn me some leverage, but whoever's pinning me doesn't fall for it. I surge against his hold anyway, and I'm gratified when he swears and has to adjust his grip. In the struggle, I'm able to get a lungful of air—but then the rope is too tight and I can't shout for help. I redouble my efforts, hoping I'll knock into a table or something will fall and summon my men from the other side of the door.

I'm not that lucky.

I can't believe I removed my weapons—all because I thought the princess was afraid. All because I thought she was in danger from her brother. I am such a *fool*. I still have daggers strapped under each greave, but they're well out of reach.

A hand grabs my wrist, and I strike out. Jory makes a small sound of pain, and I grit my teeth, hoping for another chance.

But the rope at my neck tightens, and my assailant leans down close until he speaks right to my ear. "She's the only reason you're not dead. Hurt her again, and you will be."

I go still at the words, because conviction fills every syllable. He means every word.

"Jory," he says again. His voice is still strained, as if he can barely keep me pinned. He must not be a soldier or a guard, because he's not as heavy as an armored man would be. If I could get another lungful of air, I might be able to wrench free.

But then her hand touches my wrist again, and I can feel Asher go still, watching to see how I react. He's waiting to make good on his promise, I can feel it.

I don't fight her. She draws my arm back, and she's more gentle than he was. I tighten my muscles, hoping to earn some slack later, but the man grunts.

"Hold this one," he says. "*Don't* let up. If he shouts for them, they'll hang us both."

Then they must trade, because the rope loosens marginally, and I suck in some air.

"*Tighter*," he hisses, just as he jerks the leather around my wrists. It pulls my shoulders to an unnatural angle and forces a sound from my throat. My hands are pressed together so sharply that I couldn't sketch a sigil even if there were fire to draw.

Then a new rope comes over my head, the edge cutting into my mouth. He's tied a knot in it, and it falls between my teeth, so I couldn't speak if I wanted to. With vicious swiftness, he ties this one off behind my head so tightly that I wince.

But then he climbs off my back and turns me over, pulling me upright to sitting. The garrote disappears from my neck.

A knife replaces it.

But now I can breathe. I can think. A hooded man holds the knife, the point tipping my chin up. His face is shadowed by the hood, and with the sun behind him, all I can see is the edge of his chin and the faint gleam of his eyes.

Asher. I'm going to tear him apart.

He glares back at me, as if he can sense my intent. "Make one sound, and I'll kill you." He doesn't look away. "Jory. Tie his bootlaces together. Loose enough so he can walk."

Her breathing is so quick I can hear it, fear undercutting every inhale. Is Asher forcing her to do this? Who is he? Is that why she was afraid?

She's the only reason you're not dead.

What does that mean?

But as Jory kneels to tug at my boots, I spot a flicker of motion in the shadowed hallway behind them. My heart jolts, thinking there's another assailant, but when the man shifts, I recognize his movements.

Nikko.

Oh, thank the stars.

He already has a dagger drawn, and he creeps along the wall silently. Relief blooms in my heart. My attacker will be a body on the floor in less than a second.

But Asher is too savvy—or maybe I'm just not that lucky. He notices my shifted focus, and he looks over his shoulder just as Nikko slips out of the shadows, sword drawn now.

Asher shoves Jory out of the way. I expect him to turn and fight with the dagger, but he doesn't. He leaps upward, catching the beam. He swings onto the wood in a feat of acrobatics that would be impressive if the situation were different. Nikko spins to come after him, but Asher's already ahead of him. He's barely on top of the beam before he's swinging off, using his momentum to aim a kick at Nikko's throat. Then he leaps onto my soldier's back the way he must have done to me.

Nikko swears and tries to stab back with his dagger. But instead of wrapping a garrote around his neck, Asher gets an arm around his throat. Then he snaps his head to the side.

Nikko drops like a rock.

I cry out, but the knot in my mouth captures the sound. Every muscle strains at the ropes, but I'm bound too tightly. My heartbeat is suddenly a roar in my ears.

Nikko. *Nikko.*

Even Jory is gasping. "Asher," she whispers, and her voice breaks. "*Asher.*"

But Asher climbs off the body of my fallen soldier, and he grabs my arm.

"Get up," he growls. "*Walk.*"

I don't move. I make myself a deadweight. I hope my eyes are issuing every deadly promise I can think of. I'm going to cut him into pieces and feed him each one. I'm going to pour honey into his eyes and let insects devour his face. I'm going to—

Asher leans close, until his eyes are all I see. "Get up and walk, or I will drag you into the hallway. And then I will wait for the rest of your men, and I will kill them one by one as they enter this room. While you *watch.*"

That same conviction rings in every word. He killed Nikko in a matter of seconds. One of my best soldiers. One of my closest friends.

Against my will, my eyes look away from Asher to find the body, crumpled on the stone floor.

Is his chest moving? Is he breathing? I can't tell.

Emotion grips my throat, but I shake it off and harden my thoughts. I've watched men fall in battle. I've been in bad situations. I know how to keep my wits about me.

When I look up, Jory is watching me.

"This wasn't—" Her breath hitches. "I promise. This . . . this wasn't . . ."

Her voice trails off.

"It was," says Asher.

His voice is cold.

Every emotion in my head ices over in response.

No time for regrets now. I need to wait for an opportunity.

Asher grabs my arm and gives it a tug.

This time, I stand.

Chapter Ten
THE PRINCESS

My heart is a wild thrum in my chest. I feel like I can hear every beat. Bile keeps threatening to escape my stomach, and I'm desperately trying to keep it down. I follow Asher through the king's rooms numbly, wondering how we reached this point.

He killed someone.

He *killed* someone.

I feel terribly naive, because it shouldn't be surprising. It's not as if he hasn't been clear about his occupation for years now. It's not as if I haven't seen violence and treachery before, either. But Asher stood in my chambers and tried to warn me, and I didn't listen. He showed me what he was capable of, and I ignored it. Maddox Kyronan is surrounded by guards. So am I. The thought of an assassin sneaking past our defenses to kill anyone seemed impossible.

But he did. Of course he did.

Worse: I helped him do it.

Oh, I'm such a fool. To think I cavalierly begged him to figure out a way to bring the king with us. Like we'd just lead him out of here, the way we used to sneak off to the stables. Like this would be the kind of grand adventure I've been longing for.

Asher killed one of the Incendrian soldiers. This . . . this is an end I didn't foresee.

See if you can get him alone, he said to me. *See if you can get him to disarm again. I know a way out of the royal guest suites.*

I thought he was worried about the king attacking me when I tried to explain. I thought he was prepared to act if it went badly. I just didn't realize Asher would do . . . *this.* I can't quite think straight—and I lost a minute to pure shock when he dropped from the rafters. There's a part of me that wants to shout for Captain Zale and the rest of the soldiers. There's a part of me that wants to shout for my *brother.*

But there's no relief here. We'd hang. Or we'd be handed over to Maddox Kyronan himself, because he'd be within rights to claim justice.

My eyes burn and my breath hitches, and I force myself to swallow it down. I have no right to cry. Ky just watched one of his men die, and now he's bound and gagged, being forced toward the back of the guest quarters.

I remember the moment he saw my bruised fingers. The sudden flare of protectiveness in his gaze.

He's not trying to kill me. I know he's not.

I just needed a few more minutes to figure out how to ask him.

Asher drags the king into the washroom, the hobbled boots making each step shuffle. His eyes are cold, every muscle on his frame tense. I heard what Asher said when he convinced Ky to rise to his feet, and after what he did to the first soldier, I'm terrified that he truly meant every word.

In the washroom, there's a small window above the water pump, but it's nowhere near big enough for us to crawl through—especially with Ky bound as he is. The walls are paneled with wood, and I'm startled when Asher uses his dagger to pry one open, revealing a pitch-dark gap in the wall, with a wide bricked hole in the floor.

"I'll take him first," he says to me, his soft voice tight and clipped. "We need to be fast. Pull the panel closed behind you and follow us. I'll wait at the bottom."

"What?" I gasp.

But he's already looking at Ky. "Jump, Your Majesty," he says. "It's not far."

The king glares back at him, and he doesn't move.

I remember listening to his gentle accent, watching the smile break across his face when he told me to call him Ky. I couldn't imagine how someone like that could be responsible for all the rumors spoken about him.

But now I can. The king's eyes promise vengeance. Furious, painful, deliberate retaliation. He doesn't seem afraid. He seems like he's *waiting*.

If that look proves anything, it's that this man wouldn't hire an assassin. He'd break me with his own two hands.

Asher isn't cowed, though. He steps forward with the dagger. "You can land on your feet, or I can push you. *Jump.*"

The king's eyes flash with fury, but he jumps. Whatever he lands in makes a wet, squelching sound. Then the smell reaches us, and I realize what we're about to jump into.

Asher's eyes flash to mine, and he's become so intimidating that I step back before I can stop myself.

He blinks in surprise, a tiny frown line appearing between his brows. For a flash, he's not a terrifying assassin kidnapping the king of a rival nation; he's Asher, my gentle childhood friend, the man I welcomed into my room in the dead of night.

"Jory?" he whispers.

I swallow, and my throat is so tight that it hurts. "You killed his soldier."

"No. I—" He breaks off when we hear the king take a step in the muck down below, and Asher looks aggrieved. "Remember to pull the panel," he murmurs. And he jumps into darkness, too.

Then I'm alone in the washroom, my breathing a roar in my ears. I'm tempted to pull the panel closed in front of me, trapping them down there together. I could check on the fallen soldier—or more likely, I could collapse in a pile of sobs right here. I imagine the Incendrian soldiers finding me in the washroom, leaning against the wall, choking on my heartbeat.

"What king?" I'd say. "There was a *king* here?"

A near-hysterical laugh bubbles up from my throat. This is insane.

Before I can think too closely about what we're doing, I step into the small space and pull the panel closed. Then I hold my breath, tuck up my skirts, and jump.

I expect it to be horrible, but it's worse. That hysterical laugh nearly turns into a sob. It's almost pitch-dark down here, and the smell is an assault to every fiber of my being. My eyes burn. I remember Asher vowing that I have no idea what life is like outside the palace, and I hate that this is my first taste of it. Surely being hung can't be worse than *this*. I refuse to drop my skirts. I've never been more grateful for the suede boots I chose to wear, instead of the satin slippers Charlotte usually sets out.

"Breathe through your mouth," Asher says. "Put your hand on my shoulder, Jor. I'll lead us out."

For the first time in my life, I don't want to touch him.

I also don't want to stay here, and the thought of losing track of him in the darkness is just as terrifying as everything else. I put a hand on his shoulder.

As we walk, our feet squish with every step. We find so many turns that I can't imagine how Asher learned them all. But it's not long before I learn why he insisted that we be silent: we can hear voices from above. Sometimes there are spots where the floorboards are worn and light peeks through. I listen for cries of alarm, some sign that someone has realized the king is missing.

But there's nothing. My chest clenches.

Well, of course there's nothing. Asher leapt onto his back within minutes of my arrival. We leapt into this sewer a few minutes later. I have no idea how long his men will wait before checking, but I doubt it's going to be soon.

The worst part is that I don't know what outcome to wish for. I keep my hand on Asher's shoulder, and I keep walking. The odor never dissipates. Eventually the noise of the palace fades away, leaving us in silence. I expect to come to an exit point, but we don't. It seems that we walk for *miles*. The only sound is my tense breathing and the wet slap of our feet through things I don't want to think about.

But then, almost without my being aware of it, the smell abates. Or . . . it *changes*. Instead of the bizarre cloying warmth of the tunnel, the air turns sharp and cold. Light fills the space up ahead, and I can finally see them both more clearly. Well, I can see Ky. Asher's hood is still drawn up, his features lost in shadow.

"Stop," says Asher. "Hold him. I'll see if it's safe." He takes my hand off his shoulder and puts it on the king's arm.

Hold him. I want to let him go.

No, that's stupid. Ky would surely kill us both. The rage hasn't left his gaze, and now that his eyes have shifted to me, I want to wither from the intense fury there. He left his bracers and blades back in his quarters, but he's still wearing a breastplate and greaves. I saw the hidden knives strapped to his wrists when he first disarmed, and I'm sure he has more weapons hidden.

If he gets free now, I doubt I'd have an opportunity to draw breath.

In the faint light, I can see the scrapes and bruising from where Asher choked him and pressed him into the floor. His jaw is hard and sharp, the rope gagging him so tightly that it's leaving marks, too.

The betrayal in his gaze is the hardest to look at.

"I'm sorry," I say, and his eyes seem to darken. He doesn't believe I'm *sorry* at all. It makes me rush on. "Please—you must understand. I need to explain. We had to get out of the palace. I didn't know Asher would—"

But then Asher is back. "It's clear," he says. "Come on."

The tunnel empties into a stream in the middle of the woods. I have no idea where we are, but the air is silent and undisturbed. We have to wade through a few inches of flowing water until we step up a snowy bank—a bit of a relief because it washes our boots clean, but also a bit of torture because the icy water slips past my laces to freeze my toes. The cold is almost violent, the morning sunlight doing nothing to ease the bitterness of the wind slipping between the trees.

I was relieved about the snow, but Asher looks down at our muddy footprints and frowns, then glances up at the sky. "We need to walk through the brush," he says. "We're only about a mile from the palace, and it'll be harder to follow."

A mile. That's somehow closer and farther than I expected. Wind whips around us, stinging my eyes.

Asher gives the king's arm a tug. "Come on."

This time, Ky plants his feet and holds fast. It's not just fury in his expression now, but willful determination.

Asher swears and jerks *hard*. Ky tries to catch himself, but the knotted bootlaces don't let him go far. He stumbles to his knees in the snow.

But once he's there, he sits back on his heels. His eyes are like fire.

Asher draws a blade.

I suck in a breath. "Asher."

He's not looking at me. "Get up," he snaps.

The king tries to speak around the knotted rope in his mouth, but he can't. It doesn't take an exceptional mind to figure it out, though.

Fuck you.

Asher steps right up to him and puts the point of that dagger against Ky's throat. "I said, *get up.*"

The king doesn't move. He doesn't say a word, but he doesn't have to. His eyes are dark and full of hatred, and the rigid stillness in his frame says volumes.

A trickle of blood appears at the edge of the blade, but he doesn't even flinch.

I can't keep watching Asher hurt him. Maybe I really am naive, but I never want to see him harm anyone again.

Heedless of the weapon, I step in front of him. "Asher! Stop *hurting* him."

From under the hood, his expression is dispassionate and cool, and I really don't expect him to obey. He's a vicious stranger, not the man who hung upside down from my rafters, offering to share his cookie.

But then his eyes soften, and he's Asher again. He withdraws the dagger point from the king's throat, but he doesn't put it away. Icy wind whips between us again, and my control over this moment feels very tenuous.

Asher's voice is very quiet. "They paid to kill you, Jory."

I wet my lips and look back at Ky. He's watching us both—and he makes absolutely no attempt to deny that. He wrenches at the bindings, but Asher was thorough. There's no give.

I drop to a crouch to look at the king eye to eye. The rope marks on his throat are turning purple, vivid in the sunlight, and it looks like his bottom lip has cracked and split from the pressure of being gagged.

But his eyes blaze into mine, and there's no fear. It's all rage.

This spiraled out of control so quickly. I'm not sure how to explain— or if he even deserves an explanation.

"Did you hire an assassin to kill me?" I say.

That cuts through the fury. He goes still, and a line appears between his eyebrows. He shakes his head and tries to speak through the gag. "No."

I regard him levelly. "Your soldiers, then?"

He shakes his head again, more emphatically. *"No."*

I put out a hand to Asher. "Give me the dagger."

"He wants you dead. If you cut him loose, you will be."

The king says something I can't quite make out, but it sounds a lot like *"You* will be."

"I'm not cutting him loose," I say—because it's terrifying to consider that Asher is right. "But I need to talk to him."

Asher sets his jaw, but he flips the dagger in his hand, then holds it out to me, hilt first.

When I look back at Ky, he's watching this. Taking note of it as if it's significant. It reminds me of that moment in my chambers, when he knew I'd hidden the hairpin.

Right for the eyes? That's vicious, Princess.

I'm not vicious. Not really.

But *he* is. I have to remind myself that there's a reason my father set such a far-reaching decree, banning fire in the entire kingdom. There's a reason the taverns are full of gossip.

He sat in my chambers and spoke of hope for his people, but I can't forget that Maddox Kyronan has a dangerous reputation that long precedes him.

And we took him prisoner.

I brace myself, then reach out and cut the gag loose.

Ky spits the knotted rope into the snow, and he wastes no time. "Why would I send an assassin?" he demands. His eyes are fierce, his accent biting. He wrenches at his bindings again. "If you had such a suspicion, why would you not involve your guards?"

"Assassins know how to get past the guards," Asher says flatly. "Clearly."

The king's eyes glance between us. "Who is this man, Princess? Are you working in conjunction with the Draegs?"

"No!"

"How much did they offer you?"

"Nothing!" I cry. He's getting this all wrong. "I'm not working with Draegonis."

"Then it's ransom," he says bitterly. "My sister won't pay. But my soldiers *will* find you."

"I don't want ransom! Would you listen—"

"You clearly need me alive," he says. "It's obvious you're working with someone."

"She's working with me," Asher says, and he takes an aggressive step forward. "And I'm just trying to keep her alive. She's the one trying to protect *you*. If she wasn't, I would've left your body on the floor."

"Asher."

"What?" The promise of violence is back in his gaze, and this time I don't know if it's for me or for the king. "You saw my orders. You know what I do, Jory."

I have to swallow. I don't want the reminder. I look back at Ky and try to keep my voice level. "I *am* trying to protect you," I say. "Either my father or my brother hired an assassin to kill you. We had to get out of the palace."

"Now your *king* is the one who hired an assassin?" He looks between us like we're crazy—and the sad part is that maybe we are. In the harsh silence of the woods, this entire adventure feels insane. "And instead of alerting me or my soldiers about the nature of the threat," he continues, "you felt it was most prudent to do . . . *this*."

"Yes," I say.

"I have written orders," Asher says, glaring at him. "The Crown hired me to kill you. And *you* hired me to kill *her*."

"No." Ky glares right back, his gaze burning like hot embers. "I didn't."

"I don't believe you were responsible either," I say in a rush. "But Asher has proof that *someone* from Incendar did. Once it's clear that we're not dead, another assassin will be sent. We had to get out of the palace."

Ky hasn't looked away from Asher. "Did this man tell you this, Princess? He killed my soldier. I am bound in the middle of the woods. None of this feels like *protection*."

"I didn't kill your soldier!" Asher says, aggrieved. He puts out a hand. "Give me the knife, Jor. This is taking too long. Just leave him. Come on."

I hesitate, because I'm thinking of the moment he put the hilt against my neck, a demonstration of what he was capable of. Ten minutes later, he was proving it.

"Asher." I wet my lips. "You really didn't kill that man?"

"Trust me, I know how to kill people. I don't do it for free."

I stare at him, biting the edge of my lip. My heart keeps tripping along, stumbling between fear and hope. He's never lied to me before—but he's never done any of *this* before, either.

I'm not the boy you remember.

I suppose he's proving it.

Asher's eyes go a bit sad, and he draws back, his mouth forming a line. "Fine. Believe what you want. But they'll be tracking us soon. We need to move."

That strikes its mark. I swallow and hold out the blade.

Ky makes an aggravated sound. "Do not go with him, Princess. I asked to begin with honesty, and I have. If you are not lying to *me*, then he is lying to *you*."

Asher thrusts the weapon back into its hilt. "She's known me a lot longer than she's known you, asshole. The only reason you're here is that she's trying to keep you safe. If you won't get up and walk, sit there and freeze."

"If you are *truly* trying to save my life," Ky says, "then unbind me. I can defend myself."

"No," Asher snaps. "Jory might think you're harmless, but I don't."

The king's voice drops. "I never said I was harmless, Asher."

It's the first time the king has said his name, and the low intensity of it strikes a chord in my chest, making me shiver in a way that has nothing to do with the snow. To my surprise, that purring accent seems to have an effect on Asher, too. He seems to falter, some of the disdain slipping off his face.

But as they glare at each other, snowflakes continue to fall from the sky, and I try to pull at a cloak I don't have. My breath streams out of my mouth in clouded bursts.

Asher's gaze shifts to me, his eyes in shadow under the hood of his coat. "*Please*," he says more quietly, and I can feel his urgency. "I know a place, and we need to get out of sight."

I nod quickly. "I'll follow you."

"This way," he says, turning away from Ky and heading toward the trees, forging into the brush. The black of his clothing is a stark contrast to the snow-covered forest.

But I hesitate, giving Ky one last look. His eyes are still shadowed and angry, and I have no way to undo that.

"Please," I say. "Come with us. I didn't mean for it to happen this way, but he's not lying. I'm not either. If Asher says it wasn't safe for us in the palace, I believe him."

Before I can change my mind, I turn to trail after my friend, feeling my heartbeat pound with every step. Behind me, there's nothing but shrouded silence, emphasizing that there's no turning back on the decisions I've already made.

I didn't kill your soldier, Asher said.

Oh, how I hope that's true. I've never doubted him—but then I've never seen him like this. Full of violence and ruthlessness. He might not have killed that soldier, but he could have. And now he's leaving the king in the snow to freeze.

Please, I think. *Please follow us.*

But maybe that would be worse. We did take him prisoner. He surely doesn't see me as an ally now.

Oh, Asher.

I wish I'd known it would be like this. But maybe it could *only* be like this.

Either way, after an agonizing minute, I hear the king give a ragged sigh. Then he must shove to his feet, because his hobbled footsteps are heavy in the snow as he begins to follow.

Chapter Eleven
THE WARRIOR

Most of my earliest memories include my father and a battlefield. My mother died in childbirth when I was four, leaving my father with tough choices. Victoria, my baby sister, was given to nannies and nursemaids, but from the instant I was old enough to walk, I had learned to ride a horse and handle a weapon, so my father kept me by his side. I was thrust into my first battle at age twelve, when soldiers from Draegonis attacked our encampment. I was ready. I hadn't discovered my magic yet, but I'd already spent years in my father's shadow, learning all the ways a man could wage war. Seeing all the ways a king should *lead*. I was full of pride to be the youngest in his retinue, so when I turned sixteen, I was surprised when he ordered me to return to the capital city to enlist as a recruit.

At first, I didn't mind—I had years of experience that the other young soldiers hadn't yet imagined. I expected to be the best in the training arena, and as the crown prince, I knew I'd be glorified for my skills. But instead of running drills and sparring with the others, my captain gave me every chore, every poor assignment, every torturous duty. While other recruits were practicing swordplay or galloping between army points, I was shoveling manure or cleaning sweat-stained tack. I complained about it daily, never earning a single reprieve. I finally wrote to my father, frustrated about my lowly treatment, begging to return to the battlefield where I could be of *use*.

Every duty is essential, he wrote back. *Nothing you do for your fellow soldiers is lowly. These are your people, and they risk their lives for you. Remember that when you are scrubbing latrines.*

And then, to add to the sting, the grueling assignments got *worse*. But I shut my mouth and stopped complaining—and to my surprise, the other recruits began to help me: relieving me early from long overnight guard duty, soaping up the mess hall by my side, and even scrubbing latrines. Instead of finding glory, I gained *friends*.

When we eventually made it to the battlefield, I saw that loyalty in action, as my fellow recruits did indeed risk their lives for Incendar—and for me. It led to my father's next lesson: *If you are to lead them, you must understand them.* When he brought me back to his side, I was no longer in his shadow. He'd have me walk among the regiments every day, watching training drills, listening to complaints, mediating arguments. It taught me to pay attention. I learned how to tell which soldiers were too confident, too fearful, too aggressive, too lazy. I learned how to read the signs for when someone was lying, when someone was telling the truth, and all the gray areas in between.

By the time my magic manifested, it became a tool, a weapon to wield like any other. Because my father's lessons were so deeply ingrained, I realized that the people around me were so much more important than any power I could draw from a flame. Even after he died, I continued my daily rounds. I figured out how to tell the difference between a soldier who needed a friend, who needed a king and commander, and who just needed to be left alone. I learned to spot the signs of a person who'd cave under pressure, or a soldier who'd only give his best in the heat of battle. I determined who I could trust—and who I'd have to watch.

Thanks to those skills, I've been able to form tight-knit regiments that are relentless in battle. It's how I knew Nikko would dive right back into a fight despite the torture he endured, or how I came to trust that Roman could strategize a mission with his eyes closed. It's the way I can watch Callum and Garrett bicker like siblings—with the certainty that they'll stand strong when it matters.

It's how I knew Jory's disguise was more than just deception.

Right now, it's how I know Asher *didn't* plan this—or if he did, it's a complete fucking disaster.

He has no pack, no supplies, nothing beyond what seems to be a spontaneous decision to drag me out of the palace. When he first got that garrote around my neck, I thought this might be an insidious attack by Draegonis. But I simply can't make that work in my head anymore.

A Draeg spy would *never* leave me alive.

And he might know how to kill, but Asher has definitely never been a soldier. There's a lack of discipline, of *control*, that's unmistakable. It's a disquiet behind all the belligerence. He hides it well, but once my adrenaline from the attack wore off, I could see every sign. He's defiant and hostile, but it's a bluff. A feint. He's got the vicious skill to back up his threats, and in the short term, it's clearly effective. He took down Nikko in two seconds. He forced me out of the palace by vowing to kill my soldiers.

But when I don't flinch away from his aggression, Asher clearly falters. The moment he put that knife against my throat, I refused to move—and it became clear that he wouldn't push it farther. I've had soldiers like that before: skilled men who hesitate when they meet true resistance. It's a lack of resolve. Of *conviction*. If he were one of my recruits, he's the kind of man I'd have to pair with less experienced soldiers to build his confidence—offering nothing less than candor to gain his trust.

It's no surprise that he had to attack from above and behind. I rather doubt he would've had the mettle to come at me face-to-face.

He's faltering now, too. It's in the way he left me alive, leaving me the choice to follow. Or the way he insists that he didn't kill Nikko—when he absolutely could have. There's a part of me that doesn't want to believe him, but he sounded so . . . *annoyed* when I accused him of killing my soldier. He seemed hurt when Jory doubted him. That speaks to truth. But if he left Nikko alive, that was reckless—and there's certainly no advantage to telling me. Asher should want to appear as vicious as possible.

But he's not.

He's certainly convinced Jory. She's following him willingly now, striding through the snow ahead of me, but there were moments where she seemed genuinely afraid. I wonder how they know each other. They share a casual manner that suggests familiarity—but the princess seemed truly shocked by his brutality. Not just shocked. Horrified.

That said, she helped him do this. I just can't tell if he coerced her or if she was willing.

I wonder what would've happened if I'd balked in the washroom, if I'd called his bluff *then,* before we were so far outside the palace. He vowed to kill the rest of my soldiers one by one—but I'm beginning to suspect that he wouldn't have done anything more than take the princess and flee.

Not that I'm in a position to criticize. I was distracted by a pretty girl.

By the time we finally stop, we've gone at least a mile through the brush, and falling snow has trickled under my collar to make me shiver. This cold is piercing, and it assaults us all. The princess is clutching her arms against her body, her hands tucked under her biceps. None of us have a cloak. The only person with gloves is Asher, and even his breath is trembling as he shivers. I'm still wearing the fur-lined gear I wore on the ride here, but my bare fingers feel numb, and my ankles ache from walking with my bootlaces tied together.

I don't know where I expected us to end up, but there's almost nothing here. Just a small copse of pine trees encircling a tiny hut that's practically buried in a snowdrift. If we hadn't stopped, I might not have even noticed it. Asher kicks snow away from the door, tugging at the handle.

I stand at a bit of a distance, doing my best to calculate how much time has passed. Asher said we were a mile away from the palace when we stepped out of the sewers, so we can't be too far outside the capital city. I hoped we'd hear evidence of search parties: shouting in the woods, mounted guards and soldiers trotting through. But there's been nothing—and walking so far underground will make us impossible to follow. This falling snow will obscure our tracks, too, and rather immediately.

I close my eyes and think of my friend. *Sev. Please. Find me.*

I imagine him somewhere out in the world, equally desperate. *Ky. Where the hell are you?*

The door finally gives, and snow slides from the roof to land inside. Asher gestures for Jory to enter, then stands back and looks at me. I can only see the barest glimpse of his features under the hood of his coat.

"Don't go near her," he says. "Stay by the wall."

I'm tempted to push him a little, to see how he'd react—but I suspect he might just lock me out here in the snow. I walk past him, my tied bootlaces snapping taut with every step.

Once we're inside, I hope for cloaks or blankets or *something*. But no, the walls and floor are bare planks that smell musty, with an old wood-burning stove taking up one corner. Dust and cobwebs coat the dark surface, but a small stack of aged wood sits beside it. I don't need magic to know that it's been a while since a fire burned in this room.

I sigh and lean against the wall beside a snow-covered window. I keep trying to flex my wrists, but there's so little give.

The princess is in worse shape. Her gown is thick, because the palace was so cold, but it's completely unsuitable for a hike in the snow. She tried to hold her dress out of the water, but the hem is soaking wet anyway, along with her boots. They're slim suede riding boots, not army boots, and the water from the stream likely soaked through. Despite the velvet of her dress, she's shivering so fiercely that I almost feel pity.

Asher looks at the stove for a long moment, then looks at me from under the hood. His tense deliberation practically *radiates*.

"Cold?" I say darkly.

"I'm fine."

"The princess isn't. Untie me. I can make it warm."

"By burning me alive? No, thank you." But he glances at the princess, then shoves back the hood and shrugs out of his jacket.

"Here," he says to Jory. His tone is quieter. Gentler. "Put this on."

"Th-thank you," she says, slipping her arms through the sleeves, pulling it tightly around herself, even going so far as to draw the hood up, until it's *her* face in shadow.

But I'm not looking at her, I'm looking at Asher. It's my first chance to really see him, and I'm surprised to discover that he's not some unkempt outlaw. He's clean-shaven and sharp-featured, and a bit younger than I expected—closer to the princess's age than mine. His white-blond hair is a shade I've never seen on a grown man. It's longer on top, falling into his blue eyes in a way that makes him seem almost petulant. Dark vertical lines have been inked onto his left cheek, stretching from his jaw to just below his eye.

They must be significant. I saw a few men with something similar in one of Prince Dane's battle camps, but those men only had one or two. Asher seems to have half a dozen.

He's lithe and leanly muscled, not built like a soldier at all. It explains how he was able to leap onto that beam like he was weightless—and why he struggled to keep me pinned. I probably have him by forty pounds. Maybe more.

If he were a second slower, I could've broken every bone in his body before he even knew it was happening. If the princess hadn't asked me to disarm, I could've cut that garrote and plunged a dagger into his throat before he pulled it taut.

I'm such an idiot.

Jory hasn't stopped shivering, and I'm guessing it's the soaked boots causing a problem. She's begun to stomp her feet against the dirt floor, and a little whimper escapes her mouth. She glances around the tiny room desperately, likely looking for the same blankets or cloaks I hoped for.

I refuse to let it tug at my heart. I'm still bound, and I'm not sure I believe anything they've told me.

I *refuse*.

"Take these, too," says Asher, yanking his gloves free. His voice is still low.

Jory shivers, pulling them over her hands. Her clouded breath stutters with her voice. "Th-thank you."

Oh, fine. I'm not heartless. "You need to take the boots off," I say. "If your feet are wet, you'll never get warm. Sit on the floor and wrap your feet up in your skirts so they dry."

I don't expect her to listen, but she does. She sits in a pile of lavender velvet and satin, tucking the dry parts of her skirts around her legs, the black leather and fur of his jacket a stark contrast. The worst of her shivering seems to abate.

This time she looks at me, and a hint of a blush finds her cheeks. "Thank you, Ky."

"Yes, Princess."

Asher scowls.

Jory's eyes flick to the stove, and then back to him—and finally to me. I already know what she's thinking, but I hold her gaze and say nothing.

She chews on her lip, and her eyes shift back to Asher. "We should light it," she says.

His focus is locked on me. "No."

"His hands are bound."

"I don't care."

"It doesn't do us any good if we freeze to death!" she says.

"It doesn't do us any good if we *burn* to death."

"It's freezing," she says more quietly. "Asher, please."

He draws an aggravated breath—but when he exhales, it streams out in a visible cloud, and even he can't hold back a shiver. "I don't have flint," he finally says. "Do you?"

She inhales sharply—then frowns. Of course she doesn't.

"I have flint," I offer.

Asher regards me for the longest minute, but he doesn't move. I add, "You're going to torture her because you're afraid of me?"

"I'm not doing anything to her. It's freezing *because* of you." But he crosses the small stretch of floor to stop in front of me, and our fogging breaths mingle between us. "Where is it?"

I don't answer. Garrett would spit right in his face, but I'm not quite that petty. This close, I can see the start of bruising along his chin, the slight split in his lip. I remember the bruises on the princess's knuckles. Is he the one she punched? What did he do to cause it?

My lack of an answer seems to aggravate him, because he steps closer and begins tugging at the pouches of my belt. I wonder if I have enough give in these bootlaces to kick him in the crotch and take him down. Probably not.

Instead, I say, "What do the marks on your face mean?"

"They mean I was stupid." He finds a handful of coins before he finds flint, and they jingle in his palm as he looks down at the silver. I fully expect him to pocket the coins like a thief, and I'm genuinely surprised when he puts them back.

"An honorable killer?" I say to him, and his blue eyes flick up.

"You're a killer, too," he says. "Don't try to deny it."

"I didn't."

He tugs at the next pouch, but his eyes hold mine. "I'm not a thief."

"What is your plan?" I say.

"You don't need to worry about my *plan*."

"Because you don't have one?" I say, and it earns me a glare. He finds the flint and palms it, turning away from me to kneel before the stove. When he draws the door open, a plume of dust comes with it.

"We're going to an inn," the princess says, shivering between words. "The Three Fishes. Right?"

"We can't go there now," Asher says. "We have to stay out of sight." He thrusts a dusty log into the stove, tosses some kindling on top, and strikes the flint.

The instant a spark forms, I feel it in my bones, like a surge of energy I can't ignore. It's stronger than I ever remember, but maybe the length of time away from any kind of flame made my magic desperate. The kindling catches, and I jerk at my bonds involuntarily. Every muscle in my body goes taut, my hands fighting to form a sigil before I'm even aware of what I'm doing.

Nothing. I'm bound too tightly.

But the sudden effort makes me gasp, and Asher and Jory both snap their heads up to look at me. Inside the stove, the fire catches the wood, and warmth swells into the room, quick and intense. This close, I can feel every flicker, every plume of flame, like a beckoning. Even without sigils, any fire in my presence responds to my magic, burning hotter and higher than normal, like an eager student awaiting a teacher's instruction.

Asher draws back, but Jory quickly shuffles forward on her skirts, holding out her hands toward the stove.

Asher is watching me instead. His throat jumps as he swallows. Even with my hands bound, the fire makes him anxious, I can tell.

I might be willing to tear him to pieces if I get loose, but I don't want him anxious. At any moment, he could decide my survival means too much risk to them both. I'm surprised he hasn't already.

So I lean against the wall and slide down to sitting, and I take the edge out of my voice. "So you have no plan." I tug at the leather straps trapping my arms. "I am to be your captive in this tiny room for . . . ever?"

"You're not our captive," Jory says, and her voice is quiet. She glances from me to Asher. "Asher brought me his orders, and I . . . I didn't know who I could trust."

"I am bound, and he is not. The aim of your trust is clear." Her frown deepens, so I continue, "You said you had proof of these orders. Show me."

Jory reaches into the bodice of her dress and pulls folded parchment free, then crawls in her skirts to stop in front of me. She pushes the hood of his coat back, and a few curls escape her pinned hair, leaving tendrils to twist around her jaw. She looks so small and helpless. I cannot believe this is the same young woman who helped an assassin steal me away from the palace.

Actually, yes I can. She already hid her identity once. Then I believed all her words about hope and need and wanting the best for her people. When she seemed so afraid, when she so guilelessly asked me to disarm a second time, I did it.

Bleeding skies, I am *such* an idiot.

"Look," she says, holding up the parchment.

I study the shimmering seal that I recognize from documents Dane and I have already exchanged, then look up. "Who is the Hunter's Guild?"

Asher raises a hand. "Me."

"They're assassins," Jory says, and her voice has gone a bit hushed. "They can be hired by anyone. *For* anyone."

I glance between them. "For *anyone*? And your king allows this?"

"The palace pays the Hunter's Guild quite a bit." Asher must have decided I can't incinerate him, because he's finally moved closer to the fire. He drops to sit beside Jory. He pushes hair back from his face, and the fire turns the strands to gold. "The Guildmaster approves every job before they're revealed to the Hunters. I shouldn't even *have* those. We're supposed to burn them after we read them, but . . ." He gestures to me. "*Well*. It's rumored that any killings of political import are sanctioned by the king himself—or Dane, now that he's regent. That's why there's a seal—so we know we're not risking *treason*."

"Is this how you know each other?" I say, glancing between them both. "The princess of Astranza is secretly ruthless with her pet mercenary?"

"No!" she cries, just as Asher growls, "I'm no one's *pet*."

I raise my eyebrows and look back at them.

Jory looks right back at me. "Asher's my friend," she says. "I've known him all my life."

"Just a friend?" I say. "Or more?"

"A *friend*," she says, but her cheeks flush. "He wasn't always a . . . a Hunter."

Asher says nothing. His jaw is set.

I lean back against the wall, trying to take some of the pressure off my wrists. It doesn't help. "Fine," I say. "But there's absolutely no political benefit for anyone in Astranza to kill me—least of all King Theodore, or even Dane. Draeg forces threaten *both* our countries. There's no love lost between me and your brother, but we've been working toward this alliance for months. Why kill me *now*?"

"I don't know," Jory says. She wets her lips.

"Maybe because *your* people hired us to kill his sister," says Asher.

"But they *didn't*." This feels a bit like arguing with my army captains when they can't decide on a plan of attack. I heave an impatient sigh. "Show me the other one."

Jory reveals the second page, and there it is, the order for her death, paid in Incendrian silver. A *lot* of silver. More than we would have carried with us.

I look back at Asher. "Did you see the coins?"

"No. All funds are held by the keeper of the books. No one receives their share until the job is done."

That seems convenient. I try to examine this from as many angles as I can consider, coming up with nothing. Neither Dane's order nor "mine."

"I did not do this, Princess. I swear to you. Untie me, and we can return to the palace, where you can question my men yourself."

Jory says nothing for a moment. She's stopped shivering, and her eyes are piercing as she studies me.

But then her gaze softens, and she shifts forward. I think she really is going to untie me—until Asher grabs her arm. "Even if it's not him, Jory, this order came in before dawn. Someone from his traveling party did this in his name."

"Then it's a forgery," I say to him. "Or a trick. My men were with me for the entire ride to your palace."

But as I say the words, I realize they're not *entirely* true. My men were with me until the last hour, when Sev and I split off.

But still. I can't see the other four conspiring to have the princess killed and hiring an assassin in that final hour. Not together, and not individually. They all know how desperately Incendar needs this alliance. Besides, they wouldn't bother with hiring an assassin. If any one of them wanted her dead, he just would've done it himself.

"I said the same thing about Dane and my father," Jory says. "This has to be a trick."

Asher makes a frustrated sound. "Those are both official orders, sealed by the Guildmaster. If these jobs weren't completed by sundown, the price was to be cut in half, and they'd send another Hunter. Now that we're gone, they probably already *have*." His voice turns cold. "If you return *alive*, the Guild won't receive the full pay for these assignments— and you'll still be at risk. If *I* return alive, the Guildmaster will sell me away to make up the difference. I got you out of the palace, Jory. I got *him* out of the palace." A darker note enters his voice, something hollow. Something *haunted*. Every muscle on his frame is tense. "But I'm not going back to the slavers. Not even for you."

"Asher," she whispers. She frowns and reaches toward his arm.

He immediately stiffens, drawing back. Her frown deepens, but she lets her hand fall.

My eyebrows go up. "Slavers?" I say. "There are *slaves* in Astranza?"

Jory glances at Asher, then back to me. "No. Not really."

Asher says nothing. His jaw is a hard edge. He's very deliberately not looking at her now.

"Not . . . *really?*" I say.

Jory regards him for a moment, then bites at her lip before answering. "They aren't slaves," she says, and her voice is quiet. "They're indentured. It's a debt repaid by service. Generations ago, it began with penalties for wrongdoing. If someone was found guilty of a crime, a fine would be levied by the Crown. If the criminal had no funds, there were wealthy nobles who would cover what was due and force the debtor into service until the balance was repaid. But now, *any* unpaid debt can be sold for service, and there's quite a business to be made selling the indebted citizens to those who need workers." She hesitates, casting a glance at Asher again. "Admittedly, rumor says that some are more honorable than others. But it's more equitable than leaving prisoners languishing in a cell, and fairer than leaving a family without food because of a husband's gambling debts."

On the surface, it's an intriguing concept. Making citizens work off the penalties of their crimes *does* seem fair and equitable—and beneficial to the kingdom. I can tell by her voice that she has been raised to believe in this system.

I can tell by Asher's expression that he thinks it's complete and total horseshit.

Interesting. Because they might be friends, but I'm not sure the princess is aware of how deep his tension runs. I see the longing in his eyes every time he looks at her, and I can hear the devotion when he speaks. But I watched him withdraw when she reached for him. She spoke so matter-of-factly, while the sheer mention of these slavers seems to make Asher very unsettled.

I wonder what he did to earn this *indenture,* whether he owed a debt or committed a crime. Based on this venture, I can probably guess.

He notices my focus. "Stop looking at me."

"Did the slavers give you those marks?"

His eyes narrow. "I told you to stop looking at me."

"So that's a *yes,* then."

He draws his dagger, quicker than lightning, but he doesn't move from that spot. "If you don't shut up and look away, I'm going to cut your eyes out."

I hold his gaze. "Then do it, Asher."

The princess sucks in a breath, but Asher goes very still, like a panther that's spotted its prey and is waiting for the precise moment to leap.

I shouldn't provoke him. If he actually attacks me, I have no way to defend myself. But I'd rather have him angry than anxious, and I don't think he will.

Seconds tick by while we sit there regarding each other. I think the princess is holding her breath. His dagger is a nice piece of weaponry, and it's so black that the firelight doesn't even gleam off the edge. His thumb brushes along the hilt, over and over.

But there's a point where the tension shifts, and it's clear he's not going to act. It takes a moment for him to look away, and when he does, his eyes flick to the door, to the floor, anywhere but me. He thrusts the dagger back into the hilt. The panther slinking back into the brush to wait for easier prey.

"It would upset Jory," he says.

Ah. Yes. Of course.

I don't call him out—or dwell on it. Instead, I turn the conversation back to the matter at hand. "You've shown me your proof," I say to them both. "While I do not believe it, I trust that you meant to protect me, Princess. I trust that you meant to protect this alliance."

She holds my eyes boldly. "Yes," she says. "I did." There's so much conviction in her voice that I'm reminded of why our first meeting offered so much hope.

"I trust that you believe in your friend, too."

At that, her lips part, and she nods. "I do." She glances at Asher, who's still scowling, then looks back to me. "I believe that he saved us both. I told him I wouldn't leave without you. I know this alliance is important to you. It's important to me, too. Please, you *must* believe that."

The sad thing is that I *do* believe it—or at least, I believe *her*.

"If this alliance carries such weight for you," I say, "then you must release me, Princess."

She stares back at me, and I watch her deliberate.

"If we are to be allies," I continue, "if we are to be *wed*, then allow this to be our first test of loyalty to each other. You protected me. If we are in danger, allow me to do the same. I can protect *you*."

She shifts her weight, turning to look at Asher.

But he doesn't look back. Instead, he finally looks at *me*, and his eyes are like blue fire. "I can protect her, too. I know what you're doing."

"I am speaking truths," I say.

"Bullshit." He glares at me, then turns to her. "I bested him, Jory. I bested his soldier. He needs *you* for this alliance, but he doesn't need me. If you cut him loose, make no mistake: I'll be dead on the floor a minute later—or I'll be wishing I was. Then he'll drag you back to Dane so you can be wed and he gets his alliance."

Jory's breathing has quickened, but Asher's not fidgeting now. His eyes haven't left mine. "Admit it."

"No."

That's too easy, and Asher isn't fooled. His eyes narrow, and he rolls up onto his knees to move closer to me. "Then *deny* it. Tell her I'd be safe. Tell her you'd let me go."

Firelight paints the walls with shadows, but breath still fogs faintly between us. Asher is close enough that I can count the lines on his cheek. Seven stripes, in shades of blue and violet. I really do wonder what they mean.

When I don't answer, he shifts closer, until our knees nearly touch. Through the fall of blond hair, his blue eyes are vibrant. Challenging. For a moment, I think I've grossly miscalculated—that he really *might* carve my eyes out, just to prove he's vicious enough. In any other circumstance, I'd find him intriguing. I can see why the princess seems so devoted. Despite the chaos of this venture, there's something a bit compelling about him.

"*Deny it*," he says again.

I wonder if he'd be this brave if I were unbound. There's a part of me that wants to find out.

But I think of how brutally he attacked. I think of what he did to Nikko, who might be alive—or might be dead. I think of how desperate my people are for an alliance.

I think about how this kidnapping must look to everyone else in the palace. Their princess disappeared—after being alone with me, the man they all fear.

Deny it.

I look right back into those vivid blue eyes. "No."

Jory gasps, but Asher sits back, satisfied. "Exactly. Keep him bound, Jor. He's lucky we got him this far." His eyes glitter in the light from the stove. "At nightfall, we'll take to the road, and we'll leave him behind."

Chapter Twelve
THE ASSASSIN

We could've been in the inn by now. Jory rarely leaves the palace without a full entourage, so it's not like she'd be recognized. We could've been tucked away in the corner of a room somewhere, sharing a quiet meal, making a plan for how to evade all of the people who'd be looking for her. She'd be woefully unprepared for life outside the palace, but I could've kept her safe.

Instead, I've kidnapped the most violent man on the continent. Trackers are surely searching for all three of us. If the king gets free, I'll be a charred corpse in seconds. If the Astranzan palace guards find us, I'll be thrown in the dungeon and sold off to slavers anyway. If the Hunter's Guild sends Logan or Gunnar, either one of them will kill us all.

All of these threats are very real, the weight of them pressing down until it's hard to breathe. The last thing I expect to do is *sleep*.

But I do.

When my eyes flick open, I have a moment of disoriented panic. My face is pressed into my arm, and I'm curled against the stone floor. For a moment, I think I'm still trapped in Morinstead, that all of this has been a dream. I have to remind myself that I'm not in a cell, that there are no chains to rattle when I move. There are no guards waiting to tether me over a rail while they take their pleasure, no foremen handing over coins while they sell me away to the highest bidder. The small hut has gone dim, the fire in the stove reduced to glowing embers, though it's still warm. Almost *too* warm, which is probably why I fell asleep.

Jory seems to have fallen victim to the same exhaustion. She was awake most of the night, too. She's curled up on the floor directly in front of the stove, using my jacket as a pillow.

The king is still leaning against the wall, and I think he's asleep as well, but when I shift my weight to sit up, his eyes open instantly.

Something in his expression makes me go still, and I try to shake it off, dodging his gaze. His constant focus knots up my shoulders with tension.

Not because he's a threat. Not even because of what I've done.

It's the way he watches me, his gaze unflinching. The way he *talks* to me, with no disdain or arrogance. He's very forthright. Very candid. And maybe a bit of a prick, but no more than I deserve.

If you don't shut up and look away, I said, *I'm going to cut your eyes out.*

The way he looked back at me was so piercing. *Then do it, Asher.*

I've never held anyone's focus like this. I'm barely used to anyone even looking at me—except for Jory.

"How long did I sleep?" I say softly, so as not to wake her.

There's a part of me that doesn't expect him to answer, but he does. "A few hours, maybe. I have no way to measure."

I glance over, but his features are in shadow now, the dim light pulling a glow from his hair, along with a few glints on the buckles of his armor. He's a bit striking, which I didn't expect. Jory could do worse, I suppose. I'm sure he's formidable on the battlefield, because he seems fearless. Daring, too. Between that and the purr of his accent, it's no wonder Jory melts every time he speaks to her. Last night, she seemed revolted by the idea of having a pile of children with this man, but now that she's met him, I half expect her to ask if they should start trying right here.

Allow this to be our first test of loyalty. I can protect you.

Her lips parted, and her eyes went soft. She was ready to draw a dagger and cut him free on the spot.

I don't want to be jealous. I don't.

But I am.

The worst part is that I'm not so much jealous of their attraction as I'm jealous of everything *else*. If I hadn't gotten these orders, they'd be finalizing their alliance. Jory would be allowing her ladies to stitch her into that wedding gown without a hint of resistance. The king's men would be clapping him on the shoulder and smiling. He and Jory would be riding back to Incendar in his carriage, swearing to protect each other.

Leaving me behind.

Because I'd be . . . *here*. Alone. No one's ever going to swear a thing to *me*. No vows, no promises, not even a flicker of fleeting interest. Not with these marks on my face that ensure no one will ever look at me with anything but scorn or disdain. Not when the one place that ever felt safe is going to be an empty chamber in the palace.

Stars in darkness, I have to shove these thoughts away. It's not as if I even need protection. What I *need* is to stop brooding and figure out a plan—because as much as I hate it, the king was right about that. Jory has no warm clothing, no way to travel after dark. I don't have any money. I *could* steal the king's coins, but showing up at a merchant stall with a handful of Incendrian silver will look a little suspicious. I could steal clothing from somewhere, but we're a mile away from anything, and I don't like the idea of leaving Jory alone with the king that long.

Not because I'm worried he'd hurt her. He'd convince her to let him go.

And what I told her was true. If we're caught, *she* might be fine, but I definitely wouldn't be. Even if I believe that he has nothing to do with these orders to kill the princess—which I'm not sure I do—if I'm caught by anyone at all, it would not go well for me. Right now, our only advantage is distance from the palace—and the fact that we haven't been found. Even if his men discovered the access point to the sewers, there'd be no way to follow our tracks.

And that's not even considering the Hunter's Guild. Logan and Gunnar definitely know the sewers—though they wouldn't know which way I'd go. That said, there's a limited number of escape routes, and this is one of them. My only hope is that news of their disappearance will take time to reach the Guildmaster. Hopefully, Jory and I will be long gone by then.

"Asher."

The king's quiet voice gives me a jolt, and I jerk my head up. My heart stutters at the way he says my name.

"What?" I say.

He glances at the princess and keeps his voice low. "Not to be indiscreet, but I have needs that would be better met outside this room."

As I turn that around in my head, he adds, "If I'm forced to soak my trousers, I doubt anyone will find it enjoyable."

Oh.

I stare at him, deliberating. I hadn't really considered this.

His eyes narrow, like I'm an idiot. "I need to take a piss, Asher."

What an asshole. I glare at him. "You won't trick me into letting you go."

"I know." He glares right back at me. "But I am giving you fair warning."

That sounds like the truth—and maybe it is. Because I also have needs that would be "better met outside this room." I've shared space with people left to soil themselves, and it is *not* enjoyable. Not just the smell, but the humiliation. The indignity.

I'm not doing that to someone else. Not even this man.

I shove myself to my feet and move across the small space. "Fine. Let's go." I grab hold of his arm and haul upward. He doesn't make a sound, but it must hurt, because he draws a sharp breath and scrambles to get his tied feet underneath him.

I automatically loosen my grip. "Sorry."

I say it without thinking, but his eyes shift my way in surprise, and I scowl. I should be forcing him out into the snow at knifepoint, not apologizing for being too rough.

This is why it's easier to just kill people. I only need to be terrifying for a second.

The princess shifts a little in her sleep, and the king and I both freeze. I hate that he's as worried about waking her as I am. But then she goes still again, her breath evening out.

"Come on," I whisper, dropping my voice so we don't disturb her again. I tug him toward the door and ease it open.

After the warmth of the room, the cold is vicious, the wind sharp enough to make my eyes water. A few inches of snow have joined what was there before, so our tracks are well and truly obscured. I don't see any new ones either, which means no one has come this way. The sky has gone dim, shifting to that gray that preludes twilight, and I realize it's been more than just a *few* hours.

The king shuffles into the snow beside me, hobbled by his knotted bootlaces. I think of all the brutal stories I've heard about Maddox Kyronan, and it's weird to consider that he's right here, bound and helpless, needing to pee.

Despite all those stories, however, I heard the conviction in his voice when he declared that no one from Incendar had hired the Hunter's Guild. I can see why Jory believes him.

I almost believe him, and I opened the bound orders myself. I know what measures the Guildmaster takes to verify an order—and I saw the manner of payment. Even still, there's a part of me that wishes I could unbind him, that we could flee to safety together.

But of course I can't.

When we're ten feet away from the door and into the trees, I bite back a shiver, and I turn to face him. "This is far enough."

I don't know if he expected me to untie him anyway, but I'm not that stupid. Instead, I reach for the strap of the utility belt that hangs at his hips, tugging the leather out of the buckle. It forces us close, and our fogging breath is snatched away by the wind. I don't look down at what I'm doing, because I don't want to make this less dignified than it needs to be, but he looks right back at me, his golden eyes holding mine.

Fine. He wants to be bold? I can be bold.

But then the buckle gives, and my fingers hesitate. We're so close that we could share breath, and for a moment, I'm struck by the fact that this is the first time I've been this close to another man where *he* is bound and I am not.

It's triggering a memory, and I almost shiver for reasons that have nothing to do with the cold. I frown and try to shake it off, but I have to look away. Of everything I've ever done, this is hardly the most awkward.

"Asher."

Every time he says my name, it strikes something inside of me, and I'm not sure what it is. I glare at him, peeved. "Stop saying my name."

He ignores me. "Do you truly believe other assassins will be sent to kill me and the princess?"

His voice is low, and there's no challenge in his tone. This is a genuine question.

"Yes." I tug and the belt comes loose, so I pull it wide and reach for the lacing of his trousers.

"And you believe that what you've done will keep her safe?"

He says this as if I'm not in the midst of unfastening his pants. I yank at the lacings, pulling each one free with quick efficiency. "I could have had her miles away by now," I say. "But then we brought you."

"That is not what I asked." He pauses. "I can sense your worry. It's clear you have no plan of action."

If he said it with disdain, I'd punch him in the gut and leave him to piss all over himself.

But he doesn't. He says it like a confidant. Like a friend who has to give you a hard truth.

"We'll be fine," I say flatly. His lacings finally give, and I tug his trousers wider, discovering that they're lined with fur. No wonder he's not as cold as we are. But when I go to pull at his underclothes, my fingers brush against bare skin. He gives a little flinch, a quick little indrawn breath.

I don't even know what I touched, but I flush *immediately*.

"Your hands are cold," he says, which doesn't help.

His accent turns the words to honey, and that doesn't help either.

I have no idea whether he's free enough to urinate without getting any on himself, but I feel flushed and uncertain, and I'm not looking down *now*. I give one more downward tug for good measure, then take a step back and turn away. "Go ahead. I'll be right back."

I stride through the snow until I'm ten feet away, and I unlace my own trousers to do the same thing.

When I turn back, he's dropped back a few paces, as if to demonstrate that he's done. He's kicked the snow over any evidence, too. But his trousers have slipped down his hips, revealing the pale curve of his buttocks.

I jerk my eyes away—until I realize I'm going to have to lace him back up. Heat crawls up my neck again, and I wish for my hooded jacket. There's a part of me that just wants to leave him out here.

When I stop in front of him, I don't hesitate. I just tug everything upward, my fingers brushing bare skin again. He doesn't flinch this time, so I let go of his undergarments and jerk his trousers back together. It pulls us even closer.

"Is everything where it needs to be?" I say stiffly.

"Yes," he says. "Thank you."

He's *still* looking me dead in the face. I nearly falter.

I have to look down to rethread the lacings, and I'm tempted to just thread one loop and be done with it. The only thing that makes me do it thoroughly is the fact that I don't want Jory to see him coming undone. She flushed bright red when I curled up with her in her chambers, and that was fully clothed.

I thread the lacings carefully, our breath fogging between us again. I don't think he's hard—because why would he be?—but I'm very aware of the weight of him pressing against the lacings, especially each time my knuckles brush against his warmth. I hate that he's got me so rattled. The worst part is that I *shouldn't* be. Compared to my life with the slavers, this is nothing.

But then the knot is tied and I'm reaching for his utility belt, shoving these thoughts away. He's our captive, that's it. A vicious king who'll kill me if he gets loose. He never would've spoken a word to me if I hadn't forced him out of the palace. I'm nothing. I'm no one. This is just the effect of my memories, of a life where touch and closeness could be wielded like a weapon.

I tug the belt, slip the prong through the middle hole, and tuck the length away.

"Thank you," he says again.

I grunt and turn away.

He shuffles through the snow behind me as he follows. "That was an unexpected mercy, Asher."

Something about that makes me flush in a different way. I don't know what to say.

When I slip back through the door, he follows, moving almost as silently as I do. Jory shifts again, but I hold my breath and ease the door closed. She burrows more deeply into my jacket and settles. She kept tucking her hands into the sleeves earlier, and I was kicking myself for not just kidnapping *her*. Then we wouldn't be in this mess at all.

I wish I had a quilt, or something else to give her.

But of course, I can never give her anything at all.

I glance at the small pile of wood again. I shouldn't add more to the stove. It's been hours, and I really don't want to risk anyone seeing the smoke.

But then I look at her nearly pressed against the metal legs, as if she'd crawl *into* the stove to get warm.

The hell with it. I draw a ragged sigh and bury another small log in the burning embers. I think I'll need to strike the flint again, but it catches almost immediately.

Jory blinks up at me. "Asher?" she murmurs.

"Shh," I say softly. Without thinking, I stroke a hand across her hair, my thumb brushing over her eyebrow. "All is well. Rest."

I don't expect her to obey, but her eyes flutter closed again. This time she tugs the sleeve of the jacket into her chest and inhales deeply. It settles something in my heart.

When I look up, the king is watching me, and I almost wish I hadn't touched her.

I ignore him and turn away. "Just sit," I say, keeping my voice low. "Like I said, we'll be out of here by nightfall." Then I move away from Jory and sit against the wall where I was before.

The king watches this, but he *doesn't* sit. He studies the princess for a long moment, then crosses the short space of the room toward me.

I immediately go tense, ready to spring to my feet. "I told you to *sit*," I say, fighting to keep my voice low.

"I am sitting." He leans against the wall beside me, then eases to the ground, bracing his back against the wall. It leaves a foot of space between us, and his hands are still bound, but I'm locked in place, debating whether to flee or to stay.

I have no idea what to make of this.

The king nods toward the door. "If I try to talk to you from there, we might wake her."

"I don't want to talk to you."

"You intend to drag the princess out of here in the dead of night, on foot, with no horse, no cloak, and no supplies." He looks me right in the eyes. "You are going to talk to me, Asher."

I set my jaw and turn to stare at the flickering within the stove.

"Even if you allow her to keep your jacket," he says, "I doubt her boots have dried. She won't be able to walk far."

I say nothing.

"And it leaves *you* with nothing against the snow," he continues. "Even if you manage to survive the weather, surely you know there will be guards and soldiers searching through the night."

I draw my knees up to my chest and rest my arms on them. I hate that he's right about all of it.

"*You* could leave," he says. "Take my coins and flee if you so fear the other Hunters. You are right that I need the princess to finalize this alliance—it's the very reason I followed you. And I truly can keep her safe."

"I'm not leaving Jory."

"Even if it means you put her at risk?"

That hits me like a sledgehammer, and I almost flinch. I hate that I might have put her in a more dangerous situation than she was in already.

I never should have agreed to this.

You said you would do whatever needed doing.

This didn't need doing. But she kept staring up at me with those eyes, like I could be her savior. She's the only person who's ever looked at me like that. She could have told me to throw myself off a parapet, and I would've asked which one.

When I speak, my voice is rough. "If I leave, she'll cut you loose. You'll turn me into a pile of ash five seconds later."

"No. If you choose to leave, I will not pursue you."

"Shut up." I glare at him. "Of course you will."

He looks back at me implacably. "I won't. You offered me a mercy. So I will offer you one in return."

My heart gives a little thump in my chest. I jerk my eyes back around to stare at the fire.

"If you spoke the truth about my soldier," he says, "then you've taken nothing from me but time." His eyes flick skyward, and he gives his bindings a small tug, then grimaces. "Well. Possibly the use of my shoulders, too. But my offer stands."

"No."

"If the two of you walk out of here as you are, you won't survive the night. I rode through this weather to get here. The danger is real."

His voice is so calm, so reasonable. As if to emphasize his point, a gust of wind rattles the door and whistles around the frame.

"I'll find us more gear," I say.

"And how long will that—"

"I told you to shut up," I growl, finally snapping my head around to look at him. "So stop talking."

He shuts up. But he doesn't look away. It's progressively getting more dim in the room, and the firelight gleams in his eyes.

It's too intense, and it makes me think of the way we were standing in the snow, my fingers threading the lacings of his trousers. *I'm* the one who has to turn away.

I heave an unsettled breath. I should've just killed him.

Damn it, Jory.

Less than a day ago, I was curled around her in bed. She pulled at my gloves and begged me to stay. I kissed her goodbye, and it took everything inside of me to keep it from turning into more.

Would I have been so reckless if that hadn't happened?

The king speaks into my silence. "You seemed upset with the princess when she mentioned these *slavers*."

I'm quiet for a moment because I'm not sure what to say to that. "I wasn't upset with her."

"You were."

"She rarely leaves the palace. It's not her fault that she doesn't know." It's my fault, really. I could've told her about my life at any point over the last ten years—but I didn't. I *couldn't*. "You heard her. A lot of people think like that—that it's all *fair* and *just*. Or sometimes they think it's what a criminal deserves. Either way, it's seen as . . . as *labor*. Simple tasks for a short while, and then you earn your freedom."

"But it's not?"

I scoff and look at him. "Why do you care? It doesn't matter."

"It does matter." His golden eyes hold mine. "I'm to ally with this country, Asher. I would know its faults as well as its promise."

That makes me go still. Every word is so earnest.

I don't like to think of my time with the slavers, but this conversation—or maybe this situation—has dredged the memories up anyway. I think of the men and women I've seen, waiting in the stockyards to learn their fate, how one man could be sent to work in a shop, sweeping the floor and having a bed at night, but the woman next to him might be sold to a soldier who wanted a plaything to tether to his bunk. When I was freshly exiled from the palace, charged and convicted of conspiring with a traitor, I was sold off and chained to a post that very night. I remember the men and women who would stroll through the aisles, tugging at hair, prying mouths open, ripping clothes away to reveal what was available. I'd just lost my mother. I'd lost everything I'd ever known. I remember fighting my bonds, pulling away from every prying hand, until a woman nearby whispered to me, "Don't fight. Some of them are *looking* for the ones that fight."

At sixteen, it was terrifying.

At twenty-six, it's worse. I know where I'd go and what would happen to me. I'm more agile than strong, so I'd never be picked for hard labor. I'd *prefer* hard labor. Instead, my bright hair and blue eyes would catch someone's eye. I'd be sold right back into one of the brothels. I'd spend my days chained to a rail beside a bed or a chair—or even just a dirty corner without so much as thin carpet over the wood floor.

I was young the first time I escaped, but I knew I'd be caught. No one lets a prized pet out of its cage for too long. But I didn't mind the punishment. I thought people might see that first stripe on my cheek and avoid a whore who's marked as *difficult*.

I was wrong. Instead, I discovered how many people would see a mark of rebellion and take it as a challenge.

When I was accepted to train as a Hunter, the Guildmaster seemed surprised that I didn't balk at his lessons on killing. But after my years in brothels and arenas, after my years in chains, I'd endured more than I thought I could survive. Killing meant freedom. So I did it.

The king is watching me, and I realize I haven't said a word. His voice is very low, very quiet. "*You* do not believe it's fair."

Tension has crawled down my arms to tighten my fingers. I've never found the courage to discuss any of this with Jory. She's too protected, too far removed—and I never want her to see me that way. I want her to remember the Asher she knew when we were young, the boy who'd steal cookies off a warm tray and sneak through the palace.

Not the Asher who was left naked and starving and shoved onto his knees to enforce obedience. Not the Asher who learned to kill so he could survive.

"Tell me," says the king.

I don't know why his voice has such an effect on me, but it tugs at me and makes me speak. "The slavers assign a value to everything," I say. "So if you eat, it's added to your debt. If you sleep, you owe for the time. If you need a shirt. Boots. *Anything.* So even as you work to erase what you owe, more is added. And once your debt is sold, there are no standards. You can be caged. Chained. Punished if you disobey." I hesitate. "Because you're not a person, you're a possession, and everyone is determined to get their money's worth."

As soon as the words escape my mouth, I can't believe I said so much.

To the king of Incendar of all people.

I expect him to ask why I was sold to the slavers at all, and I brace for the question. But he doesn't.

"You earned your freedom," he says.

I glance over. "I did."

"And you learned to be a killer."

He says this so frankly, without judgment, very unlike the way Jory ever mentions my work with the Hunter's Guild. It reminds me of the way I challenged him earlier. *You're a killer, too.*

So I nod. "Once you're marked, it's difficult to find work."

His eyes flick to my cheek. "Those *are* from your time with the slavers, then."

I glance at Jory and keep my voice very low. "If you escape, you earn a mark when they catch you. It's a warning to future buyers—but also a permanent sign of what you once were. Most people just want to serve their debt and be done. Once you're marked, you can't. Everyone will always know. You're questioned everywhere. It's impossible to hide."

"You escaped seven times?"

"Yes. Well . . . I was *caught* seven times. But once I had one mark, I saw no reason to avoid more."

He regards me silently for a moment, and his expression shifts, as if this answer surprises him.

"When you ran," he says, "where did you go?"

I don't intend to answer, because it's too personal, too close to my heart. But my eyes flick to Jory before I can help it.

"*Ah*," the king says, drawing out the word.

I flush. "We grew up together. I lived in the palace until I was sixteen."

"You love her."

"No. I . . ." The words freeze on my tongue, and again I think of the moment I held her against me in bed—after insisting that we should be apart. "No."

"You do."

I shrug a little. "She's the princess. There could never be anything between us."

"But she adores you. I can see it."

The words make my heart thump, and I nearly press a hand to my chest. I remember all the times I escaped my captors just to flee to her window. The number of times I wished I could hide in her wardrobe forever, letting her slip me pastries and cups of tea before the servants would find me. Sometimes I'd be injured, and I wouldn't want her to see. I'd sit on the ledge of her windowsill, invisible in the darkness, watching her read by candlelight or stand up to Dane or tuck pins into her hair.

"And you adore *her*," the king says.

This I can answer without hesitation. "I do."

"Then protect her, Asher. Flee these Hunters on your own. With fire at my hand, no one will be able to draw near. I have my best soldiers with me, and I trust *them*. We will find the source of these orders and take action. Surely you know that we have the force to accomplish it. She will be warm and safe, and you will be well away. I had no quarrel with you before this morning, and I have none with you now."

I stare at him, and I hate that every word of *this* sounds as earnest as everything else he's said.

He looks right back at me. "She said you are her friend. She will *need* friends. Head east, and cross the border into Incendar at the northernmost point, near where the ocean meets the cliffs. There is a guard station there, and if you claim sanctuary from the king, they will bring you to me." He pauses, and his voice goes very quiet. "We may have our faults, but I can promise you this: there are no slavers in Incendar. I would offer you sanctuary, Asher. I swear it."

I swear it. My heart pounds again, and my breathing feels shallow. I glance across at the princess again, and to my surprise, she's half sitting up, watching us with parted lips.

She might not have heard everything, but she heard that part.

"Please," she says.

I want to resist. *I* want to be the one to keep her safe.

But I can't. I know I can't. I've known it for hours.

Honestly, I've known it for *years*.

I run a hand down my face, then clench my fists, my fingertips digging into my palms. I draw a ragged breath and look back at the king. "You cannot leave her alone," I say in a rush. "You cannot leave your back unguarded. The other Hunters know the sewers. They can get *in* the same way we got out. Don't stay in Astranza one second longer than necessary."

He looks at me intently, like he's memorizing every word. "Understood."

"They are *fast* and they are *brutal*. Don't eat the food. They have poisons. Weapons. Disguises. And you may trust your men, but *I* don't. Someone from Incendar paid for that order." I don't even wait for a response, I just look at Jory. "Do you truly trust him?"

"Yes. Asher, *yes.*"

I clench my eyes closed. My fingernails feel like they're drawing blood from my palms. But I keep thinking about the cold. The marks on my face that make it impossible for me to go anywhere without being interrogated. Her silly suede boots that probably came close to freezing her toes off. The fact that she's never been anywhere outside the palace without a dozen guards and attendants.

I really do adore her. I would give her anything she asked. My heart aches.

I open my eyes and look at the king. "You swear it?"

"I do."

"Fine." I draw the blade buckled to my thigh, and before I can reconsider, I slice through his bonds.

The king makes a sound that's half relief, half agony, followed by a gasping breath. My heart is thumping, and I keep a tight grip on my dagger, ready to plunge it right into him. For one tense moment, I think he'll summon his magic and the room will be overcome by an inferno. But aside from the reflection of firelight in his eyes, there's nothing. He's just a man gingerly rubbing his wrists, hunching his shoulders as if they ache.

"Thank you," he says.

I swallow, because this doesn't feel like a moment for thanks. My heart is still pounding.

Jory lets out a breath. "Asher."

I sheathe the knife and turn for her, half rising on my knees to shift to standing. "Jory—"

Her eyes flare wide and she sucks in a breath, and that's all the warning I have before the king tackles me. My jaw slams into the stone floor, and my right arm is wrenched behind my back, and then his weight pins me there. I'm scrabbling for weapons, but he's too heavy, especially with his armor.

Fuck. *Fuck*.

His grip turns searing hot, and I cry out. It forces me still, and almost pulls a whimper from my throat.

Stars. I was so *stupid*.

"*No*, Princess," the king says sharply, and I realize she's drawn one of the blades from my jacket, and she's holding it up in front of him.

Good girl. I hope she stabs him.

But she shrieks and drops the blade. It's glowing red. She scrambles back, clutching her hand to her chest like it burned her.

"I'm sorry," I'm gasping. "Jory—I'm sorry."

The king grabs my free hand and wrenches it behind my back using every ounce of force I used on him. I brace myself for him to melt my hands together or something even worse, but he only tethers my wrists, likely with the same leather strap.

I'm so stupid.

So stupid.

"You will let him *go*," Jory is saying breathlessly to the king. "*Now.* I won't marry you if you hurt him. The alliance will be worthless. You need my father's magic—"

"And you need mine." His voice is tired. "I haven't hurt him, Princess." He grabs hold of my bindings and jerks me upright, until I'm on my knees, facing him.

If I had that garrote around his throat now, I wouldn't stop. Not even for Jory. I hate that I talked to him. I hate that I listened to him. I hate that I *trusted* him, even for a second. Rage is building in my chest, and I can barely breathe through it.

"I hope the other Hunters find you," the princess says to him. The viciousness in her voice is chilling. "I hope they *take their time.*"

"My soldiers will find us first," he says. His voice is cool, practical. "And you will be safe, as promised. But I cannot release a man who killed one of my soldiers and forced us out of the palace."

"I didn't kill him!" I snap.

Jory takes a step forward, until they're nearly toe to toe. In the flickering firelight, she looks every bit as dangerous as he does. "You *will* release him. You will *let him go*, or I will make sure my father's army *ends* you."

The king looks right back at her, and he doesn't back down. I'm beginning to think he never does. He lifts his right hand, then sketches a quick sigil. A lick of flame swirls right out of the stove to hover above his palm, inches from her arm.

Jory draws a sharp breath, suddenly frozen in place.

So am I.

As we watch, the flame gathers in a ball on the king's palm, reflecting off his cheeks and spinning gold in his hair. It's terrifying and wondrous and in spite of everything, I can't help but stare.

When Maddox Kyronan speaks, it's *his* tone that's chilling. "Do I seem worried?"

Chapter Thirteen
THE WARRIOR

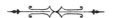

The instant we met, the princess accused me of atrocities against my people. The words were piercing—but they weren't without merit. I know exactly how much damage my fire can cause, and I saw her reaction when the first burst of flame responded to my magic. I expect that the sight of my power now will remind her just how vulnerable her position is.

The princess, however, does not stand down.

In any other circumstance, I'd be impressed at her bravery. I have soldiers who won't dare get in my face like this. But for all the ways she looked innocent and lost earlier, she looks like a vengeful queen right now. Maybe it's good that she wasn't a part of the negotiations, because she's certainly more daring than her brother.

I expect her to issue more threats—or perhaps to negotiate.

Instead, she draws back a hand to smack me.

I have a handful of flame, but she doesn't care. I can't block without the risk of setting her dress on fire, so I twist and deflect, crushing the flame out of my hand. She clips me in the jaw anyway. Her rage is relentless, because she recovers quickly enough to swing again. This time I catch her wrist before a strike can land.

She's ready for it, because she's got a hairpin in her other hand. Without hesitation, she really does aim for my eyes. She's stronger than I expect, and I'm trying not to hurt her, so the steel pin scrapes across my temple, stinging immediately.

"All *right*, Princess," I snap. This time I catch her wrists and wrestle her still. "That's enough."

Her chest is heaving, and she surges forward despite my grip. I twist hard and get her hands trapped behind her back. It leaves her pressed against my chest, my arms holding her there. Tendrils of dark hair have spun loose from the curl she unpinned, and they fall across her face. She's breathing hard, her cheeks flushed, her eyes full of fury.

As if I'm the one who bound and gagged *them* for a march through the sewers.

"You are a *liar*," she grates out. "You tricked him. You tricked *us*. I cannot believe I trusted you for a second. Dane will have his guards *execute* you. And your soldiers. And your—"

I spin her around so quickly that she gives a little yip, and I force myself to soften my grip. I deserve every ounce of her anger. I pull a spare set of bootlaces from my belt and wind them around her wrists.

She tries to kick back, but her feet are bare, and I still have my boots and greaves, so I barely feel it.

"I *hate* you," she snaps.

I knot off the cord around her wrists and sigh.

I should be relieved. I should be *ecstatic*. I'm free. My attacker is confined. The princess is safe. There should be a thrum of vindication in my chest, and there is, but it's clouded by something else.

Regret.

Asher is sitting on his heels, his breathing shallow, his jaw clenched. Rage and betrayal are all over his face, but it's his fear that's pulsing like an undercurrent in the room.

I still have no idea what to believe about his killing orders, and I won't believe Nikko is alive until I see him myself. But every word Asher said about the slavers was genuine. His *fear* is genuine. He had the king of Incendar bound and powerless, but he didn't want money or influence or even the handful of coins from my pouch.

Of all he could have demanded—of all I could have *offered*—the promise of sanctuary is what made this man yield.

And I used it against him.

I have to shove the regret away. It's hardly the worst thing I've ever done—and it's possible he deserved it. We've been gone most of the day, and people are surely looking for us. One thing is clear: I disappeared with the princess. Even if she would speak in my defense—which is questionable right now—I have no idea what anyone would believe. Too much is at risk, and I don't trust Prince Dane. Asher is the only proof that *I* have.

At least he's being quiet, though his eyes are flicking from the princess to the fire to the door, seeking a way to escape. His bitter desperation fills the air, and it pricks at me the same way her accusations do.

I tamp it back down. I can't let these emotions affect me. I need to send up a signal to my men, and I need to find a way back to the palace.

When I tie off the cord with a sharp tug, Jory gives another gasp.

I tell myself not to care about that, either. It doesn't work. "Sit, Princess."

She wrenches at the binding and speaks through clenched teeth. "I absolutely *will not*—"

I scoop her into my arms, the satin and lace of her skirts swirling around her legs. Before she can protest, I set her on the ground. "*Sit.*" I glance at Asher, who's still on his knees, glaring at the floor, his jaw set. "You too," I say. "Don't move."

He's glowering at me. "Fuck you."

I *definitely* deserve that, so I ignore him, then sketch a sigil in the air to pull another palm full of fire from the stove. Then I head for the door.

As before, the cold is shocking, biting my cheeks and making the cut from Jory's hairpin sting even more. It's begun to snow again, fat flakes drifting down between the trees. The sky above is obscured by clouds, but the light has grown even dimmer since Asher led me out here. It'll be full dark within the hour.

A low murmur of whispered conversation sounds from inside the hut, and I frown. But I can't stop them from talking, and they can't go anywhere anyway.

I hold out my hand, and the glow from the ball of flame doesn't light up much. It flickers, threatening to burn out altogether. Without fuel to burn, the magic has to draw from my energy to keep the flame lit. The long night of riding—followed by a long day of kidnapping—is beginning to catch up with me. I can't remember the last time I put a bite of food in my mouth. I feel the strain of holding the flame, like forcing a fatigued muscle to *work*.

Hopefully I can manage enough power for this. I put my hands close together, then pull the ball of fire into two, until I have one on each palm. Despite the cold, sweat blooms on my forehead from the effort. I feed the twin flames energy until they burn bright. Once they're blazing, I throw the first one high, quickly drawing a sigil with my empty hand. My magic sends it higher, until the sphere of flame bursts into a spray of sizzling sparks above the trees, sounding with a loud crack that echoes.

I'm gasping from the effort, and the remaining ball of fire flickers and threatens to die. I won't be able to do much more. But if my men are out looking, they'll hear it. If I'm lucky, they'll *see* it. Every one of them knows what it means.

But I have to throw up another, just to be sure. I wait a moment, listening, but the snow muffles everything. The remaining fire in my left hand flickers again, so I throw this one high as well, sketching another sigil. I try to feed this one more energy, and the shower of sparks is bigger, the crack even louder. But my vision goes fuzzy for a moment, and I fight off a wave of vertigo. I have to take a breath to steady myself. I can't afford to look weak. My soldiers won't be the only ones to see my signal. Anyone looking for me—including these assassins, if they're real—could follow the sound and light right to me.

When I walk back through the door, Asher and Jory have shifted closer together, but they're staring at me, their chests rising and falling quickly, their eyes wide.

"What did you do?" the princess demands.

"I sent up a signal to my soldiers," I say. Wind swirls through the opening at my back, but I don't want to close the door again. I need to hear if anyone approaches. "Once they arrive, I'll determine how to proceed."

Jory clenches her jaw, and she's glaring at me with such . . . such *indignation.*

Clearly I'm not the only one affected by hunger, exhaustion, and outright aggravation.

I look down at her. "The look on your face, Princess. Am I to be your villain now?"

"Asher *freed* you," she says. "You swore to him. You *swore*." Her eyes are full of recrimination. "You could have acted with honor. You could have kept your word and let him go."

"Honor! You speak of *honor*? I asked for truth between us. I yielded my magic. I disarmed for you. Twice! Yet you still took me by force." I stand, letting every ounce of my own betrayal fill my voice. "Have you considered that this Hunter's Guild could already be pointing fingers at *me* for what happened here? That your brother could blame Incendar for your kidnapping?" I think of my sister, and what would happen if *she* were forced to take the throne. The fire in the stove burns hotter, the flames flickering wildly, responding to my anger. "Do you have any idea what my disappearance would mean for my people? For my kingdom? For *yours*?"

She's still staring up at me, but my words have an impact. Her expression flickers into a frown.

I don't linger. Instead, I take a breath and drop to a crouch in front of Asher. He's a ball of tension with his hands bound, sitting on his heels, the firelight from the stove turning his white-blond hair to rose gold. His jaw is set, and he doesn't even look at me.

"Asher," I begin. "You should know that—"

His weight shifts, and then the heel of his boot catches me in the jaw.

I didn't see it coming, and the blow knocks me sideways. I don't even know how he *did* it. I scramble to grab him, but he's too damn fast. My fingers close on air, and he's already out of reach. He's going to be out the door in a second. Dressed in black, he'll be nearly invisible in the falling darkness.

Fuck. I should've tied his boots together.

"Go!" Jory cries, and there's a note of victory in her voice. "Asher, *run*."

He doesn't need the encouragement. He's already gone.

I don't pursue him. I could bring my own light and search him out, but I don't want to leave the princess—and I definitely don't want to walk into an ambush. He already got me once, and I'm not giving him another opportunity. I touch a hand to my lip, and it comes away with blood.

Any trace of regret has vanished. Aggravation is back.

Jory is staring at me, her chest rising and falling swiftly. I'm sure she expects me to burn him to cinders with nothing more than the power of thought. Right now, I wish I could.

I swipe the blood off my mouth. "Is that what you two were whispering about?"

She sets her jaw—but that's answer enough.

A muffled shout erupts from outside, and I brace myself, but then I hear a voice I recognize. A moment later, Asher is roughly shoved through the door. His hands are still bound, and his chest is heaving. Two of my men are behind him. Garrett has a tight grip on Asher's bicep, and Roman is right beside him, weapons drawn.

The relief that flares in my chest is so profound. The day has been too long, and I didn't realize how worried I was that someone else would find us first.

I look from my soldiers to the door, hoping the rest of my men will be right behind them—but they aren't. "Where are the others?"

Roman's analytical eyes take stock of me quickly, and then the bound princess. After assessing the surroundings, he sheathes his weapons and runs a hand through his snow-dusted hair. "Nik and Cal were searching west of the palace, but if they saw your signal, they won't be far behind."

Nik. My breath almost catches. "Nikko is unharmed?"

Garrett nods. "Yeah. He said the princess attacked you with an accomplice." He glances at Jory, who's warily staring up at them both, and then at Asher, who's scowling at the floor. My soldier's expression is not friendly. "Dane refuses to believe it, but I suppose we found the truth."

"That is *not* what happened," Jory says fiercely.

My jaw is already aching from where Asher kicked me, and the side of my face is still stinging from her hairpin—and that's nothing compared to everything else they did. "It's exactly what happened."

Asher jerks against Garrett's grip on his arm. "She was trying to save your life, asshole."

Garrett smacks him on the back of the head with a gauntleted hand. "Watch your mouth."

Asher half turns. "Fuck you."

This time Garrett punches him between the shoulder blades. Asher stumbles forward and goes to his knees.

"Stop!" the princess cries. "Stop it!"

This has the potential to spiral out of control, especially since Garrett won't stop unless I order him to. "Enough," I say. "I need him to be able to talk."

Asher sits back on his heels, breathing through his teeth. His toes are pressed into the floor, his jaw tight, his muscles tense. He's ready to spring onto his feet like he did before.

But Garrett waits behind him, and of all my soldiers, he's the most unforgiving. If Asher comes at me again, Garrett will probably break his jaw.

My lip feels like it's still bleeding, and I swipe a streak of blood away. "My men have a limit, Asher. So do I. Stay put, or I'll let them do whatever they want."

"You think that's a threat?" he says coldly. "Your soldiers doing *whatever they want*?" He looks up at me through that spill of white-blond hair. His blue eyes have gone ice-cold, every emotion locked away. I've seen that look before—in captured soldiers. "Just what do you think Dane's men are going to do?"

There's a note in his voice that tugs at the regret in my heart, but this time it's joined by a flicker of guilt.

I have to force my gaze back to Roman and Garrett. "What about Sev?"

Roman frowns. "Dane is holding him at the palace." He and Garrett exchange a glance. "He wanted to hold us, too, but we slipped out when he was arguing with Sev."

A spike of alarm lodges in my chest. *Holding.* I knew our disappearance would look bad from Astranza's side. We need to return to the palace.

A man calls from outside the hut, and I recognize Callum's voice. "There!" he says. "I see their horses."

"I knew they wouldn't be long," Roman says, just as Callum pushes through the doorway—followed by Nikko.

Relief floods my chest again. Even though I knew he survived, seeing him alive and well settles something in my heart.

It also confirms that Asher was telling the truth.

That flicker of guilt pricks at me again, but just like the regret, I have to shove it away. I can't let him go. I can't offer leniency to a man who attacked me. Who was literally ordered to *kill* me.

If this alliance is at risk, I can't afford one moment of weakness.

But when I look back at those cold eyes that are shuttered with resignation, I want to cut him free.

My soldiers don't. Their expressions haven't shifted away from stony vigilance, but I watch them all exchange a glance, and it's clear they want to tear Asher to pieces, just like I did.

I don't know how to explain everything right here, and we don't have time anyway. I have no idea what Prince Dane could be doing or saying, and if Sev is arguing with him about anything at all, it needs to end. I need to put away my guilt and regret and focus on the things that matter most. My sister. My people. My *kingdom*.

"Give me a cloak," I say. "We'll ride back to the palace. I'll take the princess." I look to Roman, then nod down at Asher. "Bring him. Make him walk."

Callum exchanges a dark glance with Garrett. "Oh, we'll bring him."

"No," I say. "You two ride with me." I step toward the princess, take hold of her arm, and draw her up from the floor.

For a moment, I think she's going to fight me, and I'm ready to physically pick her up again. But she just looks from Asher to me.

"I'll do anything you want," she says. Her eyes are piercing, her voice so desperate. "But please don't let them hurt him."

Those flickers of guilt and regret turn into a blaze.

It would be so much easier to ignore if she were yelling and making demands, instead of these desperate pleas that feel so genuine. But *she* tricked *me*—more than once! And I keep falling for it. Asher may have forced me out of the palace with violence, but violence is something I understand.

"How can I trust you?" I say to her. "Since the moment we met, all you've given me are lies."

"*Please*, Ky," she whispers. "*This* wasn't a lie. You said you would offer him *mercy*."

Too much is at stake. I force the emotion away and turn her toward the door. "I am offering him mercy," I say. "I could have told them to drag him."

Then I take a cloak from Roman, and I pull her into the cold.

Chapter Fourteen
THE PRINCESS

I'm such a fool. I should have listened to Asher to begin with. I should have just let him do what he was sent to do. We could be at the Three Fishes, on our way to . . . Well, I have no idea where we'd be.

But I wouldn't be barefoot in the snow, shivering fiercely while the king of Incendar drags me around like a captive.

The worst part about all of this is that, despite my indignant anger, despite my absolute *fury*, I also want to cry.

I can just imagine how Dane is going to react when Maddox Kyronan hauls me into the palace with my hands tied behind my back—especially when he reveals that Asher was the instigator. I watched them drag my friend away once. I don't want to watch them do it again.

Especially since it's my fault. I begged him to do this.

Against my will, a tear slips down my cheek. I try to blink it away, but it doesn't work. I have to hold my breath and duck my face, because I don't want the king to know. I definitely don't want his *men* to know. Tears feel too vulnerable. I *already* feel too vulnerable.

Luckily, the sky has grown dark, so shadows fall across us both as he guides me toward one of the tethered horses outside the hut. My toes are curling in the snow, and I stumble, my breath catching hard. Ky keeps a tight grip on my arm, and I bite my lip so I don't make a sound.

Then, to my absolute surprise, he reaches past me to pull a short knife from behind the horse's saddle, and he cuts my hands free.

I waste no time. I raise a hand and whirl.

He catches my wrists before I can hit him, and he wrestles me still. For the first time, his grip borders on painful, reminding me of every dangerous story I've heard about this man. My heart stutters.

But he simply holds me in place. His eyes roam over my face, so I know he sees the tears. "We are returning to the palace," he says. His voice is cold, that gentle accent honed to a harsh edge. For a man who can speak in low, intense tones that make my insides melt, it's a reminder that he also leads armies into war. "I would rather not bring you as a prisoner, but if that is what you prefer, tell me now."

I shiver fiercely, and I can't stop my hitching breath. "Fine," I gasp, feeling another tear escape. I dig my fingernails into my palms. "I won't f-fight you."

Without another word, he puts his hands on my waist, lifts me into the air, and then I'm astride the horse. My skirts bunch around me, leaving my lower legs bare, my stockinged thighs pressing into cold tack. Before I can grab hold of the pommel, he's got a boot in the stirrup and he swings up behind me. His hands seize my waist again, lifting me a bit, situating my weight until I'm half in the saddle and half in his lap. My lower body is trapped between his hips and the pommel of the saddle, my upper body held between his arms. I'm frozen in place, because it's shocking—and wildly unexpected, despite my layers of skirts. His breastplate presses against my spine, and the edges of his greaves brush my calves. The muscles of his thighs are right below mine, reminding me of exactly what I'm sitting against.

I suddenly can't think of *anything* else.

His entire manner is cool, unperturbed, but my cheeks catch on fire, a stunning contrast to the wind finding my tears. I keep myself ramrod straight, because I'm so busy trying to comprehend his closeness. I can't even decide if I'm cold, because parts of me are absolutely frigid, like my fingers and toes, while the parts of me pressed against him seem unnaturally warm.

When he takes up the reins and gives the signal to walk, our hips sway with the movement of the horse. The pommel of the saddle holds me in place, securing me tightly against him. I can feel everything. *Everything.*

"This is inappropriate," I say, shivering. Lady Charlotte would be horrified. "You should put me b-behind you." Snowflakes are settling in the horse's mane, melting when they strike my arms. I press my feet into the horse's furred shoulders, seeking the animal's warmth.

When he speaks, his voice is low and close to my ear. "Inappropriate, Princess?"

"I'm in your *lap*."

"I'm not sure it's safe to have you at my back."

I clench my jaw, wondering if he's mocking me. "You're not afraid of me."

"No. But you have no armor. If someone wants us dead, I don't want you to take an arrow from behind."

That's sobering. I've been so focused on Asher that I almost forgot the entire reason we left the palace at all. I can't help the shiver that rolls through my body.

To my surprise, the king swoops the cloak around us both, covering my legs along with his, twisting a steel clasp together to hold it in place in front of my waist. The inside is lined with fur, silky soft where it brushes against my feet.

"Would you rather ride with Callum or Garrett?" he says.

My cheeks burn hotter at the thought of being handed to a stranger, especially having to sit like this, thigh to thigh, hip to hip. I can't tell if Ky is teasing me or if that's a genuine offer. I refuse to dignify it with a response.

He's so warm, though, especially where his arms brush against mine. Is it his magic? Or does he just have better clothes? He did say he rode all night in this weather. Either way, I've been cold for so long that some of the tension begins to slip out of my body.

"Put your hands under the cloak," he says, his breath sparking warmth along my neck. His voice is lower, lacking an edge now. "I won't let you fall."

I don't want to obey, but my hands have a mind of their own—or maybe I'm just too cold to care. I slide my hands under the cloak, pressing them into my own thighs. The satin in my skirts must stick to the calfskin leather of his trousers, because each step and sway of the horse seems to cause friction between us. The press of his belt buckle reminds me of the moment he disarmed the first time, the gentle timbre of his voice, the slow slide of leather across steel.

Suddenly, I'm not cold at all. My cheeks must be on *fire*.

I need to think about something else. He lied. He *tricked* us. His men are probably beating Asher to death right now.

That thought throws an icy bucket of water on all my warmth.

I turn my head to see his face, but the sky has grown darker, and his profile is in shadow. His men are riding closer than I expected, one at each flank. The one on this side is Callum, I think. I'm trying to keep them straight. Callum has lighter hair than the king, but he's not as blond as Asher. The one with reddish hair and freckles on his pale cheeks was Roman. He's the one Ky told to make Asher walk. There was another one, too: Nikko, the one Asher attacked. I can't see either of them.

On our other side, that leaves . . . Garrett, then. He seems to be the tallest, with rich brown skin and hair so black it shines. When I glance in his direction, his gaze meets mine.

His eyes are so cold that I nearly flinch.

No, I *definitely* don't want to ride with one of them. I twist and face forward, my shoulders tense now. I remember how he punched Asher in the back, the way he looked ready to go after him again.

The way he chuckled as he said, *Oh, we'll bring him.*

My throat tightens. When I glance over again, he's still looking at me with that icy gaze.

I can't believe these Incendrian soldiers are so bold. I should order him to look away. If we were back in the palace, I would.

But we're *not*. I'm in his king's lap, being marched home like I'm due for a scolding. It's humiliating.

When I think of Asher, it's terrifying.

A fresh round of tears gathers. This time I can't help the hitching breath.

"Are these tears real?" says the king. His voice is still low, but it's coolly practical—and somehow that makes it worse.

"They're real," I breathe. I have to pull a hand free to swipe at my face.

"Why?" he says. "I've caused you no harm."

"But you did. You took my trust and you used it against us."

"Did you not do the same when you came to my chambers? You asked for my men to leave, then asked me to disarm."

That cuts like a blade, and it reminds me of the moment we met, when I accused Incendar of brutality. He said it was the very reason my father sought this alliance.

Since the moment we met, all you've given me are lies.

We haven't begun with faith and honesty at all.

In my silence, the king guesses, "You're worried for Asher?"

"Of course I am," I say. "You left your men to beat him to death."

"No," he says. "If I wanted anyone to beat him to death, I would've given him to these two. Roman and Nikko will follow my orders and do no more."

I wonder how true that is. I felt the aggressive tension in the hut. "You told them to make him *walk*."

"Yes, Princess. Because I don't trust *him* at anyone's back."

I want to scoff at that, but his tone is still so pragmatic. In a way, this conversation is fascinating, because I've never had a man—much less a *king*—talk to me so candidly. If we were talking about anything else, I might actually enjoy it.

"A cornered man will make reckless choices," Ky adds. "And your Asher is very determined to get you away from me."

Your Asher.

"He's not mine," I whisper.

But Asher curled against me in my bed, swearing that he'd find me, even in Incendar. Swearing that I could send word, and he'd do whatever needed doing.

He kidnapped the king for me—and cut him loose when I begged.

Another tear slips down my cheek. He *is* mine. But I could never be his.

"Asher said he once lived in the palace," Ky says. His voice is so low, his breath so warm against my hair. "How did he end up with these slavers?"

For a moment, my tongue is frozen. Asher's history isn't a secret, not really, but with him somewhere behind us being forced to march through the snow, it feels like a betrayal to talk about his past. But I need Ky to understand why I would risk so much.

"His mother was Lady Clara," I say. "My mother's first lady-in-waiting." I hesitate, because this part is always so hard to talk about.

"Ten years ago, when I was fifteen, my mother was killed in an ambush on the road while traveling to one of the northern villages. She'd admired some glass jewelry on one of the courtiers a few weeks earlier, and she wanted to examine the offerings herself. Lady Clara was with her, of course, but she survived—while my mother was killed right beside her."

Talking about it drags the memory to the forefront of my brain. Asher and I saw the attack from our own carriage. He dragged me away from the window as soon as we heard the screams, then pinned me to the floor, covering me with his body. Always the protector, even then.

But the attackers never came for us. By the time a footman yanked open the door to our carriage, my mother was dead and his mother was wailing.

I have to take a steadying breath. "It was widely believed that Lady Clara conspired in the attack. She was the only one who knew of the route, the destination. The trip was spontaneous—and it wasn't a common outing for the queen and her retinue. The attackers took nothing, not even their jewels—and one of the footmen said Lady Clara didn't have to beg for her life. They just left her alive, while my mother was dead."

My voice trails off, because the memories are surging now, making my chest tighten. Even when they threatened Lady Clara with execution, she didn't defend herself. *Spare my son*, she said. *I will confess.*

And then she did.

Ky waits, but when I say nothing more, he says, "Asher was a part of this conspiracy to kill the queen?"

"No!" I shake my head fiercely. "He loved my mother. He was my closest friend, and he was just as devastated as I was. He swore he didn't know, and I believed him. But my father declared that he couldn't allow the son of a traitor to remain in the palace. I still don't know if he really believed Asher was involved or if he just wanted to send a message to anyone else who might be planning an attack on the family. Either way, Lady Clara was executed, and Asher was sentenced, and then he was gone."

I have to swallow the lump in my throat. I hate talking about this part of my life. Within a day, I lost my mother and my best friend. The guards dragged Asher out of the palace like a criminal. I stood and watched from the parapets, sobbing the whole time—until Dane found me there and snapped at me to get myself together. He said it wouldn't do for the servants to see the princess sobbing over a traitor.

The horse stumbles through a snowdrift, and I gasp, feeling myself slip sideways. But Ky puts an arm around my waist, holding me against him. "Steady," he murmurs.

The weight of his arm has grown warmer, and there's a part of me that doesn't want him to move it. Snow continues to collect in the horse's mane, swirling down from the darkened sky above. In another time or place, I imagine I could be content to ride along like this, secure within the circle of his arm, letting him guide the horse while we sway together.

But he betrayed my friend. He's no better than my brother.

The thought feels hollow. I suppose I betrayed him, too.

"You were allowed to continue your friendship with Asher after this sentencing?" he says.

"No," I say softly. "But he knows how to slip onto the palace grounds. We explored all the time as children. After he was exiled, he began to visit my chambers." I hesitate, wondering if I've revealed too much. "In secret."

"How often?"

"Whenever he can." I swallow, thinking back, remembering the long stretches of not knowing, my worries erased in a heartbeat anytime he would appear. "Sometimes months pass, but he always finds his way back."

"The slavers would allow this?"

"Yes, of course. He wasn't a prisoner."

The king is quiet for a moment, considering that. I can't read this silence, but after a long pause, he says, "But this means you *are* more than friends."

"No!" I huff a breath. "We never—"

"*Never?*" The skepticism in his voice is thick. "I see the way you look at him. You just told me he slipped into your chambers for *years*."

"He didn't sneak under my *skirts*."

As I say the words, I think of Asher pulling me close, the press of him at my back despite the layers of blankets between us. He never tried for more, but I wouldn't have stopped him if he had.

My mouth twists into a frown. "Asher wouldn't . . . he wouldn't like that."

"He prefers the company of men?"

Ky's voice is so frank, and my cheeks are on fire again. "Oh! I . . . I don't know." I hesitate, because I never have conversations like this with anyone. Especially not while I'm sitting in their *lap*. "He just . . ."

My voice trails off again as I realize that Asher might tease me about someone catching his eye, but I've never once heard him talk about anyone *real*. I think of the way Asher stiffens or pulls away when I reach for him. Even when his lip was bleeding, he jerked away.

The king waits, and for a long moment, there's no sound except the horse's hooves swishing through the snow.

"Asher is a gentleman," I say firmly. "He never lets me touch him. But sometimes I wonder . . . I wonder if he ever lets *anyone* touch him."

My voice is so soft that the wind could carry my words away. I almost wish it would, because that also feels like a secret.

The king says nothing, but this silence is suddenly pointed. Profound in a way I can't figure out.

I turn my head to look at him, because I feel as though I've missed something, and I want to understand. But the soldier to our left speaks into the night. "Ky. Palace guards. We've been spotted."

At my back, the king's body goes taut. I peer out into the shadows. The forest has given way to open fields, and I recognize the moonlit palace walls far in the distance. Everything is still dark: no lanterns, no candles, nothing. Shadow-darkened riders are moving across the snow in our direction, but none of them carry a torch.

Ky draws our horse to a halt, half turning to face Callum and Garrett. The two leading Asher are farther behind, and my friend is barely more than a shadow. I can tell from his frame that his hands are still bound, and a long rope stretches from around his neck to one of the horses. I clench my jaw. Maybe they didn't beat him to death, but if one of those horses spooked or bolted, his neck would be broken and that would be that.

I can feel his rage from here. His panic, too. The air seems to shimmer from it.

A cornered man will make reckless choices.

I have no idea what Dane will do to him. I know what happened ten years ago, and that was bad enough. This will probably be worse.

I give a small shiver. I couldn't do anything for Asher then. I doubt I can do anything now.

Ky's arm is still around my waist, and I lift a hand to touch his. His skin is so warm, and for a moment, I'm struck by the knowledge that Asher would pull away—but Ky does not.

"Please," I whisper. "Let him go."

He inhales deeply, and when he lets it out, the breath is full of emotion that takes me by surprise. Frustration. Sorrow. Regret. "I cannot."

My heart twists, and I feel all those same emotions. "Because *I* betrayed *you*."

"This is not an act of vengeance, Princess. My soldiers said your brother is holding my captain at the palace. If Prince Dane believes Incendar is responsible for your disappearance, then I have no idea what he will—"

"We have Asher's orders!" I exclaim. "I'll tell Dane you had nothing to do with this!"

"Those same orders implicate *me*." He pauses. "Do you truly believe your brother would take your word for it?"

I inhale sharply, but then my gut clenches. My heart falls.

He's right.

Ky's voice is still low. "Asher delivered these orders—and he is the only man with a connection to where they came from. I cannot release him, Princess. I cannot risk my people for the life of one man. You have proven yourself to be a formidable opponent, so surely you understand this."

I snap my head around to look at him. For a moment, I think he's mocking me, but when his golden eyes meet mine, I'm startled by the unvarnished sincerity in their depths.

"If I were formidable," I say bitterly, "you'd be letting him go."

"If you *weren't*," he says, "I never would've removed a single weapon."

The words light me with surprising warmth, because no one's ever faced me like an equal—and right this moment, I hate him for it.

Garrett speaks from beside us. "Two dozen men," he says, his tone low and foreboding. He squints in the moonlight. "Looks like more coming."

"It seems your brother has already made up his mind," says the king. His voice sharpens, becoming an order. "Light your torches," he says, and the two soldiers beside us obey immediately. Flint strikes and fire flares to life, bringing gold to their cheeks and letting me see them both. It's clear that the palace guards have seen this, too, because shouts echo in the distance. I think I hear my brother's voice giving orders, and I wonder if he's among them.

They definitely don't sound like they're rejoicing about my safety. They sound ready to fight to the death.

"I'm the king of Incendar," Ky says to me, turning to face the oncoming guards. "I think it's time your brother had a reminder."

A chill washes through me. The king and his men might be badly outnumbered, but there's a reason his army has such a vicious reputation. I suddenly realize it's not just Asher who's in danger here. It's the entire alliance. It's all of Astranza.

I remember the fury in Dane's voice when he was scolding me about the wedding dress. *We're forming an alliance to have a chance at ending this war! I'm not starting another one!*

I don't want to start another one either.

I swallow hard. "Ky," I say. "Please. Stop this. Let me talk to Dane. He doesn't understand."

The light from the torches reflects off his face, throwing shadows along his cheeks. "And what would you say, Princess? Am I to believe you would speak in my defense to Prince Dane?"

"Yes," I whisper.

His golden eyes are so cold in the flickering torchlight. He doesn't believe me. It's *clear* he doesn't believe me.

What's worse is that I can't blame him.

The palace guards draw closer. At our back, his soldiers' torches seem to blaze hotter for a moment, a reminder of the power he wields. I shiver.

"He has the princess!" a man cries—and I'm shocked to realize it's Dane. The voice is full of outrage, and maybe a little fear. Was he worried about the alliance, or was he worried about *me*?

Ky's arm tightens on my waist, and it makes me gasp. I can't decide if the movement is protective or possessive—a threat or a promise. Maybe both. He sketches a sigil and draws a flicker to his palm, holding it right in front of me. It's tiny, dancing like the flame of a candle. I stare at the light, fascinated despite myself.

Another cry goes up from the palace guard, and Dane shouts an order. Weapons are drawn, but Ky's soldiers don't flinch. Neither does he.

"Dane was not responsible for this," I say in a rush. "And you have every right to be angry. With me, with Asher, with Dane himself. But it was my choice to remove you from the palace. *Not* his. Do not unravel this alliance because I saw a threat and took steps to protect you. Do not risk all of our people because my brother doesn't *understand*."

Against me, the king goes rigid. I can see his expression in the firelight, and his jaw is tight. His two soldiers are watching him, waiting for a signal—but they're ready to fight. I can see it. The ones coming up behind probably are, too.

"Six archers," says Callum from the other side. His hand slips to the back of his saddle, reaching for a bow.

"Hold," says Ky. His eyes are still on mine. That ball of flame blazes above his palm.

I wet my lips. "Perhaps someone in the palace *is* plotting against you—just as someone from Incendar might be plotting against *me*. But this alliance is bigger than that. You say you want to protect your people. If that's true, then you will douse your flames and you will allow me to speak to Dane. You will not put all of this at risk over a petty grievance."

"Petty!" he exclaims. His eyebrows go up, and he laughs a little under his breath, but not like anything is funny.

But I stare right back at him, because nothing is. I think of the secrets I know about my father, and everything that's at stake. I think of Asher, who risked his life to protect mine, and just like before, he'll pay the price.

Be brave, be strong, be smart.

My heart gives a wrench, and my eyes grow hot. But tears won't help me, and they definitely won't help Asher. Not now. I steel my spine and keep my eyes on the king.

He sobers, then runs a hand across his jaw. "How can I trust you?" His eyes narrow. "It's clear you don't trust *me*."

Maybe he's right, and we'll never trust each other. But I remember that moment when we were alone in my chambers, that single flicker of connection I felt when he spoke of protecting his people, and I wanted to protect mine.

"I don't trust you," I say coolly—because it's likely I never will again. "But I won't risk *my* people over the life of one man either." I pause. "Surely *you* understand this, Your Majesty."

The king studies me for one eternal second. A new emotion lights in his gaze, and it's so rare that I don't recognize it for a moment: regard. "As I said," he murmurs. "Formidable."

And then, before I can react, he crushes the flame out of his palm and turns to face my brother.

"Prince Dane," he calls sharply. "Have your soldiers lower their arms. Your sister would like to talk."

Chapter Fifteen
THE ASSASSIN

No one stays in the palace dungeon for long. If your crime is bad enough, you're executed. Otherwise, you're marked and turned over to the slavers.

Despite everything I've endured, I've really only been here once before.

This time is just as bad as the first.

When the guards hauled me away, I couldn't look at Jory. My heart was a wild rush in my ears, my thoughts consumed with panic. I kept hearing the king's low voice when he promised sanctuary, the way my blood pulsed with longing. How for one shining moment I wanted to believe there was a way out of Astranza, away from the threat of slavers and the torment of killing. The way I allowed a spark of hope to form in my heart.

The way I believed every word.

But that was a trick. A lie. There is no sanctuary. There's no hope.

Once we were down below, the guards cut the bindings on my wrists. It should've been a relief after trudging through the snow, but it's not, because they replaced the leather strap with ice-cold steel shackles. My ankles get the same. Then they cut every stitch of clothing away from my body, a true torture, since the dungeons are freezing. The decree against fire hasn't been lifted, because it's pitch-dark, too. Only a few dim shadows form in the moonlight that filters through the tiny barred windows.

They left me in a cell. No water, no food. Just frigid stone against my skin. I've curled into a ball, but it doesn't help. My shaking breath clouds with every exhale. I might be alone now, but I won't be for long. A man is sobbing somewhere nearby, but I don't try to look to see what's happening to him. Maybe he's starving, maybe he's being tortured, maybe a bored guard is taking advantage of him.

It's never good to know.

At some point, the glow of a fire flickers along the walls, and I remember the king pulling a ball of flame into his palm. I have the bizarre momentary hope that Jory has convinced him to come for me. But that's foolish, because Jory can't help me—and the king of Incendar doesn't care. All of his promises were a means to an end.

I am to ally with this country. I would know its faults as well as its promise.

I should have killed him. I should have taken her away.

Maybe I would have ended up here anyway.

I just have to survive. I've escaped the slavers before. I can do it again.

But this time, there will be nowhere to go. Jory will be gone.

When two guards return, I have no idea how much time has passed. The sky outside the windows is still inky black and I haven't frozen to death, so I doubt it's been *too* long. I go slack when they drag me through the doorway to the cell, but once we're clear, I seize the only opportunity I have: I surge against their hold, getting in one strike with my shackled hands, swinging the chain at the other in an attempt to knock him out.

But there's a third I don't see waiting just outside the gate, and he knocks me in the jaw with the hilt of his dagger. I'm hungry and tired and stiff from so much time in the cold, and the blow brings me to the ground. Blood fills my mouth.

"What's this one getting?" the guard asks, and his tone is bored. A prisoner fighting back is nothing new.

At first I don't understand the question—but then I hear a strike of flint, and new shadows find the walls. They're lighting the forge.

A sob threatens to form in my chest. I choke it back and force my mind to go blank.

Because I forgot about the brand. The marks on my cheek didn't hurt terribly much, but I forgot the one on my shoulder—the one put there with fire-hot steel, like an animal. Prisoners destined for the slavers are branded with an X on their shoulder. I've seen men and women with multiple brands, people who've paid their debt only to be charged with another crime. Sometimes the scarring blends together, forming a horrific pattern across their skin.

So far, I only have one. Unlike the stripes on my face, I expected it to stay that way.

I watch the fire in the forge grow, the bar of steel beginning to glow orange. The guards are gossiping with each other, ignoring me. I can barely hear what they're saying. My eyes only see the fire.

I should've killed him. I should have run.

When they grab me again, I fight, because I have to fight. But it's futile. There are too many of them and only one of me. They press the brand into my shoulder, and I don't want to scream, but I do. The pain is blinding, searing, stealing every thought from my head. It only takes a moment, but somehow it also takes forever.

When they did this the first time, I was sixteen. I vomited the contents of my stomach all over the boots of the men holding me. This time, my stomach is empty, but I dry-heave anyway, coughing spit at the floor. They haul me back to the cell, where I roll onto my back, hoping the cold stone will ease the burn, but it's *worse*. I cry out again. I might be sobbing. I might be keening. Again, I have no idea how much time passes, but my thoughts won't organize. My shoulder is nothing but agony. My mouth still tastes like blood. The king's words won't stop ringing in my ears.

I am offering him mercy.

No. He didn't. No one ever does.

"You. King Theodore has sent a summons."

I don't realize the guard is talking to me until he repeats it, and even then I'm still trying to make sense of the words when he kicks me in the side. "Put these on," he says, and a pile of fabric is dropped in front of my face.

When I don't move, he kicks me again. "Put them *on*," he snaps. "Or I'll find a hot poker and see if that doesn't help you move."

I move. Every shift of my arm is agony. The guard unchains one limb at a time so I can pull my hands and feet through the loose trousers and tunic. The rough muslin brushes against the fresh brand, and it nearly sets me dry heaving again.

I can't believe that I woke up in the princess's bed this morning, and now I'm all but vomiting in the straw of the dungeon tonight.

What's more shocking is that I ever thought this could end another way.

When the guard orders me to get up and walk, I do it.

The torches of the palace are blazing now, throwing shadows over the walls as we pass. I have no idea how late it is. It's odd to be led through the palace like this. I'm so used to creeping through secret passageways and springing from alcove to beam like a cat. I don't even know where they're taking me, but we're not going fast. The chain between my feet is short, making my steps small and shuffling.

I don't know why King Theodore would have summoned me. Jory had my orders, so perhaps she was able to give them proof of why we fled the palace. But surely Dane would deny *his* involvement—and Maddox Kyronan would deny his. I may adore Jory with every fiber of my being, but I know how powerless she is here.

Could the king of Incendar have done something? Said something? Spoken in my defense?

As soon as I have the thought, I banish it from my thoughts. He tricked me. He *lied*. I've already been caged and branded like an animal.

Maybe I've simply been summoned to prove that they're delivering punishment, that justice will be served.

By the time the guards draw me to a stop, the pain in my shoulder has settled into a dull ache. We've reached a set of massive wooden doors flanked by additional guards, and I realize they've brought me to the throne room.

My heart thumps hard, and my feet seem rooted to the ground. Am I to be executed? Is this what happened to my mother?

A guard raps with his halberd, a man calls for us to enter, and then the doors are drawn open. As they half lead, half drag me inside, I don't just find myself facing the king. I'm surrounded by more than two dozen people.

Jory's father is on the throne, and even if I didn't know he was sick, I might suspect it. His skin is pale, his eyes a bit yellowed. Dane is on a smaller throne beside him, looking healthy and hale, with eyes that I've hated since I was old enough to know how much bitterness hides behind them. They're both backed by more guards, and to their right is a man I know well: the Guildmaster.

Master Pavok is a large man, with a thick head of gray hair and a gut falling over his belt buckle. I'm shocked to see him here. Did they summon him to verify my orders? Maybe he'll be able to set this all straight. I've been loyal to the Guild since he took me on, and he knows it.

But as my eyes sweep the room, I realize that the king of Incendar is here, too. His five soldiers surround him, but a tiny sphere of fire catches my eye. He's passing it back and forth, palm to palm, the way an antsy child might fidget with a ball. His gaze falls on me, and I'd swear I can see that same firelight flicker in his eyes, as if that magic lives inside him.

Rage lights up my veins.

They don't need another Hunter, I think. *I will find a way to end you.*

As if he heard me, the ball of flame goes still. I jerk my eyes away from him.

"Asher." Jory's voice comes from somewhere to my right, full of shock—or maybe pity. I don't know what I look like, but I doubt it's very good.

I have to search for her, because I didn't see her in my first glance at the room, but she's there, seated on a chair by the wall, her lady Charlotte beside her. She's been dressed in a new gown, all silk and satin perfection, her hair freshly arranged. Her cheeks are flushed, her eyes red like she was crying.

Well, that's not encouraging.

"Jory," I say, and my voice is barely more than a rasp.

One of the guards cracks me in the shoulders, and it's no better than when the soldier did it earlier. This time my knees hit the stone floor, the chains of my shackles rattling. I have to catch myself on my hands.

No, this is definitely not good.

"Guildmaster," Prince Dane says. "Do you know this Hunter?" His voice sounds bored, but it sends a fresh bolt of rage through my heart.

But Master Pavok nods. "Yes, Your Highness. This is Hunter Asher."

"Was he given an order to kill Maddox Kyronan, as Princess Marjoriana claims?"

I hold my breath. Maybe this *will* help prove my innocence.

"No," says Master Pavok. "Hunter Asher has not been seen by the Guild for more than three months."

I jerk my head up. "No! I was there this—"

One of the guards punches me right where the brand seared my shoulder, and I forget how to speak. I hear a horrible sound, and I think it comes out of me.

"Stop!" Jory shouts, her desperate fury ringing through the room. "Dane, I have repeatedly told you that Asher was not responsible for this. You will *stop this*."

Nothing stops. The pain is dizzying. I breathe through my teeth.

"You have had your time to speak," says Dane. "Pavok, proceed."

"As I have said," the Guildmaster continues, "the Guild would *never* accept an order to kill a member of the royal family. I suspect these orders are fraudulent, possibly fabricated in an attempt to conspire against your alliance. This Hunter has been gone for quite some time, with no explanation for his whereabouts. His last assignment was in Morinstead, which is to the north, near the border, so it would stand to reason that he could be conspiring with agents from Draegonis—"

One of the Incendrian soldiers swears under his breath. The king crushes that ball of flame into nothing in his palm. His eyes lock on me again.

"No," I gasp. "No, that's not—"

The guard hits me in the brand again. I see stars. When I blink, my forehead is against the stone floor, and I'm gasping.

"No!" Jory says. "Father, stop this! Asher is not working for the Draegs. I *know* he's not."

"You do *not* know," Prince Dane says. "You have been deceived. For *years*, if I am to understand correctly. He coerced you into allowing him into the palace, Marjoriana."

"He did not *coerce* me," she snaps, enraged. "And you very well know—"

"Then you participated in an act of treason? You knowingly allowed an armed man to bypass the guards and access the palace? A known *traitor*? You deliberately endangered the life of your king?"

The entire room goes completely silent. Jory is glaring at him, her jaw tight, her eyes like fire.

Be careful, I think. *Please, Jory. Do not admit to this. Not even for me.*

After an eternal moment, she speaks through clenched teeth. "No. Of course not."

Dane continues, because he knows he's got her. "As I said, he coerced you into allowing him into the palace. He could be sentenced for that alone."

"Hunter Asher," says Master Pavok. "Where have you been for three months?"

"Morinstead," I say, and the word comes out of me like I'm speaking through gravel. "I completed my duties." I have to pause to inhale, and I fight not to flinch when one of the guards shifts his weight.

"Your duties should not have taken more than a week."

"I was detained. Captured by a bondsman who thought I'd escaped. He thought my Guild ring was a fake. It took time to verify."

The silence in the room is so thick. The king of Incendar is looking at me again.

I hope they execute him.

Unfortunately, it seems that only one of us is on trial here.

"It's a good story," Prince Dane finally says. "I'm almost convinced."

"It's not a *story*," I growl. "Interrogate Rachel. Interrogate Hammish. *He* saw me. Maybe they're the ones working with Draegonis—"

"I did," says Pavok. "They deny seeing you."

My head is pounding. I don't understand it. Are they protecting Pavok? Dane? Themselves?

Dane rises from his chair and crosses the room to stand over me. "Which do you think is more likely?" he says, his tone mocking. "That you received orders to kill King Maddox Kyronan and Princess Marjoriana on the day we were to seal an accord between our kingdoms—orders allegedly given by the two people with the most to gain from an alliance?" He leans in. "Or does it make more sense that someone with a questionable past and secret access to the palace was hired by Draegonis to undermine it all?" He claps me on the cheek, and it stings. "Truly, Asher, it's a great mystery."

I spit right in his face.

He backhands me so hard that I taste blood before I hit the floor. Jory makes a sound, but there's a quick round of hushing from her lady.

The guards haul me upright, and I don't know if it's the burn to my shoulder or the punch to the face, but my vision goes a bit spotty again.

That's all right. I don't need to see Prince Dane to let my hatred show on my face.

I just . . . don't know why the keepers would claim they didn't see me. I don't know why the Guildmaster would claim to have no knowledge of these orders.

Did someone trick *me*? Or did someone trick *them*?

Could Draegonis be working to undermine the alliance somehow?

None of it makes sense. My thoughts are too twisted up with anger and fear and betrayal. When I look across the room, Maddox Kyronan is still watching me, his eyes cold and hard and expressionless.

I know what *he* thinks of Draegonis.

Jory's father speaks, and his voice is softer than I remember. "What of the alliance now?"

Prince Dane has stepped back from me a bit, and he spreads his hands to address the room. "From where I sit, the alliance can proceed. Princess Marjoriana was duped by an old childhood friend, a known traitor to the kingdom, but no real harm has been done." He looks at the Incendrian king. "You were able to escape, Your Majesty. You returned my sister to the palace, for which you have our gratitude. This man will be punished for his crimes. My sister is naive to the nefarious actions of Draegonis, so you can see how she would—"

"*I am not naive!*" Jory snaps. "And Asher is not—"

"*Silence*, child!" her father says sharply. The room falls silent in a way it *never* would for Dane. "I would like to hear Incendar's answer."

Every eye shifts to Maddox Kyronan, who still hasn't spoken. He's drawn a new ball of fire from somewhere, and it passes from palm to palm in a mesmerizing pattern that's hard to look away from.

But then it stops. He spins a finger through the flame, which sizzles and burns into nothing.

A few people gasp. The Guildmaster is one of them. I think Dane is, too.

I don't. I'm not amazed anymore.

The room is absolutely silent, tensely waiting on his response. The king's eyes shift from me, to Prince Dane, to Jory, and finally to King Theodore.

"I agree that no true harm has been done," he finally says. "Thanks to Princess Marjoriana's willingness to prevent a greater conflict."

My eyes flick to Jory. Whatever she did, she doesn't look like she was very *willing*.

The king continues, "As such, our alliance will proceed—"

The gasps this time are louder, but they're not shock. They're sounds of relief.

Dane smiles. "Well! Grand tidings, then—"

"I'm not done," says the king, and silence crashes down again, like a guillotine. "The alliance will proceed, but not today. In one month's time. Until then, Princess Marjoriana will be my guest in Incendar, where she can determine whether this union between our nations is an alliance she can commit to." He pauses, and he stares right across the room at Jory. "With full faith and honesty, and nothing less."

The words are pointed, and her entire demeanor darkens. "So I'm to be your prisoner."

"I'm rather certain I just said you would be my *guest*."

Prince Dane glances between them. He's not smiling now. "Your Majesty—this is not part of our agreement—"

"Neither was my kidnapping," the king says. "And while this attempt on my life may have been thwarted, I am not fully convinced that Princess Marjoriana is as committed to this arrangement as you are."

Jory half rises from her seat. "There will be no faith," she declares. "You have already proven that you cannot be trusted."

"Enough," says her father, and he gives a short cough. The room falls silent again. "Marjoriana, you will go. Maddox Kyronan, if you find my daughter suitable, I expect you will seal this alliance in thirty days."

"Done," says the king.

My heart clenches.

"No!" cries Jory. "Father, you don't understand—"

He waves a hand, then says something softly to an attendant. Lady Charlotte tries to shush Jory. She's clutching her hand.

Prince Dane looks at the two of them. "Your attendant will join you," he says after a moment. Charlotte straightens in alarm.

"*No*," says Jory. "You will not commit innocent people to be tormented in Incendar."

"I will not send my sister without a chaperone, either."

Jory inhales sharply, but Charlotte leans in, and whatever she says makes the princess's mouth form a line.

Prince Dane turns to the guards at my back. "Return this man to the dungeon. His debt will be set to one million silvers—"

One million. I was focused on Jory, on what this meant for *her*, but Dane's words are like a steel bolt shot right through my chest. My breathing becomes a sudden roar in my ears, and I can't even hear what he says after that.

I'll never earn out a million silvers. Not in a brothel, not in a fighting arena, not on my back or on my knees for the richest citizens of Astranza.

Never.

But another round of gasps goes up around the room, and I realize Maddox Kyronan has spoken.

Prince Dane is staring at him, and his eyes are wide with shock. "What did you just say?"

"I said the debt is owed to me." The king pauses and folds his arms. "Is it not?"

Dane's mouth works like this question has never been asked before. "I—I suppose you could see it that way, Your Majesty, but—"

"You will not grant your *slavers*"—he says this word like it's distasteful—"A profit of one million silvers. Nor will you line your own coffers. Not when the crime was committed against Incendar, and most especially if this man is an agent of Draegonis."

My veins fill with ice. I can't move.

"Forgive me, but I do not believe you understand the intricacies of how justice works in Astranza—"

"Do not patronize me." The king's voice is low and intense. His fingers form a sigil, and a new swirl of flame appears in his palm.

The tension in the room thickens again. Even Dane falters.

In the silence, Maddox Kyronan continues. "This man shall be subject to Incendrian justice. *Not* yours."

Prince Dane hesitates, and for the first time, he looks directly at me. His face has gone a bit pale. We've all heard every story of how Incendrian *justice* is meted out. I watch that fire dance on the king's palm, and sweat collects between my shoulder blades, making the burn sting.

I know how badly that brand hurt, and I have no doubt the king could do something a thousand times worse.

"I'm not working for Draegonis," I growl. "Believe what you like, but my orders were—"

"Silence him," Dane says. This time the guard takes a gauntleted fist and drives it right into my stomach. I find myself dry heaving over the stone floor of the throne room. Breath rushes in my ears again, and I can't focus on anything at all. Voices are speaking, but nothing is clear until I hear Jory.

"If you do this," she's saying, her voice low and vicious, "I will *never* marry you."

It draws my gaze up, but the king isn't impressed by her vow. "You shouldn't be surprised, Princess. You keep speaking of my brutality." His eyes flick over me one more time, dispassionately, and for as warm as his eyes looked in the flickering firelight, they're bitter and cold now. "Alliance or not, rest assured, Incendar knows what to do with Draeg spies."

Chapter Sixteen
THE WARRIOR

Once again, I'm riding in a slow procession across the snow-covered fields of Astranza. I thought I'd be returning to Incendar with a new bride in a carriage and a flutter of hope in my chest, but now I'm bringing a woman who hates me and a prisoner who wants me dead.

Sev is silent at my side again, my soldiers trudging along behind us, the carriages creaking and rattling as we pass over uneven ground. The clouds overhead have shifted, allowing the moon to beam down on us all, promising another endless night.

It's reckless to travel again so soon. We're all exhausted and hungry, driven by nothing but duty and desperation, the worst combination for any soldier. But we need to get away from the palace. We need to get out of this *kingdom*. I have no idea who I can trust, but so far it seems to be *no one* in Astranza. Dane spoke a lot of words to point the finger at Draegonis, but I don't believe any of them. It was too neat. Too easy. I couldn't challenge him, however. Not with such a small group of soldiers. Not without risking my sister being left alone. It was bad enough when I thought Dane's men were going to attack in the snow.

On the way here, I remember wishing I'd brought the whole army—and just now, I'm regretting that we didn't. If I had more soldiers, I'd send runners ahead to have troops waiting at the border, just in case.

But I don't, and I'm not sending any of my men away. Not while I've got a vengeful princess in one carriage and a chained-up assassin in the other.

When Jory arrived in the palace courtyard with half a dozen trunks and her lady-in-waiting by her side, her expression was cold and her eyes were fierce. I offered them both a hand to climb into the carriage.

The princess completely ignored me. She climbed inside on her own.

Her lady's eyes were just as stony, but she offered me a curtsy. "Lady Charlotte, Your Majesty." Then she ignored my hand herself, and climbed in after the princess.

I could feel my men watching this, but they weren't smirking this time around.

Asher is in the other carriage, the chain between his ankles looped through the wooden rail that supports the seat. It's clear the palace guard roughed him up. His movements were slow and awkward, his face full of fresh bruises, right down to a spot of blood where his lip was split. I've seen how quickly he can move, so I had Callum hold a weapon on him while I adjusted the chain. I expected him to spit profanity at me the whole time, but he was silent as a dead man, his eyes locked on the floor of the carriage.

Every muscle on his frame was taut, however, and I'm no fool. I clicked the shackles closed with a little more force than necessary. "Behave," I said, and then I dropped the key in the pouch on my belt.

I waited for him to tell me off—or even spit in my face, the way he did to Dane. But he did neither.

Despite that—or maybe *because* of that—a twinge of regret flared in my chest. The same twinge that's been poking at me since the moment I tricked him. I hesitated before closing the carriage door.

"What happened to your shoulder?" I said, because he was still sitting crookedly.

His jaw tightened, but he didn't respond.

"Dislocated?" I guessed. Asher didn't move, so I glanced at Callum. "Check. Fix it."

That got a reaction. Asher's eyes flashed up, and he drew back into the shadows of the carriage. For a second, he looked like a wounded animal, cornered and ready to attack. "Don't you fucking touch me."

I was too tired and too agitated to deal with a fight, so I sighed. "Fine. Suffer." Then I shut the door.

So now we're all riding, all freezing, all irritated.

All starving, too. After Asher put the notion of poison in my head, I wouldn't touch a bite of food from the palace, and I wouldn't let my men eat anything either.

I really didn't think anything could be worse than the way we traveled last night, but apparently it can.

Maybe the silence is too much for Sev, because when he speaks, his voice is aggrieved. "Are we going to talk about it?" he says.

It's the first thing he's said in miles, and I look over. "Talk about what?"

He's got his cloak drawn up against the cold, the fur pinned in place to cover half his face and keep out the wind. But his eyes find mine. "The fact that we were supposed to stay a week but we barely even stayed a *day*? The way you didn't *marry* her? Or how about the Draeg spy you've got in a velvet carriage instead of shipping his charred bones back to the border?" He pauses, and his sarcasm thickens—or maybe it's anger I'm hearing. "Perhaps something about how they *stole our king*, yet we're escorting them to—"

"Sev."

"I could go on."

I give him a look.

From behind me, Callum calls, "How about the fact that we're all hungry enough to eat one of the horses?"

Sev snaps his fingers. "That too."

I frown.

Ahead of us, the snowy landscape stretches on for *miles*. A burst of icy wind whips between us all, and someone at my back mutters, "*Fuck.*"

Behind them, Roman says, "I have a few strips of dried beef left in my pack."

Garrett and Callum both inhale sharply. Even Sev looks back. "Leave it to Roman to be prepared," he says under his breath.

"Divvy it out," says Garrett.

"I didn't say I was *sharing*."

Hooves shuffle in the snow. Garrett and Callum must be whirling their horses around. "Well, we didn't say we were *asking*—"

Sev gives a brisk whistle through his teeth. A call for them to come to order.

They all fall sharply silent. Shuffling hoofbeats return to an even cadence. But I can *feel* their agitation.

Any other night, this would be lighthearted teasing, especially from Roman. Of all of them, he's the most easygoing, the slowest to anger, the last to argue. Tonight, everyone's voice bears an edge. I can only imagine what they'll be like in a few hours.

"Five more miles," I say to Sev, and I make sure it's loud enough for them all to hear it. "We'll find an inn for the night."

"We left the palace to find an *inn*? What are we going to do with the prisoners?"

"The princess isn't a prisoner," I say tightly. My own agitation is flaring, because I don't know what to do with Asher yet. "And I'm not convinced Asher is working for the Draegs at all—though maybe this Hunter's Guild is. Either way, Dane's claims don't quite fit. He's been an ass all along, and if there were any truth to those orders, he could have been protecting *himself*."

"Sure—or this assassin and the princess could have been working together. Holding you there. Waiting for others from Draegonis to claim you—or your body."

I think about that, turning it around in my head. Jory definitely believed Asher—no question. Her worry for him was genuine, too. When we rode back to the palace, her emotion—her *tears*—seemed real. I saw her flare of panic when Dane issued Asher's sentence.

And she was worried for *me*, too—at first. I heard her breath shaking when we first emerged from the tunnels under the palace. She stepped in front of Asher when he had a dagger in his hand.

Asher! Stop hurting him.

So that leaves Asher himself. While I might believe that a skilled mercenary could convince a young woman to help him kidnap a king . . . that doesn't seem to fit any of what happened. He left me in the snow—and it was *my* choice to follow them. He didn't even want me there. He felt he was risking something to protect Jory. Not just from assassins. From me, and from her brother. That all seemed genuine, too.

But he was so worried about going back to those *slavers*. I heard it in his voice when we spoke, and I saw it in his face when Dane set the price of his crime to one million silvers.

My fingers tighten on the reins when I think about that part. *A million.* I doubt any man could work that off in a lifetime. If I'm understanding their justice system correctly, the funds would go right into the royal family's pockets. It's almost enough to make me think Prince Dane set this entire thing up himself.

The thought strikes me like an arrow, and I freeze.

But then I shake it off. Too complicated. And I *know* Astranza needs my magic and my army. Why risk the alliance? He could set Asher up for an attack on anyone else in the palace without needing to risk everything we've been working toward.

I don't trust any of this.

"Do you want to have any of this deliberation out loud?" Sev says, and his voice has the same edge as before.

I don't want to bicker with *him*, so I say, "It wasn't like that. Asher wanted the princess to leave me behind. He wanted her to run." As I've been turning over the events in my thoughts, I keep tripping over the fact that Asher really didn't kill Nikko.

"And he left Nik alive," I add. "A Draeg spy wouldn't do that."

"If he wanted to run, what stopped them?"

"They weren't prepared." I pause. "He had ample opportunity to kill me, Sev. We know what the Draegs would do with me. There's no way they would have let me go. And I don't like how quickly Dane laid the blame at their feet. It's too easy."

"Well, *you* didn't hire an assassin to kill the princess."

"No." I keep thinking of that moment Asher said one of my men could have hired a Hunter. But I can't make *that* work out in my head either. I've known them too long. We're too close.

Sev is still musing. "If you think he lied about Draegonis, does that mean Dane hired one to kill *you*? Why bother? We were outnumbered in the palace. You had no fire. He could have set the army on us when we arrived."

"I know." I glance over again. "That's why we're getting the hell out of here. But the princess could still be a target. That's why I brought her with me."

He falls silent again, contemplating.

Behind us, Callum calls, "Why'd you bring Stripes?"

I glance back. "Stripes?"

"The guy with the lines." Garrett gestures at his face. "If we're not sending him back to the border in pieces, what are we doing with him?"

I inhale to answer—before realizing I have no idea what to say.

Because the princess loves him. Because I need her to trust me. Because I don't want her to hate me.

It's more than that, though. It's about Asher, too. I don't know how to explain that I simply couldn't *leave* him there—just like I couldn't leave *her* there. Individually or together, they're both intriguing. Compelling. Striking, if I'm being honest with myself.

But they're also exasperating. Complicated. *Messy*. Between Asher's complete lack of a plan to kidnap me and the fact that Jory convinced him to do it, I can't decide if they're the bravest pairing I've ever met, or if they're so wildly chaotic that they might one day lead each other straight off a cliff. Something about these two makes all of my protective instincts flare. Dane grabbed her arm, and I threatened to declare a war. When he backhanded Asher in the throne room, I wanted to set him on fire.

It settles something inside me to know I have them both in a carriage, safe and sound.

Even though they both hate me for it.

I've been silent for too long, because Callum is saying, "I know what *I'd* like to do with him."

His tone is low, but it's not full of promised violence at *all*. Beside him, Garrett snorts. "Leave it to you to lust after the Draeg spy because he's *pretty*."

"I didn't say I want to build a life with him," Callum says, aggrieved.

"Just that he's *pretty*," Garrett grunts.

"Actually, *you* said that he's pretty—"

"Enough," I snap, and they shut up.

As soon as I say it, I regret it, because I don't sound commanding, I sound resentful. Sev's eyebrows go up, and he glances over, but he says nothing.

I'm not even sure which part of that little bickering match sparked it. Callum flirts with anyone, and he's attracted to everyone. He teased me about the princess being beautiful, and she absolutely is. I'm not surprised to hear him make a comment about Asher.

I'm more startled by my reaction. Am I annoyed? Protective? Or something else entirely?

I remember Jory's voice, so soft in the drifting snow.

Sometimes . . . sometimes I wonder if he lets anyone *touch him.*

Between the violence and the circumstances, I hadn't thought about Asher being pretty. Intriguing, yes. A little bit fascinating—while also somewhat tragic. I don't know what's happened to him, but I've begun to build a picture of it.

Sev looks over and studies me for a solid minute, then turns back to stare out at the snow. When he speaks, his voice is low. "I know that look," he says. "But—"

"What look?" I demand.

"*That* one. The one on your face right now." He pauses. "They attacked you and took you prisoner, Ky."

"I know."

"*Violently.*"

"I know."

He makes a frustrated sound. "They could have—"

"Sev! I know."

"Oh. Well!" His eyes flick skyward. "As long as you *know.*"

I set my jaw, but I'm not angry. Not really.

He glances over and drops his voice even further. "After a few hours, I started to wonder how we were going to control Victoria."

My sister. She's so innocent—and so dangerous. My chest clenches.

When I speak, my voice is rough. "It would be no different if I fell in battle."

He snorts and tugs at the scarf covering his jaw. "Trust me, I don't like to think about that either."

Under his flippant tone, I hear the genuine worry. I haven't really spared a moment to think about what this must have been like from *his* side—and I should have.

I look over again. "You might have to. One day."

I've said this before—and he never responds. He doesn't respond now. His eyes are still fixed on the snow ahead of us. But I can tell he's thinking about a decade of fighting at my side. Ten years of battles where we've both gotten into situations that were so close to life-or-death that we don't even discuss them anymore. So many close calls where I saved his life—or he saved mine.

Until this morning, when I vanished from the palace, and there was nothing he could do about it. I imagine how I would have reacted if our roles were reversed, and my chest clenches.

I put out a hand. "But not today."

He gives me a look. "Yeah. Not *today*." But he reaches out to clasp my hand in return. In his grip, I feel the weight of his worry, and I realize how deeply unsettled he must have been.

Especially because he doesn't let go immediately, and he holds my eyes. "You truly don't believe they're working with Draegonis?"

"No." I think of Jory and Asher and how very desperate they were, and my voice goes quiet again. "I've never liked Dane. You know that. But being in their court . . ." I shake my head, thinking of those bruises on Jory's wrist. Thinking of the way Asher went pale. "Everyone here is wary of Incendar. Of *me*. Astranza is supposed to be the jewel of the continent, but something is wrong *here*." I hesitate, trying to figure it out. Maybe Astranza cloaks *their* wickedness in shadows, disguising anything distasteful. Maybe their brutality isn't obvious, the way mine can be. Perhaps King Theodore hides Astranza's corruption behind well-fed citizens and unpaid laborers.

Slavers. Bleeding skies. If I'd known about that, I might have had a few more demands for this alliance.

I glance over again. "I couldn't leave them there, Sev."

He looks right back at me. "I know," he says. "I felt it, too."

But then he heaves a sigh, because my soldiers have resumed their bickering.

"Don't be jealous, Gar," Callum is saying behind us, his voice low and mocking now. "You're pretty, too."

"Shut the fuck up."

"Just the prettiest soldier in all the—"

His voice cuts off on a choked sound that tells me Garrett punched him—and it wasn't playful. They grunt and swear when Callum hits back, and hooves shuffle in the snow as the horses adjust for their scuffling.

Those two will end up grappling in the snow in a second. They might share a bed again later, but they'll try to kill each other first.

I turn my head a little. "Roman! Take second. Callum, move back."

The scuffling ceases immediately, but it's only a minute before I hear muttering behind me again.

"You're not getting my fucking pack," Roman is snarling at Garrett.

I can't take much more of this.

I look at Sev. "Forget what I said. Let's find an inn *now*."

WE DON'T EXPECT to find one nearby, but after another mile, Nikko spots a faint glow across the snow, and a plume of smoke from a wood fire spills into the sky. The smell of roasted meat greets us when we draw close, and my stomach lets me know that it's been a *long* time since I put food in my mouth. When we reach the small cluster of buildings, the snow is tamped down underfoot, and our horses aren't the only ones here. Some are tethered out front, and there appears to be a stable behind. Maybe others were desperate for a hot meal, too.

Once we stop, I open the princess's carriage first. Jory and Lady Charlotte are sitting on opposite benches, and much like when they climbed in, they don't look at me. Behind me, the soldiers are trading barbed words while they tether the horses, but the two women are stock-still.

Oh, that's right. She still hates me.

I hold back a sigh. "My soldiers need to eat," I say. "We've reached an inn."

Jory keeps her eyes on the opposite wall. "We will remain here."

"You're going to avoid a hot meal and a warm bed just to spite me?" I say.

Her expression doesn't flicker. "Yes."

I glance at Lady Charlotte, and her expression is equally stony. Clearly a coordinated effort here.

My eyes shift back to the princess. Even in a cloak, with velvet gloves, she seems to be holding back a shiver. I could draw her into my arms and make her warm immediately, but I think she really would put a hairpin in my eye.

I've run out of patience, so my voice goes sharper than I intend. "My soldiers barely slept last night. They spent most of the day searching for *me*. Thanks to your Hunter's warnings about poison, no one has eaten, either. But for *spite*, you're going to make me order one of them to stand in the cold and guard your carriage—"

Behind me, the bickering soldiers shut up *quick*.

"I'm not making you do *anything*," the princess snaps. Her gaze returns to the wall, a clear refusal to move. I'm tempted to drag her out.

I lower my voice. "Hate me if you like, Princess. But my men don't deserve to—"

"Please close the door, Your Majesty."

Rage swells in my chest, but I slam the carriage door closed and turn away. I don't care that it seems petty and juvenile.

Behind me, she turns the latch that locks it.

Fuck.

The others are watching me with guarded expressions. They've pulled their packs and weapons for the night, but it's clear that every single one of them was listening to that exchange, and they're bracing for my orders. Wondering which one of them is going to have to be cold and hungry because Princess Marjoriana is being a royal—

I cut off those thoughts before they can fully form. But if she expects to be my queen, she's not exactly endearing herself to the army. Maybe that's not surprising. I doubt *she* has ever gone hungry.

I glance behind them at the inn. Smoke curls from the chimney, and the smell of cooked food is strong from here.

I let out a breath and fetch my quiver and bow from where they're tethered behind my saddle. Then I strap on the quiver, hang the bow over my shoulder, and put my back against the carriage. "I'll take first watch," I say to them. "Go. Eat. Arrange for rooms. Whatever is available."

None of them move.

Sev sighs, then hangs his own quiver over his shoulder. He steps away to come stand against the carriage beside me. "*We'll* take first watch," he says. "Go." When they still don't move, he adds, "That is an *order*."

They turn to obey, with the exception of Garrett, who approaches me and Sev. He glances at the other carriage. "What about Stripes?"

I try to imagine Asher's reaction if he hears them call him that—and I fail. "He's injured and chained to the seat," I say. "He hasn't made a sound. I don't think he'll cause any trouble."

But as I say the words, the latch behind us clicks open. The princess appears in the doorway.

Her eyes are cold when they meet mine. "I did not fully consider your men," she says icily. "I should have." Her eyes flick to Garrett, who's stopped, probably ready to listen to another argument. "Forgive me," she says.

His eyes widen, just a bit, and I can tell she's surprised him. He gives her a nod. "Yes, Your Highness."

"Charlotte and I will join you." She moves forward, ignoring the hand I offer, climbing down from the carriage herself. Her lady follows closely behind, and she ignores me just as effectively.

As they move past, the princess stops and looks at Sev. "Captain Zale. You will escort us."

Sev inhales sharply, and his eyes snap to mine. I'm sure he expects me to be annoyed, and I am, but I'm mostly just tired. "Go ahead," I say.

He clamps his mouth shut and offers his arm. "Your Highness?"

Jory rests her hand on his elbow, and I clench my jaw.

"Your king has told me that he plays the role of a soldier," she says to him, as if I'm not standing right there. "So as to not make himself a target."

"I am not *playing a role*," I grit out.

Garrett is still watching this exchange, and his eyebrows go up.

She doesn't even look at me. "I will do the same, Captain. You will call me Jory. Charlotte and I will be ladies of the court, sent to prepare for the princess's arrival in Incendar." She pauses. "And you will tell your king that my acquiescence now is no indication that I trust him or his deceitful actions. I am looking after his loyal soldiers, not *him*."

Sev stares at her for a long moment, and when it's clear that she seriously expects him to parrot this information, he looks back at me, bemused. "Ah . . . the Lady Jory says that—"

"I heard her."

Jory is still looking at him. "And you will tell your king that I expect Asher to have a warm bed as well. He will not be chained in a cold carriage all night."

Again, there's silence, and Sev inhales heavily. "Lady Jory also expects—"

"*Sev.*"

He lifts a shoulder in half a shrug, and they turn for the door. I expect her to look back, to say something equally taunting, but she doesn't.

"Maybe a warm bath for him, too?" I call after her. "Some chocolates for his pillow?"

"That will do," she calls back, just before they go through the door and into the tavern.

My fists are clenched the whole time.

What a great start to our *alliance*.

But they're gone, and I'm left in the snow with Garrett, our breath clouding in the night air. I'm painfully aware that my soldiers have witnessed her attitude toward me, and I'm sure they're all having *thoughts* about it.

Especially Garrett, who's watching me expectantly.

"Not a word," I say.

His lip quirks, but he's silent.

I move toward the other carriage. I have no idea how the owners of this establishment will take to us bringing a prisoner inside. I wonder if Asher will be docile enough to bring along unchained. I consider his injuries, the way he favored his right side like his shoulder was dislocated.

But then I consider his vicious skill. The way he bested me, and then Nikko.

The way he'd surely risk everything to get Jory away from me.

The way he likely wants me dead.

"If I *were* going to say something . . ." Garrett offers.

"Don't."

He laughs under his breath.

But I pause with my hand on the carriage door. It's absolutely silent inside the carriage, and I wonder if Asher has fallen asleep.

So I look at Garrett. "All right, *what?*"

"Sometimes the fighting makes it better." He pauses. "In the end."

I scoff. "She hates me."

He grins. "I know."

I give him a look, then pull the door wide. For a second, I see nothing: just a pile of blankets and scraps of splintered wood. No Asher.

"Fuck." I grab hold of the doorframe to lean in. I have no idea how he could have escaped without us noticing. *"Fuck."*

But then a shadow moves and a fist comes out of nowhere to crack me in the face—followed by a kick to the chest.

I fall back, scrambling for weapons.

But I'm too slow, or maybe he's just too fucking fast. Asher explodes out of the carriage, and before I can blink, he's got a chain around Garrett's throat.

Chapter Seventeen
THE ASSASSIN

I thought they were never going to open the stupid door. When I heard that asshole argue with Jory, I thought for sure he was going to stand guard in the snow, leaving me locked in here all night. I broke the seat support an hour ago, and at first I was worried they'd hear it and drag me out. But the wind and the snow must provide for good insulation, because no one stopped the carriage to investigate. I thought about trying to slip out while we were moving, but the king was right about one thing: I have no boots, no cloak, *nothing*. Just the few woolen blankets they left me with. If these Incendrian soldiers didn't kill me, the weather would've taken care of it.

So I hid deep in the corner of the carriage, tucking myself against the velvet seams.

And then I waited.

When the door opens, I spare one second to enjoy the king's surprise when he realizes I'm "missing," and then I explode through the opening. I've got the steel links of my shackles wrapped around the knuckles of one hand, and he snaps back when I hit him. It gives me enough distance to land a solid kick to his sternum, and that clears the doorway. My branded shoulder is screaming at me, but I grit my teeth and try to ignore it. That soldier Garrett is swearing, already reaching for weapons, but I'm too quick. I grab hold of his armor, leap onto his shoulders, and get that chain around his neck.

Just as the king summons a handful of fire.

I freeze, tightening my grip, my knees pressing into the soldier's armor. We're all breathing hard, breath fogging in the night air.

Well, Garrett's not doing so well with that. Not with the tension I have on this chain.

"Asher," says the king. "Let him go."

"So you can melt this chain through my arm?" I saw the way he made Jory drop the dagger. I have no doubt he could do it to this chain, too—if I didn't have it wrapped around his soldier's throat. "No, thank you. You already tricked me once."

"I didn't *trick* you, I was making sure a man who attacked me didn't have the opportunity to do it again."

Garrett is wrenching at the chain, but I dig in with my fingertips, using my knees to grip tight to his back. He's even bigger than the king, and every muscle in my body is reminding me that I've been hit a dozen times today—and I haven't eaten anything since that cookie I shared with Jory. Spots keep flaring in my vision, and I redouble my grip.

Then Garrett tries a different tactic. He whirls to slam me into the carriage. The hard wall collides with my shoulder, and I cry out, my suddenly slick fingers losing a few links. I scramble to regain purchase, to pull the chain taut again.

But now Garrett has a grip on it, and he dives forward into a roll. I see it coming and let go, trying to spring free so he doesn't drive me into the ground.

Unfortunately, he's too strong, and this time *I'm* the one who can't break loose. I barely have time to tuck my head before he pulls me into an awkward somersault. My shoulders slam into the ground—and then he lands right on top of me.

I take his full weight: armor, weapons, and all. It knocks the breath right out of my chest. Those spots in my eyes turn to flaring stars.

Well, this went poorly.

I've lost track of the chain. I've lost track of how to *breathe*. I barely realize when he rolls off of me, because I'm so focused on forcing air back into my lungs, and I feel like I've swallowed my tongue. I definitely taste blood in my mouth. Before I know which way is up, I'm dragged onto my knees in the snow, and the horizon spins. I don't know what's worse: the frigid snow against my bare feet, the fact that the king still has a ball of fire ready to incinerate me, or the soldier who's found a blade and now has it against my throat.

"Garrett, *hold*."

The king's voice slices through my awareness, and his soldier goes still. Garrett's eyes are dark and furious, though. His own throat is scraped raw from where I got him with the chain. He's standing over me, his free hand clutching the neckline of my shirt, holding me still. Breath clouds between us, equally rapid.

He wants to finish what I started. I can see it in his face.

But he obeys the king's order. He draws back an inch, but his gaze is locked on mine, his focus on the dagger.

So I wrap the chain in one fist and use both hands to punch him in the crotch.

Well—I try. The king grabs hold of me before I can make impact. He shoves me hard, the movement forceful enough to make me fall back in the snow.

Garrett glares down at me. "Please, Ky," he says. "Let me break *something*."

"Not yet." The king reaches for my tunic, and I try to scramble back, but my body won't respond quickly enough. When I swing for *him* with the chain, he grabs hold and pulls me upright. It wrenches at my shoulder and makes me gasp.

I wait for the chain to sear into my skin, but it doesn't. Instead, he glares down at me. "You had my sympathy for about five minutes," he says, that velvet accent clipped. "Now you're just being a pain in the ass."

I don't know what to say to that, and he uses the grip on the chain to jerk me closer. I'm still on my knees, so it puts me on eye level with his belt.

Then he reaches for the buckle.

My eyes widen—then narrow. "I know you bought me from Dane, but I'm a little surprised you want my teeth anywhere near your—"

"I didn't *buy* you." Instead of unfastening the buckle, he unfastens the pouch beside it, and now he just sounds aggravated. "Bleeding skies, Asher."

He withdraws a small key and unlocks the cuff on my left wrist. I should probably take the opportunity to punch him, but I'm so startled by this that I don't move.

Especially when he clicks it onto his own.

After years with the slavers, and then years in the Hunter's Guild, it takes a lot to shock me. This does it. I thought he was going to burn me into a pile of soot. Not . . . whatever this is. My eyes shoot from his face to the steel band tethering me to him.

It shocks Garrett, too, especially when the king tosses the key in his direction. I think the soldier's eyes are as wide as mine.

"I've been more than fair," the king says. His voice is low and resolute and leaves no room for argument. "I'll remind you that I have a limit. Get up. Walk."

More than fair, my ass. I'm not one of his soldiers, and he can go right to the pit of hell.

I set my jaw, sit back on my heels, and don't move.

"Get up," he says again.

The snow is making my feet go numb, but I glare up at him. "Fuck you."

Maddox Kyronan takes a step closer, until his boots are right at my knees. "Asher. *Get up.*"

"I said, *fuck you.*" The words sound juvenile and petulant, and I don't care. "Make me."

His expression doesn't flicker, and his tone doesn't change. "Do you want me to make you?"

Somehow the question makes my mouth go dry, and I'm not entirely sure why. But the words are spoken with low intensity, and my heart suddenly beats hard. Maybe it's the way his voice isn't tight with anger, just quiet conviction. Maybe it's the focus of his gaze or the fact that I'm on my knees at his feet.

Maybe it's because this doesn't feel like a threat, it feels like a choice.

As I stare up at him, I realize that we were in almost this exact position hours ago, except our roles were reversed. I had a dagger in my hand, a blade at his throat. He didn't yield.

Something tells me he won't yield in this instant either.

Do you want me to make you?

He could. I know he could. Either through magic or force or even if he just dragged me by the chain. But seconds tick by as he waits for my decision, as if his patience is eternal. As if he genuinely wants me to weigh the simple choice between him breaking all my bones or me getting up as he commanded. I don't know if that makes him more terrifying or less. Either way, I'm off-balance. I don't want to choose wrong.

He hasn't moved, and those fierce eyes haven't left mine.

Before I realize it, I'm shaking my head.

"Good," he says, his voice unchanged. "Get up."

This time, the command sparks something inside me, and I scramble onto my feet so roughly I nearly stumble into Garrett. The movement jars my shoulder, and I clutch my wrist to my belly, my breath coming in short bursts. A sudden sweat slicks my back, some combination of pain and humiliation—and maybe a little bit of something else entirely.

He made me yield without lifting a finger. Without even raising his voice.

The king is watching me, as if anticipating my rage. "Don't fuck with me, Asher." He nods toward the tavern. "Walk."

I hate him. I hate everything.

But I walk.

Chapter Eighteen
THE ASSASSIN

The inn sports a tavern on the first level, and it probably wasn't crowded when we arrived, but the addition of the king's men, along with the princess and her lady, means the room is rather full when we walk in. Warm, too. Jory spots us almost instantly, but so do the other soldiers. This is already humiliating enough, so I grit my teeth and keep my head down. I still feel every pair of eyes in the tavern look from the king to me, and then to the chain linking us together.

I wish I had my jacket, so I could hide under the hood. The Incendrian soldiers might be unfamiliar, but I know what this looks like to every single citizen from Astranza. I've got a shackle on my wrist and seven stripes on my face. Probably a fair share of bruises, too. The spot where Dane split my lip still stings.

I hear a sharply indrawn breath, and I glance up to see a mix of shock and anger wash over Jory's expression. I have no idea what she finds the most infuriating, whether it's the blood that's surely on my neck or the bruising that's left over from my treatment in the dungeon. Or maybe it's just the chain tethering me to the king. Her hands are planted against the table, and she looks ready to march over here to punch him in the face.

Ah, Jory. She couldn't stop her brother, so I doubt she can do anything now.

I never wanted her to see me like this.

The tavern keeper stops in front of us, blocking her view. He looks from the king to Garrett, and then, very briefly, to me. He's an older man with a heavy paunch and thick gray hair that's thinning on top and pulled into a knot at the back of his head. His eyes aren't unkind, but he looks tired.

"As I told the other soldiers," he says apologetically, "we don't have much left. Everyone's been after a hot meal since the decree was lifted, and it's late. But we've got ale, and we've got a bit of stew left over the fire." He casts a dubious glance at the others, then back at us. "It *should* be enough to share, if you don't mind meager portions. A few loaves are left, too, but we'll have more in the morning."

Meager portions. My stomach clenches hard. I've seen the size of his soldiers. That means I won't be eating.

Nothing new there.

"We'll make do," the king says. "You have our gratitude."

The tavern keeper glances at the crest of Incendar in the center of his armor. A worried line appears between his eyebrows. "Ladies of the court are with you. Will your king be coming through tonight as well?" His hands curl together, his knuckles showing white. "We're all very worried about our princess. Your king is such a harsh man, and Princess Marjoriana is such a kind creature . . . or so the stories say."

"You have nothing to fear," Ky says. His tone is resigned, and something about that is surprising. "Our king will not be stopping on his journey. And no harm will come to your princess."

"Good!" the tavern keeper says, clearly relieved.

This man is the king, I want to shout. *Right here! There are enough of you. Kill him while you can.*

But Ky would probably break my jaw before I could get all that out. I know Garrett would.

I need to get away from them. If I can get away, I can figure out a way to get *Jory* away.

Being chained to the king is going to present a problem. As usual, I'm powerless to help her.

I clench my jaw and glare at the ground again.

The tavern keeper continues, "I can have my son take your bonded man to the stable."

The king is silent for a moment, and I hear the confusion in his voice when he says, "The footmen will see to the horses. If you could send a meal to them as well, I'd be grateful."

"No, your *bonded man*," the tavern keeper says. "Unless . . ." His eyebrows flick up suggestively. "Unless he's of the kind you like to keep at hand."

The king is staring at him like he's speaking a different language. A frown line on his forehead deepens. "I'll . . . keep him at hand," he says.

"Ah, yes. Very well, then. I'll see to your meals." The tavern keeper turns away. "If you take a seat at the end, I can bring you a straw mat. If you like."

The king glances at Garrett, who looks just as puzzled, and is maybe a bit angry about it. Poor baby.

This would be hilarious if I weren't the one being discussed like a piece of livestock.

The king runs a hand over his face. "Why would I want a straw mat?" he demands.

"Oh!" says the tavern keeper. "Of course." His eyes flick to the lines on my cheek. He must catch a glimpse of the blazing fury in my eyes, because his gaze skips away immediately. "No mat for this one, then. I shouldn't have assumed."

I scowl. The man dashes away before saying anything else.

The king sighs, but he must be too hungry and tired to care *too* much, because he turns toward the table. I follow because I have no choice. Garrett moves to the far end, but the king heads for the closer side, across from the princess and his captain. She refuses to look at him, glaring at the wall behind him instead, her eyes iced over.

Good girl. I hope she kicks him in the crotch.

There's a short bench here, and the king slides down to sit across from the princess, leaving enough room for me. That's a little surprising—but I can't take it. Instead, I drop to sit cross-legged on the floor beside the table. It puts me right beside the boots of the king and his captain, and I can barely see Jory and the others beyond the edge.

Maddox Kyronan draws up the chain sharply, then glares down at me like I'm deliberately being difficult. "Asher. *Sit*—"

"I *can't*," I snap, and my voice is louder than I intend. "It's forbidden."

He stares back at me. So does his captain. Even the tables nearby fall silent, watching. They're probably expecting him to backhand me across the face, which is exactly what would happen if he were my keeper and I really had been sold by one of the slavers.

But the king's eyes are locked on me. "Explain," he says.

Heat crawls up my cheeks, because Jory is looking, too. This is degrading in a new way, and I didn't expect it. If Jory ever left the company of royalty, she'd know. If the king were Astranzan, he'd know. His gaze is so intense, and I have to look away, glaring past him. "If I sit at the table, the innkeeper will make me move. It's forbidden. That's why he offered the straw mat. Look." I nod across the room, where a man sits at a table near the hearth and a middle-aged woman is curled up on a stretch of fur at his feet. She's not chained, but the position is clear.

The king is absolutely silent. I have no idea what expression is on his face.

"I will *un*forbid it," Jory whispers from beside Captain Zale. "You will not sit on the *floor*, Asher."

Lady Charlotte leans in to murmur. "If you make a proclamation, it may give away your identity." She pauses, glancing at me briefly before looking back at the princess. "And he's right. It *is* forbidden for a bonded citizen to sit at the table."

Jory clenches her jaw, and her angry eyes flash to the king. "You will unchain him, then."

"No." His voice is flat. "He destroyed my carriage and tried to kill Garrett. And that's just in the last five minutes. I'm not putting anyone else at risk."

Jory's eyes swing back to me, but I refuse to look up.

None of the others say anything, but I can feel their focus, too.

A barmaid appears with a tray laden with steins of ale and baskets of small muffins and loaves, and thankfully, that breaks the strained silence. She doesn't acknowledge my presence, which is unsurprising. The room is warm from the hearth, but the cold of the stone floor begins to seep into my joints. I can smell the steaming bread, and I swallow and stare at the legs of the soldiers under the table. Captain Zale has a long dagger in a sheath strapped to his thigh, and it's right in front of me.

Tempting, but I'm not *that* stupid.

I might be later, though.

When the king reaches for his ale, the chain rattles against the edge of the table, tugging at my wrist. Hunger and thirst claw at my gut, and

I fold my other arm against my belly, keeping my eyes locked on the boots under the table.

"Asher." The king's voice pierces my awareness, and just like every time he says my name, my insides feel a tug. "Here. Drink."

When I look up, he's holding out the stein.

I don't reach for it. He tricked me once, and this feels like a trap. Like I'll take the stein and he'll knock it into my lap.

But my mouth is watering, and I can't help but swallow.

"Don't refuse just to spite me." The edge has faded from his voice, and his accent turns every word to honey again. "Take it."

I obey. This feels like a different kind of yielding, and I hate it. It makes me want to take the tiniest sip possible and shove it back at him.

But as soon as the taste fills my mouth, that's not an option. I can't remember the last time I had a drop of water, and this is good ale, sweet and cold, with a hint of sugar. I drink like a child, wild gulps that are too fast.

"Easy," says the king, and his voice is still mild. "I don't want to drag your drunk body around. Here." He's got a small loaf of bread this time, and he breaks it in two, holding out half toward me. It's so fresh that steam pours from inside. The ale has made my hunger flare, and my stomach gives a wrench. But after the way he acted in the snow, I'm waiting for *him* to fuck with *me*. I set down the stein and clench my fists so hard that my nails dig into my palms.

He exchanges a glance with his captain over the table. When he looks back at me, his voice is even lower. Softer. "I'm not tricking you. Eat."

I snatch it out of his hand because I resent the note in his voice. But when I bite into my portion, it's a reminder of how long it's been since I've eaten, because this simple bread topped with salt and rosemary feels like the best thing I've ever tasted.

From the corner of my eye, I can see that Jory is eating her own portion of bread, but she's watching me.

I dodge her gaze. I've spent years hiding this part of my life from her, and it was all for nothing. Now I won't be the Asher she remembers anymore. I'll be the man relegated to the stone floor, receiving scraps of food like a chained dog.

But as the others eat and hunger eases, the food steals some of the tense wariness from the air—even mine. I'm tired and sore, and it's warm, and there's a part of me that wishes I *did* have a straw mat, because I'd curl up on the floor and let sleep take me away from the fact that any of this is happening.

At the front of the inn, the door swings open wide, with enough force to slam it against the wall with a bang, wood cracking. I jump, but three of the soldiers are instantly on their feet, weapons drawn. Beside me, the king already has a blade in his hand, and I didn't even see him draw it. Alarm cracks through the room, and I don't know if people are more afraid of whatever threw the door open, or the Incendrian soldiers who suddenly look ready to level the place.

But there's no threat. I peer past the rough and ready soldiers to see a boy who's red-cheeked and windblown, carrying an armload of firewood. Wind and snow whistle through the doorway, and the innkeeper rushes to slam the door closed against the weather.

The soldiers exchange a glance, sheathe their weapons, and sit back down. Jory must have grabbed hold of her lady's hand, because she lets go, taking a long breath. The king slips his dagger out of sight, but a muscle twitches in his jaw when the boy clatters the firewood onto the hearth. I wonder if he's still worried about assassins—or if he's worried about a *real* Draeg spy.

"A Hunter isn't going to throw open the door," I mutter, and the king gives me a look. But some of the tension eases out of his body.

By the time the barmaid brings bowls of stew, the wariness has evaporated altogether, and the bread and ale have eased sharp tempers. The soldiers at the other end of the table have begun exchanging good-natured barbs. Even Lady Charlotte smiles when the one called Roman tells Garrett to stop eating like he's been led to a trough.

The only one not smiling is Nikko. I can barely see him over the edge, but he's not laughing, not teasing, not talking.

He's watching me. The expression on his face is definitely *not* pity.

I fix my gaze on the floor again, on the scuffed boots of the king and his captain. *This* end of the table is deathly silent. When a steel bowl appears in my vision, I blink in surprise.

"Eat," says the king. "I know you're hungry."

I don't reach for it. "It's yours."

"I don't eat before my people."

That makes me scowl—and also ache. I've never heard a ruler in Astranza say something like that. "I'm not your people."

"You're mine for now. And there's plenty. Astranza clearly has a different meaning for *meager portions*." When I still don't move, he adds, "I'll share with Sev."

His captain was eating a spoonful himself, but he automatically pushes his bowl to the middle of the table, between them. The king sets the one he was offering on the side of the bench, right in front of my face. Then he picks up the spoon from the other and ignores me.

Fuck it. I take the bowl and shovel some into my mouth. Like the bread, right now it's the best thing I've ever tasted.

Jory is glaring at the king now, her eyes narrow and fierce. "You won't win my trust this way."

The king pushes the spoon toward the other side of the bowl for Captain Zale. "I won't watch a man go hungry either."

"I know of your reputation," she says coolly. "You won't convince me otherwise. I know you torture prisoners."

The king's voice is just as cold. "I don't *starve* them."

His captain takes a mouthful of food and then pushes the bowl back. "For what it's worth, Your . . . ah . . . *Lady* Jory, the Incendrian army rarely takes prisoners at all."

A foreboding note hangs in his tone, and I'm reminded of the savage stories I've heard. There's a reason Incendar might be the smallest country on the continent, but Draegonis hasn't been able to gain a foothold. The implication of violence hangs over the table for a moment.

"But if we do," he continues, "they're never starved." Captain Zale cuts a glance at me, and his voice turns dry. "Not even Draeg spies."

I bristle, but the king just scoops another spoonful. "He could barely organize a kidnapping, Sev. He's not a spy. Someone else is behind this."

I can't believe this asshole is defending me and insulting me in the same breath. The worst part is that I agree with him.

The captain takes a swig of his ale and says, "Well, you've chained him to your wrist, so I hope he doesn't prove you wrong in your sleep."

The king scoffs. "And then what? He has to drag around a dead body?"

"I'll just cut your hand off," I mutter.

At that, they *all* snap their heads around to look at me. Every single stein of ale or spoonful of stew goes still.

"Asher," whispers Jory.

I don't take it back. I'm still glaring at the king.

He stares right back at me. "No," he says. "You won't."

We're frozen in place for a moment, and the tension between us is just like that moment in the hut when I said I'd cut his eyes out. He called my bluff, and I didn't like it.

I don't like it now. Every time he does this, it stirs me up, especially after the way he forced me to get up out of the snow. It makes me want to grab that dagger from Captain Zale's thigh and stab it right into him. I can already feel the weight of the weapon, the minimal effort it would take.

But the king just shrugs and takes another spoonful of stew. "I can always chain you to whoever takes first watch."

The others are absolutely silent, as if debating whether that's a veiled threat or a warning or just an attempt to break the tension. I'm not even sure myself.

Garrett finally offers a dark smile. "Cal volunteers, don't you?"

The note in his voice makes me flush immediately, especially because I didn't expect it. It triggers something in my head, because there was a time in my life when I knew how to use any flicker of attraction to my advantage—but it's been too long, and I hate that part of myself. I've spent years burying those instincts.

But Callum isn't even looking at me; he's gazing at the opposite side of the tavern, where a lone young woman is nursing a stein of ale in the corner.

"That was half an hour ago," he says. "I've moved on." He pauses as the solitary woman looks over, and a slow smile spreads over his face. "Someone else is taking first watch, right?"

At that, Garrett reaches across the table to punch him in the shoulder.

Callum doesn't even wince. Without looking, he reaches out to pat Garrett on the cheek. "Don't worry, Gar. *You're* still pretty." But then he's up, moving away.

The captain looks after him. "If someone else takes first watch," he calls, "that's when you're supposed to be *sleeping*."

"I'll be in a bed. It counts."

From farther down the table, one of the other soldiers speaks, and I think it's Roman. "Here, Ky. I had plenty." A moment later, a bowl goes sliding along the table. The king catches it, automatically pushing the other back to his captain.

I'm struck by how casual they are with each other. These soldiers must be high-ranking officers if they're traveling with the king—or at least men of importance. I've been around Astranzan soldiers before, and I've never seen this kind of easy camaraderie.

Jory seems to have noticed, too, because she's also studying them. Some of her ire has melted away, replaced with curiosity.

Garrett notices her focus, and he pushes a basket of bread in her direction. His voice is gentler. "We have plenty of bread, too, Lady Jory."

She blinks in surprise, and I watch her eyes flick to the marks on his neck. I'm sure she's thinking of what the king said about me. She gives him a nod. "Thank you."

When she looks in my direction, I finally meet her eyes. I'm not sure what she sees in my expression, but her own turns troubled, and she mouths two words at me.

I'm sorry.

I shake my head, then look away. It's not really an apology at all. It's resignation. She can be as icy as she wants to Maddox Kyronan, but she's still going to Incendar. He needs her for this alliance.

But he doesn't need *me*.

A day ago, I was watching her bite a cookie right from my fingertips, wishing she could escape the palace with me, that we could disappear into the shadows together.

I frown. It was an empty wish. It always is. If I'm going to wish for anything, I should wish for escape.

But even that is probably fruitless. I doubt I can get her away from him—and I don't even know that I *should*. If nothing else, the king really will keep her safe. So that leaves me. I clearly can't go back to the Hunter's Guild. And with these marks on my face, it would be nearly impossible to find work—if I didn't get picked up the way I did in Morinstead.

I would offer you sanctuary, Asher.

I swallow. I wanted to believe those words so badly.

None of these thoughts are helpful.

"What happened to your shoulder?" says the king.

"Nothing." I look down at my bowl and scrape the last bits of stew from the sides.

"You've been favoring it all evening." His hand brushes against the neckline of my tunic.

I jerk away, the chain rattling. The empty bowl clatters to the stone floor, and the chain goes taut between us.

I glare up at him. "Don't touch me."

His arm is suspended from the tension I'm putting on the chain. "You're also leaking through your shirt."

"It doesn't matter."

"Is it a burn? Let me see."

"No."

His men have fallen silent, ready for trouble, their focus locked on this end of the table again. Even from across the room, Callum has looked over. Jory leans around the captain to peer at me, too.

I clench my jaw. I wish the king had told the innkeeper to have his boy lock me in the stables after all.

The taut chain is straining my shoulder, and I realize I probably *am* leaking through my shirt. The mark aches like I can still feel the heat of the metal. It'll weep and sting for days. I remember.

"It's nothing," I grind out. "It'll heal."

The king glances at the princess, and then back at me. "Asher," he says, his tone lower. My gut clenches when he says my name. "They did something to you. Show me."

My breathing feels too fast. If he were threatening me or ordering his men to hold me down, I'd know how to respond. I'd snatch that dagger right off Captain Zale's thigh and fight the whole way. His men would eventually overpower me or he'd use his magic to force me into submission, and then he'd rip the tunic free and look at whatever he wanted. No one would stop him. Half the people here would probably watch.

But this is like that moment outside. He hasn't made a threat, and he hasn't raised a hand. He just waits, his golden-brown eyes holding mine. No expectation, no demand, just those simple words hanging in the air between us.

They did something to you. Show me.

I can see why his men are so loyal, because there's a shadow of guardianship here, of *protection*, that's completely foreign to me. It reminds me of the moment he asked about the slavers, or the way he promised sanctuary. The way he said he would know Astranza's faults as well as its promise.

The way he said, *You're mine right now.*

Like he'll start a war if he doesn't like what he sees.

Sudden longing tightens my chest, and it's so unexpected that my breath almost catches. Fuck. *Fuck.*

Because I hate him. He already tricked me once, in exactly this way. But something deep inside me craves every emotion that his voice evokes. Something inside me *trusts* him, despite all he's done and all that's happened. I've been broken a thousand different ways, but never like this. Never with *choice*. Never with *patience*.

So I let the chain go slack, link by link, and I crawl forward, returning to where I was. I lower my head so he can see, bracing myself.

When his fingers brush against the nape of my neck, my heart gives a jolt. Sweat has gathered in the small of my back, and my mouth goes dry. I realize I'm holding my breath.

This is foolish. I force myself to exhale, and it sounds like I've run a mile.

The king hasn't moved his hand any farther. He's waiting, his fingers warm against my skin.

"I don't know what's been done," he says to me, and his voice is even lower. "But I won't hurt you."

That tightness in my throat refuses to let go, and I can feel every muscle in my body, taut and ready to spring. But his hand waits, a warm pressure on the back of my neck, and after a moment, my eyes fall closed. My palms press into my knees. In another place or time, I could almost imagine myself as something other than a bruised captive chained on the ground. I could be a friend seeking comfort. A lover offering his body. A warrior kneeling at the feet of his king . . . and his queen.

But this man is not my king, and Jory isn't my queen. I'm nothing to their alliance. I'm nothing to the *war*.

I'm no one. A shadow.

It's almost enough to make me shrug off his touch. But I can't quite make myself pull away. My breathing has slowed, some of the ready tension easing out of my muscles.

"May I see?" he says. My eyes are still closed, and his voice is so quiet that we could be the only two people in the room.

I nod, feeling drunk on his touch. Is this his magic? It must be.

He tugs at the neckline of the prison tunic, and I didn't realize how much the wound wept, because pain sears through my back as the fabric begins to pull away. I choke back a yelp, catching the sound in my fist, my teeth pressing into my knuckles. The captain swears under his breath, and behind me, Jory inhales sharply. Somehow I'd forgotten our audience, and I didn't realize she'd moved. Every muscle goes taut again, ready to jerk away.

"Easy." The king's hand settles over the nape of my neck, his thumb brushing through the hair behind my ear. "Be still, Asher."

It's so unexpected, and it grabs my focus. Then he does it again, and the motion of his thumb is soothing and gentle and I don't want him to stop.

All the vicious stories we've heard about the king of Incendar, and he's holding me in place with nothing more than a few words and the weight of his hand.

"Asher," Jory whispers, and I can hear the tremor in her breath. That, more than anything, tells me how bad it looks.

But then her voice tightens right up. "I told you," she says, low and furious, and I realize she's speaking to the king. "I *told* you to let him go."

"And I told you why I couldn't," he says, his voice just as low. "You *know* why I couldn't. Meanwhile, you accuse me of torture, while the royal family of Astranza enslaves their citizens and brands them like livestock."

"That is *not* the way of things here," she snaps, and my heart thumps.

It *is* the way of things here.

"Then explain it to me." The king's voice is still low, but his fury matches hers. "Your brother might not hold the iron, but he surely gives the order. See for yourself. It's hardly the first time it's been done."

I go rigid, because I don't *want* her to see. But the king's thumb brushes through my hair again, and it holds me still.

Then I feel the brush of Jory's skirts against the bare skin of my feet. She touches my shoulder, her fingertips light and cool, such a contrast to the king's. It sends another jolt right through my body. Both of them touching me at once strikes a chord deep in my heart, making this shared stroke of fingers against my skin far more intimate than it should be.

I never let anyone touch me—I never *want* anyone to touch me. But just now, I don't want them to let go. For a flicker of time, I imagine their hands exploring further. Her cool fingers tracing their way down my chest, his strong hand buried in my hair, holding me still, just like this. Without warning, my cock stiffens, and my breath catches.

"*Enough.*" I jerk my head back and smack his hand away. The chain rattles and goes taut again.

My desire has no place here. I'm a prisoner, nothing more. They're destined to marry *each other*.

They're looking at me in surprise, and my heart keeps slamming against my ribs. It's only then that I realize Lady Charlotte is beside Jory. Two of the soldiers have risen from the table to flank the king, as if this . . . *discussion* might turn into something more. There aren't many patrons left in the inn, but we have the full attention of everyone remaining—including Callum and his companion, who are still watching from across the room. Even the woman on the mat has sat up to watch.

I glare up at the king. "I don't want your pity." Anger and shame and humiliation war in my chest, and I swing my head around to look at Jory. My voice is still rough, and I snap at her before I can stop it. "I don't want *yours*, either."

She jerks back like I struck her, and her breath catches.

Fuck. If I weren't chained to the king, I could slip into the shadows and disappear. I'm almost ready to cut my *own* hand off.

Captain Zale looks between the three of us, and he lets out a breath through his teeth. His eyes flick to one of the others. "Roman. Which rooms did they give us?"

Roman nods toward the staircase at the back of the tavern. "The two at the north side. They should have laid a fire already."

"Ky," says the captain. "Maybe you want to finish this privately."

The king looks at him, and then back at the princess, and finally to me. "Fine." He stands, extending a hand to her. "After you."

Her mouth forms a line, but she doesn't move. She looks at Charlotte. "I will not be remaining with him for long. Please ensure the other room is adequately prepared." She heads for the back wall of the inn.

But then she hesitates and turns back. She unlaces the small purse from the sash at her waist, and she hands it to her lady. "And find out how much that woman owes," she says, nodding toward the bonded woman on the fur. "Pay the man so she can be free of sleeping on the floor."

Without waiting for a response, she turns toward the staircase. I stare after her. So does Lady Charlotte.

The king sighs and runs a hand over the back of his neck, but then he looks down at me. Again, I wish for a hood and the shadows, because if I weren't tethered to him, I'd vanish in a heartbeat. My thoughts are jangled up and twisted, and for every part of me that wants to grab that dagger from his captain's thigh, there's another part that wants to return to the moment his thumb traced a path through my hair.

His eyes are sparking with anger, but I don't think it's directed at me. When he speaks, his voice is resigned. "You've hidden too much from her, Asher."

"I'm not hiding anything."

But as soon as I say the words, they sound hollow. Untrue.

He knows it, too.

"You are," he says, and his tone is grave. "But if she is to be a part of this alliance, she should know what has been done to her people. If she is to be a *queen,* she should know what has been done to *you.*" His eyes shift to his captain. "Make sure Lady Charlotte has enough silver to accomplish her task."

Then he turns toward the staircase, barely waiting for me to follow.

This time, I don't fuck around. I scramble to my feet before I have no other choice.

Chapter Nineteen
THE PRINCESS

My heart is pounding, refusing to settle. The men have followed me to the stairs, and their emotion radiates in the air around us. The king is angry, but Asher is almost worse. He's never snapped at me before, and definitely not like that. His anger rattled something inside my heart. I'm angry too, but my stomach is churning. I don't want to be alone with them.

Not because I'm afraid. Because I'm worried their anger is *justified*.

Asher dropped to sit on the floor like he was used to it. He didn't even look up when food was brought to the table, as if he didn't expect to be fed.

The weight of everyone's focus presses down on me as I take each step, and I wonder what they're all thinking—either about *me* or about Astranza. The king's words about branding citizens like livestock are burning in my thoughts, and I wonder how many people heard that. For hours, I've been angry about the righteous fury in his voice when he mentioned Incendrian justice to my brother. I've been furious about the way he ordered me to leave the palace, barely giving me enough time to gather my belongings.

But I saw the severity of Asher's wound, the deep purples and blacks from where a brand scorched a mark into his flesh. That had nothing to do with Incendar, and everything to do with my own kingdom.

It's hardly the first time it's been done, Ky said.

My heart gives an anguished squeeze. The older scar on Asher's shoulder was barely visible, but I saw the edges of the raised welt that formed an X, just above the new one. Did that happen when he was first exiled? I never knew. He never said a word.

As we climb the steps, Captain Zale gives some sort of signal, and Nikko and Roman step away from the table.

Before they get far, Ky pauses on the stairs. "I don't need guards, Sev."

The other man snorts. "Humor me," he calls back. "I know what happened the *last* time you were alone with these two."

Ky sets his jaw, but he continues up the steps behind me. His two soldiers follow closely behind.

I still don't know if I can trust him. He deceived us once. But that churning in my stomach won't stop, and I can't bear to look back at them. Their steps are heavy behind me, and that's bad enough. Asher takes the stairs one by one, the chain between his ankles rattling on each board as he passes.

I open the first door that I come to, ready to storm inside—until I discover that this is a room meant for multiple people, with two small pallets along the wall and a straw mattress spread across each one. I stop short in the doorway.

The king comes up behind me, and I all but *feel* his presence at my back. "The other room is likely the same, Princess. But we can move to the other, if you'd rather."

"It's fine." I square my shoulders and force my voice to be mild, completely unperturbed. But against my will, a blush crawls up my throat. I've never traveled without a royal retinue, and I've never slept in an inn. Until this moment, I hadn't thought about *all* of us sharing rooms, much less beds.

I remember Asher gently scoffing at my idea of escape, saying I had no idea what life was like outside the palace. At the time, his manner was lighthearted, but now that I've seen him crouched on a stone floor, I wonder what else I've missed.

I think of that woman curled up on the fur. Asher never mentioned *this* either. I told Charlotte to pay for her release, but that's more about my guilt than anything else. Is that kind of thing happening to people all across Astranza? If we'd arrived at the Three Fishes, would he have had to do that? Sit at my feet like a prisoner?

I swallow tightly.

Ky follows me in, with Asher in tow. The two soldiers are right behind them, but they stop in the doorway.

"When we retire," Ky says to me, "you and your lady can have one of the rooms to yourselves, Princess. I don't expect you to share with my soldiers." He pauses. "Or with me."

Aside from the nights Asher snuck into my bedchambers, I've never shared my sleeping quarters with anyone else at all. But much like the moment I realized his men would go hungry if I chose to take a stand in the carriage, it feels equally selfish to demand one room for myself when there are nine of us traveling together.

"We can share the space," I say, though I'm not sure if I mean it. "Your men have been quite respectful. I was simply . . . surprised."

His eyes narrow, but he only glances at his soldiers. Ky taps two fingers under his right eye, then draws one finger down his cheek. Roman nods, then taps two fingers against his shoulder, his eyebrows up, questioning.

The king nods in return, and Roman turns to shift through the door.

Nikko doesn't. He's glaring at Asher.

Or maybe he's responding to the fact that Asher is glaring at *him*. "Want a rematch?" Asher says darkly.

I watch the soldier draw himself up, and violent potential seems to swell through the room. But Roman turns back, grabs hold of Nikko's armor, and drags him out.

Once the door is closed behind them, Ky looks at Asher, aggrieved. "Stop provoking my men."

"I didn't provoke him."

Ky takes a breath and runs a hand down his face like he's exasperated with both of us.

Good. I'd rather feel annoyed than angry and intimidated. "Secret signals?" I say to him.

"Yes."

"Something else from when you pretend to be a soldier?"

His eyes flash when he glances at me. "Yes, Princess. More of my imaginary soldiering."

I tap two fingers under my eye, then drag a finger down my cheek. "What does that mean?"

"Keep watch," he says, tapping under his eye the same way. He regards me levelly, as if he's not sure he wants to give away all their secrets. But maybe this isn't *too* private, because he holds up one finger. "One"—he drags it down his cheek—"to stand guard."

Fascinating. I'm intrigued in spite of myself. Just when I'm about to ask about the shoulder tapping, Asher says, "I know a good hand signal."

Ky gives him a look, then unclips the clasp of his cloak and tosses it at the end of one of the pallets. "Sit, Asher."

His voice isn't forceful, but the command in his tone is clear. Asher's blue eyes are heavy and inscrutable, fixed on the king. I'm still a bit shocked that he allowed Ky to touch him, especially since he turns to stone every time *I* reach for him. Especially in a way that seemed so... vulnerable. I've watched them jab at each other with words and actions all day, but when Ky's hand fell on his neck, Asher seemed to give himself over completely, even if it was only for a moment.

He yields now, too. The chain between his ankles rattles on the wood as he sinks onto the pallet, and the one tethering him to the king is short enough that it keeps his hand partially raised.

"Unchain him," I say. "You can't accuse me of enslaving my citizens while you've got Asher chained to your wrist."

Ky reaches for the buckles of his bracers. "Downstairs, he couldn't keep his eyes off Sev's dagger. The instant I release him, he'll go for a weapon—or he'll be out the window."

"No, no," Asher says, his voice flat. "I'll be good. I promise."

Ky snorts and tosses the first knife-lined bracer toward the hearth—well out of the assassin's reach.

This verbal parry is different from earlier. Less barbed. I wonder if it's the food, or if it's what just happened, the way Asher submitted to his touch. I told the king he wouldn't earn my trust this way, but it wasn't quite true. He began earning it back the instant he handed over his meal.

Asher. Eat.

Just the memory of his soft tone makes me shiver. He's so harsh and fearsome that it makes him downright captivating when his voice goes quiet.

But he betrayed us once. I'm terrified he's going to do it again.

Though . . . maybe he feels the same way about me. In the hut, he said that all I've offered are lies. The words keep pricking at my heart.

Because I don't *want* to deceive him. I've been trying to *protect* him. Just like I want to protect Asher.

But maybe it doesn't feel that way from his side. Maybe all he sees is deception.

Considering what I know about my father and his waning magic, maybe that's all there is to see.

I don't know how to undo any of this. Especially not when the king keeps lighting these little flames of attraction. They started the moment we met, when he defended me in front of Dane, and they continued all the way into the hut, when he made that vow to Asher. In that moment, I thought this alliance could truly work, that we could find accord. When he tricked us, I thought he doused any chance of us ever coming to terms.

But another flicker of interest sparked to life when he called me formidable—and he had his men lower their weapons. It blazed hotter when he handed over his food, and it flared through me when his voice went soft and he called Asher to kneel at his feet. I'm reminded of the way Ky pulled me into his lap when we sat astride the horse, his breath warm against my hair, his arms protective around me.

The king's bracers are piled by the fire with his sword, and he quickly works the buckles at his rib cage to pull his breastplate free, leaving him in a knit tunic that clings to the broad muscles of his chest. It's the first time I've seen him without his armor, and I can't help but stare. He's such a contrast to Asher, who's as lean and agile as an acrobat.

The king pulls a dagger from a sheath in his greaves, but he doesn't toss this one with the rest of his weapons. He straightens, keeping it in his hand.

That ready tension snaps back into Asher's body, and the chain goes taut. The balls of his feet press against the floorboards.

"Relax." The king flips the dagger in his hand, then holds out the blade to me, hilt first. His voice is low, and maybe a little sad. "Here, Princess. He'll trust you. Cut the rest of the tunic free."

"No," says Asher.

"Yes. It's already sticking to the wound, and it'll only get worse. You're risking infection. It needs to dry."

Asher's blue eyes seem to darken. But he swallows, which makes me think the king's words are true.

"Would you rather pull it over your head?" says Ky. "I'm sure it wasn't enjoyable when they put it *on*."

Asher looks away, and his voice goes very quiet. "I don't want her to see."

I frown. "Maybe . . ." My own voice has gone thready. Again, I think of all the times he avoided my touch, how I thought it was propriety. Chivalry. In the last day, I've begun to realize it's something else. Something much darker.

I don't want your pity either.

My stomach clenches again.

"Here," I say to the king. I move to hand the dagger back. "Maybe you should do it, then. I'll . . . I'll go."

Asher whips his head around. "No. Stop. Just—" He makes a frustrated noise, then sets his jaw and glares at the fire. "It doesn't matter. Just do it, Jor."

That sounds more like resignation than acceptance, but I move to kneel beside him. The straw of the bedding shifts under my knees, and I can see that he's leaked through his shirt a little more, probably from all the movement. Even covered, what I can see of his skin is red and angry, the swelling spread well away from the brand. It must be agonizing. I remember the guard punching him in the shoulder, the sound he made. My belly gives a clench, and I swallow.

Everything between us seems so precarious—and Asher just said he doesn't want me to see. "Are you sure?"

His eyes don't leave the fire. "Yes."

I put the blade against the neckline of his tunic and it slices right through, razor-sharp. I'm slow and careful, trying not to cut him, but also trying not to pull at the fabric. He went pale when the king barely tugged at it downstairs. But as the tunic begins to fall away, every inch reveals the smooth, muscled curve of his shoulder. I haven't seen this much of his bare skin since we were young, when we used to sneak out of the palace to swim in the deep creek that runs through the woods. We'd lie in the sun to dry, always in varying states of undress. Never anything *too* bold, because he was raised as a gentleman, and we were still children. But I remember the summer he suddenly turned into a young man, his knobby shoulders gone, his frame fuller, his jaw sharper.

His shoulders are broader now, of course, cords of muscle running down his arms, surely an effect of whatever training he endures. But the memory is potent, and I rest a hand against his skin, my fingers falling into the dip and slope just inside his good shoulder.

He stiffens at once, inhaling sharply, and it gives me a jolt. I think of the way he whirled on the king downstairs—just after I touched him then, too.

I jerk my hand back. "I'm sorry," I say in a rush. "I'm sorry." I'm not sure what else to say. "I know—I know how much you hate that."

A moment passes, and he says nothing. But he's not glaring at the king anymore. He's cast his gaze over his shoulder, that white-blond hair falling across his forehead.

"It's not that I hate it," he says, his voice so quiet. "I'm just . . . broken, Jory."

I stare back at him. As the tunic has begun to fall away, I've spotted more bruising, some of which he must have earned in the palace dungeons. But scarred tissue mars his skin in places, too, and there are older bruises that have turned yellow and blue. Older scars, older wounds, older injuries—and I never knew about any of them. His body tells a story I've never heard.

They must have done the first brand right after his mother died. Right after *my* mother died. I was sobbing at my brother's feet, and I thought nothing could possibly be worse.

For Asher, it clearly was.

I'm just broken.

My throat is tight.

The king has drawn closer, and he speaks from right beside my shoulder. "The rest is stuck to the burn," he says. His accented voice is so practical, cutting right through whatever emotion hangs between me and Asher. "Brace yourself."

Asher scowls and looks back at the floor. Without hesitation, the king reaches out and rips it clean off. I gasp, because the full wound is even more vicious than what I could see. Bright red and blistered, with darkened bruising that makes me a little dizzy to even *look* at it. Asher doesn't make a sound, but his right hand has grabbed hold of the bedding. He's clutching so hard that his knuckles are white, his muscles trembling. A sheen of sweat has broken out across his shoulders, and I don't think he's breathing.

Ky reaches out, his palm falling over the nape of Asher's neck, the way he did downstairs. "Breathe," he says softly. "Just breathe. It'll pass." His voice has the quiet reassurance of a man who's seen a thousand injured soldiers try to swallow their pain. His hand settles there, unmoving, until Asher lets out a breath, gasping like a winded horse. Ky shifts his thumb, his finger brushing through the hair at his nape, and Asher's taut muscles seem to ease, just a little. His hand unclenches. His shoulders droop and his forearms pull against his abdomen, and he almost seems to curl in on himself.

For the longest time, silence settles around us as Asher's breathing slows. His skin glows in the firelight, gleaming where sweat bloomed. The king's hand hasn't moved from his neck, but after a while, Asher ducks his head away. The links of the chain jingle as Ky lets him go. But Asher keeps his back to me, his eyes on the fire.

That feels deliberate.

I swallow thickly. I could barely hear him, but Ky's words from the dining room are haunting me.

If she is to be a queen, she should know what has been done to you.

I lift my gaze to look at him. "You knew," I say. "Even before the guards took him. You knew something had been done to him."

"Yes."

"How?"

"I've seen the effects of torture before, Princess."

It's as pragmatic as everything else he says, but the word makes me shiver, and my breath catches before I can help it.

Asher snaps his head up. His voice is sharp. "I told you I don't want your pity."

I shift on the pallet until I'm facing him. I don't feel very formidable right now. A part of me wants to hide.

"Why haven't you ever told me?" I say, and my voice almost goes soft on the last word.

His blue eyes go hard. He says nothing.

My heart pounds. "I need to know," I say. "I need to know what my brother has done."

Nothing. His jaw is set.

Silence pulses between us, and I'm so aware of the king at his side. Those shackles bind them together, but I suddenly realize there's an invisible link, too. A shared comprehension that I can't quite understand.

But I want to. I never knew how much he was hiding, and it's making my chest tight, my eyes hot. "Asher, you're my best friend. My only friend." My voice breaks. "I would've done anything for you. Why wouldn't you tell me? Why, Asher? I could've helped you—"

"No!" He whirls to face me, and his voice is sharp and loud, like the crack of a whip. "You couldn't."

The force of his anger makes me snap back. I can't catch my breath.

"How would you have helped me?" he demands. His eyes are so fierce. "How, Jory? You saw what they did to my mother. What do you think they would've done if they knew I was sneaking into the palace?"

My eyes fill, and I try to blink the tears away.

Asher shifts closer. "And what would *you* have done?" he says. "What would you have done if I'd shown you the brand on my shoulder? What would you have done if I told you what it was like to be chained to a post and traded away like property? What *could* you have done?"

My breath catches. "Asher—"

"You say you want to know," he says. "But you don't even know what you're asking for." His eyes are so hard, his voice so cold. "Do you want to know what it's like in the brothels? The way they'll starve you if you don't perform? The way they like it if you fight, because they can be as rough as they want? Do you want to know what it was like to have men and women from the palace—men and women I once *knew*—

hand over a palmful of coins to have me on my knees? Or on my back, or bent over a rail—"

"Asher."

The king's voice is quiet, but it makes me jump. My breathing is shaking, and my palms have gone damp. Everything inside me feels tight and afraid.

I'm remembering our conversation when we were curled up in my bed and I admitted my inexperience.

Do you think it will hurt?

The way he said, *It shouldn't . . . if it's done right.*

Later, when I asked about his own experience, he said, *I don't want to be indelicate.*

I thought he was being coy. Not . . . not hiding something like this.

But now I'm thinking of the way he flinches every time I touch him. I'm looking at the scars on his body, or the areas where he has older bruising. I'm remembering the first time I heard one of my ladies called the bondsmen *slavers*, and I'm wondering if I should have paid more attention.

I'm thinking of that woman downstairs, curled up on the fur.

And as soon as I have the thought, I remember how long Asher was away, my relief when he finally returned to my chambers after months with no word. I teased him about a woman catching his eye, and he denied it. He never really said anything at all.

But now he's got a body full of bruises that aren't fresh, but certainly aren't very old.

Were you injured?

Not really.

A tear leaks out of my eye to make a hot path down my face. "Asher," I whisper. "I know you weren't working with the Draegs. What really happened in Morinstead?"

The question startles him, because he recoils slightly, his eyes flicking away. But his jaw remains set, every angle of his face bearing a sharp edge.

"Tell her," says the king. His tone is quiet, the words simple, and to my surprise, Asher obeys.

"I was given a job," he says, and his voice is tight. Controlled. "Just as I said. But I had to travel, and sometimes that's . . . challenging. In Perriden, I don't have to worry about getting picked up by the slavers." He scoffs. "Most of them *know* me. But outside the city, bondsmen see the lines on my face, and they think I've escaped. They think I'm a *problem*. They see a man who lies, who refuses to obey, who refuses to submit. You saw the way the innkeeper acted downstairs. I had a Guild ring, but in Morinstead, the bondsmen didn't care. They said it was fake—and they decided I needed to be put in my place. They locked me in a cell and . . . did whatever they wanted." His eyes flash dangerously at the king. "I'll spare you the details."

Ky doesn't flinch from his tone. "How did you get away?"

"I know how to be patient," he says, and his voice is somehow belligerent and heartbreaking at the same time. It makes me think of all the other times he was delayed.

"Why wouldn't you tell me?" I say.

"Because I loved you, Jory!" he says, and his voice is so rough and broken that I almost flinch.

"I loved you back!" I say desperately. "I *always*—"

"No." He draws back, running a hand across his face. "You loved someone who didn't exist."

The words hit me like a fist to the gut.

Asher's not done. "You think I wanted you to see me as a whore? A criminal? A killer?" He rattles the chain that keeps him tethered to the king. "An animal to be kept on a chain?"

"You're none of those things." My voice is barely more than a whisper.

"I'm all of those things!" He looks so vicious, and it makes my breath catch. "I know who you are, Jory. Our paths have *always* been set in opposing directions. Always! The only difference is that now *you* see *me*. And you will *never* see me as anything else."

I think of every moment he appeared in my chambers. The times he held me after Dane did something upsetting. The way he'd make me laugh when I felt so lonely.

The way he risked his life to save me. The way he shrugged out of his coat when I was cold.

The way he lit the stove, even though I know he was terrified of the king's magic.

I was so cavalier, asking him to help me escape. Asking him to rescue the king. With absolutely no regard for what he risked—because I didn't know. "I do see you, Asher," I whisper. "I do. And you're none of the things you said. None of them."

He draws back, silent. His eyes don't meet mine now. It's clear what he believes.

"Please," I say. "Forgive me. I didn't know. I should have—I should have *protected* you—"

"You *can't*."

That hits me like a slap, and emotion swells to fill my chest. Another tear snakes down my face, and I hastily swipe it away.

A muscle twitches in Asher's jaw, and he swears under his breath. "I don't want your fucking *pity*, Jory."

"It's not pity." But it is. I swipe another tear away. I inhale sharply, ready to beg, to plead, to find a way to fix this—even though I have no idea how. "Please—Asher—"

"Princess." The king's voice is low, quiet. I look up in surprise, and he adds, "He's had enough. Leave him be."

That makes me look back at Asher, and I realize he's pulled his arms against his abdomen, his hands gripping his elbows. His jaw is set, every muscle tight and bunched. His eyes are dark and shadowed, and that faint sheen of sweat has broken out across his shoulders again.

A pulse of regret pierces my heart. "I'll fix this," I whisper. "I swear to you, Asher. I'll find a way to fix this."

He says nothing.

I suddenly realize he doesn't believe me.

But of course he doesn't. I couldn't fix it when he was dragged out of the palace the first time, and I couldn't fix it tonight. I was powerless when Dane backhanded him in the throne room, then set his penalty to a million silvers—and if Ky hadn't demanded that Asher should be subject to Incendrian justice, he'd be back in the dungeons right now.

The thought gives me a jolt. With a start, I look up at Ky, reevaluating everything that's happened since the moment he drew me aboard that horse. I begged him to release Asher, and he refused. He demanded my presence for a month, and I hated him for it.

But I consider what my life would've been like if Maddox Kyronan had *left*. The way Dane would have blamed me for unraveling the alliance. The way Asher would be back with the slavers, with no end in sight.

Instead, we're here, and we're safe.

The king is staring down at me placidly, his arms folded, his golden eyes revealing nothing.

"The day has been long," he says, and his tone is cool. Official. It cuts through the heady emotion in the room. "You both should rest. Princess, I would feel safest if you would remain here, on the other pallet—but if you would prefer to take the other room, I will have Sev make guard assignments."

"Fine," I say, though I'm hardly listening. I can't stop thinking about the way I've spent hours hating him for his betrayal . . . all while he was taking steps to get us safely away from Dane.

"Thank you," I say to him.

"For what?"

For protecting my friend. For protecting me.

But I can't say that. Not right now. Not when I feel so powerless. I'm not even entirely sure if it's true. Not when Asher is chained to his arm, and I'm not sure what either one of them would do if he got free. Asher's anger is still a potent force in the room, and I'm afraid to consider how much of it is directed at me.

But we're here and we're safe, and this is nowhere close to where I thought we'd end up.

I look back at the king. "For your kindness," I say.

He seems struck by that, but only for a moment, because he blinks it away, any softness vanishing from his demeanor. The formidable warrior is all that remains.

"Yes, Princess," he says, giving me a sharp nod, leaving me to wonder if he even knows what I'm thanking him for.

And before I can respond, he turns away and calls for his guards.

Chapter Twenty
THE WARRIOR

It's late and it's dark, only embers glowing in the hearth. Asher is asleep to my right, curled on his side, his arm half extended from the chain that still keeps us tethered. After everything that's happened, I don't think he'd try to run, and I don't think he'd convince the princess to leave with him . . . but I also didn't want to risk it. It's the same reason my weapons aren't strapped to my body where he can reach them, and instead they're on the floor beside me.

The princess is sound asleep on the other pallet to my left, her chest rising and falling with each breath. Her lady Charlotte is on her other side, sleeping primly with blankets pulled up to her chin. Callum should be outside the door now, because I heard the low rumble of his voice when he changed shifts with Roman.

Otherwise, the inn is quiet, and it has been for hours. I should be sound asleep, too. Bleeding skies, I'm tired enough. But nervous energy has me longing to call a bit of flame to drift between my fingers, and that's never a good idea when I'm lying in bed. Just one wayward spark and the whole pallet could go up. When I was young, I nearly burned down half an encampment. My sister Victoria already causes enough problems in Incendar. I don't need to start any here.

We aren't safe in Astranza. I can feel it. I've been feeling it since we rode through the swirling snow to reach the capital. My men drew blades when that boy came crashing in with the firewood, so I know I'm not the only one. It's likely Sev is awake on the other side of the wall, staring into the darkness just like I am. If I weren't chained to Asher, I'd join him. He knows me well enough that he'd probably have a deck of cards waiting. I'd make a candle burn too bright, and we'd stop each other from finding sleep at the bottom of a bottle.

But I can't. Instead, I'm lying here thinking of Jory, bold and glaring, convincing me to lay down my arms and speak to Prince Dane.

Or Asher, kneeling in the snow, wounded and defiant, ready to fight to the death even though he had no hope of winning.

Or the two of them, sitting in the firelight, revealing unspoken truths. So desperate to protect each other that they can't see the harms they're causing. They're so wildly chaotic. It's no wonder they're in love with each other. It's a miracle they haven't gotten each other killed.

But the dynamic between them has shifted, just a little. Somewhere along the line, they each forged a connection with *me*, and I didn't expect it. It's a thin and fragile bond, as frail as gossamer thread, but it's there. It's not trust, not yet, but there's a glimmer of it.

I glance over at the princess. Her fingers are curled against the coverlet, her hair loose and spilled across the pillow. Callum said she was beautiful—and she is. But I've known beautiful women. I've known brave women. That's not what keeps tugging at something deep inside of me. It's the way she convinced me to speak to her brother, despite how deep her distrust ran. It's the way she thanked me for kindness. *Kindness.*

Because I'm not kind. I'm ruthless. Vengeful. Practical. I handed over her best friend because I won't risk this alliance I so desperately need.

But the word lit a glow in my heart that refuses to dim.

And Asher . . . he has every right to hate me. He seems to have a right to hate *everyone*. Even if Jory hadn't said anything, I could see it myself. The Draegs torture any Incendrian they can get their hands on, so I've seen the effects, the way touch can be warped and twisted until it only brings pain.

Each time my fingers landed on his neck, Asher went so still, braced for torment. I wonder how long he's gone without simple human contact, because as much as he pulls away, he seems to crave it, too. Every time he yielded, it was unexpected—and a bit gratifying. Like coaxing a wolf out of the shadows to take a piece of meat from your hand.

He told the princess he was broken. But he's not.

I turn my head to look at him, only to discover that his blue eyes are open, watching *me*.

I give a little jump, and it makes the chain between us rattle.

His eyes search mine, but it's too dark for me to make out much of his expression. He's wide awake, like he hasn't slept either. Those stripes on his face are obvious even in the shadows, but so are the subtle hollows of his cheeks. When we sat at dinner, he clung to that bowl like a man who doesn't know when his next meal is coming. He's got enough muscle on his frame that I know he's not starving, but it's clear not *everyone* in Astranza is eating their fill.

He hasn't said a word, and there's something in his gaze that makes me glad the weapons are on the floor. Though it might not matter. I've seen how fast he can move.

Maybe I'm wrong about that glimmer of trust.

"Go back to sleep, Asher," I murmur.

"Why did you take me from Dane?"

His voice is a low rumble, almost softer than thought, and after everything, the question takes me by surprise. Though maybe it shouldn't.

I shift onto my side to face him, so my voice won't wake the princess. "My words to Prince Dane were true. I will not watch Astranza collect a bounty for a crime committed against me."

He's quiet for a moment. "You could have had Jory to yourself."

"To *myself*?" I say. "If I can't earn her affection without letting her brother imprison and enslave you, then I likely don't deserve it."

Asher's expression doesn't flicker. The room is heavy with unspoken emotion, and I wish I could parse it out. But if being a soldier has taught me anything, the cloaking solitude of night is the time we all wrestle with demons that others can't see.

"You've already earned her affection," he finally says.

"Perhaps."

"You have. I know her. I've seen the way she looks at you." He pauses. "*Ky.*"

The way he says that is interesting. Almost aggressive. I haven't invited him to call me by my given name, much less a nickname, but he throws it down like a challenge.

I don't pick it up. I throw down my own. "Are you jealous?"

"No." But he is. A little.

As the word hangs between us, his gaze sharpens. "She's innocent. You should know . . . she's never . . . she hasn't—"

"I know." It's obvious. She was so startled when I drew her aboard my horse. *This is inappropriate.* And I could see it when Asher finally unleashed his truths: her wide eyes, the sudden flush on her cheeks when he mentioned being on his knees or bent over a rail.

Asher narrows his eyes, studying me. "She's afraid you'll hurt her. That you'll force her."

He might be angry, but he's still so protective. I wonder when she told him this, but it must have been before she met me. I wonder if *he's* the one who's afraid I'll hurt her.

I keep my voice low. "I'm no blushing virgin, Asher. But I've never forced anyone to my bed. I have no intention of starting now."

I have no idea what part of that affects him, but his pupils seem to grow darker, and his eyes hold mine for the longest moment before skipping away. His voice quiets further. "Are you going to let me go?"

There's a wariness to this question. An uncertainty. At first I think the reason is obvious: he doesn't want to be held captive. He doesn't want me to fuck with him. It's possibly even deeper than that: he doesn't want to be dragged back to Incendar, where he'll be put to death or forced to watch the princess marry *me*.

But as I inhale to tell him that *of course* I intend to let him go, I realize that this might not be the right answer at all.

Because there's no freedom for Asher in Astranza. He's a marked man, and he certainly can't go back to the Hunter's Guild. If I release him, I might as well give him back to Prince Dane myself.

I've taken too long to answer, and his gaze sharpens, his voice turning a little belligerent. "Or are you just going to set me on—"

"Hush." I reach out and rest my hand against his neck, and Asher goes abruptly silent. Emotions flash across his face. First the flare of panic that someone has touched him, quickly followed by an odd mix of rebellion as every muscle in his upper body goes taut. But I leave my hand there and he exhales, his frame softening. The wolf, settling under my hand.

This is different from the way I touched him before. Because of the way we're lying, my hand has fallen against the side of his neck, and it puts my thumb right over his windpipe, just in the hollow of his jaw. It's intimate and vulnerable in a way I didn't quite intend.

I can't quite make myself let go, however. There's something addictive to this. I move my thumb along his chin, feeling the start of beard growth there, softer than mine would be, which is rather intriguing. It's rare that I touch another man like this, especially in the dark, in the middle of the night. Especially in *bed*. In truth, I've been with a man once before, but it was years ago, and nothing like this. Then I was newly king, and barely a man myself. It was aggressive and reckless and occasionally violent—and very short-lived, for all the same reasons.

I'm older now, and this is nothing like that. I'm not entirely sure *what* this is. But I let my finger drift along Asher's skin, feeling his pulse beat under my palm.

"You're mine for now," I say.

He swallows, and his breath trembles. Good? Bad? I can't quite tell. Maybe he's not sure, either. It warns me to tread carefully.

I trace another path along his throat. "Sleep, Asher. We'll leave at first light."

He nods.

I move to pull away, but he catches my wrist. His eyes catch the barest gleam of light, and they hold mine, unflinching. But then he tugs my arm a bit closer, and he tucks it against the mattress in front of him, both hands loosely wrapping around my forearm. I don't understand his intent, especially when that's *all* he does, and his eyes simply fall closed.

But then I think about the way he snapped at the princess when she asked why he wouldn't let her help him. I think about the way *sanctuary* made him yield, when money and power held no sway.

I think about the fact that Jory demanded that I unchain him, but since the moment he followed me into the inn, Asher hasn't asked. Not even once.

His breath is already evening out, and I study him in the darkness. I can't quite believe how much has changed in the space of a day. From the way the princess hid her identity to meet me, to my kidnapping and subsequent escape, to the prospect of nefarious dealings within Astranza that led to our immediate departure.

But perhaps the most surprising is the vicious assassin who started the day by taking down one of my best soldiers and forcing me out of the palace—and is now falling asleep beside me, clutching my forearm the way a frightened child would hold on to a doll.

Chapter Twenty-One
THE ASSASSIN

I don't know what wakes me, just that *something* does. I'm no stranger to the sounds of the night, so I lie in the dark and listen. Wind whistles against the shutters, but inside this room, silence hangs heavy. The king is beside me, his breathing soft from sleep, the princess and Lady Charlotte nothing more than quiet shadows on the other pallet.

Beyond that, nothing.

Maybe I'm just cold. The hearth seems to have dwindled, and I can't bear the weight of these woolen blankets against the raw flesh of my shoulder.

I turn my head to look at the king. *Ky.* His sharp features are soft from sleep, his breathing slow and even. There's a part of me that's shocked he drifted off. His weapons are on the floor, hardly out of reach. I might be chained to his arm, but I'm quick. I could cut his throat and disappear in the night before any of them even knew I was gone. He didn't even keep another soldier in the *room.*

But I won't. And maybe it's obvious I won't. Maybe that's why he's asleep at all.

I can still feel the weight of his hand against my throat. The slow stroke of his thumb under my chin. Just the memory of it sends a shiver through me.

I've spent enough time in enough brothels to recognize desire, but this . . . isn't it. Not quite.

I do know I can't stop thinking about it.

Or perhaps this is just my brain refusing to think about what happened with Jory.

I've never snapped at her. Not like that. She didn't even deserve it. I've loved her forever, and even on my worst days, it settled something in my heart to know she was in the palace, safe from harm. The last person in the world who still saw me as I was.

And now that's gone. The loss pulses like a new wound, raw and weeping like the brand.

Princess. He's had enough. Leave him be.

Fuck. My throat is tight. I stare at the ceiling and force the thoughts away.

Beside me, the king's body jerks, and I look over again. A small sound comes from his throat, and he draws his arms closer to his body.

It's so dark that I can't see his expression, but I don't sense that he's awake. His arms twitch again, and he inhales sharply.

He's dreaming.

He makes another sound that's closer to a whimper.

Not a dream. A nightmare.

I reach out and put a hand over his forearm, pressing gently with my fingers. He wakes with a start, his eyes snapping open, and I jerk my hand back.

For a moment, we lie there staring at each other. The belligerent part of me wants to mock him. *Poor baby. Scary dreams?*

The deeper, darker, more vulnerable part of me wants to put a hand back on his arm.

And then I hear a sound, the soft scrape of wood against stone. It's so quiet that I could've imagined it—but I know I didn't.

The king sucks in a breath, but I slip a hand over his mouth and clamp down hard.

"Don't let them know you're awake," I whisper, my voice barely more than breath against his cheek. If a Hunter has come after us, he'll be watching to make sure no one moves. That said, this complete darkness can work in my favor, too.

The king nods. His eyes are dark pools in the shadows.

"No magic yet," I warn—though I don't actually know if he can. The hearth is dark, which makes me wonder if Hunters smothered it from the chimney. "If we can see, they can see."

The king nods again.

I slip my hand away from his mouth, and I try not to consider the way his face feels under my fingers. A little rough, a little warm.

Especially since his voice is all business. "Asher. Hunters?"

"No idea."

He exhales, and he sounds a little aggrieved.

"But probably," I add. "Unchain me."

"Garrett has the key."

Well, shit. That's not going to go well for either of us.

His eyes return to the darkness, so mine do, too. I hold very still, waiting. Listening. The king's weight shifts, and I realize he's reaching for one of the weapons he laid beside the pallet. I wonder if he'd give me one.

But then I hear another scrape, another whisper of sound. The king's body goes still, and I know he heard it, too. The darkness shifts, air moving somewhere between us and the door. A shape dropping from above.

With no warning, Ky is moving, nearly as silent as I am—which is impressive. I'm quick to follow, because he's already got a weapon in hand, but he's still chained to me. I don't want to hinder his efforts. His other hand lifts, beginning to sketch a sigil, and I don't know if I should be grateful or terrified at the prospect of fire blazing to life in this room.

But it never forms. Another attacker drops from overhead, slamming into his shoulders, knocking the king to his knees. It's a common move—and I should have expected it. Whoever the Guild sent already has a garrote around the king's neck, and it chokes off any sound he was about to make.

So far, the attack has been so silent that the women are still sleeping.

The first assailant pays me no mind whatsoever, and I don't know if he can't see me in the dark—doubtful—or if he simply thinks I won't interfere.

He's wrong. I've already got one of the king's blades in hand, and I bury it between the assassin's ribs. His body jerks, but I'm not done. I yank the dagger free just as the king summons two handfuls of fire. The flames are smaller than I expect, but I don't have time to wonder. The king grabs hold of his attacker's wrists, and the man inhales sharply to scream.

I cut his throat first. The blade is sharp, and blood flows, pouring over my hand. I give him a shove, and the king's breathing is suddenly loud and ragged.

"Where's the other one?" he says.

The smell of burned flesh is sickly sweet in the room, but the fire has gone out. My eyes search the shadows just as fabric rustles to my left. The princess and her lady are beginning to shift, mumbling about the noise, but I've lost the other man in the darkness.

No, I haven't. He's there, about to leap onto Jory.

I don't think. The chain rattles and jerks tight as I leap over the king, skidding into bed beside the princess. Jory cries out, disoriented, but the man lands on top of *me* instead of her. My branded shoulder scrapes across the mattress, and every bruise on my skin flares to life. I grunt through the pain and jerk the chain high, bracing it between the fist of one hand and the dagger in my other. His blade comes slashing down, but I deflect with the chain. Steel rings against steel in the silence of the room.

The man growls and lifts his blade for another strike. "Asher, you—"

The king slams a dagger right into the side of his rib cage. The words choke off. The body jerks twice, and it doesn't feel voluntary. It feels like the king is twisting the blade, going for the heart.

Yes, he's definitely more brutal than I am.

"Guards!" he's shouting.

I'm still straining under the weight of this attacker. From his voice, I think it's Gunnar—and I know he won't stop until he's well and truly dead. He's still bearing down on the first blade, but I can see his other arm scrabbling for something else he must have in his jacket.

The door swings open, but the king's men aren't going to be fast enough. The king is fighting one-handed, since this chain is all that's keeping Gunnar from driving that dagger right through my throat. I grunt under the pressure, especially when I feel him slip a smaller blade free.

Shadows move in from the side, and for an instant, I think maybe that's it. The king and I are both a bit pinned, so if there's a third assassin, we might be lost. But then I see the fluttering fabric of a sleeping shift just as the princess throws herself at the pallet. A sound of rage pours from her throat, and then her fist connects with the man's head so hard that he snaps to the side. The chain goes slack as he slides free.

But he still has a weapon in his hand, and he's as swift as I am. As he slides away, he swings his arm in an arc, aiming for her throat instead.

"No!" I shout. I'm tangled under the chain, under his weight.

Lady Charlotte is right behind her, and she grabs hold of Jory—but the princess has already jerked back. The man's blade slices through the air, harmless, and the sudden slack in the chain gives the king enough leverage to yank the dagger free. This time he makes sure it's done. He cuts Gunnar's throat.

The Hunter collapses onto me. Blood immediately pours over my skin, and I want to shove him away. My shoulder is aching, and everything smells like copper and burned flesh.

Ugh. This is why I hate to use a blade.

"Asher." Jory's voice. "Are you all right?"

"Yes," I grunt, though I'm not entirely sure.

Shadows have moved into the room through the door. I can't see faces, but I recognize the captain's voice. "Ro. Fetch a lantern. Ky—are *you* all right?"

"Yes." But the king doesn't wait for a lantern. He sketches another sigil, pulling flame from somewhere else in the inn to make another ball of light appear on his palm. I finally manage to shove Gunnar off of me, and the body slumps to the ground.

The scene is grim. The first attacker—Logan—is dead on the floor as well. Blood has already spread to coat the floorboards. A good bit of it poured down the king's back too, turning half his tunic black in the shadows.

Gunnar's blood slicks the front of my chest and most of my arm, along with half the length of chain. A lot more has already soaked into the straw mattress covering the pallet. In the glow from the light, I can see that blood speckles the king's face, and I'm sure it's on mine as well.

The princess is staring at both of us, her chest heaving. I doubt she's seen violence like this since the day her mother died. She's clearly unsettled—as is her lady. They're gripping each other's hands, their eyes wide.

I remember she was terrified of the king's brutality.

I wonder how she feels about seeing mine right beside it.

Then again, she was the one to leap onto the bed and punch Gunnar in the face. She leapt into the fray right alongside us. Fearless.

She proves it now, too, because she might be pale and wide-eyed, but her voice is steady. "Where did they come from?"

"The Hunters Guild," I say. "These are the men who would have been sent if I didn't finish the assignment."

The assignment that the Guildmaster said wasn't real.

But I don't say that. They already know it.

I look up, toward the crisscrossed beams lining the ceiling, then toward the windows, which are both closed. That makes me frown. I don't usually close a window once I'm *in*. It's just one more obstacle to getting *out*.

Could they have been inside the inn all evening? I can't quite make that work out in my head. They would've had to know we would stop, and even though I wasn't privy to the king's decisions, this doesn't seem like a planned location. Then again, they could have followed our tracks in the snow. Could Logan and Gunnar have come down the chimney after snuffing the embers? I glance down at the bodies. They don't *look* like they came down a chimney.

"There could be more," the king is saying. He looks to his men in the doorway. Sev and Callum have stepped into the room, and their expressions are grave. Roman appears behind them with a lit lantern.

The king glances at me, and then to the closed windows as well. He uses his secret signals to give the men another order, and Roman and Callum both give him a sharp nod, then step back through the door, leaving the lantern.

Jory is watching, and curiosity must have broken through her panic. She swallows. "What did those mean?"

Ky inhales, but his captain's gaze narrows. "Perhaps we can share strategies another time," says Captain Zale. "When others might not be listening."

I don't know if he means *me*, or if he suspects that there might be more assassins in the inn, but either way, it doesn't matter. I reach down and push the other Hunters onto their backs.

The king's voice is low. "Do you know them?"

"Yes." They're both in their mid-thirties, and neither looks particularly noteworthy, though one has a bit of a gut straining at his jacket. I point to him first. "Gunnar." Then the second. "Logan." I hesitate. "You're lucky they weren't sent *first*. They were two of the best."

"The best?" says the king. "Then this felt too easy."

"They're good at *killing*. Not fighting."

Captain Zale has joined us now, and he's looking down at the bodies, too. "Clearly."

I bristle. "It's not as if we meet much resistance. Your king would be dead in his bed if I hadn't woken him."

The king's eyes meet mine, and I know he's remembering the moment just before that, when my hand fell on his arm.

"I would've been dead, too," Jory says softly. "And Charlotte."

The captain looks up, and I watch him taking in the new marks on the king's throat, clearly left there by Gunner. His gaze shifts to me, and I wait as his eyes flick over the blood, the chain that still links us together, the blade that's still hanging loosely in my hand.

His eyes narrow, and I remember what he said at dinner about potential Draeg spies.

But I'm also remembering the moment I first opened my orders from the Guild and saw that the princess's death had been paid with Incendrian silver.

Someone wrote those orders.

"They went after you first?" Captain Zale is saying to the king.

"Yes."

His eyes flick back to me. "We were stationed at the door. Why didn't you call for help?"

Oh. That question is a little piercing. The sad truth is that it would never occur to me. I can't remember the last time I was ever in a position where I could cry out for help and expect someone to answer.

But I resent the note of suspicion in his voice, and my eyes narrow. I say nothing.

The captain glances between us again, and he sighs. He puts out a hand. "Fine. Give me the dagger."

My fingers tighten on the hilt. I don't want to. It's stupid and petulant, but much like when I glared at the king in the snow, I don't care.

"Asher," says Ky.

Fuck. *Fine.* I flip the weapon in my hand, wipe the blade on my bloodstained trousers, and hold it out—to the king.

"Nice weight," I say.

"Thank you." He crushes the flame out of his palm and takes the dagger.

Captain Zale lowers his hand, but he lets a breath out through his teeth. He's looking at the king like he wishes they could exchange more than military commands through silent signals.

Eventually, he turns away, saying, "I'll wake the others."

But he doesn't have to. Garrett and Nikko appear in the doorway next. Their expressions are cold. Hard. I wonder if the other soldiers woke them when they left. I watch as they glance from the princess, to their king, and finally, to me.

It's clear that the captain isn't the only suspicious party.

Jory speaks through the tense silence. "We should search them," she says. "They might have orders similar to Asher's."

"They won't," I say.

"We'll search them anyway," says Ky. "And when Roman and Callum return, we'll see what they've been able to discover, if anything."

"And then?" she presses.

The king sighs, looking from her to me. "Well, Princess, your brother said Asher's orders were fake. So did your Hunter's Guild. These men seem to prove otherwise. It's clear that *someone* wants me dead—and you as well. I can't see any reason why Prince Dane would be the aggressor here, but our sudden departure was unplanned. Few people outside the palace would have known. Prince Dane and King Theodore may be committed to this alliance, but someone in their circle isn't."

Jory swallows, but she straightens, looking him dead in the face. She's so brave. "Has this changed your course?" she demands. "Is your intent to return me to the palace?"

I can't tell if she wants that—or if she fears it. But the thought of being taken back to the palace makes my heart want to curl up and hide.

The king hesitates, running a hand across his jaw. After a moment, he shakes his head. "No. I don't know who's behind this, but I won't spend one more moment in this country without a regiment behind me." He glances down at the dead men on the floor, then looks to me. "They failed. Will more Hunters be sent?"

"Probably."

"We're only a few hours outside Perriden," the captain says. "If they were due to check back, it won't take long for someone to know."

"They could also have someone waiting ahead," Roman says, by the door.

The king and his captain exchange a glance.

"Can we ride straight through to the border?" says Jory. "How far are we from Incendar?"

"Twelve hours," says Roman. "Possibly more, if this weather continues."

There's a heavy weight in his voice, as if the weather is a clue—or a threat. Could King Theodore be hindering our journey so Hunters have an opportunity to catch up? Did the weather force us to stop last night? But why? I hate Dane, but he really *did* seem to want this alliance.

I watch as the king and his captain exchange another glance, and it's clear I'm not the only one with questions.

Ky sighs, then nods. "We'll leave at first light."

Chapter Twenty-Two
THE PRINCESS

We set off before dawn, and this time, everyone is on horseback. Ky gave his footmen a supply of silver, along with orders to leave the carriages and make their way back to Incendar separately. At first I don't understand, but he explains that he won't put civilians at risk. Not when it's clear that someone has been sent after us.

Armed with this knowledge, I made the same offer to Charlotte, and she hesitated—then shook her head. "Prince Dane was correct. You should not be without a chaperone."

I remembered how shocked she looked when Dane ordered her to join me. "Truly," I said gently. "Dane should not have forced you to come at all." I remembered the way my ladies were so terrified of Maddox Kyronan and what his visit could mean.

I shifted closer to her and dropped my voice. "I know you were afraid of the king and his soldiers."

"Prince Dane did not force me." The strength in her voice reminded me of the way she always stood strong in front of my brother, despite the other ladies, who would cringe. "And the king and his men have been . . . respectful."

As she said the word, she glanced at the captain, who was fastening a buckle on his horse's bridle. When he noticed her attention, he gave her a nod and a smile.

Charlotte lifted her chin, and her eyes shifted back to me quickly, but I couldn't help but notice the sudden spot of pink on her cheeks. Before I could say anything, she gave a definitive nod. "I said I would remain by your side," she says. "If you are to ride, I will ride."

So now we're all mounted, bundled up in borrowed gear. Ky didn't want anyone to be able to discern our identities from a distance, and it makes me think of the way he wears the same scarred armor as his men. Charlotte and I had trousers in our trunks, but nothing appropriate for twelve hours riding in the snow. Instead, we're all outfitted in Incendrian leather and fur, right down to the breastplate that Ky helped buckle to my chest. These fur-lined trousers are too long, so one of his soldiers helped me tuck them flat inside my boots, showing me how to double wrap the laces so nothing would move. Even Asher has leather and buckles shaping his frame, making him take up more space than I'm used to.

There's no trace of Astranza left on any of us—and I worry that's an omen.

When I asked Ky if he intended to go back to Perriden, I wasn't entirely sure what answer I was hoping for. I still don't believe my brother would try to kill Maddox Kyronan—and after everything that's happened, it's obvious Ky isn't trying to kill *me*. But it's clear that *someone* is trying to kill both of us, and continuing on this journey will keep us in danger.

The king and his men must think so, too, because we don't ride as a group. Instead, his soldiers have worked out a complex formation where two men always ride alongside the king, one rides well ahead to play lookout, and two ride behind to watch for any followers. They change often, horses galloping point to point when they swap. Their movements are seamless and well-executed, and I can't even tell what signals the change. I realize I'm seeing why Incendar might be the smallest country on the continent but Draegonis hasn't been able to breach their borders.

The cold pierces every spot of bare skin it can find, and the chill in the air makes my lips ache. When a particularly cold blast of wind whips among us, one of the soldiers mutters a comment that King Theodore's weather magic doesn't seem very useful if it can't grant us easier passage. I think it's Callum, but I've begun to lose track of who's who when they're bundled up so tightly.

Ky snaps at him to be silent, but I'm glad I heard it. It's a thought that hasn't occurred to me, and it sets a wedge in my thoughts. Why *wouldn't* my father lessen the cold and snow to make it simpler for me to get to Incendar? Does he not care? Or is this a sign of his waning health?

Or could it be the opposite? When I saw him on the throne yesterday, he seemed weak, his skin pale. Is he trying to prove that he's still healthy and strong? A show of force so Incendar knows Astranza isn't powerless?

There's certainly no one to ask. I can't mention his status to Charlotte, and it would be impossible to have a quiet conversation with Asher—if he's even willing to talk to me.

He suffered. For so long. And he never said a word.

Regret gnaws at my gut. I think about that woman on the mat, and I wonder if she's treated the same way.

I couldn't help her either. Not really.

Asher's mood has been distant and remote, and he's barely glanced in my direction since we left. It's obvious the Incendrian soldiers still don't fully trust him, despite the fact that he defended their king and saved my life. He's no longer in chains, but when Captain Zale brought him a horse, the reins were knotted up, out of reach, and the captain wasted no time tethering the animal to Ky's saddle.

I watched Asher absorb that, and he looked at the king. "You still think I'm going to run?"

Ky swung aboard his own horse. His voice was mild. "If you do, it's going to be on foot. Mount up."

I expected belligerence, but Asher obeyed, and he's been placid ever since, only speaking when Roman rode alongside us for a while, grilling him about the Hunter's Guild, asking about their training, their directives, their methods, their resources.

"How many of you are typically assigned to an order?" Roman would say.

Asher's answers were brief, his tone clipped. "One. Hunters rarely work in pairs."

"Never a team?" Roman pressed. "What about more detailed assignments?"

"We didn't *have* more detailed assignments."

I'm puzzled by his sharper tone, his ongoing silence. But after hours in the saddle, I see him flex his shoulder and grimace.

Oh. He's in *pain*.

My heart gives a tug. I want to approach him, but his words from last night are still haunting me, and he's barely looked at me all morning. Every time I try to catch his gaze, his eyes skip away.

I don't want your fucking pity, Jory.

A distance has formed between us, and I'm not sure how to close it.

I want to ask the king to slow the pace—but maybe that's unreasonable. The tension among the soldiers is like a silent companion on our journey. We all heard Roman's comment about potential assassins waiting ahead. Every time we catch sight of a town, we veer away, giving it a wide berth. I wonder if it's making the ride longer than it should be.

As we get farther from Perriden, the harsh weather seems to lessen. By the time we stop near a stream to eat and rest the horses, I haven't seen a snowflake in at least an hour, and the wind has slowed as we've traveled south. Charlotte and I make use of a small copse of bushes for privacy, but then she tells me that she'd like a few extra minutes to herself. I don't need any more explanation than that, so I join Ky near the banks to refill my canteen. The water isn't iced over at all, and in some spots along the banks, the sun has melted the snow down to the earth.

I wonder if this is an indication that we've reached the outer limit of Father's power.

I hope it's not an indication that his power has begun to fail.

The king and I have hardly spoken since last night. After everything Asher and I said to each other, I've been waiting for tension to form between me and Ky, but . . . it hasn't.

Beside me, Ky has pushed back the hood of his cloak, and when he glances over, his golden-brown eyes are warm.

But then I see flecks of blood in his hair, plus a streak of dried blood along his hairline. There are more streaks along the black leather of his armor, too.

It's a stark reminder of what happened, and I jerk my gaze back to the water. Asher offered me a way out of the palace, and I thrilled at the chance for adventure. The king called me *formidable*, and I believed him.

Now that I see the faults in my kingdom, all I feel is naive and unprepared.

I haven't said a word, and the king looks over. "Princess?"

I have to shake myself. "You still have blood on your face."

He pulls off a glove to swipe at the wrong side of his face, then looks at his hand.

"Here. Let me." I uncap the canteen, pour a little water on the corner of my own cloak, then reach for his face.

His eyes flare in surprise, but he holds still. I dab the damp fabric along his skin, very aware of his closeness. His *warmth*, which is so unexpected when the day has been so cold. The bruises and rope burns along his neck are stark against his skin, first from Asher, and then from the man who attacked him.

Breath fogs between us. I want to speak, because the silence has grown too intense, and the bloodstains on his face are too stubborn, making this take longer than I expected.

To my surprise, he's the one who speaks into our silence. "Who taught you to fight?" he says.

Warmth crawls up my cheeks, and I wish I could will it away. "I don't really know how to fight."

He touches his temple, where there's still a scrape from where I got him with a hairpin. "Your aim would suggest otherwise. And I saw you throw a punch."

That warmth turns into a flare of heat. "Well." But then I'm not sure what to say about that. "Dane has allowed a few sessions with the man-at-arms. But that was more . . . desperation."

"Your desperation serves you well."

I don't know what to say about that either. I dab more water from the canteen onto the corner of my cloak, then reach for his face again. But as I swipe at the blood, my eyes flick past him, looking toward the tether line. Asher is standing near his horse, and he doesn't seem to be looking over here, but I feel the weight of his focus all the same.

I frown.

"You seem unsettled," Ky says.

My gaze snaps back to his. "No. I'm fine."

"Are you worried about the Hunters? We've had no sign of anyone at our back. Admittedly, they could follow our trail in the snow, but if they are, they're keeping their distance."

That's a bit chilling. But I shake my head.

His eyes search mine. "You're troubled by Asher," he guesses.

"What? Oh. No. I—" He sees far too much. My flush deepens. "He's so angry at me."

"It's not anger," he says quietly. "Give it time."

He says that with such certainty—and with such care. It's coolly reassuring, and it reminds me of the way he put a hand on Asher's neck and said, *Breathe.*

I lower my hand and study him. He's been so quiet and still since I began, and there's something so surprising about that. Maybe because I've already witnessed the violence and savagery I expected to find in this man—right alongside the candor and empathy I did not.

"What?" he says.

You're so much kinder than anyone knows. Why do you keep that a secret?

But of course I can't say that. I touch the cloth to his forehead again, even though most of the blood is gone. "How much farther do we need to travel?"

"We won't reach the border until after sundown, I'd think. Once we're safely within Incendar, we'll break for the night and set off at dawn tomorrow."

"And then how much farther will we have to go?"

"From the border, it's less than a day's ride to Lastalorre. After we reach the palace, I'll have Sev send runners to the front, to see how the army has fared since I've been away. From there, we can determine how to approach your brother about the attack—and how to proceed."

Lastalorre. His capital city. A little shiver goes through me. Days ago, I hated the idea of Maddox Kyronan dragging me across the border, but now it feels like we can't go fast enough.

But then I realize what else he said.

From there, we can determine how to approach your brother.

We.

At every step, he treats me as an equal, and it's so unexpected—

especially since I've seen the power and force he can wield. It's clear that Dane and my father have no interest in what I have to offer, so their attitude has never been a surprise. But even though Asher has never been dismissive of my views, he's still treated me as someone to be guarded and protected. Someone to be sheltered.

I wonder if Asher always longed for that protection—all while I was desperate to escape it.

The blood on Ky's skin finally yields, so I lower my hand.

"Thank you," he says.

"You're welcome." As I say the words, heat sparks on my cheeks again. Something about this feels more intimate than it needs to be, like we're talking about something other than the journey. He keeps lighting these fires of attraction that refuse to dim.

I duck my head, swiping my hands on my cloak. I'm suddenly aware that we've earned the focus of his men, though they're trying not to be obvious about it. Behind him, I see that Asher is watching this interaction now, too.

I have to clear my throat, because I'm self-conscious now. "When we arrive, what will Princess Victoria think of everything that has transpired?" I say. "Will she demand that you reconsider the alliance?"

Ky frowns, and a glimmer of emotion passes over his expression. "As I said, Victoria has no interest in politics."

My mouth forms a line. I remember how he expected *me* to be stoic and uninterested, so it makes me wonder if that's exactly what I'm going to find in his sister. "Not even when your life is at risk?" I say.

He sighs. "My life is always at risk, Princess." I inhale to press further, but he turns away. His voice rises as he calls to his captain. "Sev! I want to make sure we reach the spire lookout by dusk. Have them mount up."

When I turn back to head for my horse, Asher isn't watching me anymore. Instead, he's glaring at his own mount like it's an adversary. The bruising along his jaw and up the side of his face is worse today, but I know that's not the worst of it. The armor is likely pressing into the burn on his shoulder—or maybe the countless other injuries he earned in the dungeon.

I can't take this distance between us. Not when so much of his pain is my fault. I square my shoulders and join him beside his horse.

He doesn't even look up.

I hesitate, then wet my lips. "Asher."

"Jory."

The silence between us practically screams. I want to ask if he's all right, but it's obvious that he's not.

"Ky said we'll cross the border around nightfall," I finally say.

"Oh, good." His voice is flat. "Another six hours of this."

"I can ask the king to slow the pace," I offer.

His mouth twists. "I'm fine."

I frown and move closer. "I can tell you're in pain," I say quietly.

That gets his attention. He draws himself up, but then he scowls a little, glaring past me toward the others. "So can they. Garrett offered to tie me to the saddle if I need help sitting upright."

My mouth forms a line, but the soldiers are drawing closer, returning to the line of tethered horses.

Callum whistles through his teeth when he sees Asher looking. "Chin up, Stripes." His voice is darkly taunting. "We could always drag you."

Stripes. I inhale a breath of fire, ready to snap at him.

"Jory!" Asher's voice is low but sharp. "Leave it."

I clamp my mouth shut. "You saved their king," I whisper tightly. "They should see that."

"I kidnapped their king right out from under them. They saw that, too." He puts his foot in the stirrup and stiffly swings aboard.

"My lady," calls Charlotte. "Our horses are ready."

"I'll be right there," I call. But I can't move away from Asher. Not yet. I shift a little closer and look up at him. It's still so unusual to see him in the daylight. His skin is so much less pale than I remember, his hair picking up flecks of light from the sun. Even his blue eyes are vivid, vibrant above the lines on his cheek.

He glances down, and I realize I was reaching for his knee. I bite my lip and adjust my motion, patting the horse on the shoulder instead before I turn away.

Quick as lightning, Asher catches my hand. I stare at his fingers wrapped around mine, and my breath catches. His grip is gentle, and I'm frozen in place, my eyes lifting to meet his.

"Jory," he says. His voice is as soft and low as it was in the darkness of my room. I don't know what I'm seeing in his expression, whether it's regret or longing—or something else entirely. His cool fingers are soft against mine.

I'm not the boy you remember, and you're about to marry another man.

My chest aches. I was focused on the second part of that statement, but I should have paid attention to the first.

I wish I'd known. I *should* have known.

He gives my hand a squeeze. "I'm still here," he says, and the words give my heart a tug, softening everything inside me that feels wound up tight.

But then he drops my hand, and the motion is so abrupt that I almost jump. Ky has returned, and he's swinging onto his own horse beside Asher. I wonder how much of that interaction he saw, because I can suddenly feel the weight of his gaze as if I've been caught at something.

The king says, "Princess? Is all well?"

The words sound more like a challenge than an inquiry, and I turn to look up at him.

As soon as I do, I regret it. The king's hair finds hints of red and copper in the sunlight, and he wears his armor like he was born for it, not a single buckle or weapon out of place. Astride his horse, he's easily ten feet tall. I can't believe I just dabbed blood off his forehead, because he seems ready to spill more if the occasion presents itself. Beside him, Asher is equally intimidating. He's drawn up the hood of his cloak again, leaving his eyes heavy and shadowed. Combined with the black armor broadening his frame, he couldn't look more like an assassin if he tried.

Side by side, they're a little captivating, and for a heartbeat of time, I'm transfixed. Are they rivals? Enemies? Allies? Adversaries?

It's truly unfair that fate has put us all together.

My mouth has gone dry, and I have to shake myself. "Yes, Your Majesty," I croak out, bobbing a curtsy before I realize that I don't even have skirts to flare. "All is well."

His eyebrows go up, but I'm already turning away, striding to Charlotte, taking the reins to my horse.

I have no idea what expression is on my face, but she studies me closely, then looks past me at the men. Her voice drops. "Which one am I to hate now?"

She sounds so earnest that it startles a smile through my tears. She was always so loyal in front of Dane, so I'm not surprised to find that she's the same in front of Ky. Despite everything, I'm glad my brother sent her—even though everything seemed so much easier when Charlotte and I were locked in the carriage, hating King Maddox Kyronan because he seemed so evil.

But I consider everything I've learned about Asher—and about Astranza.

Nothing was easier. It just seemed like it was.

"You don't need to hate either one, Charlotte."

Her eyes haven't left them, and her tone turns musing. "Are they no longer hating each *other*?"

My cheeks won't cool. "I . . . don't know."

Charlotte huffs a breath. "Well, they're being too bold."

I look at her before I swing aboard. "They are? How?"

"They're both *watching* you."

I can't look. I can't.

I'm not sure what it says about me that I desperately want to.

"What about the captain?" I tease. "Who's he watching?"

She huffs a breath—but her eyes snap past me, and Captain Zale *must* be watching, because her cheeks flush as pink as my own must be.

Yesterday, I would've agreed with Charlotte. This all would have felt too bold.

Today, I'm not sure I mind.

I bump her with my shoulder. "Let them all watch," I say. Then I swing aboard the horse, take up my reins, and ride out.

AS WE TRAVEL south, the snow fades away entirely, leaving lush grass alongside the roadway. A chill still hangs in the air, but it's not stinging my face anymore. The soldiers have shed some of their outerwear, tucking fur gloves and caps into their saddlebags. As the road becomes less flat, we ride over hills and down through shadowed valleys, always avoiding towns and settlements. Eventually even the grass begins to turn sparse and thin, the ground turning hard enough to make the hoofbeats echo. Ky's soldiers wordlessly change their patterns, hanging closer as the sunlight begins to fade. No words are spoken, but bows are unhooked from saddles, quivered arrows sitting ready.

Their vigilance is contagious, and Charlotte and I fall silent, our eyes searching the darkness, watching for danger, too.

At twilight, we crest a hill, and there, in the fading light of sunset, I see the distant mountains of Incendar. To our right, the sky is still a vivid red that melts into purple behind the mountain range, with the first scattered stars flecking the sky overhead.

"*Oh,*" I breathe.

Ky looks at me in surprise. "Have you never been to southern Astranza?"

"Not this far." I can't look away from the mountains. I've seen paintings, of course, but that's nothing compared to the massive earthly formations that somehow seem to be right in front of us, yet also a hundred miles away. It feels like something else Dane has kept from me.

I look at Charlotte, and her mouth is hanging open. At least I'm not alone.

Beside Ky, Asher is also staring, but there's no awe in his expression. Just wariness.

"Have you seen the mountains before?" I say to him.

"From here, yes. Never up close."

"This is nothing," says Ky, as we descend into yet another valley. Shadows have grown longer as the sun sets, and the mountains shrink over the crest of the next hill. "Wait until you're looking up at them."

Up ahead, one of his soldiers gives a shout, and my breath catches. I look up in alarm. It's hard to see much detail in the fading light, but it seems like two dozen armed men have appeared from *nowhere* to block the road. For an instant, I'm fifteen again, clinging to Asher while bandits attack our carriage procession.

Captain Zale touches his heels to his horse's flanks, and the animal sprints ahead.

Beside me, Charlotte's eyes are searching the horizon, too, but her voice is cool, the only sign of her worry. "Are we in danger?" she says.

"No," says Ky. "They're mine. Border guard."

As he says it, Captain Zale reaches the group of armed men. They're all too far to hear any words exchanged, but they shift to form a line on either side of the path, standing at attention. I expect Ky to hurry the pace, but instead, we stop in the hollow of the valley and he reaches down and untethers Asher's horse from his saddle. Then he unwraps the reins from where they're tied by the animal's head, holding them out.

Asher looks startled.

"I don't want gossip that we brought a prisoner back from Astranza," Ky says. "Don't make me regret it."

Asher takes the reins. "No promises."

Ky gives him a look, but the rest of his soldiers have caught up, so we ride on. At the crest of the hill, the border guards stand at attention as we ride past. All motionless, all silent. They're all in the same black armor as Ky's soldiers, and I feel the weight of their gaze as they take stock of me and Charlotte. In these clothes, it would be impossible for them to know which of us is the princess. The king says nothing, so I don't either.

At the end of the line, a man steps forward, and his bearing tells me that he's likely an officer. He holds out a hand to Ky and says, "By fury and flame."

Ky catches his hand and grasps it. "For valor and truth."

The men behind us slap a hand to their armor. "For Incendar."

It makes Ky smile, and the relief in his expression is profound. "For Incendar," he says in response.

Riding past the border guard seems to lift a weight from our group, as if Ky's soldiers have all released a collective breath. They're on their own soil, with allies at their back.

But Asher glances back at me, and the tension still clings to his eyes. He's not relieved. Not yet.

Neither am I.

The king nods down at his officer as we pass. "Hold the border, Lieutenant." Then he taps three fingers on his opposite shoulder, and rides on.

But as my own horse begins to move away, I'm still looking at the guards, so I see the lieutenant's eyes widen slightly. There's a new alertness to his stance, and he turns to the other men and repeats the three-fingered gesture. "Hold the border," he says sharply. None of them say a word in response, but I see the same awareness in their figures as they shift to move into new positions. Ky's own soldiers fall into line to follow us, but their bows are strapped to their saddles again, their vigilance less urgent.

My eyes shift to the king. "What did you tell them?" I say.

"To hold the border," he says dryly. I huff a breath, and he adds, "No passage into Incendar."

"And what was the *secret* order?" When his eyebrows go up, I tap three fingers on my shoulder.

He looks back at me and says nothing. His expression is still easy, but now there's a cunning look in his eye that I absolutely cannot ignore.

"The morning we met," I add, "you said that once we were in Incendar, you would show me anything I desire."

"I'm not quite sure that was my promise."

"Please?" I say sweetly.

The king heaves a sigh, then lets it out through his teeth. He glances at Asher. "Is this how she convinced you to force me out of the castle?"

Asher keeps his eyes forward, and his voice is flat. "Yep."

I scowl, but when the king looks back, he smiles. "Very well, Princess. It's not really an order at all. It's a measure of severity." He holds up one finger, then taps it against his shoulder. "Hold the border—but use your discretion. Question merchants and travelers, and let them pass if it seems legitimate." He holds up two fingers, then taps them as well. "Hold the border, but restrict access. Don't allow anyone through without a valid reason to be here. Inspect wagons, search carriages, that kind of thing." He shrugs a little and repeats the two-fingered gesture. "Basically, *don't pick a fight, but stand your ground.*"

I remember he tapped two fingers last night, when Roman and Nikko were moving into the hallway to stand guard. Now I understand.

"You used three," I say, and this time Captain Zale glances back, over his shoulder.

"Yes," Ky says. "I did." A note in his voice tells me his lesson is over.

But Asher was paying attention. He taps three fingers. "Hold the border," he says. "Use lethal force."

The king says nothing. His captain says nothing.

But that says more than enough.

Asher glances back at me, and there's a look in his eye that reminds me that the king and his men seem relieved . . . but Asher doesn't.

I remember the way the king tricked him, then let my brother's guards take him away—to protect himself, and to protect his soldiers.

I consider my very first impression of King Maddox Kyronan, the way he stood in my chambers and faced me, somehow knowing that I had a weapon hidden in my palm.

The king must sense the weighted silence between us, because he looks back at me, and his eyes search my face. He's been gentle with me, and honestly, he's been gentle with Asher, especially in moments when my friend likely didn't deserve it. I thanked the king for his kindness—and I meant it.

But I've also seen his other side. I dabbed that blood off his face, but I know how it got there. Behind that honeyed voice and those searching eyes is a man who knows how to put emotion aside. A man who knows how to be vicious.

Hold the border. Use lethal force.

That doesn't just mean Hunters who could be on our trail. That means *everyone*.

Astranza's army. Palace guards. My brother. My *father*.

Anyone who might want to harm me—but anyone who might need to protect me, too.

I look back at Ky, holding his gaze. "I am committed to this alliance," I say, feeling my heart beat hard in my chest. "So is my family."

"So am I," he says equably. "But someone isn't."

Chapter Twenty-Three
THE PRINCESS

We ride on for another three hours, until the grass turns crunchy underfoot and the moon is high overhead. The footing has turned even more treacherous, especially in the dark, with many rocky outcroppings, and a few spots where we have to weave, single file, through narrow ravines that seem endless. There's a scent in the air I don't recognize, though it's not entirely unpleasant: some mix of burning leaves and smoked meat, reminding me of the fall harvest in Astranza. My stomach has been hoping for food for hours. Based on the scent in the air, I expect we're close to another inn, so I'm surprised when we come to a dip along the wall of one of the ravines, and the king calls for a stop.

"We'll camp here," he says.

"Camp?" I say in surprise. I'm still off-balance from our exchange at the border, when I realized that I've been cut off from Astranza, for good or for bad.

"Yes, Princess. *Camp.*"

Nearby, one of the soldiers chuckles under his breath as he climbs down from his horse. That makes me scowl.

The king whips his head in the man's direction. "Garrett," he snaps. "Dig a trench for the latrine."

Garrett shuts up—and so do the others.

Inside, I'm spinning. I don't know if it's the threat still clinging to my back or just the simple fact that I've never *camped* anywhere. I move close to Ky. "Wouldn't we be safer under cover?"

"Incendar has no inns or taverns this far north." He kicks at the dried grass underfoot, which is sparse and brown. "It's mostly a few roving bands of nomads, and they keep to themselves. The terrain here is not exactly hospitable." He pauses, and his expression turns challenging. "We've had several long days—and nights—of riding, Princess. My soldiers need to rest. The ravines are easily defensible—and I'll have a sentry posted."

He's right. I *know* he's right. But I'm tired and hungry, and all that's kept me going for the last few hours has been the promise of a soft bed and a hot meal. Not the cold, hard ground and strips of dried beef or whatever the soldiers have left in their packs. Emotion tightens my throat, but I refuse to let it get to me. I already feel sheltered and inexperienced. No need to prove it to everyone else.

Nearby, Asher is tethering his horse with the others, and Charlotte is tying hers a short distance away. I head over to join them.

"I know you've never been a soldier," I murmur to Asher. "Have you ever slept outside?"

"Yes."

"Well, he sent Garrett to dig a *trench*. For a *latrine*." I make a face—and I'm gratified when Charlotte looks as horrified as I feel. She and I privately relieved ourselves in the brush when we stopped earlier, but I hadn't considered anything *else*. "Asher, have you ever had to use a—"

He cuts me a narrow glance. "Jory, it would probably be quicker to give you a list of unpleasant things I *haven't* done."

Well, that smacks me in the face—and it's a reminder of everything he said last night. I frown, wishing I could undo this odd hum of tension that's formed between us. But he's already turned back to his horse, and he's stripping the gear, arranging it in a pile like the soldiers. I watch, following their patterns, doing the same thing.

By the time we finish, Asher and Charlotte haven't left my side, and the king has made his way over. Behind him, a fire has been started, and I hear the low timbre of the other men's voices.

"For a woman who seemed shocked by the idea of a campsite," Ky says, "you did rather well with your gear."

The compliment is startling, and I feel warmth on my cheeks, especially since his voice has fallen back into that silken tone. "I know how to tend a horse."

"We're in safer territory here," he says. "You can strip your own armor as well." He pauses. "If you like."

That makes me realize he's in a fresh tunic, with a cloak thrown over his shoulders. It looks like he's splashed water over his face, too.

Yes, I absolutely *do* want to get out of this armor.

I reach for one of the buckles near my waist, but my hands falter when I find straps doubled over and tucked away in a pattern I can't see in the dark.

"May I?" says the king.

My eyes flick up, and I nod.

He moves close, until I can hear his breath, and it reminds me of the moment I dabbed the blood off his face. The king's fingers brush my waist as he pulls at leather straps and tight buckles until it all comes free. Every touch of his hands makes me want to shiver despite the warmth in his touch. Maybe I've never slept outside, but there's suddenly something very primal about this that I crave, being under the stars, stripping armor and tending horses.

When cool air reaches my sweat-dampened clothes, I *do* shiver. Ky tosses the armor with my gear, then he shrugs out of his cloak. In one swift movement, he throws it around my shoulders instead. His fingers are swift and gentle at my throat as he tugs the clasp together.

Much like everything else he does, it's bold and forward, and I'm not entirely sure how to react—except I don't hate it. Just like that, another tiny flame is lit.

"I didn't mean to frighten you," he says. "At the border."

"You didn't." But my voice is a little thin, because he did—and I think it's clear that he did.

"Those assassins did not just come after me," he says. "They came after you as well." He pauses. "My intent is not to trap you here. My intent is to *protect* you."

His eyes are so determined, and his hands have gone still on the cloak at my throat. It's so different from the way Asher said, *I'm still here*—but it's also so similar.

"Come eat," he says gently. "Callum and Nikko shot some mountain elk. Sev has some whiskey." He smiles, and this time it's not cunning or challenging at all. "We're safe here." His thumb brushes against my throat, and then he lets me go. "*You* are safe here."

"Even Asher?" I say.

The king's eyes lift, shifting in Asher's direction—reminding me that he's been at my back this whole time, watching our interaction.

"That," says Ky, "depends on him."

THE CAMPFIRE IS surprisingly inviting, and the cooked meat unexpectedly tasty. We've fallen into small paired clusters that form a circle around the fire: me and Charlotte, the king and his captain, Garrett and Callum, Nikko and Roman. Only Asher sits alone, though he's to my left, a little closer to me than to Roman. His expression is still tight, and his wound wept through yet another tunic during our ride. He's shirtless now, with one arm through the sleeve of a fur-lined jacket, his branded shoulder and left arm bare to the night air. It's buckled at the waist, holding it all together. He must be cold, but he's hardly said a word.

After a day on the road together, I've begun to piece together the soldiers' personalities, and I find them all a bit fascinating. Captain Zale is clearly a close friend and confidant to the king. They exchange glances often, and it's obvious that more is being said than what I'm allowed to hear. I can't help but notice that Charlotte seems taken by the captain, because I've caught her watching him a few times—to the extent that I want to ask if *she* needs a chaperone.

I've heard Garrett and Callum bicker all day, with a few remarks that might've sparked a fight if the king didn't snap at them to stop. But they also seem to share a deeper intimacy. Last night, Callum flirted with that woman in the inn—but tonight, he's on a low, flat rock by the fire, with Garrett leaning back against his legs. At one point, Garrett finished the piece of meat he was eating, so Callum tore his remaining portion in half, then held it out. Garrett bit it right from his fingers.

Nikko and Roman don't bicker at all, but they don't seem as tightly bound as the others. Roman is something of a strategist for the king—or maybe a tactician. He's the one who arranged their riding patterns after the attack. He's quieter. More easygoing—I think.

Nikko is quiet, too, but his silence is different. When he speaks, his voice is always low and unnaturally rough, like he's inhaled a mouthful of smoke. He's very still, and very watchful, and it hasn't escaped my notice that he seems to resent Asher's presence.

Every time Nikko's dark eyes settle on my friend, I'm reminded of Asher's comment when we stopped.

I kidnapped their king right out from under them. They saw that, too.

Small steel cups of water are passed around while we eat, but the king was right about Captain Zale's whiskey, because that's shared with much more enthusiasm. In Astranza, I would *never* be invited to drink liquor with a group of soldiers, so I don't expect the bottle to come my way at all. But the king passes it to Lady Charlotte—who immediately hands it to me. I automatically turn toward Asher without taking a sip.

But once the heavy glass bottle is in my grip, I hesitate, biting my lip. I'm half-turned to face Asher, and when he sees me reconsider, his eyes flare in surprise.

I raise my eyebrows at him, wondering if he's going to tell me to stop.

He doesn't. "Dane would have a *fit*," he says. His voice is quiet and low, and it sounds like a dare.

After hours of silence and tension, it's the lightest thing he's said all day, and it lights a tiny spark of hope in my chest. "Exactly."

To my right, Charlotte gasps out loud. "*My lady*," she says. "I must object to—"

I tilt the bottle back and drink.

A lot.

At first, it's sweet, like warm cinnamon, and it's probably why I gulp two swallows. The burn hits me a moment later, and I pull it back from my lips, sputtering—but not before a third swallow makes its way down my throat. I have to wipe my mouth in a way that is certainly not ladylike. Asher is watching me, but his expression isn't daring now. In the flickering firelight, his gaze is full of heat.

To my right, Ky is watching me, too. His eyes are gleaming and fixed on my mouth. Warmth crawls up my jaw, and I have to lick the last of the liquor off my lower lip. Something in his gaze instantly tightens.

Oh. *Oh.*

I shiver, but it has nothing to do with the chill in the air. I'm definitely blushing now.

For an instant, the soldiers are silent, and their eyes go from me to the king to Asher and back. Their moods have been lighter since we've eaten, bolstered with confidence now that they're back on their own soil. I can't tell if they want to tease or if they want to start trouble.

The temptation for mischief must be too strong. Callum grins and says, "You won't have *any* trouble sleeping outside if you keep drinking like that."

I laugh a little, abashed—but pleased. "Well, I think I'll need a good bit more before I use the trench."

That makes them all laugh, including the king, and I smile. When I turn to pass the bottle to Asher, he takes it with one hand, then reaches up with the other to brush a damp line of whiskey off my cheek.

"Don't be *too* brave," he murmurs.

The touch is brief and his fingers are cool, and I'm sure that's meant to be a warning. But I'm so aware of him to my left and the king to my right.

Especially since none of the soldiers are grinning now.

I force my eyes back to the fire. This whiskey has struck a match to my insides, and I'm not sure what to do with it. I didn't realize it was possible to feel so hot and cold at the same time. Do they hate Asher? Do they hate that he touched me? Is this part of their loyalty to their king, as if I somehow suddenly *belong* to him?

I don't like the track of these questions.

Asher doesn't take a sip at all, and he just continues passing the bottle, half-rolling onto a knee to hold it out to Roman. The soldier seems ready to reach for it, but Nikko, beside him, smacks him on the arm, and Roman goes still.

"What's wrong?" Nikko says to Asher, his voice rough and quiet. "Too good for our whiskey?"

Asher hasn't withdrawn the bottle, but his eyes narrow. "No."

"Then why don't you drink?"

At once, everyone's focus tightens. Asher's gaze flicks around the circle, his finger tapping against the glass of the bottle.

"Maybe I want to keep my wits about me," he says.

"Why?" says Garrett. His voice is casual, but his eyes are sharp. "Worried something will happen?"

For the first time, I realize that *we* may have stripped our armor and gear, but most of the Incendrian soldiers haven't. There are still plenty of weapons, plenty of armor, plenty of ways for this evening to turn from lighthearted banter into . . . something very bad. My heart gives an uncertain beat in my chest, and I glance at the king, wondering if he'll intervene or call his men to order, the way I've seen him do several times now.

He doesn't. He pulls meat from a bone and watches. His golden eyes are shadowed and intent.

Callum whistles, low, through his teeth. "Is Stripes nervous?"

"No," says Asher. He looks coiled and dangerous, like a snake waiting to strike. The bottle is hanging loosely from his hand, and I watch him carefully set it on the ground.

I'm regretting that healthy swallow of whiskey right now. It's churning up my insides.

"Hey, Nik," says Garrett. "Didn't he offer you a rematch?"

"He did," says Roman.

Asher hasn't moved, but his body is practically vibrating with violent potential. I wonder if they can see it, if it's adding to the heightened tension, or if I just know him so well that it's only obvious to me.

Nikko hasn't responded. His eyes are locked on Asher now.

Asher, who's still in pain. I've been watching him move stiffly all day. So have they.

Beside me, Charlotte reaches out and grips my fingers.

"It's all right," she whispers. But I really don't think it is.

The king eats another piece of meat, but says nothing. Captain Zale leans in to murmur something to him, and Ky goes still, then shrugs.

I look around the circle. "Whatever you're all doing, you will *stop it*."

For half a second, I have their attention. The threat in the air seems to hesitate. But then their eyes shift to the king. It's clear who will give the order here.

Ky glances my way, and his voice is mild. "Asher did offer a rematch," he says. "He can withdraw the challenge if he likes."

My breath catches, and I wait. *Withdraw*, I think. *Withdraw*.

But Asher says nothing. His eyes haven't left Nikko.

The king speaks into my silence. "He has not asked for your defense, Princess."

I almost flinch. I don't think he would. I've never been able to help him before.

"You said we would be *safe*," I say, a little desperately—but it's not really what he said at all.

He said *I* would be safe.

"If he wins," says Garrett, "he'll be perfectly safe."

Throughout all of this, Asher and Nikko have been completely still. I'm not even sure they've taken a breath.

My heart feels like it's stopped beating, as if it's not sure it can handle this.

Nikko is the one to break—and when he moves, he's *fast*. He's off the ground, sword and dagger drawn, and Charlotte gives a little shriek—just before she grabs my arm as if she's going to pull me out of the way.

Or maybe she's stopping me from jumping between them.

Asher still doesn't move, and Nikko barrels down on him. Those blades will be buried in his chest before I can do anything about it. But at the last possible moment, Asher dives under the weapons, skidding through the dirt beside the fire. He's shirtless, and I realize he must have unbuckled the jacket before he leapt. Maybe that's what took the extra time. Nikko is already spinning, but Asher rolls, avoiding the blades again. His shoulder collides with the ground, dirt sticking to the burn. He grunts and falters midroll, letting out a sharp burst of breath. It gives Nikko an opening to swing his sword arm down.

I gasp in alarm, but Asher twists inside the movement, getting closer, and the sword scrapes dirt behind him. Asher surges off the ground and grabs hold of the soldier's breastplate with one hand, then throws a handful of ash from the fire in his face with the other. A few glowing embers flare in the night air, and Nikko jerks away, sputtering.

It only buys him a second, but Asher clearly needs less than that. I barely see him move, but he's used that grip on the soldier's armor to swing onto his back. Asher gets an arm around Nikko's neck, the edge of a blade tucked tight against his throat.

I don't even know when he got a weapon.

Everyone is frozen in place, and I'm straining against Charlotte's grip, ready for the other soldiers to explode off the ground and go after Asher. Two of them are already on their feet. Boots scrape in the dirt, and hands flicker toward daggers and swords.

But Asher doesn't move farther. He grips the blade right up against Nikko's throat, but he hasn't broken skin. A bloom of sweat coats Asher's upper body, mixing with the dust and grit from the ground, and I realize he's panting, his chest heaving hard.

Nikko, on the other hand, isn't breathing at all. His face is turning red from Asher's grip. The soldier drops his weapons in the dirt, then taps two fingers against the palm of his other hand.

"Asher," says the king. "He yields." His voice is low, his expression reserved, a complete contrast to the strain in the air.

Without hesitation, Asher withdraws the blade, then uncurls his arm to spring to the ground. He's still breathing hard, and I can tell he's well aware of the other men watching him. I don't want to imagine how much that hurt—or how much effort it took.

The soldiers don't look threatening anymore. Now they're just staring.

Nikko doesn't take his eyes off Asher, but he swipes gray ash off his face and coughs hard, then fetches his weapons from the dirt. When he straightens, Asher holds out the blade he stole from somewhere. Nikko blinks in surprise—then does a double take.

It's only then that I notice the sheath on his outer thigh is empty, too.

Callum whistles through his teeth again, but this time it's not taunting. "Stripes is *fast*."

Asher makes a derisive sound. "No. Lucky."

Nikko surveys him for a long, quiet moment. "That was skill. Not luck." He doesn't seem happy about this, but he takes the offered blade and slides it home, then turns to sit back down.

Captain Zale's gaze is more assessing, his voice cool. "You said you Hunters were trained to kill, not fight."

"I said *they* weren't trained to fight." Asher returns to where he was sitting, but I notice that he doesn't pull the jacket back over his skin. A dozen bleeding abrasions run up the side of his back opposite the burn scar. He still seems to be breathing too hard, especially for such a short fight, and his skin seems a little pale in the firelight.

I wonder how close that really was.

He glances at me. "What's with the look?"

I want to tell him that I was worried he'd get himself killed. I want to say that he's so fast and agile that it's almost poetic. I want to tell him he's my only friend, and I can't lose him now, like this.

But then I remember everything he said last night. I remember the way he took my hand and said, *I'm still here.*

I consider what he looks like right now, half-glistening, half-dusty, cords of fatigued muscle bunched across his shoulders.

Friend suddenly feels like the wrong word. I need to stop staring.

The gulps of whiskey have fully hit me, so what I end up saying is, "That was very brave. And very *stupid.*"

Asher chokes on a laugh as if I've genuinely surprised him—and so do a handful of the soldiers.

Ky doesn't laugh. He's looking between the two of us. As always, his eyes are intense and unyielding, the fire reflecting off his features to paint gold in his hair. Is he angry? Jealous? I can't tell.

Asher sobers, regarding him. For a heartbeat of time, emotion flickers between *them,* and my heart stutters. It feels like a challenge. A warning. The air shifts, and Asher's form takes on that ready stillness again. So does Ky's.

My breath catches. The king won't go down as easily as Nikko. Not in front of his men. Not in front of *me.*

I can't watch that again. I can't.

But the king shrugs one shoulder and sits back, his posture almost lazy in the firelight. "You've earned a rest, Asher." His accented voice is low and silky, easing through the tension in the air. "Take it."

At that, Asher blinks, as if the simple words catch him by surprise. But he swallows, and the aggressive bracing in his body melts away. He pushes sweat-damp hair back from his face, then picks up the abandoned bottle of whiskey and holds it out to Roman. This time, the soldier takes it.

I'm still studying the king, however. Asher's fight took my breath away, but there's something so fascinating about *this*, the king's quiet resolve. The way he's able to unravel tension before it spirals into something worse. I've seen it for days, in the way he spoke so thoughtfully when tears were on my cheeks, or how he was prepared to stand in the snow and guard my carriage, simply because his men were hungry and tired. It's in the way he put a gentle hand on Asher's neck, or offered food from his own dish.

Maddox Kyronan has a reputation that long precedes him, and from everything I've seen, that reputation is hard won and well deserved. He slaughtered those assassins like it was nothing, and he still wears armor bearing their blood. But what I find so surprising is that the most formidable part of his character seems to have nothing to do with his magic, or his soldiers, or his strength.

Instead, I'm discovering that the most powerful thing about him—in fact, the most *compelling* thing about him—has nothing to do with violence at all.

Chapter Twenty-Four
THE WARRIOR

If anyone has been stupid, it's me.

My comment to the princess about our need to camp in the ravines wasn't quite true. I know at least half a dozen inns and taverns within two hours' ride from here. But we rode for miles after we crossed the border, and the grass is still brown and dead, with no sign of resurgence—not even near the streams, where it should be lush and vibrant. If the grass is this bad, I'm sure the crops are worse.

Or the *lack* of crops, I should say. If we found an inn, I doubt I'd be welcome.

Victoria, I think. *Please tell me you haven't made anything worse.*

This alliance needs to proceed. King Theodore's weather magic will renew our crops and keep them safe from damage. If the miles of snow convinced me of anything, it's that he's powerful enough to do as he promised. Once the princess and I are wed, my people will be able to stop worrying about how to survive the next season. I'll be able to help his soldiers hold their borders more effectively, protecting the citizens of Astranza from invading forces. We *need* each other.

But in the back of my mind, one threat has been left unanswered: those Hunters still came after us.

Sev has been fit to be tied all day. There haven't been many opportunities for truly private conversation, but I know he's still suspicious of the princess and her motives—to say nothing of Asher.

"This could all be part of a carefully laid plot to infiltrate the palace and kill off anyone in power," he said earlier, the first time we had a moment to ourselves. "Asher could still be working with these Hunters."

"If it is," I said, "then it's a poorly laid plan. Why invite suspicion on himself first?"

"Then how did anyone know where we stopped?" he says.

"How would Asher have alerted anyone at all?" I counter, frustrated. "He was chained to me the whole time!"

But as soon as I said it, I remembered, *again*, the way Asher was so sure that one of my own soldiers could be behind this. I still can't make that work out in my head. They're too loyal. I've known them too long. And they've had ample opportunity to harm the princess. There'd be no reason to hire anyone at all.

Later, when we stopped to rest, Sev saw Jory and Asher talking quietly, off by the horses. "Further plotting?" he muttered to me.

That time, it was obvious that my soldiers had noticed, too.

But when I approached Jory and Asher, it didn't seem like plotting at all. It seemed like an uncertain princess and a captive assassin sharing a moment of doubt.

"They're friends," I said to Sev later.

"Oh, right. I look at *all* my friends that way."

He's not the only one who's wary. My soldiers have been watching Asher all day, and I've heard some of their barbed comments. They're protective, so I understand it. Tonight, they bristled when he touched the princess, and I watched every pair of eyes swing to me, waiting to see if I'd react.

But I didn't. And when Garrett mentioned the "rematch," I almost called them to order. Asher is wounded and sore, and it's no secret from anyone.

Then Sev leaned in to murmur, "They're either going to fight here, where you can see it, or they're going to wait and do it when you can't."

I didn't like it, but he was right. I wouldn't like it if I found Asher in a broken, bloody pile outside of camp later, either. So when Jory protested, I gave Asher an out, and I fully expected him to take it. For most of the day, sheer force of will was all that kept him upright on the horse. If he withdrew his challenge to Nikko, any of them would have understood it. Honestly, a little wounded humility might have bought him some mercy.

Like an idiot, he didn't take it.

The fight lasted less than a minute, but it was the longest minute of my life. I spent the whole time weighing the repercussions.

If Nikko kills Asher, the princess will never forgive me.

If Asher kills Nik, the men will tear him apart.

But then it was over. No one was dead. Asher was springing to the ground. My soldiers were looking at Asher with a little less fury—and a lot more regard.

Sev leaned close. "That man is more than just a hired killer, Ky."

His words lodged in my thoughts and stuck there.

It's later now, and bedrolls have been laid out close to the fire, almost everyone wrapped up for the night. Garrett sits sentry a short ways off, perched on a stone outcropping that lets him see both paths into the ravine. His bow is in his lap, his quiver strapped over his shoulder. The rest of my men are already asleep—or at least their eyes are closed. Even Asher has stretched out on his bedroll, his face turned to the fire. The others are deeply tucked into their bedding, but Asher lies half-exposed, his back bare to the cold sky. The brand is red and weeping again, and the friction of the armor clearly didn't help. A line of fresh abrasions from the fight runs straight up the opposite side of his spine, and I can already see new bruises beginning to form.

I'm sure it hurts like hell. I can't believe he was ready to tangle with me next.

Actually, I can. Brave and stupid, like the princess said.

I've unrolled my own bedding at my feet, but I'm nowhere close to sleep. The princess seems to be the same, though Lady Charlotte has already curled up in her own blankets. The woman holds herself aloof, but I've been impressed at her bravery—both in the way she agreed to come along for this journey, and the way my men don't intimidate her.

As time goes on, the night sky grows heavy, and I become very aware of the fact that Jory and I are the only two left awake.

I wish I could read her thoughts. She's so bold, and there are moments when I worry she'll demand that I return her to Astranza. She seemed so shocked by the prospect of *camping*, which took me by surprise and reminded me of how sheltered she must be. But this morning, she leapt into the fray when those Hunters were attacking. An hour ago, she glared at my soldiers and issued an order as if she's been commanding armies her whole life. When Nikko stood ready to fight with Asher, I thought she'd jump right in front of him.

But that's not what's fixed in my brain. Instead, it's the way Asher caught her hand earlier—and the way she went still. She seems to long for his touch. They might be a little raw from what he revealed about his past, but that'll ease. Some of it already has.

Last night, I asked Asher if he was jealous.

Right now, I think *I* am.

Maybe that's better, though. I fully intended to go into this marriage as a matter of political strategy, and there's no reason I can't. The princess deserves a gentle companion, not a jaded soldier who spends his waking hours walking across blood-soaked battlefields. There's no place for . . . for *softness* in my life.

But I keep feeling her delicate touch as she carefully washed the blood off my face. A few tendrils had escaped her braid, and her cheeks were so pink from the wind, but her hands were warm and tender. She didn't flinch from the violence—or the result. With every stroke of her fingers, I found myself wishing she wouldn't stop. I remember the way she sat in my lap astride the horse. She was so angry, yet so determined. The memory of it sends a flare of desire through my belly, and my trousers go a bit snug.

I have to shove the thoughts away—but they're immediately replaced with thoughts of Asher. He bested Nikko so fluidly that it was almost artful—then yielded when I called him off. He tries to be vicious and cold, but it's so clear that he craves trust and security. He craves *certainty*—and I think there's a part of him that regrets he could never fully find it with the princess. I've seen him flinch from her touch, but every time I put a hand on him, he goes so still.

I glance over at him again, watching the firelight paint shadows across the smooth, muscled arc of his shoulders.

Fuck. I need to think about something else. It's foolish to lust after either one of them. They're in love with each *other.*

But I can't help glancing over at the princess. A breeze whips through the ravine, lifting the tendrils of her hair, and she shivers, tucking her hands into her sleeves. The camp has truly fallen into the heaviness of sleep, but I keep my voice low anyway.

"Cold?" I say.

She glances my way sheepishly. "I shouldn't complain. It was far worse in the hut when we kidnapped *you*."

"Yes," I agree. "But here, my magic is not bound." I sketch a sigil and pull a small blaze of fire to my palm, then shift to sit beside her. We're close, yet not touching, and the princess stares at the flame. Firelight flickers off her cheeks, making her eyes sparkle, and I draw a little more power. The warmth of the flame pulses almost in time with my heartbeat, and it only takes a moment before her hands pull free of her sleeves.

"Can I touch it?" she says.

"Carefully." I hold it a bit closer. "It's real fire, Princess. It'll burn whatever it finds."

She lifts a hand, reaching out delicately, like it's a ball of glass. Her hand flickers along the edge, making the fire gutter and spark. But then her eyes light with daring, and I can see she's going to push too far.

I twist my hand to crush out the flame before she burns herself.

I'm too late. She gives a sharp yip.

I swear under my breath and put out a hand. "Here. Let me see."

She offers me her hand, but it looks like she only burned the tip of her middle finger. It's red, a tiny blister already appearing.

I tsk, then hold up her hand to blow on her fingers like she's a child who touched a glass lantern.

She blushes. "I should have listened."

"Probably."

Lady Charlotte shifts in her sleep, and the princess goes still. For a moment, I wonder if I should move back to my spot, but Jory hasn't withdrawn her hand from mine—and in fact, now her fingers have curled a little around my own. I can't quite bring myself to let go.

I drop my voice. "Is Lady Charlotte going to rap my knuckles if she wakes?"

Jory's blush deepens. "We're just sitting."

"She had no idea about Asher's nighttime visits to your quarters?"

Jory shakes her head quickly. "He was very stealthy—and I was never willing to risk it."

I glance at the woman curled in the blankets, and I wonder if Prince

Dane specifically ordered her to make sure I kept my hands off his sister. "She seems very loyal. Is she a friend?"

"No. I . . . I don't think so." The princess frowns, her expression shifting. "None of my ladies have ever been a friend. Usually they're too frightened of Dane to be truly loyal to *me*." She pauses. "But not Charlotte. Maybe . . . maybe she *could* be a friend."

There's a note of longing in her voice that drives home how lonely she must have been in that palace. No wonder she and Asher were so desperate for each other's company.

She nods down at our hands, which are loosely linked together. "Show me again. I'll be careful."

I draw another sphere of fire to dance on my palm, and this time she doesn't reach for it, she just gazes into it. "So much danger, from something so small and beautiful. No wonder the rumors about you are so terrifying."

Terrifying. I crush the fire in my palm again, choking off the energy that keeps the flame lit. "You learned the sigils yourself?"

The princess makes a face. "Yes." She lifts a hand and sketches a *summoning* sigil—or at least an attempt at one. "It's been years," she says sheepishly.

I take hold of her hand, and her skin is so cool against mine. "This way," I say softly. I fold her fingers into the right pattern, then keep hold of her hand to carefully sketch the symbol in the air. A faint shimmer appears, immediately caught and pulled into nothing by the wind.

But the princess gasps. "That's never—*oh*." Her cheeks turn pink. "I used to do this with Father. The sigil is summoning *your* magic."

"Perhaps." I fold her fingers, then do it again. The shimmer reappears, glittering above her fingers before vanishing. "You try, Princess."

She sketches the sigil more accurately this time. For a heartbeat of time, I think nothing will happen, but there, in the space between breaths, the tiniest gleam hangs over her fingertips.

She stares at me, her lips parted. "Was that me . . . or you?"

I'm startled by the wary hope in her expression. She must have been very disappointed when she did not inherit her father's talents.

"Try again," I say. "You surely have magic in your blood, if you're King Theodore's daughter."

"It's never been of any use before." But her expression shifts, turning determined. She sketches another sigil.

This time nothing happens at all, and she frowns.

I reach out and take her hand, then move her fingers through the pattern again. I add a little nudge of my own power, and this time the sigil burns brighter before disappearing altogether. "If you have magic that responds to mine, it's possible yours will manifest," I say.

But as I say it, I know it's a thin hope. Any magic usually makes itself known during adolescence.

She knows it, too, because her frown has deepened.

"We have scholars and historians in Incendar who may know sigils you haven't tried," I offer.

That softens her expression—but only a little. "That's very generous," she says.

"If you find a way to harness your father's power, it benefits us both." I pause, then nod down at her hand. "Do it again."

She scowls like an indignant schoolgirl, but she attempts the sigil again—and this time she manages the faint glow on her own.

Her breath catches again, but then she casts a glance at her opposite hand, still linked with mine. "I'm still touching you," she says ruefully.

"It took me years to gain control, Princess. Do not give up hope yet."

"When it comes to magic, I gave up hope years ago."

I frown, but she reaches down to trace her fingertips across my skin. The motion steals my words, because I feel it right down to my core, heat pooling in my abdomen. I need Sev to wake up so he can come smack me on the side of the head and tell me to focus.

"You're so warm," Jory says.

"I always have been, even before I knew I had a talent for magic." Without warning, a memory strikes me. It's not a bad one, but my childhood wasn't easy, and memories often tug at parts of me I'd rather leave untouched. "When we were young," I say, "Victoria used to curl up beside me and tell me I was warmer than the hearth."

Jory draws back, studying me. "You and your sister are close," she says, and she sounds stunned.

I frown a little and shake my head. "Victoria is . . . we are . . ." My voice trails off, because if there's anything I need to discuss with care, it's my sister. "We were raised separately. I was on the battlefield with our father from a very young age. She was . . . is . . . better suited to life within the palace."

Her eyes search mine. "But you care for her."

"Of course. Very much. She is . . ." My voice trails off.

She is my sister.

The answer should be obvious. A foregone conclusion.

But Jory has a brother who doesn't seem to care for her very much at all.

The realization seems to strike her at the same time, because her mouth turns downward. Another gust of wind swirls through the ravine, and she shivers again.

I automatically shift closer, until we're thigh to thigh, arm to arm. I want to pull her against me, but I'm not sure if she would welcome it.

I consider her comment about losing hope for the magic. I consider her life in the palace and wonder if Prince Dane's cruelty and discouragement is the real reason any power refused to manifest. I know as well as anyone how closely magic and temperament are intertwined.

"I am sorry your brother was not a protector," I say quietly.

She swallows and glances away. "He loved our mother. I think he resented her for having another child to dote on. And then she was killed, and he resented me even more." She pauses, and her voice goes very soft. "I sometimes wonder if he punished Asher so severely as a means to punish *me*. I survived. She didn't."

"You truly believe Asher had no knowledge of his mother's involvement in the attack?"

She shivers, and this time I don't think it has anything to do with the cold. "I do. Sometimes I wonder if that's even true—if his mother ever had any real involvement. There was no evidence, and my mother certainly couldn't speak to her guilt. At the time, I was too young to question it, but as I've grown older, I sometimes think that perhaps

Lady Clara was executed to give the people a clear signal that justice had been swift and the royal family was safe—not that a crime was actually solved."

I twist that up with everything else I've learned since coming to Astranza. More deception? Or simply rulers making a careful choice to prevent civil unrest?

I glance at Asher. His form is still, his breathing slow and even, but I'm not entirely sure he's asleep. He could be listening to every word she says.

Jory is studying me carefully. "Dane wouldn't like me saying these things."

I shrug. "It's no secret that rulers often feed lies to their people."

"Truly?" Her eyes lock on mine, full of intrigue. "What do *you* lie about, Your Majesty?"

Everything.

But I can hardly say that. It's not even true—though some days it feels like it is.

The princess flushes and glances away before I say anything at all. "Forgive me. I shouldn't be so bold. It's the whiskey, I'm sure."

"I like you bold," I say, and I mean it. I find it maddening that Dane kept her locked in the palace for so long. I doubt our alliance negotiations would have taken half as long if she'd been part of them. I look over and smile. "I should see if Sev has another bottle."

She gasps in feigned outrage, then turns to swat me on the arm, but I block the motion, batting her hand away lightly.

It's an automatic response, the way I'd react if Sev or one of the others did it, but her eyebrows go up as if I've surprised her—as if it's a *challenge*.

Her gaze turns a little rueful, and she swats at me again—so I deflect a little harder. The third time, she throws some real strength into it, so I do the same. It's still playful, but her breath is a little more quick, her gaze flickering with uncertainty. I can't tell if she's shocked—or eager.

Maybe both.

"You want to tussle?" I say.

"No, I do not want to *tussle*."

But she does. I can hear it in her voice.

"Forgive me," I say. "You seemed curious."

"I assure you, I am not."

She is, though. I can tell. She doesn't look half as outraged as she sounds. Instead, she looks like she wants to do more than tussle. Her cheeks are pink, and I'm thinking of the way she dressed as a maid in defiance of her brother—or the way she helped Asher force me out of the palace.

I wonder how often she has to swallow her emotions to play a role.

I wonder if she's doing it *now*.

The night wind whips across the camp, making the fire snap and gutter. When I look over, she's biting at her lip.

I remember what Asher said to her, before she drank the whiskey.

"Dane," I say softly, "would have a *fit*."

She inhales sharply, and her head whips around to face me. For an instant, I think I've pushed too far—or maybe I've completely misjudged.

But then I realize that she's balled up a fist, and she's swinging for my face.

I block, throwing her arm wide, but she's quick and she has her other fist ready. When I block twice, she changes tactics, grappling for my face. Somewhere along the line, she figured out how to be ruthless with her thumbs, because there's a moment where it's unclear if she's trying to gouge out my eyes or my windpipe.

At first, she's smiling, her efforts tentative, but I match her strength and I don't yield. It doesn't take long for her to realize that I'm not going to be like whatever guard or soldier has been assigned to give her a few sessions of "training." Hell, she's probably been taught by someone who's been ordered to let her win without much effort. Someone who's never let her feel the power of a true victory, or the physical release of a real fight.

I feel the moment when our tussling shifts, when she throws her heart—or maybe her rage—into it. Her swings become more sharp, her attacks more pointed. We've been mostly silent, mindful of the sleeping soldiers surrounding the fire, but now we're grappling with some force, and the sound of our breathing is heavy between us. At some point, her nails dig into the skin of my neck, and she's so determined that I suddenly can't tell if she's enjoying this or if she hates me for suggesting it.

When I shove her off, she scowls and comes at me full force. This time, I let her tackle me, and we go skidding backward into the dirt. When we roll, she ends up straddling me, and I want to ask what happened to the princess who declared I was being *inappropriate* a day ago. Her thighs press into my waist, and I immediately forget that we're tussling at all. But her expression is all battle now, and I'm impressed at her ferocity. Luckily I have enough training to fend off her attacks. When she tries to grab a handful of dirt to throw in my face, I catch her wrist, flip her onto her back, and pin her.

It leaves me on top of her, pressing her forearms into the dirt. Her eyes are a bit wild, and she scrabbles for purchase, breathing hard.

"Easy," I say softly. "We're not *really* fighting, Princess."

She stares up at me. Her cheeks are flushed, her hair in sweat-damp tendrils around her face. Her chest is heaving under mine.

"Oh," she says between breaths. "Oh. Forgive me."

"*Forgive* you?" I brush a thumb over the inside of her wrist, then let go, bracing my hands in the dirt. "That was impressive."

I expect her to roll away, but she reaches for my throat. Her thumbs trace over my skin where her nails dug in. "Did I do this?"

Every stroke of her touch is impossible to ignore. "Better there than my eyes," I say.

Her blush deepens, and her fingers are so soft on my throat. "I've never fought with anyone like that before," she says.

"I'll fight with you anytime you like."

Her eyes flare a little in surprise, but that curiosity hasn't dimmed. Without warning, she swings for my face, and I barely catch her wrist before she makes contact.

"Like right now?" she says. She smiles, and somehow it feels like a reward.

I laugh a little, under my breath. She's so different from Asher, and I find it fascinating, especially considering their connection. He's full of violence and rage, and it's completely unbound. Every time he settles under my touch, it's like taming a wolf.

The princess is the opposite. This feels like freeing a caged falcon and hoping it returns to your hand.

Her wrist is still in my grip, but I've loosened my hold, so her fingers drift along my chin. It forces me still, especially when her eyes narrow a little, her fingers tracing through the beard growth as if it's captivating.

I wonder if she's ever touched a man like this. The thought is striking, especially because her eyes have gone dark, her breathing quickening. I'm suddenly very aware of the fact that her body is caged beneath me, that I could shift my weight a few inches and this would be an entirely different kind of tussling.

As soon as I have the thought, I'm as hard as a rock.

Her breath catches, and we're pressed together so tightly that I'm sure she can feel it. But the instant I begin to pull away, she grabs hold of my tunic, holding me in place.

I have to remind myself of her innocence. This is not a seduction. This is not a courtier angling for political sway, and it's not a soldier looking to stay warm for a few hours. We're under the stars, surrounded by my men. She's a *princess*, destined for an alliance. She deserves a slow and careful courtship, not impassioned rutting in a ravine.

But her eyes are wide and trusting, her lips parted slightly, her fingers exploring my jaw now that I've gone still. A strain has built in my shoulders from the effort of holding myself above her, but it would take a bolt from an arrow to convince me to move.

When her thumb runs along the ridge of my lower lip, my eyes fall closed, and I inhale a ragged breath. Her hips shift beneath me, and it's almost my undoing, especially when she gasps.

I put a hand to her waist, holding her in place. "Princess . . ."

But instead of going still, she arches a little under my touch, her body moving against mine. I shift my grip to pin her there, and she gasps—and then we scuffle. Her chest swells with each breath, and her eyes have lit with challenge again. Her fist is still clenching the front of my tunic, but this time it's all eagerness, and not entirely about fighting at all.

It would take almost nothing for my hand to shift, for my fingertips to find the sensitive bud of her nipple. Then scuffling turns to grappling, and the choice is made for me. My thumb slides along the warm curve of her breast, and I drop my weight to pin her again. Her lips part farther, this little gasp even sweeter than the first. When she arches into me again, her breast fills my hand. I thrust against her without meaning to, and desire sparks in her eyes.

But there's a flicker of uncertainty hiding there, too.

That reminds me to tread carefully. Her palm is still against my face, so I turn my head to kiss her hand. Then her wrist. Her fingers drift along my ear, brushing through my hair.

"I thought you didn't want to tussle," I murmur.

"I want . . ." But then her eyes flick left, and she inhales sharply. "Asher."

I freeze in place, then cast a glance in his direction, too. He's no longer facing the fire, but he's still lying on his stomach, propped on his elbows. His expression is in shadow, unreadable.

I have no idea how much he saw or what he thinks is happening, but I'm rather clearly pinning her to the ground—and I have been for a while.

"Ky," she says swiftly. I can't quite figure out the note in her voice, whether it's guilt or regret or simply shock. "Let me up."

I do. The princess shifts to sitting, but her cheeks are still red. Mine aren't. Hostility sizzles in in the air, and I wonder if Asher is going to make me finish that fight he tried to start earlier.

But he doesn't move. "Did he hurt you?" he says softly.

She looks up. "Asher. We weren't—it wasn't—"

"I know what it was," he says, and his eyes flick to me. His words, however, are for her. "Did he *hurt* you?"

"No."

"Did he force you?"

"No!" The color in her cheeks deepens. "Asher, that is not what we were—"

"Do I need to stab him for any reason?" He still hasn't looked away from me, and his gaze is so piercing, even in the shadows. "The rest of them are asleep, so it's the perfect time."

Bleeding skies. I can't tell if this is jealousy or anger or just plain belligerence, and I'm pretty sure he can't either. But I've begun to learn that all of Asher's posturing is really just a mask to hide a man who's terrified of losing the few things he's been able to hold dear.

He's still propped on his elbows, glaring up at me, so I roll onto my knees until we're close. Before I can think better of it, I touch a hand to his chin, letting my thumb drift right below his lip.

"Your princess is safe," I say softly.

He's stopped breathing, probably the instant I touched him. His eyes are glittering in the moonlight. When his gaze shifts, I realize the princess has rolled to her knees beside me.

She touches a finger to his chin beside mine. "I'm safe," she says softly.

His throat jerks as he swallows. But then he turns away, pulling free of both of us.

"Fine," he says, and his voice is rough. "You win." He shifts on his bedroll, turning to face the fire again.

The princess studies him for a moment, but she frowns. She tucks the loose hair behind her ear and looks at me. "It's late," she whispers. "We should sleep. I know you wish to depart at dawn."

"I do," I say.

She bites her lip and nods, then retreats to her own bedroll by Lady Charlotte.

Before she lies down, however, she looks over. "Dane really would have a fit," she says.

It makes me grin. "I look forward to the next time, then."

She smiles in return, and the heavy organ in my chest feels lighter than it has in days. Weeks. *Months.*

But then I glance toward Garrett, sitting at the opening of the ravine, watching for any sign of trouble. I remember why we're camping here at *all*, and the weight of tense worry crashes into my chest again.

Garrett must sense my focus, because he turns in my direction, then signals a query. *All well?*

I nod, then shift onto my own bedroll between Asher and Sev.

Asher is facing me, but his eyes are closed, and his arms are curled in tight to his bare upper body. Every muscle is bunched, and there's enough fire for me to see gooseflesh all over his skin.

Fine. You win.

I don't want to touch him again, because I know it makes him anxious, despite how badly he seems to want it. When I speak, I keep my voice soft. "Asher."

His eyes flick open, finding mine in the darkness. Dark and piercing, just as before.

"We are not at odds," I say quietly. "This is not a competition."

"I know," he says. "Like I said, you've already won her affection."

Maybe—but it doesn't feel like something I've *won*. I think of the slow drag of her fingers through the scruff on my chin, the way it was almost inquisitive. It stirs something inside me—and I'm surprised to realize it's not different from the way I felt about doing the same thing to *him*.

I hold his gaze. "That does not mean I'm stealing it away from you."

He says nothing to that. Another gust of wind whips through the ravine, and he bites back a shiver. I watch him try to tuck his arms closer.

"You're cold," I say. "Move closer if you like."

His mouth forms a line. He says nothing and turns back to the fire.

"Or not," I say. I sigh, adjust my blankets, and rest my head on my arm. I don't think I'll sleep, but it's been too many long days and nights in succession. Exhaustion eventually claims my thoughts.

Sometime later, I wake, and I realize that Asher's face is all but pressed against my arm. The moon is still high, and the air is still cold. I lie there and wait to remember whatever nightmare woke me. I wait for visions of my soldiers dying, Draeg soldiers ripping them limb from limb. Bodies strewn on a battlefield, my own soldiers responding with equally vicious violence.

But for the first time in a while, I can't remember a single dream. No blood, no death, no soldiers being torn apart while I watch, helpless. I'm warm and safe, sleep already calling me back.

Especially since Asher is quiet and still, his bare arms tucked between us, his wounded body stretched out alongside my own.

Chapter Twenty-Five
THE ASSASSIN

When we ride out, the air is sharp and I'm still sore. This much riding is often reserved for the nobility or the cavalry, and I'm neither. If there's any spot of relief, the burn on my shoulder has mostly stopped weeping, and new scabs have begun to form. It makes the weight of the leather armor less bothersome. I'd rather not wear it at *all*, because it's heavy enough to slow me down in a fight, but the soldiers' angry glares and muttered comments seem to have shifted into grudging acceptance. I'll strap leather to my body if it makes them keep their distance.

But maybe *I'm* the one keeping my distance. They're all clearly less worried about an attack now that we're in Incendar, so we're riding in more of a pack today, and everyone seems to have fallen into similar pairings as last night. Nikko and Roman are at the front, followed by the king and his captain, Jory and Charlotte, and finally Garrett and Callum.

And then me.

In a way, I don't mind. I'm used to being alone—and I'm glad I'm not tethered to anyone anymore. My horse drifts along behind them, well trained to follow a formation. We've been riding through dried grass and sparse vegetation for hours. Narrow ravines are frequent, but so are open fields of . . . *nothing*. I've heard rumors of the poor crops in Incendar, and I suppose I'm seeing the proof. From time to time, the air seems thick with woodsmoke, but then the wind will shift and I'll think I imagined it. We haven't come close to a single flame since we buried our campfire. When we pass villages and settlements, they're always at a distance—but maybe that's on purpose. I don't ask, because I don't care. No one is looking to me to navigate. Not even the horse. I suspect I could fall asleep and this army steed would continue plodding along until we stopped.

It's tempting. Being awake is giving me too much time to think.

My thoughts are full of the princess—and the memory of the king on top of her.

I wasn't trying to stare. I wasn't even trying to spy. But they'd gone quiet for a little too long, and then I heard the rough breaths and scuffling. I remembered how frightened she'd been in her chambers.

When I looked, he was pinning her to the ground, but Jory did not look afraid. Her hand was on his face, and there was no disguising the flicker of desire on his. There was no disguising the desire on *hers*. She seemed flushed and eager from their "fight," completely contrary to the prim and proper princess I know from the palace. Maybe it *started* as sparring, but it certainly wasn't going to end that way.

For one blinding second, they didn't see me, and I had an opportunity to look away. To go to sleep. To pretend I'd seen nothing. I've lived in a dozen different brothels, so I'm no stranger to any level of intimacy happening right beside me.

But then she saw me, and so did the king. I was caught, my eyes wide open.

Fine, I said to him. *You win.*

He caught my chin. *We are not at odds. This is not a competition.*

Did he mean that as a warning? A statement that he's the king, so there's no competition to be had?

Or did he mean it in another way? Some way I can't seem to figure out?

It shouldn't matter. I shouldn't even be here. She's sealing an alliance. If anything, I should be happy that they're finding some kind of accord. I have no part in this.

Then again, I promised Jory I would look out for her. Despite everything that happened in the throne room with the Guildmaster, despite everything he *denied*, Hunters came after us anyway. I have no doubt more will follow us into Incendar, either to kill him, or to kill her. I just can't figure out *why*.

Could it have anything to do with King Theodore's illness?

I can't make that work out either. That's the whole reason they need Maddox Kyronan.

Ky.

I haven't found the courage to call him that again—despite the fact that I've now spent two nights sleeping right beside him. This morning, I woke before the sun, my body lying flush against his, my cheek pressed against his bicep. He was so warm that I didn't want to move.

I don't know what's wrong with me. Normally I hate sleeping near anyone at all. And when people *touch* me, I usually want to stab them through the arm. But the king barely has to say my name or touch his fingers to my skin, and I'm no longer a trained killer, I'm a fucking lapdog. I'm never like that with anyone but Jory.

I thought maybe he was having another nightmare, but he was warm and still, his breathing soft between us. I moved away anyway. I'm not chained to his arm anymore, and I didn't want his soldiers to find me there. Hell, I touched Jory's face and one of them tried to kill me. I have no idea how they'd react if they saw me curled up against their king.

I have no idea how *Jory* would react.

Or maybe I do. Her fingertips were so cool against my chin, right beside his. Like that moment in the tavern, the touch of their hands at the same time stirred up my insides and filled my veins with honey.

Ah, Jory. I rub at my eyes. I need to stop thinking about this.

"Hey," Callum says. "Stripes."

I jerk my hand down. He and Garrett are both looking back at me. I can't decide if they're calling me that to be annoying or if they've just decided it's going to be my nickname.

I also can't decide if I care.

"What?" I haven't talked to anyone in hours, so my voice comes out rough and wary.

They exchange a glance that might mean mischief—or it might mean trouble. I defeated Nikko last night, but these are the two I really need to watch out for. Of Ky's soldiers, they're the biggest, the most aggressive, clearly the brute force of this small team. There's also a *sharpness* to them that warns me to tread carefully. It's like the way Garrett flipped me into the snow when I was choking him with the chain. The move could've broken his neck, but he went for it anyway.

"Stop following us like a ghost," says Garrett.

"Yeah," says Callum. "Ride up here."

This isn't an invitation. It's a challenge.

Fuck it. I touch my heels to the horse's sides, and the animal jogs up to ride abreast with the two of them. Just ahead, Jory glances back, and then the king, but I don't need them to hold my hand. I ignore them both.

Callum is closest to me, and when he looks over, blond hair falls into his eyes. Like the others, he's practically dripping with weapons—more than I wore as an assassin. I suppose it makes sense, since they apparently ride into war, and I . . . don't. A long dagger is strapped to his thigh, and I know a sword is on his left hip. I remember that their bracers cover an array of knives buckled to their forearms, and there are likely more weapons tucked under their greaves.

I still have nothing.

"How did you learn to fight like that?" Callum says to me.

The question sounds genuine, which takes me by surprise—and that's probably what makes me answer.

"Some of it was the Hunter's Guild," I say. "One of the first lessons is how to kill someone before they have a chance to fight back." I shrug. "But some of it was the slavers." I gesture to my face. "After I earned a few lines, I'd sometimes get sold into the fighting rings. I'm not big, but I'm pretty fast. They only broke a few ribs before I learned how to get out of the way."

My voice is flat, because I don't think much of this—I honestly preferred the fighting rings to the brothels—but Jory whips her head around, horrified. *"Asher."*

I look back at her. "You said you wanted the truth."

She clamps her mouth shut.

Garrett is giving me a more appraising look. "We have fighting rings here, too," he says. "It's a good way to make some coin if you've got a bit of skill."

Ahead, the captain snorts. "And if you're not afraid to lose a few teeth," he calls back.

Callum gives me a similar once-over, and then his eyebrows go up. He hits Garrett in the arm. "Gar. We should take him to the arena at Mossnum. Can you imagine the side bets?"

Garrett considers, then chuckles darkly. "No one would see it coming."

Jory is still looking back, but her gaze turns fierce. "Are you talking about Asher? You will not force him to *fight*—"

"Who said anything about force?" says Callum. He turns to look at me again. "It's good silver, if you've got the mettle for it."

At that, the king glances back. "Mossnum? That arena runs a rough crowd."

Callum scoffs, and Garrett's eyes flick skyward. "Just who does he think makes it rough?" he mutters.

"What was that?" Ky calls.

Callum raises his voice. "We were just saying you're an amazing leader."

The king gives an aggrieved sigh and turns to face forward.

Callum shrugs and adds, "Besides, Stripes wouldn't have to worry. We'd look out for him." He claps me on the shoulder. "He could probably earn enough to—oh. Shit. Sorry."

If he tried to punch me, I could've blocked, but I wasn't prepared for friendly camaraderie. But now I'm gripping the horse's mane, breathing through my teeth. My vision has gone spotty. For the first time, I'm somewhat grateful for the armor, because if he'd smacked me directly on the brand, it might have knocked me off the horse. It takes a full minute before I can straighten.

The worst part is that I genuinely don't think that was intentional.

"Asher," says Jory, and her voice is very soft.

"It's fine," I say roughly. I taste blood in my mouth, and I wonder if I've bitten my tongue. "I'm fine."

They're all completely silent for the longest moment, and I just want them to stop looking at me.

Then Garrett glances over. "If you think that's bad, just wait until he accidentally punches you in the balls," he says dryly.

"That was *one time*, Gar—"

Captain Zale whistles through his teeth, and they shut up.

"*Thank you*, Captain," Lady Charlotte says primly. But Jory giggles.

Callum looks at me again. "So how about it?"

I still can't quite make sense of this. Maybe he really did knock me off the horse. "How about . . . what?"

He glances at Garrett and then back at me. "We'll have a few days' leave in a week or so. Provided no one from Astranza shows up to kill you all, do you want to go earn a bag full of silver?"

I stare back at him. Last night, they all wanted to kill me. Two days ago, I wanted to kill *them*. Someone from Astranza presumably wants to kill *all* of us. But now Ky's men want . . . Well, I'm not sure, exactly. This must be like the slavers—they see me as a means to earn a little extra silver.

But there's a tiny phrase that Callum said. *We'd look out for him.*

My heart thumps hard against my ribs.

Roman looks back. "Did he say yes?" he calls from the front of the line. "Because I'm in. I'd pay to see that."

"You're all insane," says the captain. "You couldn't pay me to *go* to Mossnum."

"He hasn't said anything yet," says Callum.

"Because you broke him," says Garrett.

"Would you shut the fuck up—"

The captain whistles at them again.

Jory is looking back, studying me, her expression bemused. Honestly, I'm sure mine is the same. Do I want to go fight with random strangers I've never met in some city I've never seen?

Probably not.

But Callum is looking at me again, waiting for an answer. I think a lot of them are waiting for an answer, including the princess.

And in that moment, I'm struck by the fact that I've been given a choice—a *true* choice, for the first time since I can remember. No chains, no threats, no orders, no assignments.

The king is looking back now, and I realize he's curious about my response, too. They might be violent and vicious, but there's something different about the people here—or at least his soldiers. Something very honest, very *real*, that I crave. It's the exact way the king was able to convince me to release him.

There are no slavers in Incendar.

My chest has grown a bit tight, and I have to shake it off. I cast my gaze forward and shrug, keeping my voice nonchalant.

"Sure," I say to Callum. "If we survive that long, I suppose it could be fun."

He whoops. "Man, I bet we'll need to rent a wagon for all the silver you'll take in."

That makes me smile. "You've only seen me fight once. You might need to rent a wagon to bring back my body."

"Please." He starts rattling off on his fingers. "You blew through the king. Then Nikko. Then you—"

"He did not *blow through me*," Ky snaps. "That was—"

"Right, right," Callum calls. "You were 'disarmed.'" He flicks his eyes skyward. "I forgot."

That startles a laugh out of me—and I can't remember the last time that happened.

"You were chained to Ky, and you killed those assassins." Callum jerks a thumb at his friend. "And Gar won't even tell me how you did that to his neck."

"It was the chain," I say.

Garrett heaves a sigh. "Here we go."

Callum's eyes light up. "The *chain*?" He looks at the other soldier, and he gives him a wolfish smile. His voice turns sultry. "Did you like it?"

"Not a whole lot, no."

Lady Charlotte whips around. "Gentlemen, *please*."

The soldiers go completely silent, but their eyes are still sparking with devilry.

Jory is smiling, though, glancing between them, and her cheeks turn faintly pink. I'm not sure what about the expression is so unfamiliar, until I realize that she looks *happy*—and that feels so rare. We've had so many secret moments, but it's been so long since we were together, like this, with wind and sky and easy companionship around us. I don't know if the soldiers feel it, or if they'd even understand it. But I do. In my heart, I feel her emotion as strongly as I feel my own.

For all our differences, Jory and I have always had one thing in common: our aloneness. Our solitude. She was my only friend, as I was hers. When she demanded truths from me, I thought that might have erased all of it. I thought I might have *lost* all of it.

But to my surprise, she *doesn't* seem to judge me for it—and it's clear that the king doesn't. Somehow, they each have the talent to wake something inside of me, a flame I thought I smothered years ago. When I was with Jory, I knew how to keep my distance. I knew how to lock everything away.

Out here, with the two of them, that somehow feels impossible. I'm still raw. Bare.

But maybe it's like the brand. Maybe it needs to breathe so it can begin to heal.

BY MIDDAY, THE terrain begins to change, long valleys of dried grass giving way to steep hills lined with granite outcroppings. In some spots, the trail is so narrow that we have to ride single file, and at one point, I think we'll need to dismount and lead the horses through. But these Incendrian horses must be used to the footing, because they step carefully, and we ride on.

It makes travel slow, however, and I can't escape the prickle on my neck that reminds me *someone* is on our trail. We've gone more than a day without any sign of more Hunters, however, and the tense anticipation among the soldiers seems to be melting away. As we descend into yet another valley, I wonder how far we are from the king's palace in Lastalorre. It would probably be easier for an assassin to attack while we're traveling, before we reach a location thick with guards and servants. Then again, I consider how I would approach this assignment. I'm not sure I'd want to risk confronting six soldiers out in the open. A skilled archer could do it from a distance, but we're all in armor, making that tricky. One failed shot would give a Hunter away.

When we stop at the base of the valley to water the horses, the scent of distant smoke is stronger. I wonder if Incendar always smells like this, or if it's some effect of the king's magic baked into the very earth. I lift my gaze to scan the sunlit hills surrounding us. There are times when I can see for miles, but sometimes in these valleys, the line of sight is interrupted by the crest of the next hill. A Hunter would probably struggle to find cover out here, since we all—

"What are you doing?"

The king's voice interrupts my thoughts, and I blink in the sunlight. I've hardly spoken to him since we woke, and my thoughts are still tangled up in the space between finding him on top of Jory—and finding myself curled up against him.

Every time I earn his attention, it sends little sparks through my veins, and I'm still not sure what to do with it. I shrug and keep my focus on the terrain. "Thinking about how I'd kill you," I say.

He doesn't take the bait—though I'm beginning to think he never does. He follows my gaze to the hills surrounding us. "How would you?"

"We're too exposed—but a Hunter would be, too. If it were me, I'd wait for a city, or nightfall, or both. Somewhere I could make an attack without being seen, and without triggering a response."

"They didn't attack last night."

"You posted a sentry—and you fell asleep beside the fire. You weren't alone." I don't mean that the way it sounds, and I have to look away again before warmth crawls up my neck. "There was no easy escape route from the ravine, and anyone following will know we defeated the last Hunters. It would've been a risk to attack there."

He considers this. "We'll be in Lastalorre before dusk."

I offer half a shrug. "It's easy to hide in a city. Out here, a Hunter wouldn't have many options. I think the greater risk would be in Lastalorre."

Roman has overheard our conversation, and he leads his horse over. "What are the other options?"

Before I can answer, a sharp sound pierces the air from the east. We freeze.

Jory looks over, her eyes a little wide. "Was that a scream?"

Just as she says it, the sound echoes again. Definitely a scream.

"Mount up," says Ky. "We'll check it out."

But I grab his arm before he can turn for the horse. "There *was* another option."

He looks back at me, and as always, I'm startled by the intensity of his gaze, the way he seems to truly *see* me.

"Tell me," he says.

That scream sounds again, and I realize the scent of smoke is even stronger. I look back at him. "A trap."

Chapter Twenty-Six
THE PRINCESS

The soldiers hold a different formation as we ride up and out of the valley. I was ready to go galloping over the hill when I heard the scream, but it's clear that Ky and his men are wary after Asher mentioned a trap. I probably should be, too, but I heard the desperation in that cry. The soldiers hold the pace at a walk, with Charlotte and me in the middle of the group. Ky is to my left, and Asher is to our right. Only the captain has ridden ahead, and he's waiting at the crest of the hill—likely for some invisible signal from the king.

To the east, smoke curls into the sky, thick and black. When I inhale, I can taste it.

"What's in that direction?" I say, keeping my voice low, though we're still not over the hill.

"Not much," says Ky. "We're still a good ways from the sea, and you've seen the state of my grazing lands."

Nikko looks back. "There are usually some Suross settlements out this way," he says in his rough voice.

Callum nods. "I've led patrols out here. There aren't many, but I've seen them, too."

"What are Suross settlements?" I say.

"Incendar has a few traveling bands of nomads," Ky says. "A hundred years ago, they lived in the mountains, but as more and more people mined for iron, they dispersed into the hills." He pauses. "My father used to say they were a blight on Incendar, because they refused to fight in the war." He shrugs a little. "But I can't use soldiers who don't want to be there. There aren't many of them. They don't cause too much trouble, so I leave them alone."

Callum scoffs. "They're a little crazy."

"And they hate outsiders," says Nikko.

"They're still my people," says Ky—but he sighs.

We've drawn closer to the crest of the hill, and he lifts a hand to signal to Captain Zale. Another scream peals over the mountain, and it tugs at my heart. The pain in the sound is piercing.

And then I realize why: it reminds me of the moment my mother died.

"It doesn't matter who they hate," I say. "Someone clearly needs help."

"Or someone is *pretending* to need help," says Asher.

I grit my teeth and nudge my heels into my horse's ribs anyway.

Ky grabs my horse's rein before the animal can take off. I glare at him and try to yank the rein free while the horse prances underneath me.

His expression is resolute, his grip tight. "We are not riding heedless into danger, Princess."

Asher glances between us, but he says nothing. Up ahead, Captain Zale rides to the top of the hill and surveys the valley below. After a moment, his horse whirls, and he jogs down to us.

"It's a small Suross encampment," he says. "Two of their huts are on fire." He pauses, and I can feel the weight of unspoken communication between the king and his captain. "It's spreading. They're pulling buckets from the stream."

That scream won't stop echoing in my head, and I can't tell if I've heard it again or if my thoughts just won't let it go. My heart pounds hard against my ribs, and I try to jerk my rein free again. "Then we should *help*." When Ky's grip doesn't give, I snap, "You just said they're your people! You can stop the fire!"

He ignores me, his hard gaze shifting to Asher. "Draeg forces often try to lure me out by torturing my people with fire. Would your Hunters know to do the same?"

The words send a chill through me, but Asher lifts one shoulder in a shrug. "I've never hurt someone else to get at a mark," he says. "But that doesn't mean another Hunter wouldn't."

I grit my teeth. "If you won't help, *I* will."

"I didn't say I wouldn't help them, Princess." Ky looks back at Captain Zale. "Did you have a clear sight line?"

He nods. "The whole valley. They seemed panicked. It doesn't feel like a trap."

Ky gives a decisive nod. "Nikko. Hold the crest. Cal, keep the perimeter. We'll check it out." He finally looks back at me. "*Stay here.*" His eyes shift to Charlotte. "Both of you."

She gives a dutiful nod. "Yes, Your Majesty."

But I glare back at him. "I'll stay on the crest of the hill with Nikko."

He runs a hand across his jaw. "Fine. Asher—"

"I can help, too." He says this a little bitterly, like he expects to be told to remain at the crest with me and Charlotte. But Ky just nods, whirls his horse, and leads his soldiers away.

The billows of dark smoke are getting thicker, clouding the sky. From the crest of the hill, the damage is worse than I expected. The straw roofs of two mud huts are entirely ablaze, but the fire has spread to the dry grass, blazing red flame crawling through the brush like something alive. As I watch, a gust of wind blows sparks onto a third hut, the straw catching immediately. Two trees have also caught, fire climbing the trunks, reaching for the dry branches. Ky was right that the settlement seems small. Only a dozen people can be seen running with buckets to the stream, sloshing half out on their way back to try to attack the fires.

But then my eyes fall on the woman who's screaming, because she stumbles away from a burning hut, where she's trapped by a field of fire. She wasn't visible a minute ago, so it's possible Ky and his men haven't even seen her. Her circle of safety is quickly dwindling, and I watch as the king and the others reach the bottom of the hill. I wait for Ky to sketch the sigils that will bring all of this fire under control, so she can run to safety.

But . . . he doesn't.

He's calling orders to his men, but he's too far for me to hear the words clearly. The soldiers have leapt off their horses, and they start going for buckets, too. I look to Nikko, my heart suddenly in my throat. "Why isn't he stopping the fire?" I demand. "Why isn't he using his magic?"

Nikko frowns a little, like I've asked an unexpected question. "His magic *summons* fire," he says in that rough-quiet voice. "He cannot stop it."

Charlotte gasps, and my breath stops in my chest as those words sink in. I remember the king summoning a sphere of fire to hover above his palm.

It's real fire, Princess. It'll burn whatever it finds.

The world tilts a little. I thought he'd ride down and stop the flames. I thought he and his soldiers would be safe from harm. That he would swiftly rescue these settlers and this would be an easy solution.

Another gust of cold wind sweeps down through the valley, blowing sparks and flames along the dry grass. I blink, and suddenly there's twice as much as there was before, blowing toward the people gathering buckets. The soldiers are shouting, people scrambling to avoid the flames.

That trapped woman screams again. The wind has blown flame onto her dress, and she's panicked, beating her skirts against the ground. Her circle of safety has shrunk to half the size. She backs toward the hut, but that's no better. Flaming bits of straw are falling from the roof.

Another woman is on the other side of the burning grass, and it sounds like she's shouting to the trapped one. She looks ready to stride right into the flames.

I look toward the king and his soldiers, who are on the other side, heading toward the stream.

"Oh," I whisper. "Oh no." Then I raise my voice. "Ky!" I shout. "Ky, there's a woman—"

But I break off. He can't hear me. The shouts are too loud, and I'm too high.

That woman disappears from view again.

I think of my mother, of the way Lady Clara screamed. I think of Asher, racing to help the king and his men.

My heart is a caged bird, wildly flinging itself against the bars.

Suddenly I'm not thinking at all. Not anymore. I've drawn up my reins and dug my heels into the horse's sides. Nikko and Charlotte shout behind me, but I barely hear their words. I'm already flying down the hill.

THE HEAT FROM the flames hits me like a wall, making my eyes burn and the air hard to breathe. This army steed must be used to confronting fields of fire, because my horse is bold and unflinching, even when another gust of wind sends sparks and flaming bits of debris in our direction. A glowing ember lands on my arm, and I shriek and smack it away.

It's possible I've been too bold.

Then I realize Charlotte has followed me, her horse cantering through the flaming grass at my side, her expression marked with determination.

She's so brave—and she really doesn't have to be. I think of that moment Ky asked if she could be a friend.

Yes, I think. *She definitely will be.*

I've lost track of Asher, but I spot Ky among the scrambling people, and I aim the horse right for him. One of the other soldiers gives a shout of warning, and the king whirls in surprise. I haul on the reins to bring the animal to a sliding stop, but I'm already leaping out of the saddle. Charlotte is half a second behind me, breathless and winded, her horse fighting her grip on the reins.

The king catches me before my feet even hit the ground, his strong hands secure on my waist. His eyes are full of concern, but his expression looks like thunder. "Princess, I said—"

"There's a woman," I gasp, breathless. "You didn't see her. She's trapped—"

"Where?"

I point. "There! Behind the—" The wind changes, and I get a mouthful of smoke. My words break off and I cough hard.

The king takes stock of me quickly, then looks to my lady. "Charlotte," he says sharply, his voice full of command. "Help them. Join the line." He points at his soldiers, who are already pulling buckets from the stream, but his eyes return to mine. "Princess. Show me."

I cough again, then grab his arm and pull, and he follows me around the hut. The woman has even less space now. She's younger than I thought, probably not more than thirteen or fourteen. She's sobbing, pressed up against the wall of the building, sparks raining around her from the roof. Her friend has made it to her side, but the edges of her skirts are singed and dark with soot. Both their faces are bright red and awash with sweat, their clothes damp and flecked with charred spots.

"Please," I say to Ky, my voice cracking with panic. "Please help them."

He sketches a sigil, and it pulls a patch of fire right off the ground, leaving scorched, dry grass in its wake. I gasp. "But you—I thought—"

"Walk at my back, Princess," he says, cutting me off. I don't understand how his voice can be so cool and commanding while everything inside me feels as hot and agitated as the flames. "But you must stay close."

As he says the words, fire surges into the area he just cleared. He crushes the flame from his palm and summons more from the ground, opening another path. As soon as we step into it, fire begins to crowd into the space he cleared.

Stay close. Got it.

My breathing roars in my ears as he begins to walk. Flames are already beginning to swoop into the space, so I match my footsteps to his. Step by step, he summons a handful of fire, then crushes it away—but there's always more ready to burn and replace what he's taken. It's like trying to watch someone empty the ocean with a bucket.

A desperate thought occurs to me. When I sat with him and practiced a sigil, the air glowed for a moment. Can I do that again? Can I *help*?

I touch a hand to his back, then move my fingers in the pattern he practiced. As before, a faint glow appears in the air, but nothing more.

But it's *something*. I try again, and this time the sigil glows brighter, hovering in the air. The tiniest lick of flame flares just at the edge, and I gasp.

Ky glances back over his shoulder. "No!" he says, his tone sharp with warning.

He sounds so severe that I almost flinch back—before I realize I'm stepping into rejuvenated flames.

Ky catches my arm before I can. Sweat coats his forehead, too. "You're unpracticed," he says. "You could *hurt* more than you could help."

That's sobering, and I curl my hand into a fist, then nod. He turns back, swiping another handful of fire so we can proceed. Sweat slicks my back by the time we reach the girls. The first has slid down to sit against the hut, and her eyes are heavy lidded. Thick smoke surrounds us, making it hard to breathe, and it's grown difficult to see in the hazy shadows. A spark lands on the girl's skirt again, but this time she doesn't move to do anything about it.

"Ky!" I say sharply, but he's already moving his hand, drawing the tiny spark away.

The other girl looks up at us through the scorching flames, and she cringes back.

They hate outsiders.

"It's all right," I say to her. "We're going to help you."

Ky reaches down to pick up the girl on the ground, scooping her into his arms. "Keep her close, Princess."

The other girl is sobbing, but I pull her close to me, then put a hand on the leather of his armor again. When my hand brushes against a rivet in his armor, it burns my palm. We move through the flames as slowly as we began, fire reaching for us with every step. The girl's breath hitches against me, but I tug her close, keeping her between me and the king.

"You'll be all right," I murmur. "You'll be all right."

As I say the words, I really don't know if any of us will be all right. The air has grown so thick with smoke, and I can't remember the last time I took a deep breath. When I blink, I see nothing but flames. We seem to be surrounded by blazing arcs of red and yellow. Has the fire grown higher?

But then something cold splashes against me, shocking my awareness. We've made it to the edge of the flames, and the soldiers and the Suross people have reached us with their buckets. The king is passing the girl to one of the men who've come forward, and an older woman takes the second girl from me. She clings to the other woman, gasping through her sobs.

Ky's soldiers throw their buckets on the flames as well, cutting a line through the fires and making a pattern. It takes me a moment to realize that they're soaking a circle, keeping the fire from spreading.

The king notices my attention, and he says, "We have a lot of experience stopping fires, Princess."

I shiver and nod. Water has gone into my boots and soaked half my trousers. But I look to the girls, who are still clutching the people who must be their family. "Are they all right?"

"They will be."

I look around. "What about Asher? Where's Charlotte? Are they all right?"

Garrett is carrying a bucket toward the flames, and he nods as he tosses it wide. "Stripes is filling buckets at the stream. Your lady is helping. We got them to set up a chain."

"Princess." Ky nods past me, to one of his soldiers. "You and Lady Charlotte should return to the hill with Nikko—"

One of the older women puts a hand on his arm, cutting him off. "*You,*" she says, and her accent is thicker than his. "You will take your soldiers and *leave.*"

He instantly bristles. "We came to help—"

"I told the first one," she says. "I told him soldiers are not welcome here. And yet you came. And now look at what you've done."

I glance past her at those sobbing girls. They're all watching Ky and the other soldiers suspiciously.

The king inhales a sharp breath, and I remember what Nikko said earlier. *They hate everyone.*

But Ky also said they were his people. If I've learned anything on this journey, I know how much that means to him.

"We *helped* you," he's saying tightly. "We didn't *do* this—"

"But we'll leave," I say quickly. His soldiers seem to have the flames more under control, as they're throwing buckets at the mud huts now. Ky looks at me in surprise, and I drop my voice. "We're *frightening* them."

He seems struck by that, because he falls back a step. He casts a gaze around at the Suross people, some of whom are soaking wet and shivering, some of whom are exchanging anxious glances. There's a sense of *otherness* to them, and I understand why Ky leaves them alone. I suddenly realize they have no weapons at all.

I wonder if they know who he is, or if it's just the mere presence of soldiers that they find unsettling. He hasn't even announced himself, but the older woman who was arguing with him looks ready to cower if he draws a blade.

I put a hand on his arm and tug him back another step. "Go," I say quietly. "Gather your men. I'll find Charlotte and head back to the crest of the hill." I give the woman a gentle nod. "Forgive us. We just wanted to help."

She says nothing. Her gaze stays wary and hard.

I give Ky's arm one more tug, then move away. At my side, I hear him sigh, but he begins giving orders to his men.

As I head toward the stream, I look for Charlotte and Asher. I don't see my lady, but I eventually spot Asher at a distance, responding to the king's calls. He must sense my focus, because he looks over, and when he spots me, his eyebrows go up. He's too far to shout, but he mouths two words to me. *All good?*

The question gives me an unexpected burst of warmth. Despite everything, he and I are all right. I nod quickly and move on.

As I move toward the stream, I pass several other huts like the one that burned beside the girls. They're very small, not much bigger than the space we shared after Asher and I kidnapped the king. Ky said these people are nomads, and I wonder if the huts are so crudely constructed so the Suross can move at will, whenever they need to go.

Near the stream, I spot Charlotte just as I move to pass a final hut. It's set a little ways off from the others, well out of the path of the flames. As I walk by, a noise catches my attention, something soft and low, like a whisper or moan. Is someone else hurt? My steps hesitate, and I peer into the shadowed doorway.

Without warning, a hand latches on to my wrist, and I'm jerked into the shadows of the hut. It's so fast and unexpected that I don't make a sound—but then my instincts flare, and I *fight*.

When I swing a hand back, the man grunts, but he's easily as big as Ky, and he wrenches my arm back so hard that I cry out. I inhale sharply to scream for the king and his soldiers, but cold steel finds my throat. The man clamps a hand over my mouth. I freeze.

Asher did this once before, and it was terrifying.

This time, it's worse.

"Quiet," says the man. "I've got you." His accent is different from the king and his men. Is he part of the Suross? Or have I been caught by another Hunter?

My heart is in my throat, my thoughts narrowing down to nothing more than that blade. The man's breath is against my cheek, and he smells like leather and soot. From the pressure at my back, it seems like he's wearing armor, too.

I don't want to whimper, but I do.

Did Charlotte see him grab me? What about Ky and his soldiers? Asher? A full minute ticks by, and I hear voices outside, but no one close. I pry at the man's arm, but he's too big, too strong. Another whimper squeaks out of my throat.

Is he waiting? Am I bait?

Am I *leverage*?

Desperately, I try to sketch a sigil—but Ky is nowhere close, and nothing happens. The man redoubles his grip. He's pinned my head back against his shoulder, so I can barely struggle. His hand is so tight over my mouth that I can't even part my lips to bite him.

A cool wind rushes through my thoughts, and I think of the way I sparred with Ky. For a few minutes, I felt so strong, so powerful.

I'm not. I'm helpless.

But as soon as I have the thought, I remember Asher fighting Nikko. He had no armor and no weapons, just sheer determination and grit.

Ky called me formidable. He called me *vicious*.

I've never thought of myself as either, but my hand slips down, brushing cool steel along the man's leg. *A dagger.*

I don't think, I just grab the hilt.

And then I slam it into his thigh.

The man roars at the sudden pain, jerking away. Metal scrapes against my skin, and I'm panicked, terrified that I've sliced my throat, that I've done this assassin's job for him. But I stagger forward, slapping a hand to my neck, bursting out of the hut into the sunlight.

Ky catches me. He must have been right there—or my attacker's shouting summoned him. But I fall against his chest, gasping.

"Steady," he says, his voice low, like we're just sitting in the firelight again. But he's also turning, shifting me, pushing me away. "Help her."

Someone catches me, and I realize it's Asher. I can't look at him, though, because I whirl, keeping my eyes on Ky. He's already got weapons in hand, and he's now responding to the man who followed me out of the hut, blades drawn. My attacker doesn't stand a chance against the king. Before I can blink, Ky has driven a sword right into the man's side, just at the base of his armor. The man keeps coming, and I gasp, but Callum is thirty feet away, loosing an arrow from the back of his horse. It's so smooth and practiced that their movements could have been choreographed. The arrow catches the man in the back of the neck, and he pitches forward, falling into the dirt. Dead.

Suddenly, all I can hear is my roaring breath.

But then Charlotte's voice breaks through. "Is she all right? Let her go. Let me see."

"She's all right," Asher is saying. "She's all right." But there's a grave note in his voice—because nothing is all right.

I finally peel myself away from him to look down at the dead man on the ground. He's in brown armor, his black hair thick with sweat. His face is pressed into the dirt, but I caught a glimpse when he attacked Ky, and nothing about him seemed familiar. He seems older, too, with gray threading the hair at his temples.

I remember what the Suross woman said.

I told the first one.

"You put that blade in his leg?" says the king.

My eyes skip to the man's thigh. The dagger is buried right at the juncture of his hip, a little twisted from the way he's lying against the ground. I swallow, then nod.

"As I said: vicious, Princess."

He says it like a compliment. Just this moment, I'm not sure it feels like one.

"Who is he?" I say, my voice low. I look at Asher, who's soot-stained and damp from carrying buckets to the flames. "Asher—is it another Hunter?"

"No," he says. "At least . . . I don't think so. I don't know him."

"It's not a Hunter," says Ky, and his voice is grim. "He's not from Astranza at all."

"Do you know him?"

"Not personally." Ky kicks the man onto his back. An agonized sound bursts from the man's lips—which tells me he isn't dead. But I doubt he'll be alive for long. Not with the tight fury in Ky's voice, or the way Callum has another arrow nocked and ready.

Not with the bolt that pierced him straight through the neck, or the dagger lodged in his thigh.

My eyes fall on the crest in the center of his armored chest, a winged shield emblazoned with two crossed keys.

I suck in a breath. "What's that crest?" I say—but I know.

Ky looks over. "Draegonis." His eyes scan the empty fields around us, and then he looks back to the old woman. "He wouldn't be alone. Where are you hiding the rest?" he demands.

"We are hiding no one!" she says quickly, shaking her head. "He said he was looking for the rest of his crew. I thought that was *you*."

Ky scowls and casts another look around. "Garrett. Fetch Sev. Cal, search the other huts. Make *sure* he was alone." His eyes shift back to me, and like before, his manner is so severe I take a step back, colliding with Asher.

Something in that must take the king by surprise, because his expression softens, but only a fraction. His gaze drops to the cut at my neck. "He hurt you," he says.

A note in his voice tells me the Draeg soldier will be a pile of ash in a second if I say *yes*. I shiver, and Charlotte moves close to take hold of my hand. "I'm fine," I say breathily to both of them, even though my pulse hasn't stopped racing. "I'm *fine*."

That old woman has come closer. She's pointing at Ky. "You must leave. You and your soldiers are not welcome here."

Callum scoffs, shoving his unfired arrow in the quiver. "That sure doesn't sound like *thank you*."

"You want my thanks?" the woman snaps at him. She points at the man on the ground, then gestures at the scorched earth all around. "You are not *welcome* here! You all brought your warmongering ways—"

"More soldiers could come after him," says Ky. "We won't be here to help you again."

"Then we will return to the stars," she says. "And we will be at peace."

Ky's expression twists, revealing a flicker of sorrow behind all his lethal aggression. I remember the last thing he said about the Suross, just before he rode down the hill.

They're still my people.

And they don't want his help.

"We'll leave," I say. The Draeg soldier hasn't made another sound, and his eyes have rolled back in his head. It also looks like he's soiled his trousers.

"*Now*," says the woman.

So we go.

Chapter Twenty-Seven
THE PRINCESS

As we ride, the king's manner is tense and uncertain. It's clear that he and his men are unsettled by the Draeg soldier, especially considering that the man was alone. But they found no evidence of others—though the Suross people were quick to chase them out of their settlement. We couldn't search *everywhere*.

"You didn't tell them who you were," I say to Ky once we've made some distance from the attack. We're all damp and soot-stained and exhausted, so it's the first thing I've said in an hour.

He hesitates, then shakes his head. "No, Princess."

"Why not?"

Captain Zale glances over, but the king keeps his eyes on the terrain. "It would not have helped—and in fact it may have agitated them further. They barely recognize my rule."

I think about that for a little while. "Could *they* be working with Draegonis?" I say. "Or someone among them?"

He shakes his head. "They're not a warring people," he says. "It's more likely that he knew we were nearby, and a fire would draw me out . . . which it did."

He sounds rueful, like he's angry he was caught in a trap—and I suppose we were.

"How do you think he got past the border?" I say.

"I have dedicated patrols," he says, "but they're not limitless. I cannot guard the entire border between Incendar and Astranza. I don't have enough soldiers—and of those I do have, they're more desperately needed at the border with Draegonis."

It takes me a moment to figure out what he's saying, and when I figure it out, I gasp. "You think he came through Astranza?"

"I do." He pauses, and this silence is grave. "He attacked while we were worried about Hunters on our trail. That's too much of a coincidence." He pauses. "I worry that Draeg spies have already breached Astranza's borders, and I suspect that he—or his superiors—are behind these falsified assassination orders."

At that, Asher looks over. "You think they infiltrated the Hunter's Guild."

Ky nods. "Possibly."

Charlotte speaks up from beside me. "Master Pavok *was* quick to point the finger at Draegonis."

I look at her in surprise. "Yes," I say, putting it together now. "He laid the blame at Asher's feet. Was it really *him* all along?" I look at Asher. "Could that be true?"

He considers. "I've only been a Hunter for a few years. Master Pavok wasn't sharing secrets with me. I was gone for so long anyway. It's not like I would've been privy to any dealings with Draegonis—"

He breaks off, his face twisting in thought as if he's solved a puzzle.

"What is it?" I say.

"I was gone for months," Asher says, musing now. "Maybe Pavok would have denied these orders from anyone—but my return from Morinstead gave the Guild a golden opportunity to accuse Draegonis and pin the blame on me."

Ky glances at him. "Exactly."

I roll these thoughts around in my head. "I *knew* Dane was committed to this alliance," I say, and despite how terrible my brother can be, it's a bit of relief to know that he wasn't behind *this*. Astranza still needs this alliance—and so does Incendar. Dane is still working to the benefit of both countries.

Then reality comes crashing down. We might have solved this puzzle, but my father is still dying. This entire alliance is based on a false promise. Incendar might be able to help Astranza, but I have no idea how long we can support them in return.

But Ky looks over at me, and I'm surprised by the spark of hope in his eyes. "Your brother is still committed to this alliance," he says. "And so am I."

I look back at him, and my heart twists. So much between us has shifted, changed. Despite everything that happened, my body hasn't stopped humming from the feel of his body on top of mine. Not just the way he almost kissed me. It was the sparring, the way he let me feel powerful. The way he let me feel *his* power when his muscled body pinned me to the ground. The way he folded my fingers so gently and let me try his magic. The way he kept me close when we rescued those girls. The way I found the courage to seize that soldier's dagger.

Somehow, Ky has lit a flame inside me that I've never felt, something very different from the sparks that fly when I'm with Asher. I've loved Asher for as long as I can remember, but he's always made me feel safe. Protected. Treasured.

The king makes me feel like a weapon. Powerful. Capable. Worthy.

I can't betray him. I *can't*.

"So am I," I say to Ky, but the words sound hollow in my heart.

Especially when Asher looks over at me. I know the truth will be in his eyes, and I can't face that right now.

So I turn my face forward and ride on.

IN ASTRANZA, THE capital city of Perriden is flat and compact, full of narrow alleys, angled streets, and so many winding pathways that it's easy to get turned around and lost if you're unfamiliar. Shops and vendors and food stalls are around every corner, with so many scents and sights that you could spend all day wandering the city and never get bored—or so I've heard. Anytime I left the palace, it was with a full contingent of guards and carriages and an entire entourage, so wandering was never an option. But I've heard a thousand different stories from Asher, and he always made the city sound like a grand adventure, even when he was held by the slavers.

Now that I know the truth about Asher's life, my memories of those stories evoke an unpleasant sensation, like finding a beloved old quilt has become infested with insects. But I can still picture the cobblestone streets in the rain at night, or the broken windows in the poorer districts that always let in the cold, or the bright rooftops in the summertime, laid out with flowers in every color. Asher's stories brought them all to life.

When we approach Incendar's capital, I'm surprised to discover that the city of Lastalorre seems to be the opposite of Perriden: wide and sprawling, set in a high valley between two mountains. A huge stone castle sits near the center, spires stretching into the sky, stained glass windows glittering in the sunlight. We must still be miles away, separated by acres and acres of dried grasslands, but I can see the blues and greens from here. Far ahead, gates flank the road into the city, but they stand open, guards posted by the massive stone pillars.

"It's so high," I say to Ky, just as a gust of wind blasts between the mountains to lift my hair and tug at the horse's mane. The scent of woodsmoke is stronger here, carrying more of an edge. Several small homesteads dot the hills, and I wonder if they're homes or farms. I can't see any livestock, but as before, we aren't traveling too close to any structures. Instead, we're passing through fields, the horses' feet crunching in the dried grass. The underbrush is unusual, too, acres of different stages of underbrush that seems almost organized. If we were in Astranza, I'd think these were crops, but these fields are too dry, stems and leaves flaking away into nothing as the horses trudge through them.

"It is high," the king agrees, drawing my gaze back up. His tension still hasn't dissipated since the fire in the Suross settlement, but his voice is casual. "And easy to defend. Several of my other large cities are situated similarly. It's part of why Incendar has managed to hold its ground for so long. One day soon I'll take you down to Marrowell. Their cliffs overlook the ocean."

"There are *cliffs* over the ocean?" I say.

Ky gives me a startled look. "Princess, if you've never seen the ocean, I'm going to ride back right now and shoot Dane for that alone."

That makes me smile. "I've seen the ocean on the northern side of Astranza. But we don't have cliffs."

Ky nods. "In the summer months, the tides are calm. There are several rock formations with pools that are good for swimming. Not so much now, though. Too rough."

I give him a quizzical look. "And surely too cold."

"Princess." He glances at me, then sketches a sigil. Flame gathers on his palm, flickering in the wind. "I can heat a pool of water."

My eyes grow wide, because I hadn't considered that. Even Asher looks startled.

Captain Zale glances back. "Wait until you see the Hall of Stars in the palace. It's the best at this time of year."

I frown, because I don't know what that has to do with pools of water, but Ky shakes his head. "Wait," he says. "That one is better left a surprise."

There's an eager note to his voice that makes him sound almost boyish, and for an instant, it cuts through the anxious uncertainty. For a little while, I thought perhaps the attack by the Draeg soldier was going to sour his emotion, but instead, it seems that solving a minor mystery has settled something within him.

Guilt churns in my gut, and I need to shove it away. My father might not have *long* to live, but he's alive *now*. And Dane is so committed to this alliance. Father can surely help during the time he has left.

I smile back at the king. His eyes are gleaming in the light from the fire, and I'm surprised to feel a blush crawl up my cheeks. "I look forward to seeing it."

My horse stumbles a little in the underbrush, and even though I'm not unseated, it draws my gaze back to the ground to check the terrain. I suddenly realize that the fields don't just look dry, they look . . . burned.

Ahead of us, a distant shout rings out, followed by another. My head snaps up, my heart fluttering with alarm, but then I realize what they're yelling.

"He has fire! It's the king! The king approaches!"

At least an acre separates us from the nearest structure, but I can see a half dozen people have gathered in the sunlight—and their shouts must have summoned others, because a few men and women come out of another distant building.

My smile widens. We're close enough to Lastalorre that these people won't be like the Suross, distant and reserved, rejecting their king.

The citizens from his capital city will likely be rejoicing that Maddox Kyronan has finally returned.

I turn back to Ky, sure his expression will have brightened further, that he'll be proud to let me see his people now that we're safely arriving. Maybe he'll even make a bigger display of magic to flaunt his power, the way Father will sometimes summon clouds to form a perfect array of sunbeams over the royal family when we travel.

But to my surprise, Ky scowls, crushing the fire out of his palm like it's displeasing. Instead of sitting straighter, preparing to greet his people, his shoulders have drooped. He looks like he'd almost rather turn back.

The captain glances at him. "We've seen the damage. You had to know."

Ky nods. Any hint of a smile is gone from his face. His expression is all hard lines and stormy eyes.

"Know what?" I say.

They exchange another glance and say nothing.

Across the fields, more people have come out of their homes and outbuildings. They're up a hill, barely more than silhouettes with the sun at their back. From the size of the people, most of them look like men.

"What have you done?" they shout. "Nothing will grow! Don't you see? Don't you *see*?"

Around us, the guards have gone stony-faced and silent.

I fix my eyes on the king and shorten up the reins to my horse. "Ky. Why are they shouting? Tell me."

He sets his jaw and says nothing.

I reach out and grab his rein, hauling both our horses to a stop—exactly the way he did to me.

The king is stronger, and he wrenches free, whirling to face me. Before he does, I realize Asher's horse has all but slid to a stop beside mine. He's so close, his knee brushing my knee. They're suddenly facing each other like adversaries again. King and killer. Warrior and assassin.

Ky's soldiers have shifted, responding to the sudden hostility.

"Stand down," says Captain Zale—and to my surprise, his tone is mild. He taps his knuckles to the king's arm. "Ky. The Suross didn't know you—but these people do. You need to tell her *something*." He jerks his head toward the gathered people, a few of whom now appear to be running down the hill toward us. "Or they're going to do it for you."

I look at Ky, and he stares right back at me. His jaw is still set, his shoulders tight, no inch of give in his expression.

But the barest flicker of emotion in his gaze takes me by surprise. It's so unexpected and vulnerable I almost don't recognize it: *Fear.*

Running downhill, the people don't take long to reach us. It's only six of them, and they're older men, dressed in loose linen and calfskin, with scuffed boots—definitely farmers or tradesmen. No soldiers. But Callum and Garrett swing down from their horses to block them from getting any closer.

"It's gotten worse!" one is shouting at Ky. He kicks at the ground. "Look what's happening! Don't you see?"

"You swore to fix it!" shouts another. He plants his hands right on Callum's chest and gives a solid shove. The soldier shoves him back so hard that the man nearly goes sprawling, but Callum doesn't pursue him. He casts a glance up at the king.

"I *will* fix it," Ky grits out. But he taps two fingers to his shoulder, and Callum gives a sharp nod.

I remember his lesson about their signals. *Don't pick a fight, but stand your ground.*

The first man takes a swing at Garrett, but it's easily blocked. When he spits at the soldier, Garrett grabs his tunic and hooks his ankle. The man sits down hard.

"Be civil," Garrett snaps at him.

The man glares at him. "Tell the *king* to be civil," he growls, surging off the ground to get in Garrett's face. "He's letting his magic kill us all."

The next two men are the oldest, probably nearing fifty, and they haven't advanced on the soldiers like the others. More shouts are coming from the hill, and I realize more people have gathered together between the farmhouses and outbuildings, and their shouts seem to be drawing attention from the gates leading into the city. Far ahead, others have begun to come through the gates, stopping to watch. It's too far to see how many people are there, but it seems like a lot.

One of the older men looks back at the crowd near the farmhouses, then shifts his gaze to the crowd forming outside the city gates. Tension sizzles among us all, and I realize others are beginning to run down the hill, all shadowed figures in the fading sunlight.

After a bare hesitation, the man looks back to the guards blocking his path to the king.

The king, who still hasn't explained what's happening.

The man grits his teeth and draws a long dagger.

Quicker than thought, Nikko and Roman have arrows nocked—and Garrett and Callum have weapons drawn. The closest men scramble back, but that one violent motion has triggered a dozen others, like the spark from a hearth launching an inferno. The men are suddenly wielding their tools like weapons. Two have real daggers, but the others are armed more crudely with hammers or axes—tools they must have been in the midst of using. They're shouting at Ky, they're shouting at the soldiers, and I sense that they're not going to wait for those reinforcements coming down the hill. I look past them, expecting more armed men, but all I see are swirls of color. The newcomers are shouting, too, but their voices are tiny and high-pitched, unlike the men in front of us. The crowds gathering outside the city gates have grown.

"If you can't help us," one man growls at Ky, "what *good* are you?"

Another one surges forward with his dagger. "Maybe we should solve the problem right now."

He slams into Garrett, but the soldier snaps the blade right out of his hand, then slams him to the ground—more aggressively than before. Blood blooms on the man's lip.

I suck in a sharp breath, and Lady Charlotte gives a little yip of alarm. "Your Highness," she breathes at me. "We must run."

But we can't. We're trapped between the king and his men and the citizens running down the hill. There must be more than a dozen of them—with more waiting outside the gates to the city.

We've been braced for silent assassins for days. I never thought we'd walk right into an assault from Ky's own people. In a moment, we're going to be surrounded.

But then I realize that the people coming down the hill aren't calling for more violence. "Stop!" they're shouting. "Stop this!"

They're not armed reinforcements at all. They're women, they're children, they're two dozen people shouting for the others to *stop*.

Ky's soldiers are completely still, braced for violence. Waiting for an attack—or an order.

The king is already moving his hand toward his shoulder. Three fingers this time.

Lethal force.

"No!" The word comes out of me like a crack of lightning. I don't wait to see if the king listens, or even if his soldiers do. Heedless of arrows and swords and whatever else they might have, I swing to the ground and stride between the horses and soldiers.

Behind me, I hear swearing and regrouping, and a hand grabs for my jacket, but I slip free. I don't know if it's Asher or the king, or maybe even Charlotte. A man mutters, "Stars in darkness, Jory," and then boots hit the ground.

That is definitely Asher.

I don't care. I keep going.

Garrett and Callum have swords drawn now, but I step between them. The older tradesmen are braced like they're going to surge forward and attack, regardless of the consequences. The others are going to be on top of us any minute, and I sense this really *will* turn into a battle.

But these men are ready to go down fighting. A note of desperation hangs in the air, and I know they've seen the nocked arrows.

He's letting his magic kill us all.

This is different from the Suross people. They just wanted to be left alone.

These people are about to attack their king—and they don't care that he might kill them. They don't think they have anything to lose.

It reminds me of that moment in the inn, when Asher finally broke. The way he said I didn't see him. The way he said *no one* sees him.

When I step past the soldiers, the men quickly size me up—and immediately disregard me. I'm certainly not dressed as a princess, and I'm clearly not much of a threat.

But that's fine. I've spent a lifetime in my brother's shadow, and I'm not really used to anyone seeing *me* either.

"I am Princess Marjoriana of Astranza," I shout. "Tell me what has been done." I pause, looking at each of them in turn. They're all breathing hard, glaring. "Tell me what you need."

"He knows what we need!" snaps the one with the dagger. He thrusts it in the air, gesturing toward the king, but it's two inches from my face.

Garrett steps forward, but Asher is quicker—and closer. He grabs the man's wrist.

"Stop," he says, and his voice is deadly quiet. "Listen to her."

The man begins to fight him, but whatever he sees in Asher's face makes him go still. I forgot how lethally terrifying he can be when he wants to be.

"*Listen* to her," Asher says again. "She came here to help you."

Their gazes snap to me again. A crowd has gathered as the others have made it to us, but they stop, too. More men, ranging in age, including one who can't be out of his teens. Three women, one of whom looks so pregnant that she might give birth before we finish whatever we're doing here. Also three children, none of whom are older than ten.

They all have stones in their hands.

It makes me swallow. Do they *hate* him? Do the Incendrians hate their king?

In a flash, I remember all the terrifying stories about Maddox Kyronan—and the horrors he visits on his citizens. It was one of the very first things I challenged him about. As I've come to know him, I couldn't imagine any of it was true . . . but then we faced the Suross, and he didn't tell them who he was.

And then I saw these burned fields, which are clearly growing no food.

And now we're facing his people, who are armed and ready to fight.

"Tell me what you need," I say again. I hope my voice sounds strong, but I'm worried that dismay has begun to creep into my tone. "I have come from Astranza to help you. Please. Tell me how."

The women exchange glances. The men are still glaring. The oldest girl looks fierce, like she's desperate to throw her stones at *someone*.

But no one is talking, and the air still rides a knife's edge of tension.

So I take a step toward that little girl, and her fingers tighten on the rocks. "We were heading to Lastalorre," I say. "I've never been here. Perhaps you could show me the rest of the way." I glance up, past her, at the rest of the people who are dubiously watching this exchange. "And maybe you could tell me why everyone is so angry at your king."

Her face twists, like she can't decide whether to help me—or to scowl. But she doesn't move.

A younger girl with dark blond pigtails steps forward and drops one of her stones to take my hand. "I'll show you," she says, and I'm captivated to hear that lyrical accent in her tiny voice. "It's not far."

"Thank you," I say.

That spurs the older girl into motion. "I'll come, too." She drops both her rocks.

A little boy of about seven walks up beside her. "Me too."

I give him a nod. "You have my gratitude."

The girl with the pigtails gives my hand a tug, and I begin to follow, but then I worry that I'll simply be leading the children away while the adults finish trying to kill each other.

I look to my left. Callum still has weapons in hand. From the corner of my eye, I can see that the others still have arrows nocked. Ready for war, I suppose.

"Put up your weapons," I say sharply, trying to fill my voice with the same effortless authority the king always seems to have. I remember the way his men hesitated last night, then looked to him. I don't know if they'll listen now. "They came with grievances first, not violence. If Astranza is to ally with Incendar, I will hear from these people."

Ky's citizens shift and exchange glances uncertainly, as if they're not sure what to make of this. I hear a few muttered comments, but I can't catch their words.

Callum hasn't moved. He's looking back at me. Weighing this.

He's not going to yield to me. I can feel it. None of them are. Rage at their defiance and admiration for their loyalty go to war in my gut.

But then Ky says, "You heard the princess. Stand down."

Callum slams the weapons home. So do the others.

"Good," I say. "Charlotte, come along. The rest of you will follow at a distance."

Charlotte swings down from her horse, but I don't wait. I simply turn to obey the child tugging at my fingers. We stride into the sunlight, dried grass crunching underfoot.

The boy looks up and over my shoulder. "What about him?"

"I follow the princess," says Asher, and he says it so simply that it makes something in my heart sing. Despite everything that's changed between us during the journey to Incendar, *we* aren't broken.

"Is he a guard?" says the older girl.

"He doesn't have any weapons," says the younger one, squinting at Asher in the sunshine.

"He's a Hunter," I say, thinking it will be the simplest answer to give children.

But of course the boy immediately says, "What does he hunt without weapons?"

"Whatever the princess wants," says Asher, and my heart gives another tug.

"Maybe it's rabbits," whispers the littlest girl. She drops her other stone, then reaches back to take Asher's hand, too.

"Did you mean that?" says a woman to my left. When I glance over, I realize it's the one who looks ready to give birth at any given moment. Her hair is thick and full, twisted into two braids that hang down over her shoulders, but plenty of tendrils have escaped to frame her face. "That you care to hear our grievances?"

"Yes," I say. "I did."

She glances at some of the others. They aren't all armed, but the ones who are have put their weapons away. "The king's magic has destroyed most of our crops," she says, gesturing at the grounds surrounding us. "Now he's turned on the grazing lands."

I remember the rumors I used to hear in Astranza—the ones that made me fear Maddox Kyronan before I ever met him. But then the king sat in my chambers and spoke so passionately about how badly he wanted to *protect* his people. How desperately he wanted to feed them.

"I've heard this before," I say to her. "But when your king first came to me, he was desperate to *help* you. Why would he turn his magic against you?"

"We don't know," says a man. He casts a dark glare over his shoulder toward the king and his soldiers. "They say he's lost control of it."

"We all know that once a fire begins, he cannot stop it," says another man.

"What good is his magic on the battlefield," says an older woman, "if it just kills us more slowly at home?"

I hear the pain in their voices, and it tugs at me. It reminds me of Asher's voice when he finally told me the truth about everything that had been done to him—the truth about Astranza.

But I heard the same pain in Ky's voice when he spoke of Incendar.

"I hear your suffering," I say. I glance at Asher, then back at them. "I see your pain. I saw it when you first approached. But your king risked his life to come to Astranza. He spoke passionately about caring for his people—"

"He was just going to kill us!" a man near the edge cries.

"You *did* come at him with weapons drawn," I respond, my voice dry. "He could have summoned fire, and he didn't."

That makes them all go silent, and I see glances exchanged.

I have their attention now, but I'm not sure if I'm doing the right thing. The king and his men have fallen back to follow at a distance. Ky *was* ready to let his soldiers kill them all. I think of the child clutching my fingers, and I have to shake off a shudder.

The king just risked himself to save those girls at the Suross settlement. But they didn't know who he was. Would they have attacked him similarly, if they'd known? And would Ky have killed the children here, just because the tradesmen came at him with tools brandished like weapons? I don't want to consider it.

I remember a conversation I had with Asher ages ago, about his duties as an assassin.

So your brother and his soldiers can be killers on the battlefield, but you save your contempt for me, just because I'm not in uniform?

This isn't a battlefield.

Has Maddox Kyronan spent so long at war that everything has begun to look like one?

These people were furious, and they did come running down the hill, but even I can see that they're simple farmers and tradesmen and their families. Yet the king and his soldiers responded so swiftly—bracing for violence as if we'd walked right onto the front lines. I've been marveling at Ky's hidden kindness for days, but maybe I should have been paying closer attention to *this* side of him: the ruthless, brutal, practical man who dragged Asher through the snow and threatened my brother with Incendrian justice.

I can't look back at him. I'm terrified to consider what I might find.

"I cannot speak to the past," I say to his people. "But I am here to help, if you'll allow it. My father, King Theodore, has magic that allows him to control the weather, and it helps keep our farmland prosperous. Once the alliance is struck, it will help restore your fields as well."

As I say the words, a twinge of guilt tugs at my heart.

"And if the king's magic brings more fire?" says one of the women.

"My father will summon rain to put it out," I say simply. "We have no droughts in Astranza."

That makes them fall silent again.

"Are you to marry our king?" says the pregnant woman.

If she'd asked me an hour ago, I would have said yes. I was ready to seal this alliance, because I know how desperately Astranza needs Ky's abilities on the battlefield—and I know how desperately they need my father's magic, despite the fact that his health is waning.

But I think of everything I've learned in the last fifteen minutes, and I glance over my shoulder at the king, who has obeyed, and is riding about twenty feet behind us.

He's too far, and I can't read his expression. I don't know if I want him to see mine.

I glance at Asher, and his expression is just as blank. He's waiting for my answer, too.

Oh, this is too complicated. Especially now. I turn my eyes forward and swing the little girl's arm playfully. "Marriage?" I say. "We'll see."

Chapter Twenty-Eight
THE WARRIOR

They're too far for me to hear anything they're saying.

That doesn't stop me from trying.

My soldiers are trying to listen, too—or maybe they simply know I am. They haven't made a *sound*. They're all braced for this to go badly. Every quiver is still strung across their backs, their reins tucked in one hand, their bows held ready in the other.

Jory looked almost *wounded* when Callum didn't obey her order to put up his weapons. Talk about bold—the very idea that she would expect to command my best soldiers is nonsensical. But she clearly expected them to obey, and they didn't. In that moment, she almost faltered.

But her conviction is so *strong*. My men considered it. Only for a heartbeat of time, but they thought about it.

She didn't see that—but I did.

Sev looks over at me, and he keeps his voice low. "How long are you going to let this go on?"

I study the small crowd ahead. There aren't more than two dozen people, with Jory and Asher at the center. A little girl of about six years old walks between them, every now and again swinging from their arms. Lady Charlotte walks just behind. No one's voice is raised. No weapons are in hand.

I'm still waiting for it, though. When I lift my gaze to the gates to Lastalorre, there are others waiting, drawn by the shouting. I would have preferred to enter the city quietly. I can't believe I was so reckless as to draw flame to my palm.

And then the princess walked right into the fray. We're lucky there are so few of them—and that none were more heavily armed. If she knew what the last few years have been like, she never would have dared. There's a reason I didn't tell the Suross settlers who I am. There's a reason we took circuitous routes to get here.

A month ago, a man came at me in the middle of the night, when we were riding back from the Draeg border. It was pitch-black, and I didn't see him until the last second. He meant to put a dagger into my thigh, or maybe my waist, right at the gap in my armor. I twisted in time, and instead, it went into my horse's flank. The animal reared—then collapsed, nearly crushing the man, and me with him. We ended up grappling in the dirt, half tangled in the tack, the horse flailing around us.

"Your magic is killing us," the man snarled in my face, right before I drove a blade into his body.

"It's not my magic," I said, but he was already dead.

The memory fills my head more often than I like to admit. Every time I do, shame curls around my thoughts, and I have to shove it away.

Jory and Asher swing the little girl again.

That same shame is curling around my thoughts *now*.

I didn't see the children as they were advancing down the hill. I didn't see the pregnant woman.

Maybe the attack by the Draeg soldier was too fresh in my head, but I just saw attackers. Adversaries.

"Ky."

I rub at my eyes, then look over at Sev. "What?"

He frowns, and I realize I didn't answer his question. I don't know *how* to answer his question.

Because Jory simply got down from the horse and . . . walked up to them. Heedless of danger. Asher right by her side.

Daring. Chaotic. Admirable.

Sev tries a different tack. "We're twenty feet back. The princess is—"

"Thirty feet," says Roman.

"Thank you. *Thirty* feet back. The princess is unarmed. Defenseless."

My eyes flick to Asher. I saw him take down my soldier.

I watched him slide under an assassin to take her place.

Then I saw the princess stab a Draeg soldier in the thigh while a knife was at her neck.

"She's not defenseless," I say.

Sev makes an aggrieved noise and keeps going. "You have *no idea* what they're telling her."

That hits the mark. I look over at him.

His eyebrows go up. He knows he's got me. "Are you just going to let her walk into Lastalorre like this?"

Let her. She almost took control of my soldiers right out from under me. I'm beginning to think there's not a whole lot I can stop the princess from doing.

I turn and look at him. "No."

He lets out a breath, clearly relieved. "Well, good, because—" He breaks off sharply as I swing down from the horse, midstride. "Ky! What are you—"

"Take my horse." I toss him my reins. "I'm going to join her."

IT DOESN'T FEEL like thirty feet. It feels like a mile. Once I'm on the ground, jogging out from the horses, the gap between my soldiers and my people seems like a chasm I don't know how to cross. I'd lay down my life for Incendar, and I've watched thousands of soldiers do that very thing at the border with Draegonis. But my people *here* believe I'm harming them instead of helping them. They attacked without hesitation. Their fury—fury at *me*—was clear.

I knew it. I *expected* it. I just didn't expect it to be this bad.

Jory glances back, looking over her shoulder, and she seems surprised to see me on the ground, halfway between her and the rest of my soldiers.

Many of the others notice her reaction, because sudden tension flares among the people surrounding her. I immediately feel like I've made a misstep, and my steps slow. For an instant, I wonder if I've made all the wrong choices here, and they're going to draw the few weapons they have and we're going to have a battle anyway. My hand is automatically beginning to sketch a sigil, calling fire in case I need it.

But the princess leans down toward the little girl and says something quietly, and suddenly the child is sprinting across the distance toward me.

I shuffle to a stop, nonplussed.

The girl gives an exasperated huff when she reaches me. "Come on," she says, grabbing my hand before I finish that sigil. "Princess Jory says that if you want to walk with us, you have to keep up."

Her fingers are so tiny and cool against my own, and it's almost jarring. I can't remember the last time I was this close to a young child. "I . . . yes, Lady."

She gives me a tug, so I jog by her side until we reach the group.

I can only imagine what Sev thinks of *this*.

If I expected a kind reception, I don't get one. Every gaze is a bit cold, but there's an undercurrent of fear, too. They know who I am—and they know what they just did.

There was a time when my people *never* looked at me this way.

"See, Mama?" says the little girl. She still hasn't let go of my hand, but she's looking up at the pregnant woman. "He didn't hurt me."

Well, that stings like a dart. My jaw goes tight.

"I see." The woman is a little pale, and she holds out her own hand. "Come walk with me now, Hannah."

The little girl drops my hand and skips over to her mother.

Even the princess seems a bit frosty. Her eyes are cold and challenging, and with Asher at her shoulder, she looks every inch a rival queen, here to negotiate for resources before we abandon pleasantries and go to war.

"Your Majesty," she says coolly.

"Princess."

"Have you come to walk with us?"

"I have."

"Good." She turns and starts walking again, and it seems like the people around us are holding their breath, waiting to hear what we'll say.

I fall into step beside her, but my thoughts are already categorizing where the men are, and which ones have weapons.

Jory reaches out and takes my hand, and it's so startling that I almost jump. But her fingers close around mine. There's a part of me that doesn't like it. I want both hands free.

But Jory's voice is calm as she says, "These people didn't come to fight with you." She glances at me. "And once these gentlemen began scuffling with your soldiers, their families came to stop them—not to heighten the tension."

She's clever in the way she says that, assigning blame to no one.

I'm not sure I like it.

I'm also not sure she's wrong.

She continues, "I have been telling your people that you spent months negotiating with my brother, Prince Dane. That you hear their worries, and you have been taking steps to protect them."

"Yes," I say gravely. "I have."

"Well, you haven't done enough," one of the men snaps. "Your magic has been scorching the fields."

"It's not my magic," I say.

"It's *fire!*" says another.

My jaw is tight again. None of these are unfamiliar arguments. "I cannot control the wildfires—"

"They aren't just wildfires," says a dark-haired woman near the back. "These fires come from *nowhere*—"

"And no one can *stop* them!" the pregnant woman cries.

"We keep running out of food," says one of the children, and the others begin to echo it, like chirping baby birds.

"And now our livestock are going to starve," a man calls from the edge of the crowd. "Once the cattle and chicken die off, we won't have—"

"I *know!*" I say, and my voice is a crack like thunder. Sudden silence falls. I stop and gesture out at the dried fields we just rode across. "I am your king! You think I don't see the state of my kingdom?"

Two of the women flinch. Several of the men are glaring again.

The little boy's face crumples, and he starts to cry.

Fuck.

I would give anything to be sent back to the worst battle on the border, right this very second.

"I have spent *months* trying to find accord with Astranza," I say, speaking into their scowling silence. "I yielded everything I could to satisfy Prince Dane. I know our fields are nearly bare. I know our food stores run empty. I know you have heard stories from Netherford and Covepoint about the barren crops. I know you are *desperate*." I look from face to face, making sure they hear me. "But know this, too: Draegonis waits at our eastern border, watching for every sign of weakness. You have heard *those* stories, too, from every soldier who comes home. If you think you can rip me off the throne and solve your problems, the Draeg army will be happy to give you a new one."

They're frozen in place. Some appear chastised—while others look more angry. Behind us, Sev and the rest of my soldiers have drawn closer, and it does nothing to dispel the tension. I have no idea how to unravel anything that's happened here. I certainly don't think I've made anything *better*.

I look at Jory. "Princess, you have my gratitude for keeping this conversation civil." I look back to the people. "The next time you wish to air your grievances, approach me with fewer weapons and more consideration, and I will listen." To Jory, I add, "We have neared the city of Lastalorre. For your safety, you and your lady should ride."

Now it's her jaw that's set, and I'm not sure what part of that earned *her* ire.

"Fine," she says. Her eyes are still cold.

At her shoulder, Asher is studying me, too, but his gaze isn't cold at all. Instead, he looks curious, intrigued, like he's stumbled upon a puzzle he can't figure out.

I can't make sense of that, and now I'm too twisted up and angry. I turn for my horse.

Someone in the crowd mutters, "We'd be better off if Victoria took the throne."

No, I want to snap. *You wouldn't be better off at all.*

But I can't say that. Not now. Maybe not ever.

So I set my jaw, give the horse a nudge with my heels, and we set off.

AS WE RIDE up the hill and into the city, my soldiers hang close. No one is speaking, and the tension between me and the princess is *thick*. It's clear she has thoughts—but she either doesn't want to voice them or she doesn't think I'll give her honest answers. I remember what Sev said right before the people approached us, and I'm sure she does, too.

Ky. You need to tell her something. Or they're going to do it for you.

He was right. They did.

Shame won't stop curling through my gut, hot and unpleasant.

Welcome to Incendar, Princess. Everyone feared me in Astranza, but everyone hates me here.

It wasn't like this when I was young. When my father would return to Lastalorre, people would line the streets. He was welcomed like a hero. When my mother died, the people grieved with him. When he died, they grieved with *me*. It wasn't until the weather began to shift, leading to the dry months, that people began to worry.

It wasn't until fires began to spread that my people began to *blame* me.

But as Jory discovered, my magic can only call fire. Once it begins, it burns everything in its path. I can't stop it.

Now I dread coming home.

Dozens of citizens have gathered, but they yield a path as we ride through the gates. I hear muttered comment, but no one says a word to us directly. My people stare—or worse, they glare.

I know the princess sees all of it. Asher rides behind us, but I'm certain he does, too.

My soldiers, of course, are used to it.

Maybe Lady Charlotte can't take the silence, because she begins chattering to Sev.

"Ah . . . Captain," she's saying. "The architecture here is so unique. Our buildings are not so high in Astranza. Do you have many stonemasons?"

Sev is never one to shy away from attention from a lady, so he navigates his horse closer to hers. "It's not the stone," he says, "it's our iron. All the buildings are fortified with it. They have been for over a century." Sev points to the corner of a building, where brickwork has chipped away, revealing the ironwork below. "The wind through the mountains can get fierce. Our cities can take a lot of damage without falling." He pats the leather armor on his chest. "Iron plates are stitched into the leather, too. Impervious to arrows."

This seems to have caught Jory's interest, because she glances at Sev. "Why not steel armor? That's what soldiers wear in Astranza. Surely it's simpler to forge."

"Simpler, yes." He glances at me. "But if you're surrounded by fire, plain steel gets hot fast."

Her eyebrows go up. "Ah."

"This moves a lot better, too," Sev adds. He pats his armor again. "It takes longer to make than a plate of steel, but we have no shortage of metalsmiths here."

Behind us, Callum snorts. "Throw a stick and you'll hit one."

"No wonder your weapons are so fine," Asher says, musing. It's the first thing he's said since we left the people near the city gates.

Jory looks at him in surprise. "Are they?"

He nods, then shrugs a little. "Nicer than mine, anyway."

"Incendrian steel costs a *mint* in Perriden," says Lady Charlotte, and there's a hint of envy in her voice. "One of the courtiers in the palace had a set of hairpins, and she never let us *touch* them."

"You can get a dozen hairpins for a few coppers here in Lastalorre," says Sev, and Lady Charlotte gasps.

"Iron is heavy," I add. "It's difficult—and costly—to transport a lot at once. Incendar does not export much." I don't add that we're often wary of our weapons getting into the hands of Draeg forces. Sometimes the strength of our steel is the only advantage we have against their army, which has three times as many soldiers as I have.

"But you have a lot here," Jory says, looking up and around at the buildings as we pass. Another gust of wind whips through the buildings to tug at the tendrils of her hair that have pulled loose from her braids. She still looks so fierce and beautiful, and I wish I could erase the tension that has built between us, but I'm not sure how.

"Iron is everywhere in the palace," I say to her, encouraged by the fact that she's talking. "Some of the metalwork is centuries old. It's really quite beautiful."

She turns cool eyes my way. "Did you know your people were so angry?"

Maybe I shouldn't have been encouraged at all. I let out a breath. "Princess—"

"You asked me for truth between us. Perhaps I should have asked you for the same thing."

"I will give you truth," I say quietly. "Yes. I did know."

"Did your magic cause these droughts?"

"No."

Her eyes stare into mine, hard.

I stare right back at her. "I do not have weather magic," I say. "I can summon flame, but fire is fire—and as you saw, if there is fuel to burn, it will spread and multiply until there is none."

"Has your magic caused these fires, then?"

I hesitate, thinking of my sister. "No."

She considers this for a long moment. The horses plod on.

Eventually she turns to look at me again. "Those were simple people. Your soldiers are armed for war. You would have killed those children."

I nearly flinch. Her voice is very low, very quiet, but I'm very aware of the people in the streets, and she might as well have shouted the words. She might as well be branding them on my skin.

I think of little Hannah's cool fingers pressing into my palm as she tugged at my hand.

I imagine my soldiers tearing her apart, the way they'd tear apart an opponent on the battlefield. My brain has no trouble imagining it. I've seen worse. This will probably haunt my sleep for the next week.

My eyes are fixed ahead, but I don't see Lastalorre anymore, I see every terrible thing that's happened on the front lines of the war. I've clenched my right hand into a fist to keep from sketching a sigil, because I don't want to draw any attention to myself in front of my people. Not now. But the strain is building in my body, until I feel like I'm going to burst into a ball of flame myself.

I haven't said anything, and her expression darkens with anger. "They are *desperate*. You are their *king*. I know what you've gone through with Dane. But your people came to you with complaints, and you nearly turned—"

"Jory. Stop."

She stops short. To my surprise, it's Asher's voice.

I can't even turn to look at him. Every muscle in my body has gone taut and rigid, and I didn't even realize it.

The princess is still staring at me. Fury is a lit match in her eyes. Her chest is rising and falling like she wants to resume her tirade.

"*Jory*," Asher says again, his voice a bit sharper, a bit louder. People on the ground look up, and even Lady Charlotte inhales sharply, like she can't believe he'd dare.

Jory whips her head in his direction, and I can feel more than see her fury.

But then his voice softens. "He's had enough," Asher says. "Leave him be."

I don't expect her to listen. But maybe she sees something in his face. Maybe she sees something in mine.

Either way, her mouth clamps shut. Her eyes face forward.

And then we turn a corner, and I'm home.

Chapter Twenty-Nine
THE ASSASSIN

I grew up in the royal palace in the heart of Astranza, and when I was a child, every hallway seemed magical. The marble gleamed, the tapestries were vibrant, and there were hints of wealth and privilege everywhere, right down to the veins of silver embedded in the doorframes. Gray and white stones could be found everywhere, with wooden beams crisscrossing every ceiling in artful patterns. Even after I was exiled, I still thought it was the most beautiful building ever constructed. Once I was hired by the Hunter's Guild, I had occasion to visit very fine estates, some of which were so grand that I almost didn't dare to break into them, but nothing ever came close to my childhood home.

Until now.

The Incendrian Palace is taller than any building I've ever seen, easily ten stories high at the center—and once we get inside, I realize that's just the atrium. From the outside, the stonework is heavy and dark, which made me think the interior would be gloomy, but the room is wide and airy, with plenty of light. The ceiling of the center atrium is lined with stained glass that throws blue and yellow shadows across the floor. As we climbed into Lastalorre from the valley, it didn't seem so high, but that was clearly an illusion, a massive building dwarfed by the surrounding mountains. There's a part of me that wants to stare like a boy.

The king mentioned ironwork throughout the palace, and he almost understated it. Steel and iron are *everywhere*. Stunning patterns line the stone walls: every archway, every window, even the floor in spots. I should be reveling in the architecture, but I've spent so long as an assassin that my brain is sketching out places to hide, the paths to climb to the ceiling, and at least three ways to escape.

I expected the palace to be packed with people: courtiers and servants and guards and all the people who want to cling to royalty. Astranza's court can be downright stifling.

But the palace here is . . . not. It seems to be nearly deserted, with few guards and fewer servants.

"I was not expected back so soon," Ky explains to us, as the soldiers take the horses to the stables. Not even Captain Zale has accompanied the king into the palace proper. "I will show you to some rooms so you can rest."

His voice is cold, formal, and I don't think he's made eye contact with Jory since she started going after him as we rode through the city. I don't think he's made eye contact with anyone. She still seems furious, so maybe she hasn't noticed. Maybe she doesn't *want* to notice.

Ky leads us down a narrow hallway, and every door we pass is lined with iron in a winding pattern. We stop near the end, and he sketches a sigil to light a torch on the wall. To my surprise, it's not *just* a torch—once lit, the fire continues on a path down the entire wall, seeming to disappear behind each door and into the rooms beyond. The hallway is suddenly thrown into vivid, flickering light, and the magic would likely be awe-inspiring on any other day.

But Jory stares at the trail of flame for a moment too long, then frowns.

I wonder if she's thinking about the accusations from the Incendrian citizens.

Either way, the king notices, because his shoulders droop. This time, when he speaks, his voice is sad. "You can have this wing, Princess. I will have food sent. The fire will warm your rooms, as well as the washbasins beyond." He hesitates. "Forgive me if you find it displeasing."

Jory opens her mouth, then closes it. Her lips form a line.

The king looks to me. "Asher. I will take you to—"

"No." Jory steps in front of me. "He will stay in *this* wing. With me."

His gaze turns flinty. "Fine. I will return at sundown. *Do not explore.*"

Then he turns away, and he doesn't say another word.

Jory turns away, and she doesn't either.

Lady Charlotte looks between us all, then follows the princess.

Fine.

I pick a room and lose myself inside it.

I expect elegance, but it's better. Six people could share the bed, and a set of doors twice my height leads to a terrace that overlooks the mountains. Astranza may be stunning in the summertime, but right now, Incendar wins the view. At the far side of the sleeping quarters is a washroom that's double the size of the apartment I once rented in Perriden. The trail of fire from the hallway ran the length of the wall in my bedroom, and it stretches into the washroom as well. The fire ends in a pile of glass stones under a wide steel basin that's more of a pool than a bathtub. I pull a chain and water flows. My eyebrows go up. Within minutes, water reaches the top. I touch my hand to the surface, and thanks to the glowing glass stones underneath, it's already lukewarm.

Fine, Ky, you can win this, too. I lose every inch of armor and clothing and all but leap in.

The brand on my shoulder reminds me that this was a terrible idea—but it only hurts for a moment. Or maybe the sensation of days' worth of sweat and dirt and riding grime washing away is simply worth the pain. I sink completely under the water and hold my breath.

But once I'm there, I think of the king. I watched his reaction to Jory's words when she was snapping at him. I saw the way her accusations struck him.

I saw it when he spoke to the people. I heard it in his voice.

For days, he's been competent and commanding, in clear control: of himself, of his soldiers, of every situation we've encountered. Of *me*.

When those men confronted us, he was still in control. Just . . . more than he needed to be.

It wasn't until he gave the order to attack that I realized Ky is just as broken as I am. Not broken by slavers or brothels. Not broken by cruelty or pain.

Broken by war.

Do his people not see that?

Does Jory *not see that?*

I come up from the water, swiping it from my eyes. I try to lie back against the edge, but that *does* hurt, so I turn the other way and hang over the rim, water dripping from my hair to sizzle on the glass rocks below.

I shouldn't care if he's broken. As always, this isn't my war, isn't my alliance. They're to marry, and I'm no one. I shouldn't be here at all.

But I think of the way he let me clutch at his arm. I think of the way he let me sleep curled against him.

I think of the way he heard my fear about the slavers, and he used it to trick me to gain his freedom—but then he still rescued me from Dane.

I think of the way my heart thrums when he touches me.

I think of the way he's really quite striking, and I still kind of hate it.

I lay so long, dozing, until the water grows almost too warm for comfort, and I wonder if this stupid king's magic might actually start to cook me.

A stack of bottles sits on a small table just within reach, along with a wooden box that turns out to be a shaving kit. I lather and scrape my face clean, then randomly pour a jar of scented crystals into the water with me. The scent of lavender flares in the air, and bubbles swirl through the water. I duck under the surface again and scrub at my hair until it feels slick and clean. Then I hold my breath until it hurts.

When I sit up, Jory is in the doorway.

I startle so hard I almost overturn the bathtub. Thank the stars I put away the shaving razor. Water sloshes over the sides and sizzles on the stones, steam rising around me.

"Jory! *Fuck*." I run a hand down my face, then flip wet hair out of my eyes.

"I'm sorry!" she cries. "I didn't mean to scare you. You were under for so long!"

My heart is pounding. "Well, you don't have to worry about me drowning because I nearly leapt into the fire."

"I'll go." Her cheeks are turning red. "I just—it's nothing. I thought—I don't—"

"*Stars in darkness*, girl. Stop. What's wrong?"

She turns around so she's not facing me any longer, and even puts her hands over her eyes. "I wanted to talk to you."

"So talk."

"Asher, you're *naked*."

Sometimes her innocence is almost hilarious. She's so fierce with the king, and I saw the dagger sticking out of that soldier's thigh. But if anyone knows how sheltered she is, it's me.

"You can't see anything," I say. "*I* can't even see anything. I poured an entire jar of soap in here."

That makes her turn back around. She peeks between her fingers, and then, seeing that I'm mostly covered, she drops her hand.

Her hair is wet, clearly from her own bath, and wrapped into a ropy braid. Her skin is also fresh-scrubbed. The worn armor and riding clothes are gone, replaced with a linen dress with a green overskirt. She looks simple and innocent and pretty, and I much prefer this to the tense, formal Princess Marjoriana who lives in the palace in Astranza.

"What's with the look?" she teases.

"I'm thinking you're beautiful," I say, and there's no teasing in my tone at all.

She sobers. Then frowns. And then her eyes well.

"Ah, Jory," I say. "Don't cry."

She comes into the washroom and all but drops to her knees beside the tub, and I realize this the first time we've been alone together since the morning I received orders to kill both her and the king.

She puts her hand on the edge of the tub, and I put mine over hers.

"Be mindful of the stones," I say softly.

She swallows and nods, and a tear slips down her cheek.

I reach up to brush it away, but my hand is wet, so it just adds more. I frown. "I'm making it worse," I say.

"You're not." Her eyes gaze up at me. "Asher, I love when you touch me."

That tugs at my heart in so many ways. I've wanted her forever, but my life made that far too complicated. And she's always been destined for someone else—including right now. Last night, she was scuffling with the king, and I know where that would've led if I hadn't woken up.

But now she's kneeling in front of *me*, her eyes wide and trusting, my fingers tracing a line of water across her cheek.

Both of these images tangle up in my mind, and suddenly, my cock stiffens. I'm grateful for the bubbles.

But then she puts a hand over mine, and the rest of me goes tense. I pull my hand back automatically, without meaning to.

Jory frowns. She puts her hand back on the rim of the tub.

After a moment, I put my hand back over hers.

Her eyes flick up to meet mine, as if she suddenly understands the significance. As if she finally understands why I can touch her, though it's so very different when *she* touches *me*.

"You could have told me," she says, and her voice is so soft. "About the slavers."

My hand goes still. "No," I say. "I couldn't."

"I really would have tried to help you."

"No one could've helped me," I say, and I mean it. "Not even you, Jor."

I should tell her to leave. I *need* to tell her to leave. Touching her is reckless, because every time I start, I never want to let her go.

But I brush a damp finger along her cheekbone again, more slowly this time.

Her breath catches. Just a little. Just enough.

The king will probably kill me for this, but we're alone and it's warm and I've been in love with her forever. I lean forward, just a bit, and brush my lips against hers. I smell the lavender, I taste her tears. Her lips part, and she kisses me back. But it's small. Gentle. Soft. Nothing like the rough-and-tumble passion she shared with the king before I interrupted.

Would I want that? I don't know. I take hold of her hand, then press it to my cheek. But when her fingers land on my skin, I freeze.

She draws back, but she leaves her fingers there. I leave my face there.

"Am I hurting you?" she whispers.

"No, lovely." But maybe she is. A little. My body wants to recoil. It's exquisite, though. This pain.

She wets her lips. "Please don't stop."

The plea in her voice means we *should* stop. When I'm wrapped up in shadows, it's easy to resist her. Right now I'm naked and hard, and I'm so aware of the feel of her palm against my cheek. There's a part of me that hates it, but there's a part of me that's imagining the slow path of her hand down my body. I draw a shuddering breath. "I'm not sure the king would approve."

Her eyes turn sharp and hard. "I'm not sure I care." Her lips part. "Asher, please."

I am not this strong—or maybe my body simply knows what it wants. I surge forward and press my mouth to hers again, and this time there's nothing small or gentle or tentative about it. When I tease at her lips with my tongue, her mouth parts, and it wakes something inside me. I force myself to be slow, drawing at her lips until it pulls a small sound from her throat. When she bites at my lip in response, I forget myself. I rise up a bit and grab hold of her waist, jerking her against me.

But then her hand slides into my hair, and I break free, gasping. A tiny bit of water sloshes over the side again, sizzling.

Jory lets me go, breathing hard. "Oh," she gasps.

I slink back under the suds again, then lean against the side, my fingers tight on the edge. Wet spots are all over her dress, and I wince.

"Forgive me," I say.

"Don't apologize." She drops to her knees beside the tub again, cautious of the stones. Her cheeks are pink and her lips are swollen. "Do it again."

Fuck. I'm so hard I'm pressed into the side of the tub, and I draw a ragged breath. If she keeps looking at me like that, I'm going to drag her into this water and pull her down on top of me and she'll learn a whole lot all at once.

But then I force myself to think clearly, and I realize what she said. I open my eyes and look at her. "Jory. Do you really want—"

"Yes." Her eyes are heavy lidded.

I put a finger over her lips and give her a stern look. "You almost kissed the king last night. Do you *really* want me, or are you mad at *him?*"

That draws her up short, and she goes still. A flicker of sorrow washes over her expression.

"Both?" she says softly.

I sigh, then nod toward the corner of the room, because the water really *is* growing too warm. "Fetch me those linens, Jor."

She does, and I stand, wrapping them around me as I go. She takes one glimpse down at the outline of my cock straining at the fabric and she turns bright red—then whips around, covering her face again. "Asher!"

"Well, that's your fault," I say. "If you ever start using your teeth on a man and he *doesn't* go rock hard, consider it a warning." I step over the side and onto the stone floor. "What on earth does Lady Charlotte think you're doing over here, anyway?"

"She's sleeping. She said she stayed awake last night to make sure the king didn't take advantage of me."

I roll my eyes and take another linen from a rack, rubbing it through my wet hair. "I'm glad you were safe."

She half turns to look at me. "You seemed to be rather cozy with the king yourself."

That's so unexpected that I flush immediately.

Especially because it summons the memory of the way the king rolled onto his knees and took hold of my chin.

We are not competing.

The way Jory leaned in to touch a finger to my cheek.

I close my eyes and swallow. I'm going to be hard for an hour at this rate.

"It was just cold," I say, and I hate that my voice is rough. I force my eyes open, and I walk past her, wondering what kind of clothes I might find in the bedroom. The wardrobe is surprisingly well stocked, with dresses and trousers and tunics and underthings stretching from one side to the other. I run my hand across the fine fabrics, all silk and velvet and calfskin leather.

I haven't worn anything this nice since I lived in the palace in Perriden.

Jory hasn't said anything, but I can feel her eyes on me.

"What?" I say flatly.

"He was going to kill those children, Asher." Her voice is so soft. "He wants this *alliance* and he wants to protect his *people* and he wants to make things *right*. I believe all of that. I've seen the kindness inside of him."

So have I. I think of the king breaking his bread in half—or telling one of his soldiers to make sure Lady Charlotte had enough silver to buy that woman's freedom.

Jory continues, "But he didn't tell those settlers who he was—and this is why! When his people approached him, he was ready to kill them! He gave the order—"

"I was there." I randomly pull trousers and a tunic from the closet.

"How could he?" she demands. "How could he, Asher? Is that why the rumors are so terrible? Is that why everyone is so afraid—"

"Jory." I toss the clothes on the bed and turn to face her. "He didn't see children."

"How could he not see children? They were right—"

"He saw attackers. He saw enemies. He saw a *threat*."

She falls silent and stares at me.

I take a step closer to her, and I reach out to take her hand. Then I press her palm to the center of my chest. Even with me controlling the action, there's a moment where I go still, where my heart stutters, begging me to recoil.

She must see a flicker of it in my expression, because I can see the response in hers. It's something akin to pity, and I hate it. But I need her to understand.

"You felt that?" I say softly.

She bites her lip, uncertain now. "Yes."

"The slavers broke me, Jory. Over and over again, until my body learned that if someone touched me, something bad was coming."

"Asher." She frowns a little. "You're not broken—"

"Oh, I am. It changed something in here . . ." I put my hand over hers, tapping over my heart. "And it changed something in my head. So now, even when it's someone I trust, even when it's someone I *love*, I still feel it."

As I say the heavy words, I'm surprised to realize they're not *entirely* true. At some point, I stopped wanting to recoil when *Ky* touches me.

That's too complicated to examine. Especially when Jory's hand is so heavy against my chest.

"He's broken, too," I say. I think of his nightmare in the inn, the way his eyes were dark and full of shadows. When that boy crashed through the door with an armload of firewood, he was out of his seat, ready for an attack. When the Draeg soldier stumbled out of that hut behind Jory, I thought he might call fire and level the entire encampment. "He's just broken in a different way."

"How?" she whispers. "He's not like you."

"Not by slavers. By *war*. He's learned to see a threat—and kill it. Because the alternative is that it would kill him first. Or worse, his soldiers. You've seen how deeply he cares for them. Who knows how many he's seen die?"

I watch emotions pass through her eyes as she works that through. "Is that why you told me to leave him be?"

"Yes."

"How did you know?"

I give her a look. "Because a lot of broken soldiers visit brothels, Jor."

Her expression twists like she thinks I'm teasing—but then she must realize I'm not. "Oh," she says softly. "I don't know what to do with this."

"I certainly can't solve it. But I don't think he meant to slaughter children. I think he's a man who was *attacked* and responded in kind. They didn't just come at him with grievances. They weren't unarmed. One of those men *did* draw a weapon."

"But he didn't see the *children*."

"But *you* did, and you stopped the fight. And when you called for his men to disarm, the king listened to *you*. It's not the first time, either." I kiss her on the forehead. "Seems like a powerful alliance, Your Highness."

Her mouth opens. Closes.

"Look at that," I say. "Maybe I *can* solve it."

"But what if Father dies, and the alliance fails?" She pauses. "And what if the king's magic really is causing his fields to go barren?"

I snort. "Now, those are problems I definitely can't solve. Turn around so I can get dressed."

She gives me a rueful look. "What if I don't want to?"

"Suit yourself." I drop the towel.

She whirls so quickly she almost smacks her face right into the wardrobe. "Asher! You are *never* this bold!"

She's right, I'm not. But much like the way I mentioned the fighting rings, there's something a bit freeing about knowing my past is no longer a secret. That she finally sees me—and it didn't scare her away. Maybe that's wrapped up in the way the king doesn't flinch from my past. A new emotion has been building in my chest for the last couple days, and it's so unfamiliar that I can't even identify it. It's not confidence or courage. It's something else entirely. It's an easing. A loosening. Not all the way—nowhere close—but it's something.

I reach for the trousers. "Well, I told you about using your teeth."

Her cheeks turn pink. She says nothing for a long moment, and I work the laces.

"Can I ask you a question?" she finally says, and her voice goes a bit quiet.

I tug a tunic over my head. "Anything."

"Do you fancy Ky?"

I freeze. The question is sobering, especially since I don't know how to answer.

"I don't know how to fancy anyone anymore," I say.

Despite that, I can't stop thinking about the king on top of her. I can't stop thinking about the weight of his hand on my face, or the way he offered me a bowl of food after I tried to kill his soldier. I can't stop thinking about that moment in the tavern when they were both touching me at once, how I felt it right down to my core. Even now, it's a low pulse of heat in my belly.

I need to stop thinking about this. Since enduring the slavers, I've never wanted anyone but Jory.

"You let *him* touch you," she says quietly.

I swallow, because I didn't realize it was so obvious. To my surprise, warmth is crawling up my neck. I look over at her. "Do you fancy the king?"

"I don't want to," she says softly, but her cheeks darken, and I know she's thinking of his body pinning her to the ground, the way his hand stroked over her breast.

Fuck. Now I'm thinking of it, too. I frown, then run a hand back through my damp hair. "I don't want to either."

"You were so angry last night." She pauses. "I thought you might be jealous."

"I'm not jealous," I say, and I mean it. Whatever I feel, it's not jealousy. At least not entirely.

"Really?"

"Jory." She's still turned toward the windows, staring out at the mountains. I cross the distance between us and put my hands on her waist, then pull her flush against me. She gasps in surprise, but her body yields under my hands, and she all but melts right into me. Even clothed, feeling the warm curve of her ass against me is more intense than I expected, and it pulls a low sound from my throat.

I lean down to whisper into her ear. "Do I *feel* jealous?"

"Asher," she breathes, leaning into me. I desperately want to stroke my hands up her body. To finish everything we started in the washroom.

There's a part of me that wishes I hadn't told her the truth. The boy she knew would pull away and put some distance between us. But now she's pressing herself against me, her ribs heaving a bit against mine. Instead of slinking into the shadows, I want to hitch up her skirts and bend her over against the bed.

But then I think of the way her hand slipped into my hair. How it made me jerk back. I think of what she's longing for—and everything I'm afraid of. My heart stutters a little.

I let go and step back.

She spins, her eyes full of fire.

"*No*," I say.

This time she crosses her arms and pouts. Her cheeks are all flushed, and some of her hair is beginning to come loose from the braid.

"Jory," I say. "You are *killing* me. And your fiancé might *really* kill me. Move. I need my boots."

"Why?" she demands.

Because the king is alone—and he shouldn't be.

The thought hits me harder than I'm ready for. I shouldn't care. I *shouldn't*. That flicker of not-quite-jealousy in my gut should be rejoicing that Jory has found something about him unappealing.

But I remember the way he woke from that nightmare. I saw the look on his face after he realized what almost happened—and he heard Jory's censure.

It reminds me of all the reasons I wouldn't tell her about *myself*.

I tug a boot on and work the laces. "We should go find him. I don't think you should leave things between you as you did."

"He's probably with his captain," she says. "Or the other soldiers."

I frown and pull on my other boot. "That man needs a few minutes *away* from soldiers."

"We're not allowed. He told us not to explore."

At that, I look up and meet her eyes. "Jory. When has that ever stopped us?"

Chapter Thirty
THE WARRIOR

The palace is so quiet, even in the center of Lastalorre. It's well known that I spend little time here, and I've never seen the sense in keeping a full staff of servants and guards for an empty castle. Especially now, when I wasn't supposed to return for *weeks*.

But it's a double-edged sword, because the relentless silence is part of the reason I hate being here. At nights, I'll lie in bed, stare at my ceiling, and think of what's happening to my soldiers on the border. During the day, I'll endure endless meetings with advisers. It's interminable.

Even my afternoon was full of nothing but melancholy and dread. My chambers are lavish and well-appointed, so soaking away days of travel grit should have been calming. Soothing. But lying in the warm water was the exact opposite. Every time I ducked my head under, I came up expecting to find attackers waiting.

I can never sleep here. At the same time, I don't want to be awake.

If Sev were here, I'd be in his quarters. He'd be pouring me whiskey, and I'd be dealing cards. We'd wait out the day until sleep overtook us both, and then we'd start over again tomorrow. We wouldn't talk about angry citizens or wildfires or potentially fractured alliances, but we'd *know*, and that would be enough.

But Sev is already gone. I need reports from my other captains, and if Draeg soldiers are sneaking across the border from Astranza, I need to be prepared. Sev took Nikko and rode out almost immediately. I haven't seen Callum and Garrett, but I have no doubt they headed into the city—and Roman would have followed, if for no other reason than to make sure they didn't get into trouble.

I wish I could join them.

Instead, I'm here, and there's one part of the palace that I don't hate.

Victoria's room is down a long hallway on the second floor. I used to have extra guards stationed at the opening to the hallway, but I quickly learned that it led people to believe something especially valuable was down this way, so I had them reassigned. Now it's simply my sister's suite, and it's known among the court that Princess Victoria prefers to keep to herself, valuing her solitude, using her time to read and reflect on the state of Incendar.

It's known among my closest circle that Victoria rarely leaves her quarters at all.

When I stride down the hallway, I look for any new signs of damage. The walls are bare stone and steel, so there's nothing that can burn, not for a good fifty feet. But when her magic flares, sometimes it will spark into the palace. Today, nothing seems new.

It's not a relief. If there's no mark in this hallway, it means her magic flared somewhere *else*—like the crops we passed when we rode up the hill.

When I reach the end, the door is open, and there's an elderly woman in a rocking chair just inside. She looks up in surprise when I step into the threshold. White hair is tightly bound back from her face. One bright blue eye blinks at me in the sunlight. The other is lost in a mass of burn scarring.

"Ky," she says fondly. She was my nanny when I was a boy. That was well before Victoria gave her the scars on her face.

I dread the day she can no longer look after my sister. I sometimes worry I've kept her to this role too long.

"Norla," I say. "How is she?"

Her face breaks into a warm smile. "She's doing very well—this week. She will be happy to see you."

This week. I wonder if that means she destroyed the crops last week.

"I'll visit with her for a while if you'd like to fetch some dinner."

That smile widens. "I will, thank you." She swats me on the arm. "Your Majesty."

I lean down and kiss her on the forehead. "You have my gratitude, as always."

She squeezes my arm. "I know."

Then she's gone, and I step farther into the room.

Victoria is near the back corner, sitting cross-legged on the stone floor, wearing a simple linen dress. She has a colorful array of a hundred metal and glass tiles on the floor in front of her, and she's arranging them in patterned lines—one of her favorite games. Her hair is lighter than mine, a golden blond, and it's so long that it reaches her waist. When she was young and difficult, Norla used to cut it short, but when Victoria grew older, she grew to love having her hair combed. Now she'll sit for an hour every morning, just letting someone run a brush through her tresses.

She doesn't look up as I approach, but I know she's already aware I'm here. Our father used to get frustrated that she wouldn't greet him with excitement when he returned, but I figured out early on that Victoria seems to have an odd impression of time. It doesn't matter how long we've been gone. As soon as we're *here*, it's as if we've been here all along.

"The red and black is missing," she says.

"No, it's not," I say. I drop to sit cross-legged in front of her, the tiles arrayed between us. I'm very careful not to touch any of them. "You'll find it."

She slides the tiles around. They're very pretty, a mixture of thick glass and steel, forged so hot that the glass doesn't crack, even when she drops them against the stone floor.

"Are you hungry?" I say. "It's close to dinnertime."

"No."

"Norla said you've had a good week."

"We went for a walk."

"You did?" My heart thumps as I think about the wildfires that no one can stop.

"Yes." She picks up two tiles, one blue and yellow, one green and orange. Then she smiles at me. She's really very beautiful, and when she smiles like that, I sometimes see the young woman she might have been, if she hadn't been birthed into tragedy.

I also think about the men who've dared to try convincing me that they have the skills to "help" the princess with her condition.

"We saw two butterflies," she tells me, bouncing the tiles. "These colors."

"*Two*," I say. "That sounds very lucky."

"Norla said one was a moth. But she was wrong."

"Silly Norla."

"It's not silly. It's ignorant."

I snort, glad I sent the nanny away. "*Vic*."

She sets down the tiles. "The red and black is missing," she says again.

"It's not. You'll find it. You always do."

She surveys the tiles, moving them carefully along the stones. "Who are they?"

I frown, because for a moment, I don't understand the question—and then I remember that I have guests in the palace, and almost no staff to stop them from roaming.

I snap my head around. Jory and Asher are in the doorway. Their eyes are a little wide, a little confused, a little concerned. I have no idea how much they've seen or how much they've figured out, but it's clearly been *enough*.

Rage and panic go to war in my chest. I *told them* to stay put. I don't know what to say. I don't know how to react.

I know it would be *very* bad for my sister to have a reaction to their presence. I never know how strangers will affect Victoria.

Jory's eyes go a bit soft. "Ky. I'm sorry—"

I lift a hand and shake my head sharply.

Her eyes widen, but then she nods.

"Ky?" says Victoria.

I turn back to face her. Her eyes, the same honey brown as mine, look right into my face, never quite making eye contact.

I keep my voice low. I have to clear my throat. "Yeah."

"Who are they?"

"They are . . . friends. Jory. And Asher." I hesitate, wondering how much to share. "They will be staying with me in the palace for a short while."

She shuffles her tiles again. "I want them to sit down."

Well, I don't.

Introducing new variables to Victoria's environment is always risky. But refusing her is risky, too. Especially since she's already seen them.

"Just until Norla comes back," I say. "Then they have to leave." I look back over my shoulder. "Come. Sit. Say nothing. Touch nothing." I keep my voice soft, but I leave no room for disobedience in my tone.

"Why do you tell them this?" says Victoria.

"Because I don't want them to break your tiles."

Asher and Jory sit.

"The red and black is still missing," Victoria says.

Jory points. "It's there."

I smack a hand over my face, then drag it down.

Victoria looks up, then follows Jory's finger. And indeed, there is the red and black piece, just under her left foot.

"I wanted to find it," she says.

"Oh!" says Jory. "I'm—"

I shake my head at her, then hold my breath.

But Victoria only takes the line of tiles she's already arranged and scrambles them all up in a pile again.

"I'll start over," she says.

"That will be more fun," I say.

Jory's mouth is clamped shut now, but she looks between the two of us, then glances at Asher.

I keep my eyes on my sister. After everything that happened this afternoon, I'm not sure how to handle their appearance *here* of all places.

"Ky," calls Norla from the doorway. "I'm back. Oh! You have guests."

She sounds surprised—which I can appreciate.

"They have to leave now, Norla," says Victoria. "Because you're back."

"I'll return in the morning," I say. I reach out and tuck a lock of hair behind her ear. "Maybe we can go for a walk and you can show me where you saw the butterflies." I pause. "Or we could read a story together. One of your favorites."

Victoria says nothing to that. She places the first tile in her line, a blue and orange one. She's focused on her game now, and she has no further time for conversation.

It tugs at something inside of me, but I know better than to acknowledge it.

I look at Asher and Jory. "Out."

The princess looks back at me, and I watch pity flash through her eyes.

That is the last thing I need. So I square my shoulders and turn for the door.

I DON'T SAY anything until we're well away. It's unlikely that Victoria would hear us—or try to follow—but I won't risk it. I storm down the staircase toward the main atrium, but there *are* guards near the main doors. I don't want our words to be overheard, so I turn down the first hallway I find, and there, I finally round on them.

"I *told you* to stay put," I say, and it takes effort to keep my voice down. "Do I need to put you in a cell? Chain you to the wall?"

Jory's eyes light with fire, and she inhales like she'd set me ablaze if she could. "So I'm to be your *prisoner*? I thought I was your *guest*."

"*Guests* do not intrude on—"

"No," says Asher. "We're not starting this way."

Rage sparks in my chest. He's so defiant. So cavalier. They both are. I round on him. "*You* have no right—"

"I know, I know. You're so powerful." He puts a hand against my shoulder. Then, quicker than thought, he shoves me right into the wall.

Jory gasps, but I'm bigger than he is, and I know I can throw him off. But Asher ducks right inside my movement and jams his forearm into my throat. As always, he's remarkably fast, and the movement pins my neck to the wall, his arm pressing up against my jaw, his weight blocking me. I readjust to strike, fighting for leverage, because I have the strength to break his hold. But instead of attacking, his arm slips away and his hand slides up my neck. His thumb presses beside my windpipe, the same way I held him on the first night. I'm suddenly so aware of each rise and fall of my chest pressing into his, each beat of my heart.

His grip is looser now, and I could throw him off if I wanted to. But it's so startling and unexpected that I go still. My thoughts can't realign, can't parse out this way of fighting. I don't even know if we *are* fighting.

I don't think he does, either. Because he may have caught me against the wall, but this has shifted from aggression into something more like vulnerability. The wolf, unsure if it should bite your fingers off or lick your hand.

I keep my eyes on his, waiting to see what he chooses. That familiar flicker of challenge flares between us, but it's different now. More charged. Asher shifts his weight, and the press of his body moves against mine. Such a tiny, simple motion shouldn't affect me, but it *does*. I can't tell if he's letting me go or pressing closer. Either way, I'm instantly hard, and my breath goes a bit ragged.

Do you want to fight? I think. *Or do you want to fuck?*

Considering everything I know about him, I think it's both.

His blue eyes haven't left mine, and when he speaks, his voice is very quiet. "Ready to try again?"

"Fine."

"Good boy." He smacks me on the cheek, too rough to be friendly, then draws back, letting me go.

I'm still angry, but the edge is gone. I can't focus, and my breathing feels too fast. I run a hand down my face, willing my body to cool. "Fuck you, Asher."

The princess is looking between the two of us, both hands pressed to her mouth. Her eyebrows are up, her eyes wide. Her cheeks are bright pink.

"How did you do that?" she whispers at Asher.

"Please. Men are easy."

My pride sparks. "I am not—"

"Do you want me to do it again?"

That makes me flush, and I'm not ready for it. "No," I grind out.

"Exactly." He glances at the princess. "Jory has questions for you."

I fold my arms. "*Questions.*"

"That's why we came looking," Jory says. "But you must have somewhere better for a conversation than a hallway."

My brain can't keep up. I can't believe we've shifted from arguing to fighting to seduction to interrogation, all in the span of one minute.

Actually, considering *everything* I know about the two of them, I should have expected nothing less.

I run a hand back through my hair. After what just happened, it would be torture to lock ourselves in a cold strategy room. I definitely don't want to go back to my bedchambers.

But then I remember our conversation from the ride here, right before my people attacked us and everything unraveled.

"Come," I say. "I have just the place."

Chapter Thirty-One
THE PRINCESS

The king leads us toward the back of the palace. I'm so struck by how *empty* it is. Even when Dane and my father aren't in residence, the palace in Astranza is always bustling with people. Guards and servants and courtiers and noblemen *everywhere*. It's almost impossible to be alone.

Here, Ky's palace seems . . . desolate.

He seemed so enraged to find us at the doorway to his sister's room, but truly, the bigger shock is that he thought we *wouldn't* find him. The exterior of the palace appears suitably appointed, but inside, there are so few guards, so few servants. Asher and I thought for sure that we would be stopped or detained as we wandered through the halls, but the palace felt eerily quiet. If I'd come here alone, I would have thought it was haunted. The king claimed that he wasn't expected for a matter of weeks, which . . . fair, but still. Certainly he must carry out kingly duties from here?

Or does he do everything from the battlefield?

I keep thinking of everything Asher said. *He's broken, too. Just in a different way.*

When he told me about that, the explanation tore at my heart. I never considered. From the second Ky walked into Astranza, he carried himself as a fierce warrior—and then, over the next few days, he revealed the kindness beneath. I heard it today, in the low voice he used with his sister, or earlier, the way he took that little girl's hand. But he clearly doesn't see that kindness in *himself*. Or . . . maybe he does. Maybe that kindness terrifies him. Maybe it doesn't feel like kindness at all, and instead it feels like weakness.

When he confronted us in the hallway, I thought we were going to wage war right there. He was so angry, and it reminded me of the way he lost his temper when we confronted his people. I watched his hands flex, and even though I didn't think he'd hit me, I did expect him to sketch a sigil and call fire.

But then Asher pushed him right up against the wall, and Ky seemed to . . . melt. I was surprised to find it lit a fire in my own belly, and it still hasn't fully extinguished.

I glance at Asher. "Truly," I murmur at him. "How did you do that?"

He shrugs. "It's a skill like any other."

"How is . . . *that* a skill?"

He looks at me like I'm insane. "Am I going to have to draw some pictures of what happens in a brothel, Jory?"

That makes me flush, which is ridiculous, because, aside from the obvious, I actually have no idea what happens in a brothel. "Maybe," I snap.

"Oh." He considers that. "People come for a lot of different reasons. Sometimes they come angry, and it's better if they're . . . not." He shrugs. "Much like fighting in the arena, if you don't want to end up with broken ribs, you pick up a little skill."

Well, that's sobering. His voice is so casual, but I glance over at him, and I can't help the pity in my gaze. I realize the king is looking at him the same way.

Asher sighs. He flicks his eyes at the ceiling. "Sometimes it's easier to be a shadow."

I frown, but Ky has reached a large, ornate steel door, and he pushes through.

Cool air finds my cheeks and lifts my hair, and I realize we're outside. Well . . . sort of. The clear sky stretches overhead, and we've reached that point of twilight where stars have begun to twinkle to the east, while the last bit of sunlight still glows above the horizon in the west. The moon has risen, hanging just above the mountains, which tower above us.

But we're still clearly in a room—or perhaps a low-walled courtyard, because there's no ceiling. Intricate metalwork is on display here, too, spires and twists stretching along the wall, reaching high into the air. Flowering vines would be stunning in this room, but I wonder if the drought prevents them from growing. The floor is marble, gleaming in the moonlight, and a dozen massive square pools stretch in two rows, leading away from us. The water in each is tranquil, reflecting the stars above, creating a fascinating illusion that the sky has been captured in twelve distinct frames.

"The Hall of Stars," says Asher.

Ky looks at him. "Yes," he says, and he seems pleased.

Then he sketches a sigil, and light flares. As he did in the hallway to my chambers, he touches his hand to the wall, and the flame catches, racing along the stone. It streaks all the way around the room, coming back to where we stand at the entrance, brightening the space. But as I watch, the ring of fire does not remain along the wall. There are other, narrower paths, and flame crawls more slowly along the iron artistry, until all of it is lit and glowing. Fire has also followed a dozen small trails to light up glass stones below these pools, similar to the basin in my washroom. The entire space begins to glow and flicker, from the marble to the iron to the water itself, but the reflection of the sky never shimmers, never changes.

"Oh," I breathe, because words don't seem powerful enough to capture it. We have nothing like this in Astranza—and now that I've seen it, I never want to leave.

"I hate most of the palace," Ky says. "But I do love it here."

That gets my attention. "You hate the palace?"

He nods, as if that explains everything. "Come. Sit. You can ask your questions, Princess."

He leads me to the middle of the room, where there are stone benches and wooden tables. Some are lined with plush cushions, while others are bare. The Hall of Stars is clean—pristine even—so I can tell it's well cared-for, but the bleakness of the entire palace is shocking to me. In Astranza, a space like this would never be empty. The fires would never go cold.

Ky gestures to one of the cushioned benches, and I sit. Asher drops beside me, and I'm startled when his thigh brushes mine. The king looks down at us both for a long moment, then turns one of the wooden chairs to face us, and sits himself.

All of a sudden, I'm reminded of the morning we met. We sat just like this, and I had a hairpin clutched under my knuckles. He disarmed.

We spoke honestly—or so I thought.

"I would like to begin anew," I say, feeding him the exact words he said to me that morning.

As usual, his eyes spark with cunning, and maybe a little appreciation. But it's only for a moment, and then they turn sad. "I don't think that's possible at this point, Princess."

The word has never put distance between us, but just now, it seems to. "Jory," I say softly.

"Jory," he concedes.

Silence builds between us for a long moment, and I begin to realize Asher was right. The king can only set the field as an adversary. As if we were preparing for battle. As if this were truly an interrogation. Maybe *that's* why he keeps saying I'm formidable. Maybe he doesn't know any other way.

Very well, then.

"Why didn't you tell me about your sister?" I say.

His mouth twists, and he glances away. "Victoria is . . . well. You only saw her for a moment, and perhaps a moment was enough. In many ways, she seems to have the mind of a child—though she's *not*. That said, she can be easy to manipulate, easy to control. It would take nothing for someone with bad intentions to use her against me—or in place of me." He pauses. "She has always been kept very secluded, with private caretakers. When necessary, I can present her at court, for brief periods." Another pause. "She's very direct, and often quite lucid. She appears aloof, not addled. Very few people know the truth."

I study him. "What happened to her?"

He takes a long breath. "I don't know for certain. I was young when she was born. Our mother did not survive it. The baby was . . . very small. Very weak. They told my father she would likely not last the season. So he took me to the battlefield, and left her with a wet nurse."

"He left your sister to *die*?" I say.

"And he took you to *war*," says Asher.

Ky's frown deepens. "Again—I was young. I don't know every thought that crossed his mind." His voice sharpens a bit. "But his wife was dead, his daughter was close, and he had a son left with no mother. So yes, he took me with him."

I understand the sharpness in his voice—because I feel the same thing. "My mother died, too," I say quietly.

"And mine," says Asher.

Ky sighs, then runs a hand across the back of his neck. For a flash of time, he looks heartbroken, but then it's gone.

Oh. That's why he hates it here. This is where his mother died. This is where his most sorrowful memories are kept. So his life is split between a place like this and a battlefield where he risks his life and his people perish. He clearly loves his sister. I could hear that in every word he spoke to her—and I saw his pain when she seemed unaware of it. But she's vulnerable. She leaves *him* vulnerable—and therefore his kingdom vulnerable. He hates that, too.

I genuinely didn't think anything could be more tragic than what Asher told me about himself. No wonder Ky is so desperate for this alliance—and so relieved that we discovered the truth about the assassins.

"What else do you want to know?" Ky says to me. The sharp edge is back in his accent, emotion locked away. He's the perfect soldier again, ready for war.

"Does she have magic?" I say carefully.

"Yes."

My heart thumps. "So she can sketch sigils—"

"No." He shudders. "She's fascinated by anything vibrant, and if she knew how to summon it on purpose, I think she'd burn the whole kingdom down." He pauses again, but this one is weighted. "But her power can flare unexpectedly. If something upsets her, if she loses her temper, if she panics—anything can trigger the magic, and without training, she has no control. Often, it's small. But sometimes, it's not. I can summon fire from quite a distance, so it stands to reason that she can, too. She's burned herself, her nannies . . . there's a reason I keep her down a stone hallway."

I study him. "That's why you were so upset," I say. "When I tried the sigil in the settlement."

"Yes," he says gravely. "I know how much damage untrained magic can cause."

"Is Victoria burning your crops?" says Asher.

Ky looks at him. Seconds tick by, and the silence is painful.

"I don't know," he finally says. "It might not be her. Without training, I have no way of knowing if her magic causes fires elsewhere. I can direct fire away from me, but it took years to develop any kind of precision." He pauses. "Without rain, the land is so dry. Whether it's Victoria or not, once a fire starts, it's near impossible to stop."

And all his terrifying power can't help. I saw that myself. I think of the scent of smoke when we camped in the ravine, and I wonder if wildfires were flaring then. "Could you ban fire, the way we did in Astranza?"

"We may not have your deep snows, Princess, but it is still winter. I cannot ask my people to freeze. They already suffer enough." He pauses, his tone grave. "And how would I justify it? How could I even *enforce* it, for that matter?"

I remember our conversation about the lies rulers tell their people, how I asked what lies *he* tells. He didn't answer. But as I consider his questions, I realize that there's no good solution. I think of Charlotte bringing me the ice-cold cup of tea. A night without fire in the palace was miserable—and that was just a night.

"Could Victoria live elsewhere?" I say.

He sighs heavily. "I've tried—but she does not handle change well, which brings its own set of risks and challenges. She fears being in a carriage, so traveling could make her panic and cause her magic to flare. Once I was able to take her to the cliffs over the ocean, and I thought she might like it there . . . until she decided she had enough, and tried to walk back to Lastalorre, in the cold, in the middle of the night. We found her soaking wet, in a ravine. I had to bring her home."

I can hear the worry in every word. He's such a protector.

Unlike Dane . . . who's not.

Ky looks into my eyes and says, "Forgive me, Princess. I asked for no lies between us, and I . . . I did not intend for this to be a lie. But perhaps . . . perhaps it was an omission. You deserve the full truth. My army is fierce. Incendar is strong—for now. I will protect these borders, and I will protect you. If Dane proceeds with this alliance, I will do my best to protect Astranza. But my sister is . . . my sister. Keeping her a secret was an effort to protect her, not to deceive you. But you see why I am so very desperate for your father's help, and why I will do anything to ensure this alliance is a success."

He's so earnest. As always, he speaks with such conviction. I still don't know how Dane negotiated with this man for months, because there's a part of me that would've given him everything he asked for on the very first day.

But as I look into his eyes, I realize Asher is looking at me, and there's weight in his gaze. He's been affected by every word the king said as well.

We both know that my father can't uphold this alliance—or if he can, it won't be for very long.

Emotion wraps up my chest and draws tight. Maybe I'm being disloyal to Astranza, but I cannot lie for Dane anymore.

"Ky," I say, and my voice is so soft. "My father is dying."

He goes completely, utterly still. The fires in the room flicker and blaze for a wild moment, as if reacting *for* him. For all the warmth surrounding us, his eyes have gone ice-cold.

"I didn't know," I say in a rush. "Dane only told me the night before you arrived, and he threatened that it would be my fault if I risked the alliance—because Astranza needs you. If my father's weather magic cannot protect our soldiers—"

"You need mine to do it."

He says it so quietly. This is worse than that moment when he finally broke from strain and lost his temper. I swallow thickly, then nod.

He still hasn't moved.

"She truly did not know," says Asher.

Ky's eyes flick to him.

"I heard Dane tell her myself. I saw him *threaten* her myself."

The king's eyes shift back to me, and I watch him glance at my wrist.

I remember the bruises that were there the morning we met, and I know he remembers, too.

"How long does King Theodore have?" he says.

"I don't know. But Dane believes it will be soon."

His jaw twitches. "No wonder he dragged out the negotiations. No wonder he spent *weeks* on minor points. He was biding his time, knowing I would gain no magic, while he would get my army. And all the while, my people move toward starvation."

"I'm sorry," I whisper. I hadn't considered the *reason* for Dane's delays—and I wonder if this is worse than just sending assassins after us.

Ky sighs, rubbing his hands down his face again. "So I have struck an alliance that yields nothing for my people—and merely puts them at risk. More at risk than they already were."

"Well," says Asher. "Not *quite*."

We both look at him. We both say, "What?"

He shrugs. "No one signed anything. You're not married." He looks at Ky. "Didn't you tell Jory that you'd strike the whole thing and rewrite it with *her*?"

"Well, yes, but—" He straightens, his gaze darkening. "Wait, were you *spying*?"

Asher waves it off. "That's hardly the worst thing I've done. But if you already know the truth about King Theodore—"

"And if I'm *here*..." I prompt.

Ky looks between the two of us, considering. But his mouth is still a line.

"When was Dane to begin providing food?" I say.

"He wasn't," Ky says. "It was the very first thing I asked for."

Rage surges in my chest. "He wouldn't give you *food*? Now *I* want to ride back and shoot him."

Ky snorts. "I'll saddle the horses right now." He pauses. "Princess—your brother was quite resistant to my requests for anything that would provide immediate aid. Knowing this, it's clear that he designed this alliance with the knowledge that Incendar would be kept weak, while I would be obligated to support Astranza."

"Dane also thought he could bully me into keeping this a secret," I say. "But he couldn't." I reach out and put a hand over his. "Ky. You really *could* saddle horses right now. Our winter stores are full. Overflowing, even. You said it yourself in the inn: Astranza doesn't know the meaning of *meager portions*. We could have wagons filled and crossing the border in a matter of days—before Dane would even know. On *my* order."

A new emotion flickers in his eyes, and he puts a hand over mine. "Not *now*, Princess—because I'm not riding back into Astranza without a regiment behind me."

"Behind *us*," I say.

He takes a breath, then pulls my hand to his mouth, and kisses my palm. His fingers are so warm, and there's so much reverence in the motion, and I shiver. Without warning, I'm remembering the weight of him when we were tussling, the feel of his thumb brushing along the curve of my breast.

But his eyes are still serious. "If your word is good, then yes, Princess. *Yes*. If you will help me feed my kingdom, then whatever you ask, it's yours."

"Sanctuary," I say immediately.

He looks at me, and his eyebrows flicker into a frown. "I won't let Dane harm you. I would hope I've been clear."

"Not for me," I say. "For Asher."

This time they both go still.

Asher finally looks at me. "I'm not a part of this."

"You *are* a part of this," says the king. "You've been a part of this since the moment you forced me out of the palace in Perriden."

That draws Asher up short, but only for a second. He glares between the two of us, but his gaze stops on me. "No. I'm not." His eyes light with a spark of challenge, but maybe a little belligerence, too. "He's your future husband, Jor. It's clear you want each other."

I glare at him, but heat is already climbing up my throat. The worst part is that he's not wrong about either half of that statement. "*Asher.*" I swallow. "I don't—I want—"

But I can't finish either statement.

I don't want him to go.

I might want the king . . . but I want Asher, too.

"Please," I say softly. "Stay."

Asher glances away, his gaze locking down. "I shouldn't be here. Just lock me in a carriage and send me back—"

"Bleeding skies," Ky snaps. "The two of you are worse than Cal and Garrett." He sighs heavily. "I'm going to knock you both into the pool."

"Oh, shut up," says Asher. "You are not—"

Ky grabs the edge of the stone bench and flips it back. I shriek before I realize it's even happening, and then I'm soaking wet and sputtering.

The water isn't deep at all, and once I sit upright, it's level with my chest. Thanks to the fire in the room, it's delightfully warm—but I simply cannot believe he did that.

The king is looking between us, firelight flickering across his features. "Asher." He crosses his arms, and his voice goes low, full of honey. "I'm not sending you away."

As always, Asher goes still when the king says his name. He just said it's clear that the king and I want each other—and he's not wrong. I felt the king's hard weight thrusting against me last night. Just the memory of it sends a pulse of heat right between my legs.

But it's clear that they want each other, too.

I think of everything I've learned about Asher, and everything he said about our alliance. I think of everything he's gone through, the way his body reacts when I touch him. I think of how he reacts when the *king* touches him.

Maybe he doesn't need me to negotiate for sanctuary—and instead he needs me to negotiate *this*.

I look at him in the warm water of the pool. The firelight glistens off his blond hair, droplets of water clinging to his jaw, just below the lines of ink on his cheek. His eyes are still on the king, belligerent and wary.

"Asher," I say softly. "Kiss me."

For an instant, he freezes—but then his gaze meets mine, and he obeys. When Asher takes hold of my waist, it draws a small sound from my throat, but then he sucks my lower lip right between his teeth. It's sudden and aggressive and gentle all at the same time, and I'm gasping into his mouth. All the heat he stoked in my chambers blooms between my legs. I could drown in the taste of him.

But then my hands fall on his arms, clinging to him. I feel the change, the *hesitation*, and I draw back.

"Stop?" I whisper.

He's breathing hard, but after a moment, he shakes his head.

"Do you still fancy the king?" I say, my voice just as soft.

He holds so still, his eyes boring into mine. But then he nods.

I lean in, very carefully, and brush my lips against his. This time, he breathes, his eyes falling closed.

I finally look up at Ky. His golden eyes are full of heat, watching us both. Waiting.

"You're a part of this, too," I say. "Join us."

The king doesn't move. His eyes flick between us as if he's not sure he should dare.

But Asher takes hold of my waist and pulls me against him, and his hand slips right up my rib cage to stroke a thumb right over my breast. It's quick and hot and that tiny movement pulls a sound right from my throat. My legs shift in the warm water, and suddenly my clothes feel like too much.

"Don't worry," Asher says to him, and now his tone is low and taunting, reminding me of their moment in the hallway. "We are not competing, remember?"

Water splashes. Ky makes an aggrieved sound. "Oh, fuck you, Asher," he says. And that's all I hear, because the king's warmth is suddenly at my back, his hands are on my hips, and his mouth, hot and sweet, closes on my neck.

Chapter Thirty-Two
THE PRINCESS

It's so warm with both of them pressing into me in the heated water of the pool. Ky holds me from behind, one arm around my waist, another stroking my breast. He must have stripped his jacket and tunic before splashing into the water, because his arm is bare, and the heat of his skin pulses against my back. He's tucked me against him so tightly that I can feel the length of him, hard and erect, through my layers of skirts. Every time his finger strokes over my nipple, it pulls at something deep inside, like a chord only I can hear.

I can feel Asher, too, the hard press of him against my thigh. His kisses have slowed, his tongue exploring my mouth, and it's like he's somehow timed it with the rhythm of Ky's finger stroking my breast. At some point he pulled his own tunic over his head, and my fingers keep brushing his bare skin. I shift against them both, craving more, *wanting* more, worried that this will stop before I'm ready—and terrified that it will keep going. My legs part, almost of their own accord.

The king tugs at the lacing of my dress just as his teeth tug at my ear, and I make a small sound.

"Yes?" he says, the word gentle, careful. He pulls at the lacing again, and his question is clear.

"Yes," I say, and my answer is practically a gasp. "Please."

He tugs harder, and the ribbon comes loose. His fingers encircle the bare skin of my breast just as Asher pushes my heavy skirts aside. Asher strokes his hand up the length of my calf, then my thigh, his fingers so smooth under the water. My clothes feel like they're strangling me, and I'm suddenly panting, intoxicated from the feel of them both. I feel as though my heart might stop—or possibly take flight.

"Jory," says Asher, and I open my eyes.

The sky is full of stars behind him. He traces a thumb over my lower lip, his gaze searching mine. "Too much?"

The instant he says it, Ky goes still. Asher's eyes shift, and they must exchange a glance over my head, because the king's hands move, then let go of me altogether.

"Not too much," I whisper. But maybe I'm lying. All of my inexperience seems to have caught up with me at once, leaving me tongue-tied.

Asher studies me again, and then he kisses me on the forehead. Simple and chaste.

I want to grab him. "Don't you dare leave."

He laughs a little, under his breath. "I'm not leaving you, Jor." His eyes flick up again. "I'll entertain your king while you determine what you want."

Then without hesitation, he tackles Ky, full strength. They go skidding backward in the water, causing ripples and waves to go over the side and sizzle where water meets the rocks. At first, it's so surprising that it makes me giggle—because it's *clear* that Ky didn't expect it, and I wonder if this is like that moment in the hallway. Asher pressed the king into the wall in a way that seemed like a battle and a seduction until I couldn't tell how much of their reaction was hostility—and how much was intrigue.

But just now, they tussle and roll in the water for longer than I expect, grappling and splashing and pinning each other with enough force that I start to think they're really fighting.

"Hey," I say. "Asher. Ky. *Gentlemen.*"

I try to crawl through the water toward them, but now the dress really *is* a problem. The corset is already half-unlaced, so I shed it with the overskirts until I'm left in my muslin shift. But just as I draw close, they somehow wrestle themselves upright. They're both on their knees, breathing hard, every muscle taut. Water glistens on their skin, sparkling in the firelight. They're face-to-face, very close, and this time, the king has bested Asher. Ky has his arms pinned behind his back, and I see the strain in his grip.

For a moment, I think belligerent animosity is going to break us apart again. Asher's jaw is clenched, his chest rising and falling swiftly. But as I look at them, I realize there's no lingering aggression in the air. No hostility. Asher isn't trying to escape. Ky isn't struggling to pin him.

This isn't restraint. This isn't confinement.

This . . . this is *holding*.

Eventually, the king speaks, and his voice is very low, very quiet. "You don't have to pick a fight every time. You don't."

Asher's body gives a little jerk, and he takes a sharp breath. I expect the king to let him go, but he doesn't. He simply waits, and I watch Asher's breathing slow, every muscle relaxing, one by one.

And then he puts his forehead down against Ky's shoulder.

You don't have to pick a fight.

But much like the king and his own inner struggles, I wonder if that's the only way this feels safe for Asher. Like he doesn't trust himself to be vulnerable, so someone else has to win it.

I tuck myself in behind him, mindful of his wound, pressing my face to his good shoulder. I feel him stiffen as soon as he feels me behind him, and I almost regret touching him. But after a moment, he relaxes again.

The king adjusts to pull me into their odd embrace, resting his hand against my cheek, holding me against Asher. For the longest moment, we simply rest there in the warmth of the water, feeling each other breathe.

But then Ky shifts, moving slightly. He leans in to kiss me gently on the lips, drawing a wet finger along my chin. "Princess," he says. Then, as before, he runs a finger under Asher's jaw, too, and I feel the shiver go through my friend's body. This time, however, he leans down to press the lightest kiss to Asher's temple. "Hunter." He nods toward the edge. "As usual, you're both a chaotic mess. Come. Get out of the water. I know what we need."

WE LIE IN the pillows, and the king has a servant bring small bowls of fruits and nuts, along with a bottle of wine. The fire makes the air warm enough that my shift dries quickly, and we lie on the pillows and mats from the benches. Ky was the first to stretch out on one, and he says, "Tell me what you were like when you were young."

At first, we're quiet, because it's unclear which one of us he was speaking to. But then I realize it's *both*, because Asher says, "We drove the palace staff crazy. We were always somewhere we weren't supposed to be."

And then he's telling a story about our childhood, a time we snuck into the kitchens to steal pastries that were so hot they left blisters on my fingers for days. It leads to other memories, other stories, until we talk about the time we were teenagers in the hayloft above the stables, how the night watchman almost caught us.

Some of the stories turn darker, the months of waiting when I thought I'd never see Asher again. The way I rejoiced when he finally appeared in my chambers—and how afraid I was when he told me I had to keep his presence a secret. We talk about Dane and his cruelty, which makes me think of Ky and his sister, the way he must care for her so much, while fearing the risk she brings to his kingdom.

He tells us stories from the battlefield, the way he met Sev when he was young, how the origin of their friendship is wrapped up in memories of the loss of his father. We learn a lot—likely *too* much—about the way he's formed his regiments, the way he runs his army, how seriously he takes their training and drilling and organization. It's clear that he and his captain are very close, that they bear no secrets and their trust runs deep. Asher has been my best friend for my whole life, but I've never had *that* kind of friendship with another woman.

It makes me think of Charlotte, who's not quite a friend—but might be. I remember the way her cheeks turned pink every time she looked at the captain.

"Is Sev married?" I say.

Ky snorts. "Sev? No. His longest relationship is with his *horse*. I don't think I've ever seen him with the same woman for more than a month." He pauses. "Why?"

I wonder how the prim and proper Charlotte will take *this* news. "Just curious."

As we talk, as the wine flows, our words grow a bit looser, our thoughts a bit freer. I'm lying beside Asher on some of the cushions, and as the night has gone on, I've shifted to lie *against* him, our hands loosely intertwined. At some point, Ky moved to fetch more food, and when he returned, he sat against the foot of the bench, so he's now perpendicular to us, our heads by his thigh. At first, Ky would touch me lightly as we spoke, his finger drifting along my hairline, or maybe along my cheek. But now, lying like this, he strokes my hair, my shoulder, my collarbone. Always gentle, always simple, but it's becoming intoxicating. I've felt a pulsing warmth in my belly, and it's been building for a while. My breasts feel heavy, my nipples sensitive to the dried fabric of the shift.

But all he does is continue the chaste path. Hair. Face. Arm. Collarbone. Shoulder.

When Asher shifts closer and his face falls against my shoulder, Ky incorporates him, too. Running his fingers lightly through his hair, tracing one of the lines on his cheek. I wait for Asher to go tense, but he doesn't. He's very still, his breathing quiet. When the king's finger drifts over his mouth, and then mine, I feel Asher's cock twitch against my thigh, and I flush.

Do you fancy the king?

I don't want to.

His body does. And it's clear the king fancies us both. *I fancy them both.*

But I think of what just happened in the pool, and I wonder if any of us should be fancying anyone at all.

This is too complicated to think about. We've gone too long without speaking. "Tell us about your men," I say.

"Which ones?"

"What happened to Nikko?" says Asher.

I look over, because the question is interesting, and in a way I don't understand. His eyes find mine, and I recognize an awareness there. A perception that I lack. Like the way he saw the king's brokenness—or the way the king saw his.

"Nik was captured by the Draegs," Ky says. "Held for weeks. Most of his regiment was slaughtered. They always keep a few for torture. They burn them as a lure for me."

I remember him saying that Draegonis forces would set a fire to lure him out, but this is more brutal than I expected. The knowledge cools some of the heat in my body. My heart pounds.

"How did he get free?" says Asher, and his voice is calm, as if he's unaffected.

Ky's hand drifts over my face again, then strokes a path up Asher's cheek. "We rode in and got him."

He's so loyal to his soldiers. No wonder they're so loyal to *him*.

I have to clear my throat, because I don't want to talk about tortured soldiers. "What about Garrett and Callum? Are they a couple?"

Ky snorts. "If you ask them, they'll say no. You might have noticed that Callum is not the type to confine himself to one partner." He pauses, and there's a weight in the hesitation. "But they're very ... very close. Sometimes among soldiers there's a connection that forms. A bond that keeps pulling them back together, regardless of anyone else."

I wonder what he's thinking of. His hand is tracing along Asher's shoulder now, drifting through his hair. But Asher's eyes are on me, vivid blue and intent—and a bit heavy lidded.

I roll a little to face him, then reach up to touch his face. His eyes close, but his lips part when I stroke a finger across his mouth. I feel the hardness of his cock twitch against my thigh again, and he shifts against me. A small sound pulls from his throat.

Then he draws back. "I should leave you both."

"Please stay," I whisper—but then I clench my eyes closed, because maybe I shouldn't say that at all. I did just swear to an alliance. Saving a country shouldn't mean I have to leave someone behind.

Asher smiles, but it's a little sad. "He's to be your husband, Jory."

But Ky twists a finger through his hair and gives a gentle tug. "She's in love with *you*, Asher. You should stay."

Asher inhales, likely to protest again, but the king rolls onto his knees to lean right down over him. He puts a hand against Asher's cheek, and his voice is low and intense and sure. "Do you want me to make you?"

Asher goes completely still. His pupils seem to dilate. His lips part.

The king laughs softly and lets go of his hair, then sits back on his heels. "You're right. Men *are* easy."

"Fuck you." But Asher doesn't move.

The king smiles. "You love her back, Asher. You should kiss her."

So Asher does.

He's swift and precise, no fumbling or uncertainty at all. He takes me in his arms and I hear the king's sharp hiss of breath, and then I'm drowning in the taste of Asher's mouth. I remember what he said earlier about teeth, and the instant I feel the brush of his tongue, I tug at his lip.

I'm rewarded with a small grunt of pleasure, so I do it again.

But too quickly, Asher pulls away. His eyes are hot and daring. "Kiss *him.*"

I stare back at him for a moment, but then I turn. The king catches my waist in his hands, and he's less gentle than Asher. It reminds me of that moment we were tussling by the fire, the way Ky pressed me into the dirt and thrust against me. When his hands slide up my waist, his thumbs brush right over my nipples through the thin fabric, and my insides seem to bloom. I shudder without realizing it, gasping against his mouth.

"Slow," Asher murmurs, catching me from behind.

I lean back against him, and now I feel them both, hard and needy, pressing against me. Their breathing has gone a bit ragged, and I shift, wanting to feel them.

They *both* make a sound, and it's deep. Primal. Masculine. Asher's hands are so tight on my hips, pulling me against him—or maybe pulling himself against me. He's all but tucked into the cleft of my buttocks, and again, my clothes feel like too *much*. His mouth lands on my shoulder, his teeth pressing into my skin. The king's hand is still on my breast, but when I make a little gasp, he replaces it with his mouth, sucking my nipple into his mouth through the fabric. He's slower now, careful, but my breathing shudders anyway.

My hands clutch at his shoulders, but I trace a path down the muscle of his chest. When I trace a finger around one of *his* nipples, he makes a small sound that gives me courage. I go farther, find the lacing of his trousers, and hesitate. Then I steel my spine and stroke lower, my fingers light and delicate, exploring.

The king reaches down, wraps his hand around mine, and grips hard. Then he hisses a breath, and the sound makes my insides give a hard pulse.

There's something so carnal about it. Almost aggressive. I would never touch myself like this. It takes my breath away.

Then he does it again, dragging my hand against the hard length of his cock through his trousers.

"I don't know how to pleasure a man," I whisper, suddenly uncertain.

They both go still. The king looks right into my eyes and says, "You're bringing me quite a bit of pleasure, Princess."

But it's Asher, at my back, who nips at my shoulder, then says, "Do you want to learn?"

Chapter Thirty-Three
THE PRINCESS

The room has grown so warm that the pools are beginning to throw off steam, causing thin clouds to gather around us, making for an ethereal setting. The fires glow in every direction. When Asher tells the king to disrobe, I'm not sure what to expect, and I'm glad for the wine feeding me courage.

It helps that Asher pulls me into his lap, then says, without hesitation, "Your Majesty. Strip."

Ky looks back at him for a solid minute, as if weighing this. Then, without ceremony, he stands up, unlaces his trousers, and lets them fall.

His naked body is so simultaneously intimidating and intoxicating that I don't know if I should hide or if I want to start rubbing up against him. His body is strong, muscled, as expected for a soldier, and his erect cock reaches his abdomen. No wonder it felt aggressive to grab it. It feels aggressive to *look* at it. I can't stop staring.

"Now what?" says the king, and his voice is challenging. Asher's chest is rising and falling against my back, and I realize he's also staring, just like I am.

Maybe a man's naked body is always intimidating and intoxicating.

"Sit," Asher finally says, pointing to the bench. When Ky obeys, Asher lets go of me to situate some of the pillows and cushions on the ground around him. Then he kneels close, puts his hands on the king's knees, and parts his legs.

Ky draws a sharp breath, but he reaches out to put a hand against Asher's chest, just below his throat. Half catching him, half stopping him. A gleaming bead appears at the tip of his cock, and my heart skips.

Asher's eyes flick up. "Let me go." His shoulders are tight again, his voice just as challenging as the king's was. "Jory wants to know how to pleasure a man."

But the king doesn't let him go. He just strokes his thumb along Asher's neck until my friend sighs. His head drops. He *softens*.

Like before, the king's voice goes very low, very quiet. "Asher. Do *you* want to?"

At that, Asher looks up at him steadily, as if surprised by the question. For a moment, some of his easy confidence falters, but he nods—then hesitates. Swallows.

The king runs his finger along his neck again. The purr of his accent is so gentle. "Tell me."

"I do." Asher's voice goes so small, so soft. "But don't . . . don't touch me. During. Please."

My heart aches. "Asher."

"I won't." Ky's hand falls away from his neck. "But you don't have to—"

"I said I *want* to." Then he leans forward, takes the base of Ky's cock in his hand, and runs his tongue in a slow drag up the length.

The king hisses a breath that nearly ends in a yelp. I watch his hands curl into fists against the stone of the bench.

Asher sits back. "There," he says to me. "Start with that."

My eyes go wide.

"Fuck," says Ky. "You're going to do it at the same *time*?"

"Yes," says Asher, and Ky's fists grip tighter.

I'm more tentative, more hesitant—but I remember the way the king gripped my hand around him. Like a weapon, not a flower. So I take the weight of him in my hand, and it makes me shiver. Warm, like the rest of him. Asher moves close, his hand wrapping around mine, his forearm against my own. The skin is so soft, like velvet under my palm.

"Slow." Asher's voice is a rough rasp against my ear. "Take your time."

I'm a little afraid, but Asher did it like it was nothing. When I lean forward and touch my tongue to the king's cock, I'm rewarded with the same hissing breath. I'm startled by the salty taste of the tip, and it makes me jump, just a little.

When I sit back, letting go, Asher moves close and strokes the length of him again. This time he takes the tip into his mouth, sucking gently.

He's slow, taking his time, only going halfway down, but lingering at the tip before he lets go. Ky's eyes have gone dark, his gaze hot and possessive as he looks down at us both. Seeing it makes my insides go taut.

I try to follow Asher's lead, but Ky is bigger than I thought. I expected velvet in my mouth, but this is just warm, smooth. I was prepared to find the feel of it odd, or somehow repellent, but it's not. Not at all. I pull him deeper into my mouth, relishing the sound of his deepening breath.

When I come loose, I'm still uncertain. But his eyes find mine, and the look on his face almost takes my breath away. It's not just reverence. It's gratitude. Admiration. Wonder. Desire.

"Good?" I whisper.

"Better than good, Princess."

Then Asher takes him in his mouth again, and Ky's eyes clench closed. His fingers scratch along the stone of the bench, and his throat jerks as he swallows. "Fuck. Are *you* competing—"

He breaks off as Asher goes down farther, one hand coming up to grip between his legs, his fingers cupping him, drawing at the heavy weight of his testicles. Whatever he does makes the king's breath catch, and his legs spread a bit wider. Ky's hand almost lifts, almost reaches, but he catches himself, clamping it down on the bench.

I watch Asher's face, seeing his cheeks fill and hollow, as he goes up and down, torturously slow. Watching him fight was poetic, and this is, too. He draws at the king with the same vicious grace. His hand moves again, disappearing under Ky's body, and the king makes a sound that I could only describe as raw. Something inside me clenches, reacting to that low growl, and I'm very aware of the heat between my legs, the tautness of my nipples against this shift.

After a moment, Asher pulls free, and the king is gasping, gazing at him now.

"Asher," Ky whispers, and there's a desperate, ragged note in his voice.

But Asher doesn't look at him. His eyes are only on me. "Your turn. Don't stop."

"Wait," I say, rising up. "What are you going to—"

Asher moves behind me and grabs hold of my hips, then presses himself right up against my buttocks again. I shiver, and his hands slide up my ribs, the fabric of my shift twisting under his fingers. "I'm going to show you how a man pleasures a woman."

For a moment, I'm uncertain, trapped between them. I don't know what he intends, and this is different from when we were in the pool and they were both kissing me. But my body is so primed, so *charged*, and I trust Asher. I take Ky into my mouth again, but I'm slower now, my focus split between the two of them. I expected Asher to tug at my shift, but he leaves it on, and at first, he simply runs his fingers along my buttocks slowly, his hands gentle, tracing the distance from my upper thigh to my lower back over and over again until the tension eases back out of my body.

Without warning, he spreads me a little, his fingers pulling me apart through the shift. The sensation lights me on fire. I feel so exposed, yet so covered at the same time.

He leans in close, and I feel the weight of his bare chest against my back, his legs against my legs. It makes my entire body shiver.

Then he reaches around to press a hand against my abdomen and says, "Spread your legs, lovely."

I let out a breath and obey, but it's Ky that gasps, and I forget that his cock was in my mouth, that my cheek is against his thigh, and he's practically panting. I draw back just as Asher runs a hand up the length of my leg, from ankle to hip, bringing the shift with it. I shiver at the sudden feeling of the air, but he's still so close against me that I don't quite feel naked either. Then his finger simply, suddenly runs right along the seam between my legs, the lightest most delicate touch. No one has ever touched me there, and it gives me a jolt. I cry out.

The king puts a hand against my cheek. "Easy, beautiful."

Then Asher does it *again*, this time a little slower, his finger slipping between the folds. He rubs back and forth so lightly and I shudder, feeling my insides clench.

Then his hand moves, and he runs a thumb downward, sliding

through the cleft of my buttocks. I shiver, and then he pauses to press gently against the tight hole there.

I flush red and shoot straight upright, but he catches me against him. *"Asher."* My voice is half outrage, half plea.

Ky is staring at him over my shoulder. "What did you do?"

"Guess." Asher kisses me on the neck. "Do you want me to stop?"

"No," I whisper, and my cheeks burn hotter.

The king is watching us now, his eyes so dark. His cock is so hard, glistening a bit now from my attentions, another bead appearing at the tip. But I finally realize what he means each time he says *we are not competing*. I thought he meant him and Asher, that they were rivals for me. But they're not rivals at all. He said it clearly.

She's in love with you, Asher.

You love her back.

But I've seen his attraction to us both since the first day. I saw it in the gentle way he'd touch Asher, and the confident way he'd touch me.

He's not competing because he's been *waiting*.

Asher's voice is so low in my ear. "Do you want to let the king have a turn?"

I'm wanton now, aching, so I nod. "Please," I whisper.

Ky slides to his knees, then takes my breast into his mouth like he means to worship it. I feel his cock prodding my belly, and my legs part wider, almost of their own volition. He pulls at my shift without hesitation, baring my thigh. Asher was slow and sure, but Ky has a different kind of confidence. His hand slides between my legs, and it's so different. Asher used one finger, so delicate and precise. The king's whole hand presses against me in a way I'm hungry for. I find myself rubbing against him, and before I realize it, he slides two fingers into me.

It stings a little, which makes me gasp, but it's only for a moment, and I crave it so deeply that I don't care. I rock against him, longing to be fuller.

"Slow," he says gently. He rubs at me slowly, never going farther than an inch, and it's torture.

When Asher puts a finger against my back entrance again, I make a guttural sound and push back against him.

"Not yet," he says, kissing my neck again, stroking me there, a careful dance of push and release that's driving me crazy. "Not the first time, Jory."

The king shifts his fingers, stroking just a bit deeper. I'm so warm between them. A pressure is building in my lower abdomen, and I sink harder against his hand.

"Never?" he says, and I think he's talking to me, so my eyes flick open. But his eyes are looking past me.

"Never," says Asher.

Ky's hand slows, just a little, and then he withdraws to look at me. I feel open, exposed. My body wants him back.

"Your first time doesn't need to be *tonight*," he says.

"Please," I whimper.

At my back, Asher laughs under his breath. "Don't worry, lovely. We won't leave you like *this*." He lifts me a little, his knees kicking mine wider. Then he hitches my skirts, until I feel the swirl of the night air again, and Ky's hand slides against me. I'm slick and ready, and his fingers slide right in.

He grabs my knee and lifts it, giving him more access, and suddenly his hand is deeper. Suddenly Asher is pushing at my back entrance just a little more firmly.

Ky makes that primal sound again, and I look down to realize Asher has taken hold of his cock, and he's stroking it right against my hip, right beside Ky's own hand going in and out of me. He's not just stroking it, Ky's thrusting into it. The sight triggers something inside me, because I buck against his hand, seeking the friction, imagining his cock instead. The whole time, Asher keeps stroking my tight little hole with his free hand, every brush of his finger driving me wild. Everything inside me clenches tight, heat building everywhere. Ky grunts, his own momentum building, and begins to thrust harder, both with his hand and his cock. I feel each penetration deeply, and I begin to cry out, because the pressure is intense, bordering on painful. But then he cries out and thrusts against me so hard that it drives me back onto Asher, and his finger slips right inside my ass.

That pulls the guttural sound right from my throat. A cool fire washes through my abdomen, my insides pulsing so hard that I cry out again. I keep grinding against their hands, seeking more, and I feel like a wild animal, shameless and wanting to mate.

But my quivering eventually slows, and their hands withdraw from my body. I'm trembling, sweaty, exhausted, exhilarated. They're holding me so tenderly, and now it's *my* head that falls against Ky's shoulder.

And then, suddenly, I begin to cry.

The king gathers me in his arms, and Asher presses up against my back again, holding on to me. He kisses my shoulder. "Hush, lovely," he says gently. "Hush."

"I don't know why I'm crying," I say, weeping.

"You're just a cryer."

"Is this going to happen *every time*?"

"Maybe?" he says, and that doesn't help stop the tears.

"Enough of that," says the king, and there's a slightly amused note to his voice. "Your tears are an honor. Because you, Princess, are exquisite."

His arms are so warm, but I shiver and look into his golden-brown eyes. Those words summon more tears. I blink and he goes blurry, but he strokes at my hair until my tears dry. I'm worn out and exhausted, and the night has gone nowhere I thought it would.

Eventually, the king tucks my head under his chin. His voice is low. "Are you well, Princess?"

I nod, drowsy. But then I realize I haven't heard Asher's voice, so I turn my head to look to him. "Asher?"

He brushes another kiss on my shoulder. "Still here, Jor."

There's a note in his voice that I can't quite parse out, but he presses his cheek to my shoulder, and my heart settles, content.

After a while, Ky draws back. His hand strokes down my cheek. "Both of you, come with me. Again, I know what you need."

THE KING TAKES us to his quarters, which are down a different hallway from where he left us earlier. His rooms are large and well-appointed, which isn't a surprise, along with the same fascinating lines of fire that trace the walls and leads to the hearth. My heart skips a little when I see the bed, but Ky simply brushes a light kiss against my temple, then glances at Asher.

"Rest," he says to us. "I have limited guards tonight, so I want to see to their stations before we sleep."

Then he's gone, leaving me with Asher.

I glance up at him. His eyes have gone a bit cool, but he's so beautiful in the flickering shadows. I can't seem to look *away* from him. I've wanted him for so long; there's a part of me that can't believe we just did . . . that.

The side of his mouth turns up. "I know that look. Come on."

Asher tugs me to the bed, tucking me under the lush blankets, then curling himself around me the way he did days ago. Silk sheets and velvet covers are between us, but his breath falls warm and steady against my hair. His arm comes around me, and when I take hold of his hand, he doesn't pull away at all.

I'm warm and drowsy, but I don't want to sleep. Not yet.

"Do you think he left us alone on purpose?" I say to Asher.

He's quiet for a moment, as if considering that. "I think he wants to make sure you feel safe."

That makes me shiver a little—in a good way.

"He's very kind," I whisper, like it's a secret.

Asher says nothing to that, but he presses a kiss to my neck through my hair. "*Do* you feel safe?" he says.

I nod and give his hand a squeeze. "Is it . . . is it always like that?"

He's quiet for a moment, and then he shakes his head. "No."

There's a heavy note in his voice that I can't quite make sense of, but he draws the hair back from my neck to press a kiss to my skin. "There's plenty more to discover," he says, the words almost wicked.

It makes me laugh and shiver again.

Then he whispers, "I didn't even get to use my mouth on *you*."

My laughter cuts off. My pulse leaps. Heat swells in my belly at once.

Now it's Asher's turn to laugh, the tone low and sultry against my skin. "Sleep, Jory. There's plenty of time."

"Promise?" I say.

Again, he's quiet for a beat too long. But then he nods against me. "Promise."

He's so warm, and I feel so cherished in his arms. To my surprise, I find myself longing for Ky, too, wanting him to complete this circle of safety and contentment.

After a while, Asher's breathing turns slow and heavy. Against my will, I begin to drift to sleep as well.

But then I realize what he said, how the king wanted to make sure I feel safe.

He didn't say a word about himself.

"Asher," I murmur, turning my head slightly. "Do *you* feel safe?"

He must already be asleep, because I wait, but he doesn't answer. So I sigh and close my eyes again, pulling his hand to my heart.

He's here. He's with me. For now, that'll have to be enough.

Chapter Thirty-Four
THE WARRIOR

When I returned to my quarters, I found them curled up beside each other, the princess clearly sound asleep. At first, I thought Asher was, too, but when I slipped under the blanket beside them, his body took on an alertness that hasn't gone away. When the princess eventually shifted in her sleep, Asher moved away, letting her go. He's adrift in the blankets now, lying on his belly, because the brand is still a bit raw. His eyes are still closed, but I know he's not sleeping.

He's avoiding me.

He hasn't looked at me since the moment he said, *Don't touch me.* Not after he took my cock in his mouth to show her how to pleasure a man, not when I confirmed Jory's lack of experience, not even when the princess was so lusciously pinned between us. When he wrapped his hand around me, I nearly spilled right there. I was already so close and Jory was exquisitely clenching around my fingers and Asher's grip was . . . perfection. But his face was buried in her neck, and he never lifted his eyes.

And despite what he did—despite the fact that we've spent the last two nights all but pressed together—he's now lying three feet away from me.

It didn't escape my notice that he also left the Hall of Stars still rock hard, his trousers still laced in place. The princess wouldn't notice—likely wouldn't *think* to notice—but I did.

Maybe I should have stopped him before any of that happened. Maybe I broke whatever began. Or maybe he's simply realized that I won't stop him from being with Jory, so there's no need to continue . . . whatever we were doing.

Or . . . maybe he scared himself away.

The princess herself continues to stun me. So innocent, yet so . . .

unflinching when it comes to things that matter. I've been so hesitant to reveal the truth about my sister . . . and then she was so quietly gentle. She didn't judge me for what happened with my people, and she's ready to go take food from Astranza without even waiting for Dane to approve it. When we finally confessed our hidden truths to each other, she was ready to ride right into war that very moment. I said I wouldn't ride back into her country without a regiment behind me, and she was so quick to correct me.

Behind us.

The falcon, always free, choosing to return to my hand.

Asher, by comparison, is the wolf willing to stand at her side, to do whatever she asks—even when it costs him something. Even when it costs him *everything*.

I think of that day when he held me captive. One of the very first things I noticed was how he'd obviously never been a soldier—and if he were, I'd have to carefully build his confidence, because so much of his courage is a facade. So much of his true spirit has already been stolen away.

Though . . . clearly not all of it.

"Asher," I say, and I keep my voice low.

For the longest time, he doesn't move, though I know he's not sleeping. I don't think he's going to look at me, but I won't ask again. I don't want to make it a battle of wills. Not now.

But then his eyes flick open, more gray than blue in the shadows. He still doesn't meet my gaze.

"Can I touch you?" I say.

He says nothing, and I don't want to push him—though sometimes I think he likes to be pushed. He's just out of reach, so I shift toward him, watching his reaction, stopping when we're close enough to share breath.

He goes tense, of course, and he seems prepared to launch himself out of the bed.

"You only have about four guards in this entire palace," he says, like it's a warning. "I could escape in five minutes."

"*Escape?*" I say softly. "Do you still feel you're a captive, Asher?"

Emotions play over his face as he considers that, and it steals some of his fire. "I don't know what I am."

I remember how he didn't ask to be freed from the chain. I wonder if there was a part of him, deep inside, that *liked* it. If captivity meant safety, in an odd way. Being my prisoner meant no one else could take him.

He's so tense that he could walk onto a battlefield right now. "Would a fight make you feel better?" I say, and a tiny light sparks in his gaze that tells me it would. "Should I get some swords and we can go to the training yard?"

He looks a bit startled, but then he laughs under his breath. "Honestly, I have no idea what to do with a sword."

That's so shocking that I press up on one elbow and look down at him. "*What?*"

He shrugs. "It's not the most efficient weapon for an assassin." He makes a face. "I haven't held one in forever. They're heavy—awkward—"

"Asher." I run a hand down my face. Bleeding skies, and he's going to let them take him to Mossnum. "Can you shoot an arrow?"

"Probably? It's been a while."

I stare at him. He's finally looking at me, and some of the bracing tension has slipped out of his body. He's not prepared to leap from the bed anymore. I find it amusing that a conversation about fighting is what finally drew him out.

There was a moment when he was lying with Jory that he allowed me to stroke his hair. They both seemed lazy and content, curled up like purring cats beside me. He's not purring now, but he doesn't look ready to claw up my arm, either.

I reach out and thread my fingers through his hair.

He stops breathing, but he doesn't pull away. I do it another time, and then another, until he finally lets out a breath and his eyes close.

He's really so beautiful. They both are. When Asher and Jory were kneeling between my spread legs, I had a moment where I thought it couldn't possibly be real, that maybe I died at some point during the journey and this was the heavenlands.

I let go of his hair and run a hand down the curved muscles of his arm. When he shifts a little, his hand drifting the tiniest bit toward me, I say, "Will you let me hold you?"

I wait, and I'm rewarded when he responds, tucking his face in against my shoulder, aligning his body almost flush with mine. I can feel him breathe, the too-quick fluttering of his heart, and I shift my stroking to run along the slope of his back, mindful of his wounds. When he relaxes, he's as responsive as the princess, and I begin to let my hand drift. His back, his arm, his rib cage, his throat. I brush a thumb over his nipple, and his eyes flick open, his breath catching the tiniest bit. His skin is so warm, his pulse beginning to hum.

So I stop with my hand against his neck, my thumb right in that hollow under his jaw. "You are not my prisoner, Asher. You are free to stay, just as you are free to leave. But no one will take you away from her. No one will take her away from you. Certainly not me." I lean in, letting him hear the righteous conviction in my voice. "You are *free*. But if this is where you choose to remain, know this: *no one* will take you away from me."

He stops breathing again. His eyes fix and lock on mine.

I run a thumb across his chin, barely touching his lower lip. "Rest assured, I know how to go to war."

He's simply staring, so I lean in and brush my mouth over his.

It's the first time I've kissed him, and he responds so softly, his lips barely brushing mine, his breath light and sweet as he withdraws.

He whispers, "It must have been *really* good if you're offering to go to *war*."

It makes me laugh in spite of myself. But then I'm thinking of his mouth again, the slow drag of his tongue, the way he looked to the princess and encouraged her to follow his lead. And then the longer time, the moment he lingered, the way he pushed a finger inside me and I nearly pulsed right into his throat.

I blink and he's watching me, his eyes so dark.

"Do you want me to do it again?" he says softly.

Yes.

I almost say it—because I'm already hard, just hearing him offer.

But I realize this is a different kind of fighting for him. A different kind of challenge.

"No," I say, and I stroke my hand through his hair. I consider the way he reacted when I brushed a finger across his nipple, so I do it again. "Do you want me to do it to you?"

His breath catches, and he shivers, and I don't know if it's from my hand or from the question. He shifts closer to me, almost unconsciously, pressing himself into my hip.

But then he tucks his face against my shoulder. It's not a refusal—but it's not a clear assent, either.

I pinch his nipple between my fingers and he grunts, almost thrusting against me. There's a desperate sound to it. A wanting sound. But I also hear the fear underneath. It must be torture to live like this, to go without touch, to fear the motive of anyone who offers it even in the simplest way. I have no idea how he hid it from the princess for so long.

Actually—maybe I do. Her innocence is likely the only armor he has.

"Take yourself in hand," I whisper along his temple. "I'll hold you."

I don't think he'll do even this, but I've barely said the words before the cord is pulled and his cock is free. He strokes himself against my thigh.

The princess is so guileless that I have to guard my words, because I don't want to shock her or frighten her—at least not until she's a bit more experienced. But this is one thing I don't need to fear with Asher.

I press a bit closer and drop my voice, speaking right against his skin. "When you're ready, I'll do that for you, Asher. Perhaps I could be the one to give the princess a lesson. You could tell me what you think of my mouth."

He gasps against my shoulder.

I stroke a hand along his neck, tracing a line across his chest. "I rather liked what you did with your finger," I say. I let my voice go husky. "That's a trick I could show the princess. She certainly seemed to like it when you did it to *her*."

He makes a small sound. His hand accelerates.

"Maybe you wouldn't want to finish in my mouth," I say. "Maybe you'd like to push Jory down against the bed. I saw the way you pulled her apart. I know you want to fill her up."

"Fuck," he gasps. A sheen of sweat has broken out on his shoulders. "*Fuck.*"

I stroke a hand down his side, pressing my fingers into his hip. "Or maybe you're the one who wants to be pushed down against a bed," I whisper. "Maybe you don't want my mouth. Maybe you just want me to fuck *you.*"

He grunts hard and bites down on my shoulder, almost whimpering as he comes, jerking himself hard until he's done.

And then, to my surprise, it's his breath that's hitching, his eyes that are suddenly gleaming.

Bleeding skies.

I pull him close, kissing his temple, his cheek, his neck. "Hush, lovely," I say, a little bit teasing, but very much not. I smooth his hair. "Hush."

When his breathing settles, he doesn't pull away. I want to get him linens from the washroom, but I'll wait until he's ready.

But then he says, "I bit your shoulder. I'm sorry."

I look down, surprised to discover he broke the skin.

I kiss him on the forehead again. "That, Asher, is a wound I'll wear with pride."

Chapter Thirty-Five
THE ASSASSIN

I've been sleeping beside the king for days now, so I shouldn't be awake. It's just so odd to have him on one side of me, with Jory on the other.

Despite what the king said about freedom and protection, there's still a part of me that wants to slip out of the bed and flee the castle. I could return to the shadows, where everything is less complicated.

You don't have to pick a fight every time.

The memory of the words makes my throat go tight.

That's what I want to flee. That . . . *awareness*. Not just from him. From her, too. It's too much. Too intense. I clung to her in the Hall of Stars. I clung to him just now. I've spent too many years locking myself away, and now I feel as though every wall has been torn down.

I'm not ready for it.

Jory shifts in the bed, turning a little. Her hand, light and soft, lands on my shoulder. I'm frozen in place, wondering if she's awake, if she somehow sensed my indecision.

No, she's still sound asleep. I sigh.

But then I hear a sound, and it's so faint I could almost ignore it. Not a voice, not a scrape, just a whisper of movement.

I go completely still. I have no idea if this is a Hunter or another Draeg soldier, but if either one made it to Lastalorre, this palace has so little internal defense. Ky said he was checking with his guards before we retired, but it's clear that he sends his most experienced fighters to the battle against Draegonis.

I wait, listening for another sound. My eyes search the shadows, looking for movement.

Then a blade is drawn, and as always, I'm lucky I'm fast.

I roll, then punch, then duck when another blade comes out of nowhere. Pain erupts in my forearm, but I roll again. There's not enough light to see much, but I spot three shadows in the darkness. Jory shrieks, but the sound is a momentary distraction. I reach for her, but her shift is jerked away from me.

"It's me," says Ky. "I've got her."

Then it's not dark at all, because the king has called fire. It surges from his hand, catching anything within reach, almost too bright. I see his form, clutching the princess, and then I see one of the attackers— just before they're all but incinerated, leaving nothing more than a charred corpse on the ground. It's quick and vicious and the most horrific thing I've ever seen, and it steals my focus for a terrifying moment. I can hear the princess's heaving breath, too. As we stare, fire leaps to the wall tapestries, and smoke begins to fill the room. The princess coughs.

"Asher," the king snaps. "Get her out. The walls are stone. The fire won't spread from this room."

"There are two more," I say, because I saw them. But they're either dead in the sudden inferno—or they're hiding, using the smoke and shadows to their advantage.

I inhale a lung full of smoke, and the decision is nearly made for me.

"Asher!" the king says again, and he shoves her in my direction.

Jory shrieks, but I catch her, and I drag her into the hallway. The steel door slams shut behind us.

Suddenly we're cloaked by silence.

Jory stares at me, shaking. "We have to help him, Asher. We can't leave him in there."

I look back at the door. As usual, I have no weapons. No protection against the flames.

I reach out and touch the handle anyway.

"Fuck," I snap, jerking my hand back. It's too hot to grab.

Jory stares from the handle to me. "He can't stop it," she whispers. "He can only start it."

I swallow. I don't know what to do.

I remember the captain demanding to know why I didn't call for help. I haven't even done it *now*.

"Guards!" I shout. "*Guards!*"

But no one comes.

I wonder if the assailants killed them first.

Something thumps against the door. A minute later, it's pulled wide. The heat of the flames inside is intense, and we rock back.

Ky has a burning tunic wrapped around the handle, and he's dragging a blistered body. He's also panting heavily. The door falls closed behind him, and he shoves the body against the wall.

Then he drops himself right next to it. His hair is threaded with sweat, but he doesn't look like he's been injured.

"Asher," he says to me. "Do you recognize her?"

That makes me look, because I hadn't realized this was a woman. The burns are already too bad. But not only is it a woman, she's still alive.

Barely.

"I don't know her," I say, but that's more a factor of the injuries than anything else.

"Who sent you?" Jory demands.

The woman says nothing.

Ky rolls onto his knees and summons a handful of fire. "Talk," he says.

The woman says nothing again, and Ky draws the fire closer to her face. She tries to flinch, but that must be painful, because she doesn't move.

"Talk," Ky says again. His voice is vicious, and it makes me shiver.

"He's bargaining with Draegonis," she gasps. "He's killing you for *them*."

"The Guildmaster," says Jory. "Is he directing this?"

"No," says the woman. Her voice has grown very weak. "They want you back. That's part of the . . ."

Her voice trails off. She slumps over.

Ky crushes the fire out of his palm and grabs her burned tunic, pulling her upright. But her head lolls. She's dead.

Jory looks between me and the king. "They want me back? Did she mean Astranza?"

Ky frowns, then lets go of the woman. "Come," he says to us both. His voice is tight. Hard. A military commander, ready to take action. He glances at the princess, then me. Assessing damage, looking for weakness. "I need to check Victoria. I'll take you to a safe place."

But Jory stands. "No. I need to check on Charlotte."

Ky draws a sharp breath, and I can already see this is going to turn into a standoff. "I'll go with her," I say to him. "Go. See to your sister."

He considers for less than a second, and then he gives me a sharp nod. Without a look back, he turns and departs.

THE HALLWAYS ARE cool and dark, and I can hear Jory breathing heavily. We inhaled too much smoke, and my lungs feel tight and scratchy, so I wonder if hers are the same. We have to cross through the massive atrium to reach the other hallway, and our footsteps echo.

There are no guards posted. A chill goes up my spine. There was one earlier. I'm sure the king has already noticed.

"No guards," Jory whispers.

"I know," I say softly.

She glances at me, and her expression is tense and worried. "They're going to keep sending people, aren't they?"

"It certainly seems that way."

"Do you think they got to Charlotte first?" she says. She draws a shaky breath. "She's been so brave for *me*. I should've been in that room."

"Most Hunters won't go after someone who isn't a target."

She glances at me, her soft features barely visible in the shadows. "That Draeg soldier attacked the whole settlement."

My mouth forms a line. There's a part of me that wishes I'd returned from Morinstead a week earlier. Would I have learned about the Guildmaster's treachery? Would I have suspected something?

Would I have been able to warn Jory, preventing all of this?

There's just no way to know.

And as I consider everything we've been through together, I wonder if it was better this way.

We turn a corner, and a shadow shifts. Without hesitation, I shove the princess behind me, then tackle the other person into the wall. A woman gives a sharp cry, and I freeze.

"Oh!" says Jory. "Asher, it's Charlotte!"

Fuck. I withdraw, letting the woman go. She's so pale. She rubs at her sleeves and peers at us in the darkness. Her breath is shaking, like she's afraid. I suppose that's my fault.

She offers Jory a hasty curtsy. "Your Highness," she says in surprise. She glances warily between us. "What are you doing here?"

"There's been another attack," Jory says. "Charlotte, I was so worried. Were you harmed?"

"No. No, I'm fine." Charlotte looks back toward the darkened hallway. Her hands twist together, fidgeting. "There's been another attack?"

Her tone is so hollow, and I frown. She doesn't quite seem afraid. It's something else, and I can't put my finger on it.

"Yes," says Jory.

"What of the king?" she says. She glances back a third time.

"He survived," says Jory. "He's checking with—"

"Jory. Wait." I grab hold of her wrist sharply, pulling the princess behind me. Jory breaks off, sucking in a quick breath. I'm not sure why my instincts are warning me about this moment, but they are.

And then I figure it out.

Your Highness. What are you doing here?

She wasn't surprised Jory was gone. She was surprised to *find* her.

And she keeps glancing down the hallway.

Just as I put the pieces together, another shadow shifts, somewhere to my left. I move to block, but this time Charlotte tackles *me*, shoving me into the wall. It's completely unexpected, but I'm able to throw her off.

Unfortunately, it allows the real attacker to slam me into the ground. The stone floor scrapes against my branded shoulder, and someone lands on top of me. I cry out. "Jory, *run.*"

But she gives a sharp shriek, and I know they've got her. Panic grips my heart as I fight my assailant, desperately seeking a dagger. Desperately seeking *anything*.

So much Incendrian steel in the palace, and I never asked the king for a weapon.

Light flares, fire filling the hallway. It's so blazingly bright that I can't see anything at all. But then I hear the *snick* of a crossbow, and the man pinning me to the ground jerks hard. A second later, a booted foot kicks him off me.

Ky stands over me. He's got a handful of fire in one hand, and a crossbow in the other. Two guards are at his back, swords drawn.

They're all pointing at Charlotte.

Jory is gasping, shoving her own shot attacker to the ground. Blood is all over her chemise, and I quickly draw her to me. "Where are you hurt?" I say in a rush. "Jory, where?"

"Not mine," she says. "Not mine."

We scramble to our feet. To my surprise, the two men on the ground *are* familiar. Though maybe it shouldn't be a surprise, if Pavok is working with Draegonis. Beyond them, Charlotte is cringing against the wall, backing away from the king's fire.

"Please," she's saying. "Please. He made me."

"Charlotte?" says Jory. Her voice is small. "Charlotte, *who* made you?"

She shakes her head quickly. "No. Please. You must understand." Her voice drops to a whisper. "He'll kill me."

I frown. "Master Pavok?" I say.

Charlotte shakes her head.

"Then it's someone from Draegonis," says Ky, and his voice is dark. The fire on his palm flickers, emphasizing his fury. "One of the generals? If they've infiltrated Astranza this deeply, I will have to—"

"*No*," says Charlotte. "But Your Highness—you should know. You are in danger."

"Then who?" demands Ky.

Charlotte wets her lips, then glances down the hallway as if she'd like to run. "Not like this," she says. "Please. Not like this."

It's exactly what my mother said, when the queen's carriage was attacked. The words hit me like a knife—and I know they're doing the same to Jory. Her lips part.

Ky steps forward, lifting the ball of fire. Lady Charlotte flinches back.

"No!" says Jory. "I'll hear what she has to say."

For a moment, there's no sound aside from Charlotte's panicked breathing.

"I cannot," she finally says, her voice barely more than a whisper. She stares into that ball of flame, then shudders.

"If you fear for your life," Ky says, "you should be aware that you are no safer from me than from whoever bears this threat."

Charlotte blanches. The silence stretches on. One of the Hunters on the ground makes a low moan. I don't know him well, but I think his name is Rancal. I kick him.

"Fuck you, Asher," he says.

"Fuck you back." I kick him again.

Jory puts a hand on my arm, though the king looks like he wants me to do it again.

"Charlotte," says Jory. "I will spare your life. No matter what you say." Her tone is bold and confident. The princess who will be queen. She looks to Ky. "Tell her."

He hesitates, then nods—though he doesn't look happy about it. "If the princess will spare your life, then I will as well." He pauses, and that ball of fire crackles and pops, making Charlotte flinch. "But only if you speak the truth, and now."

Charlotte shudders. "Your Highness, you should know—you should know I have always tried to be loyal. I have always tried to be—"

"*Now!*" Ky snaps.

The woman cringes against the wall. "Dane," she whimpers. "He told me to leave a trail on your journey. I left scraps of my clothing when we stopped."

"That's a lie," Jory says. "Dane is allying with the king of Incendar. We already know Draegonis is involved."

Charlotte shakes her head quickly. "It was Dane. I swear it. Astranza needs Maddox Kyronan dead to keep up their end of the bargain."

"What bargain?" says Ky. "He is bargaining with *me*."

Charlotte falls silent again, and Ky draws the fire closer to her face. "I am not bound by the princess's vow unless you tell the truth."

"Dane is the one bargaining with Draegonis," Charlotte gasps. "He's killing you for *them*."

Ky goes very still.

"And me?" says the princess. "Did he send you to kill me as well?"

"No," says Charlotte. A tear slips down her cheek. "They want you back. That's part of the—"

"*Enough*." Rancal surges off the ground to drive a dagger into her gut.

Jory shrieks. Ky fires his crossbow, but it's not fast enough. Charlotte is already collapsing.

Jory catches her, easing her against the wall. "Charlotte," she whispers. "Charlotte—I wish you'd told me—"

"Your Highness," she gasps. "Forgive me. Please, forgive . . ."

Her voice trails off.

Jory's face crumples. "She was supposed to be my *friend*. I promised her. *I promised her*."

The king looks down at the carnage, then looks to me. "I'll deal with this," he says, his voice low. "Take her back to your quarters. I'll find you shortly."

I nod, and he claps me on my good shoulder. He does it so casually, like I'm one of his soldiers, and of anything, that takes me the most by surprise.

But I have to shove that away and look after Jory.

Before I do, I turn back to the king. "Ky," I say.

His eyes glance my way. "Asher?"

I put out a hand. "I've made do until now, but would you *please* give me a weapon?"

Chapter Thirty-Six
THE PRINCESS

By the time we make it back to Asher's quarters, I'm still trembling from everything that happened, and Asher wraps me up in his arms.

"How did that happen?" I say. "How did they get here? When did he convince Charlotte to do this?"

"Hunters are very skilled," he says quietly. "And you've known Dane to be a snake for years. We should be more surprised that it *wasn't* just Draegonis."

"So you think that's true?" I say.

He sighs against me. "That your brother would double cross the king of Incendar? Yes."

"Why go to all this trouble? He could have just killed him when he rode into Astranza."

Asher draws back to think about that for a moment. "He wouldn't know that Princess Victoria is . . . well, as she is. He might have feared retaliation if *he* were the aggressor. An assassin can be made to look like an accident."

I stare at him, realization dawning. "Or a *spy*. That's why he accused *you* of working for the Draegs." My heart lurches as I begin to put this together. "No one would be surprised by an assassin sent by Draegonis to kill the king of Incendar. If he made a bargain with the Draegs, he could have killed off Maddox Kyronan *and* me . . . and made himself look like a victim!"

Asher gives me a grim look. "He gives Draegonis what they want—and Dane gets left alone."

Something about that still doesn't fit quite right, but I'm shaky from the attack, and I can't puzzle it all out now.

A knock raps at the door. "It's me," Ky calls from outside.

Asher moves to open it. When the king enters, there's soot on his hands. I wonder if he burned the bodies. I think of Charlotte, and I shudder. I don't want to know.

I thought she was brave. I thought she was *loyal*.

I suppose she was. But that loyalty wasn't enough to stand up to my brother. It never is.

I have to clear my throat before emotion chokes away my ability to speak. "You never told me if your sister was all right," I say to Ky.

He nods. "Sound asleep. So is Norla. I'm lucky I don't have guards stationed there, because it looks like an empty hallway." He pauses. His expression is so hard. "They killed the few guards inside the palace. Some of the servants as well."

"Ky," I whisper.

He folds his arms and leans back against the door. "Do you believe what Charlotte said?"

"She was afraid for her life," I say. "I do."

He nods. "I do, too." He pauses. "If Astranza has truly made an alliance with Draegonis, Princess, then our positions have become rather complex."

His voice has grown cold, and I stare back at him. A chill runs up my spine as I consider what he's saying. "Would you consider Astranza and Incendar to be at war, Your Majesty?"

"If these claims are to be believed, then yes. I would."

His eyes are so fierce. But underneath all the aggression, I know this scares him. I know this *terrifies* him. His people aren't starving yet, but they will be soon. My father is dying—but he's alive right now. Dane clearly has no intention of keeping up this farce of an alliance, but my father's borders can still fend off Incendar. I may have been ready to ride with Ky into Astranza to claim food, but we can't do that if he means to launch an assault on my country.

If he even trusts that I had nothing to do with this.

I know how ruthless he can be. I know he's a man who puts his country ahead of everything—even his own desires. A cool wind of fear curls through my chest, and I'm glad I have Asher by my side.

But I remember the king looking down at me when I washed the blood off his face. I remember the way he broke that bread in half so

Asher could eat, or the way he blew on my fingers when I burned myself on his fire.

I remember every moment of thoughtful kindness I've witnessed since the moment I met him.

And then I remember that before any of this happened, I was a princess preparing for an alliance.

So I square my shoulders and look up at him. "I believe you and I were prepared to be allies against Prince Dane already."

He regards me for an eternal silent moment, and his expression doesn't flicker. I'm very aware of Asher at my shoulder, watching this face-off.

"What do you propose?" the king finally says.

"Perhaps the alliance between our countries could continue," I say. "My father has little time left. I *am* second in line for the throne, after all."

His jaw twitches as he considers this. "You would go to war against your brother to claim the throne for yourself?"

I have to take a breath, because I've never considered such a thing. Years of being under Dane's thumb almost makes me falter.

But I think of the way he plotted against both of us.

I think of those blue marks on my wrist.

I think of the way Charlotte cringed—and I realize Dane must have been terrifying, indeed.

I think of the way he had Asher dragged from the palace in chains.

I think of the way Ky protected us both.

"Yes," I say to him, lifting my chin. "I'm ready to go to war."

The king regards me . . . then smiles. "Vicious, Princess." He puts out a hand. "I will accept your offer of alliance."

I take his hand in mine. As always, I feel his warmth, the magic that he wields.

But then Asher speaks at my back, his voice like a cool wind.

"If you only need to kill the prince," he says darkly, "you don't need to go to war. You don't even need an army."

"What do we need?" says Ky.

Asher steps forward, out of the shadows behind me. He looks between us, then puts his hand on top of ours. "You need a Hunter."

ACKNOWLEDGMENTS

If you're expecting a short paragraph of acknowledgments, I am not your girl.

As always, I must start with my husband. Michael, I couldn't do this without your support and encouragement, and most especially without your ability to talk me off a ledge and bring me back down to earth when I so desperately need it. Thank you for everything. I love you so much.

While working on *Warrior Princess Assassin*, I had the luck and pleasure of working with two new editors for the first time. To Julia Elliott and Rachel Winterbottom at HarperCollins, thank you so much for sharing your vision, your guidance, and your confidence in my work. It has been a true joy to work with you both, and I am so incredibly grateful for all of your input into this story.

Tremendous thanks also go to Suzie Townsend and the entire team at New Leaf Literary. Suzie, I am so grateful to have you by my side for this publication journey. Special thanks to Olivia Coleman, Sophia Ramos, and Keifer Ludwig for your help and assistance and feedback. Thank you all so much for everything.

To the team at HarperCollins: THANK YOU. It has been such a pleasure to work with all of you. At the time of my writing these acknowledgments, we're still early in the publication process, so I know there are people working tirelessly on my behalf that I haven't even met yet. Please know that I am so grateful for all of your efforts, and I can't wait until the day I can thank you personally. You are seen, and you are appreciated.

Huge debts of gratitude for regular chats and moral support to Victoria Aveyard, Tanaz Bhathena, Maegan Bouis, Erin Bowman, Susan Dennard, Alexa Donne, Stephanie Garber, Reba Gordon, Amalie Howard, Isabel Ibañez, Amie Kaufman, Christina Labib, Jodi Meadows, Jodi Picoult, Nicki Pau Preto, Siobhan Reed, Beth Revis, Sarah Rifield,

Bradley Spoon, and Melody Wukitch, because I honestly don't know how I would get through the day without you all. I am so grateful to have you in my life.

This book was revised about a billion times (not really) (okay maybe really), and I am deeply appreciative to the friends who offered to give me fresh eyes on the manuscript when I needed them. Tremendous thanks to Jodi Picoult, Reba Gordon, Sarah Rifield, Jodi Meadows, Laura Samotin, Don Martin, Isabel Ibañez, Amalie Howard, Serene Heier, Jamie Pacton, Nicki Pau Preto, and Jim Hilderbrandt.

Tremendous thanks to readers, bloggers, librarians, artists, and booksellers all over the world who take the time to post, review, share, and discuss my books. I owe my career to people who are so passionate about my characters and my stories that they can't help but talk about them. Thank you all.

And many thanks go to YOU! Yes, you. Whether you've read all eighteen of my novels or if this is the first one you've picked up, I am honored that you took the time to invite my characters into your heart. Thank you for being a part of my dream.

Finally, as always, tremendous love and thanks to my boys. You love each other so very, very much, and I am so incredibly lucky to be your mom.

BRIGID KEMMERER is the *New York Times* bestselling author of more than a dozen dark and alluring novels like *Defy the Night, A Curse So Dark and Lonely,* and *Letters to the Lost*. Her stories always feature complex characters facing the challenges of life, both in realistic settings and rich fantasy worlds. A full time writer, Brigid lives in the Baltimore area with her husband, her boys, her dog, and her cats. When she's not writing or being a mommy, you can usually find her with her hands wrapped around a barbell.